To Mary Smitham, who searched the grottoes of my emotions and
found my fountain of creativity.

To Ron, who spotted the diamond locked in the lucite box and set it free.

PUPPET CHILD

A Novel

by TALIA CARNER

Under our constitutional system, courts stand against any winds that blow as havens of refuge for those who might otherwise suffer because they are helpless, weak, outnumbered, or because they are non-conforming victims of prejudice and public excitement.
—Justice Hugo. L Black

This is a work of fiction. The legal case, the names and the characters are all fictional. Any resemblance to living or dead individuals is purely coincidental.

Contents

PROLOGUE

RACHEL Belmore was jolted from a dream, awash with dread. "The baby!" the words crashed against her temples. Her breathing came in gasps.

Still groggy from the pill Wes had given her, she sat upright in bed and listened. No sound reached her. Wes, careful not to disturb her, must have slipped out of bed and closed the bedroom door she insisted on keeping open.

She dropped her head back on the pillow. Since Ellie's birth eleven months before, Rachel's sleep only skirted the periphery of dreams. The night before, she had lain in the dark next to the sleeping Wes, her ears attuned to any rustle coming from the nursery, her tense body ready to leap with the slightest new sound—or after a prolonged silence.

"How do you expect to keep up your strength without sleep?" Wes asked in the morning when she dashed out the door for a nine o'clock client meeting. She had been up since seven, feeding and playing with Ellie. "Certainly not with a full-time career."

Before bedtime, he handed her a vial of sleeping pills brought from his office. "Take one Saturday and Tuesday; I'll do all the getting up when no surgeries are scheduled in the morning," he said. "As your private physician, I order you to get a good night's sleep. Starting tonight."

In response, Rachel made a playful salute and clicked her heels. She loved to make him laugh; it made her feel witty, sprightly. Dr. Wesley Belmore's love for her was the mirror from which her own image reflected back at her, and where she saw a winner.

The whirring stillness of the room closed in on her. "The baby." The words continued to bang inside her head. Why hadn't Wes returned if Ellie was fine? Rachel pushed herself out of bed and rushed toward Ellie's room. In the dark corridor she nearly knocked over the sculpture stand.

At the door to the nursery she froze.

In the darkness, she could barely discern Wes's silhouette bent over the crib. To her disoriented mind, his body appeared contorted. A stranger's figure.

Was she hallucinating?

Rachel's muffled groan made Wes straighten. He turned slowly, and let out his low, throaty laugh, full of savoir-faire. Instantly, it wrapped her in its warmth.

"Are you okay, honey?"

"Is she all right?" she whispered.

His long fingers reached gently toward the soft hair on Ellie's head. "We have a beautiful baby," he replied, awe in his voice.

"What were you doing?—" Rachel clammed up. She moved closer to the crib and stared down. Ellie slept, her breathing dry and even. It was madness. Even if sleeping medication swam in her brain, she must be suffering from a protracted postpartum depression to even think—

Ellie's finely carved mouth puckered and moved in a sweet sucking motion. She stirred and brought her thumb to her mouth.

"She'll have buck teeth," Rachel said, still staggering in an air pocket of dread.

"Relax, honey." He drew Rachel to his chest and planted little kisses on her face.

"Relax?" she mumbled into his silk paisley robe. She breathed in deep. She adored his smell. "Who said, 'To have a child is to forever have your heart go walking around outside your body?'"

"She's fine." He drew her closer. "Remember, I've been through this before."

She hated to be reminded of his other daughter. Was it possible he loved another child as much as he loved Ellie? It had been several years since Stephanie's mother moved to southern New Jersey, two hours away, which made visiting with his child difficult. Whenever Wes spoke of it, it was with an atypical fury, and his eyes, pulsating with anger, scared Rachel. Accustomed to being in charge, Wes had no tolerance for events that took their own turn.

Grateful that he didn't bring up his former wife, Rachel allowed him to lead her back to bed. He spooned her in his arms. "I love you," he murmured, and rocked her to sleep.

But for months, the insane suspicion, the improbable vision of what she thought she had seen in the shadows, kept tormenting her. When she prepared a client sales presentation, Wes's image would pop up and project itself on the screen. Even while her body was swept up in his tender lovemaking, a mental image of his figure lurking in the shadows would force its way to a spot behind her eyes.

She distrusted herself, convinced her mind was deranged. Hugging Ellie, Rachel forced herself to remember how lucky she was. Their Fifth Avenue penthouse offered her a ringside seat on life, her own private show in which every act complemented the other. It was lunacy to think otherwise.

A year later, exhausted from a one-day round-trip business flight to Memphis, Rachel gave Ellie her bath and tucked her to bed. Then, wanting to keep Wes company in his study, she lay on the couch. Sometime later, through a gauzy curtain of sleep, she felt his strong arms as he lifted her and carried her to their bedroom. Gently, with the delicate yet assured hands of a competent surgeon, he removed her shoes and clothes, and tucked her under the satin sheets. She drowned in their coolness, sucked down as though by an undertow, and slept.

She hit the surface of wakefulness with a start.

She sat up.

The green glow of the digital bedside clock bounced off the mirror above the antique dresser. Three-thirty. It took her a moment to realize it was not afternoon, but the middle of the night.

Instinctively, she listened for sounds of Ellie. Lately, the two-year-old would wake up several times during the night. With Rachel's cooing and singing, she would finally fall back to sleep, but she thrashed about, getting entangled in her blanket. Rachel kept checking on her, fearing she would smother.

"People who say they sleep like a baby usually don't have one," Rachel had commented one morning after a sleepless night, and Wes responded with his open, warm chuckle.

No sounds reached Rachel now as she cocked her ear, her eyes trying to penetrate the darkness. The room was silent and still. Once again, even though she had demanded that Wes leave the baby monitor on, he had turned it off to ensure her uninterrupted rest.

What made her open the door with the stealth of a thief? What made her tiptoe ever so lightly on bare feet, sliding along the corridor wall until she reached Ellie's room?

The scent of baby lotion and fabric softener wafted to her nostrils. The faint light of the new Mickey Mouse nightlight, bought in response to Ellie's panicked crying at bedtime, outlined the doorway. Although Ellie, at almost two, couldn't speak yet, Rachel knew her baby was terrified of the dark.

She hugged herself against the chill and held her breath. She heard the tiny sounds Ellie emitted in her sleep, a cross between lip smacking, thumb sucking, and a gurgle.

Rachel peeked in.

The pale halo of light was golden, outlining Wes's back. His body was contorted in the position she had seen in her nightmare.

Silently, Rachel glided in and rounded his body.

Through the crib bars, she saw Wes coaxing his penis into the baby's mouth to suckle in her sleep.

She had seen it right that night over a year ago.

Time stopped, hovered, and quivered before it exploded into a million fragments. Rachel screamed.

PART I

"CROSS MY HEART AND HOPE TO DIE."

CHAPTER   ONE

IN the reception area of Chuck Bernstein's law office, Rachel took a deep breath and relaxed her fists. She extended her fingers and touched the white spider mums in the vase on the side table. The current issue of *Business Week*, her must reading, lay beside it. She picked it up, leafed through it, and dropped it back. She wasn't up to it. Not now.

She stood and walked around. The receptionist raised her head and gave her a sketchy smile, then went back to her typing. Rachel sat down again. She bit the side of her lower lip.

It had been three years since she had taken her daughter and fled from Wes in the middle of the night, a wild woman with the wind in her hair. Ever since, it had been Wes's word against hers. She accused, he denied, she insisted, he denied again. With her world devoid of possibilities, she was running out of legal options. What was there left to do?

Chuck touched her shoulder, and she jolted before she caught herself. As she got up, she adjusted her suit skirt. It hung too loose. And she had believed she couldn't lose more weight.

She followed Chuck into his office, cleared the files from one of the upholstered guest chairs, and sat down, dropping her briefcase on the floor next to her.

Across the desk, Chuck's kind, dark eyes gleamed bright and enlarged behind his glasses. His face, rumpled like an unmade bed, was pensive. He touched a pink memo note. "The word from Judge McGillian's office is that he won't tolerate any more adjournments. This is to be the last day of the trial."

"Hurrah," Rachel replied in a flat voice. "He's the one approving these damn post-ponements. If he delays again, I want you to move the case to another court."

"One more time—and in the middle of a trial? Do you want a new judge, who'll have no time to learn the details? He won't be allowed to review the history of the case and won't understand what you've been going through—"

She interrupted, "Neither does McGillian—"

"But he *knows* the previous charges against Wes even if they had been cleared and McGillian's supposed to ignore them. He hasn't had a lobotomy."

"Chuck, I want results."

He leaned back in his chair. "McGillian won't stop Wes from seeing Ellie, but I expect him to block Wes's *unsupervised* visits."

She sighed. "Whatever made me think that by running away I could lock the door in Wes's face?"

"Parental kidnapping is never the answer."

"You'd think I flew to the Amazon and disappeared in the jungle." How she wished she had. "It was only Jacqueline's apartment downtown, for heaven's sake. Then got my own place in Long Island." Rachel stopped. At Chuck's high hourly rates, it was no use dredging it all up.

"Nevertheless, you established a history of kidnapping." Chuck studied her. "It doesn't help when we're now up against a custody trial. But I have all the witnesses lined up—"

"More experts, pitted against one another. Another parade of social workers, doctors, and therapists." Ellie lost with each spin on the legal spiral. "I can't take losing. Chuck, no unsupervised visits. That's my bottom line."

"I know. But there are always surprises. These judges have seen and heard it all. The cases they hear are no more than a Chinese menu of grievances and wrongs: Column A and Column B. The differences are in the variety of combinations. The smells and flavors are the same."

"Great. Keep on reminding me that I feel like Chop Suey."

Chuck smiled wanly. "Look, if all else fails, we'll bring in Stephanie. That'll be our next round of ammunition. McGillian may have to allow her testimony now that she's eleven."

Rachel leaned forward. "Do you think she can handle telling it all in court? What can she remember after so many years?"

"She's testified well enough to convince the New Jersey judge to forbid Wes to even call or write her."

Rachel sighed, "I'll call her mother whenever you say. She's been a Godsend."

"We'll have to first argue the admissibility of her testimony."

Rachel's voice rose. "But it would prove what Wes is capable of."

Chuck lay down his pen. Like a broken record, he repeated the analogy he had used before. "If you robbed a liquor store on Tuesday at ten, wearing a ski mask and carrying an Uzi, that doesn't mean you were the one who robbed a liquor store on Wednesday at ten, wearing a ski mask and carrying an Uzi. That's the law in its strictest sense."

Chuck had the patience of a geriatric nurse explaining the concepts over and over as if to a dimwit. "That legal logic may make sense to you," she said, "but not to me. This is not justice."

"It's how the system works. You have to connect all the dots in each case." He peered at the papers on his desk. "And even then, you should be ready for all the possibilities."

"Don't you always tell me to entertain positive thoughts?" Rachel spoke with a forced light tone into the bald triangle on his temple. "Now you tell me not to get my hopes up. Which one is it?"

"I want you to reserve your energy for this last time."

"Sure," she said, sarcasm in her voice. "Trust that nice man—that chauvinistic bastard."

Chuck raised his gaze, their eyes locking. "McGillian knows his law; he'll see the light."

Rachel waited in the reception area while revisions were made to the documents Chuck would file in court. She stared blankly at an ashtray. How appalled she had first been at her inability to keep Wes away from Ellie legally. Her ranting and raving subsided in time as the court battles raged on, but giving up the fight had never been an option. Instead, a black hole had opened inside her with an infinite capacity to suck in emotions. Like now.

Chuck came out and placed the papers before her. He stood over her and wordlessly pointed at the places awaiting her signature.

When she was done, he straightened up. He looked shorter standing than sitting. "I just got a call from Henry Ortman. Wes's girlfriend has moved into his apartment as per Ortman's suggestion. Ortman trusts it should put our minds at ease regarding the Fourth of July visit. It won't be unsupervised."

"Ortman '*trusts*?'" Wes's lawyer was as sly as his client. "Chuck, you don't buy it, do you? They've tried it before."

"It's the best we can hope for, for now."

Rachel felt the blood rush through her. "All Wes needs do is to send her to the supermarket or to get her nails done and he'll be back to his old tricks."

"Don't you dare deny him visitation before the next hearing."

"One more denied visit won't make a difference—"

He cut her off. "It would—in McGillian's mind—when determining custody. Especially if you have Ortman's guarantee."

How could she take the chance? Rachel got up and flung her jacket over her shoulders. "Chuck, do we still have this appointment with the Assistant D.A.?"

He nodded. "I've filed the complaint in criminal court. The Nassau County D.A. hates to lose cases. In election year especially, he'll prosecute only if he can win, or he won't touch it."

"Do I have to meet with him too? I can't afford more time off work."

"You'll be back at the office by lunch." He paused. "Vince Carducci still gives you a tough time?"

"How can I explain to him the nature of my court appearances? He'll never understand—"

"No one ever does unless they lived through the justice system," Chuck said.

"He'll hit the ceiling when I tell him I'm taking another day off—even though I'm using vacation time—"

"Be there." Chuck's finger touched a thick brown curl on her shoulder. "Put your hair up, and don't look so beautiful. The red suit is too assertive. And no matter what, please don't cry."

At his words, tears gathered up behind Rachel's eyelids. She would not cry. She would wrestle her hair into a French braid. She would use a pale lipstick. But the pain within her would continue to grow fat on her misery.

At the door, instead of his customary handshake, Chuck kissed her on the cheek. "Go to the beach this weekend. Have a date with Gerald. Whatever. Just relax."

"While I send Ellie to Wes?"

"You have a whole weekend with her before Monday. Enjoy it."

"You know, Chuck, when I was a baby, every time I burped, my mother said it was the birth of a star," Rachel said. "What happened?"

He laughed. "She was right. You are a star. In my book, you light a whole galaxy."

Instead of taking the taxi back to her office, Rachel strolled up along Fifth Avenue. It was a rare summer day when the air was crisp and cool, giving vibrancy to the brushed brass and polished chrome of the stores' window frames and distilling all impurities till the displayed merchandise came to life in sharp, colorful lines. She glimpsed a moving silhouette reflecting back at her. If it weren't for the refined yet decisive stride and uptilt of the head, she would not have recognized herself in the young woman whose face was a play of shadowed planes and deep-set eyes, a face lovelier and more poised than she felt. She slowed down. Tomorrow might be another oppressively hot day, making a relaxed stroll down Manhattan streets impossible.

At the tail end of lunch hour, the suit-clad working crowd was dwindling, giving way to the multitudes of tourists in shorts and belt pouches. Rachel bought a bottle of cold, peach-flavored water. As she ambled on the west side of the street, keeping to the narrow strip of shade, she took small sips from the bottle. Careful not to jostle the tourists holding cameras to their faces, she studied the top of the buildings across the street. Exploring the architectural details stilled the scream of despair that rumbled inside her. Ever since she had taken a course about the Avenue during her maternity leave five years before, she found comfort in the beauty of the ornate windows, roof gargoyles, verandas, banisters, and turrets that decorated the upper sections of the pre-World War II buildings.

She stopped at a street vendor, his display of toys spread on a rickety table. She touched each item, turning it to check its construction and safety, and settled on a string puppet and a storybook. She'd keep the puppet for those moments when Ellie would have a temper tantrum and need to be distracted with a surprise.

At Fifty-second Street, Rachel turned east and crossed the block to Madison Avenue. With a rare lightness of step, she entered a building where she had scheduled two appointments at an advertising agency. Her corporate sales job at *Women's Life* magazine provided normalcy and the income to keep feeding the justice machine. Every sale of an ad page meant more money for filing fees, attorneys, and expert witnesses. And at the end of three years of legal battles in which she had so often been branded unstable and given to hallucinations, her work was the one place where she retained her old composed self. Once upon a time there had been weeks when work offered the background music to portentous decisions such as what shoe brand to buy, the scheduling of a weekend tennis game, or the amount to be written on a charity check. Now it was the oxygen line that kept her life functioning.

During the routine meetings with clients at both the media department and account services, Rachel shifted her emotions to neutral and navigated the discussions with ease. After two hours, she sealed a four-month negotiation with a commitment to advertise Compton Foods' new product launch.

Yet back at her office for the remainder of the afternoon, the thunder of panic over the coming trial gathered force. She must keep it all in check. Later there would be moments when her daily pressures would peel away, leaving her raw to do nothing else but feel for Ellie.

She was busy making notes at her desk when she raised her eyes to see her ad director's lanky figure leaning on her doorframe.

"What's up?" Vince asked. A lazy smile spread across his face, darkening its grooves with a five-o'clock shadow. His Nicole Miller sports-theme tie lay askew over a loosened button.

"Had a great day," she replied with remnants of the exuberance she had felt when leaving the agency. "Compton Foods is coming in with a full schedule for a new diet entree. One million dollars." There was no need to mention the obvious—her commission.

Vince let out a chuckle. "As long as *Women's Life* keeps its number one position in the field, advertisers will automatically come on board."

Rachel's old resentment rose up. "Vince, I didn't just sign up an order. You know that. If I may say so myself, it took wits and persistence to get on their ad schedule—" She caught her sharp tone and stopped.

He examined her face for a moment. "You okay?"

"I'll be all right."

"I'm your buddy. You can talk to me. Still having problems with your ex?"

She nodded, but said nothing. Vince would find the litigation, the reasons for it, tacky.

When he did not move from his position at the door, Rachel uncoiled herself from her seat and made a show of picking up a stack of stapled papers from her windowsill. "Next week I'll give you a run-through of the presentation for the Baroness account."

"Rake them in. We'll be ready with prominent positioning," he said, referring to the magazine page layout, a well-studied map of prized real estate. Advertisers vied for the most advantageous exposure for their ads. Like a prime storefront rental, *Women's Life*'s sales force secured the best spots with multi-year contracts. "Location. Location. Location," he chanted.

"It takes more than location to bring them aboard." Rachel smiled.

"You bet it does. That's what you have an expense account for." Vince continued. "You haven't done much entertaining this year. Why don't you set up something fun for the Baroness management team? Just let me know when, and I'll join you. Bring that snazzy boyfriend of yours along. Gerald?"

He left, and she plopped down into her chair. Vince never missed a major car race, new fragrance launching, yachting party, international tennis tournament, or opening night either on Broadway or in Hollywood. *Women's Life* entertained clients at all of them, but Rachel could rarely cram those events into her schedule. The few hours in the evening spent with Ellie did not make up for the missed trip to the pumpkin farm, the school play, and the Mother's Day party.

Jacqueline came in. "Your flight to Chicago week after next is all set," she said in her French-accented voice. Her eyes, dark as raisins, glanced around the room at the charts tacked to the wall and the large boards leaning against the bookcase. "I can't wait for this sales presentation to be done with. Don't you feel you go on popping them out for the same reason a hen goes on laying eggs?"

Rachel laughed. Jacqueline's streaks of merriment shot out and zapped Rachel whenever she was in her presence. "We all sing for our supper," Rachel said.

"Except that my singing doesn't pay for supper." Jacqueline had come to New York to nurture her musical career. Years later, her CDs sold only when she herself took position at Grand Central Station, singing for rush hour commuters.

"It will," Rachel said. "Anyway, I love working on presentations."

Jacqueline tilted her head toward the banter of voices carried from the corridor—Rachel's male colleagues enjoying their social time at the end of the day. She tossed her mane of black curls that looked huge on her petite frame. "Guess what? Vince is talking sports."

Rachel shrugged. "What a surprise."

"You'd think that after thirty years past his glory, a former Yankee player would get a life."

"He's waiting to retire from Sheridan Magazines. The top brass think it's hot to have his name on the executive list; they can well afford it."

"If work is when you'd rather be doing something else, then those guys must have a tough life." Jacqueline motioned with her head toward the corridor.

"They have exactly the life they want," Rachel smiled. "A neat package of work and play." And no stress.

She cast a glance at the Waterford crystal clock on her desk—last year's top salesperson award.

Quarter to five. She stretched her arms over head. Her back muscles ached with fatigue. She longed to hug Ellie, inhale her sweet smell. "My mother said that in life you stop at each station, not just pass through it. She forgot to warn me that there would be a time when it felt as if I were making the entire trip in one day, every day." She dropped her arms. "I'll have to adopt some of your French nonchalance to exit this place, as if I, too, have all the time in the world."

She got up and checked herself in the mirror on the back of her door. She put a couple of drops of Visine in her eyes to make the green appear alert, touched the shiny spots on her nose and cheeks, and applied a darker lipstick. Her face shouldn't reveal to her male colleagues that her morning had started with the weekly laundry, hours before they woke up. Or that for the past three years she'd been living a nightmare.

"What did your lawyer say that will make my day?" Jacqueline asked.

"Funny how my I.Q. drops thirty points the minute I speak to him. I can't grasp the legal convoluted logic." Rachel sighed and recited, "When it comes to 'preponderance of evidence,' we're in better shape than in prior trials."

"Pass that by me again?"

"'Preponderance of evidence' is all that's required in Family Court. If we have more credible evidence in our favor than they, we win. It's the easiest standard to meet, very different from criminal court where we have to prove Wes's guilt 'beyond a reasonable doubt.'"

"That would be an interesting twist."

Rachel swallowed hard. "But I must send Ellie to Wes on Monday, the Fourth of July."

Jacqueline stared at her.

"Until now it was a question of visits. This time around Wes is going for full custody." Rachel's stomach rumbled. "Apparently, my denying him his visits is strong legal grounds for reversal of custody—"

"What kind of system is this? Last year he admitted Ellie slept in his bed, and that turkey of a judge found nothing wrong with it."

Rachel shrugged. "No worse than when Chuck asked the next judge to forbid him from showering with Ellie. His nudity at eye level with her face—"

"In France *we do* shower with kids."

"Well, I guess this judge had French ancestry, because he said that when his three daughters were little, he, too, often showered with them."

Jacqueline's olive skin was pale. "Tell me you won't send Ellie to Wes—"

"Jacques, please. I have no choice."

Jacqueline took a step forward and hugged her briefly. Her perfume smelled of cinnamon and spicy wood. "We'll do something fun Monday. And I'll cover for you Tuesday morning when Wes drops Ellie at the daycare center, she may need you."

Rachel shook her head. "That's when I'm back in court. For the last time."

"Okay, then. I'll sleep over at your place and check Ellie at the daycare center at eight."

The familiar feelings of gratitude and awe bubbled up. "You're more than a best friend—"

Jacqueline waved her hand. "Wes has been lucky to catch a ride on this new-age trend of keeping fathers involved in their children's lives at all cost—I'm evening out the score."

Rachel dropped her face into her hands. "Can we not talk about it now?"

"Sorry."

Jacqueline left, and Rachel, collecting herself, punched in her home number. The babysitter had picked up Ellie at four. The light of Rachel's day would be their picnic dinner under coppery skies. Her heart expanded with pleasure as she heard Ellie's chirpy voice.

"Remember our picnic, Mommy? And I want to plant all the flowers—"

"Sweetie, of course I remember." She was so tired. "We'll plant the irises, but the impatiens and daisies will have to wait until tomorrow."

She hung up and started to the door. Vince was leaning on the wall outside his office.

"Leaving, huh?" His tone was laden with echoes of his past complaints about her rushing home right after work. "Want to join us for a drink?"

She turned around to face him, feigning a smile. "Sorry. Another time?"

"You said that last week. Rachel, we're a team here—"

"If bringing in more ad pages is the team's goal, then I hit the most home runs." She softened her tone. "But I have a child, and there's no time for beer parties."

"That's not what it's all about," he said pointedly, then added with a sigh, "Good night."

"Have a nice evening." Her forced polite tone sounded awkward even to her ears. She pivoted on her heel, her briefcase flapping against her knee, and walked away, feeling Vince's eyes piercing her back.

In the subway to Penn Station where she would catch her train home to Green Hills, Long Island, an errant thought wormed into her consciousness. What Vince resented the most was her intensity. His own boss, the publisher, and her male colleagues' work style was as casual as his. While she talked statistics and market share, they arranged golf foursomes.

Her pleasure came from the energy of strategizing a sale, as she was doing for Baroness, the giant cosmetics company she hoped to snare as a new client. Designing the research, writing the presentation, developing the statistical charts, and creating the video with the art department were intoxicating. The excitement was like a chemical stimulant that altered the formula of her days.

Perhaps Vince was right; she was unlike the rest of his team. She was a woman, with one child and many problems, and she could never play in their sandbox. Even if she loved her work more than they did.

On the train, finally alone with her emotions, Rachel tucked her briefcase between her head and the window, leaned against it, and closed her eyes.

That's when the pain seared through her. She could feel its physical presence, an inflated balloon painfully contained within her ribs. She'd have to send Ellie on Monday. She wished she could trust Ortman's promise that Wes's girlfriend would sleep in his bed, not Ellie.

Rachel rearranged herself in the seat and listened to the train's steady chant of steel rolling over steel. The train came out of the tunnel, and a bright red sun hovered above the western end of Long Island Sound, presenting itself with pride, like a teenager showing off her prom dress. There would still be enough daylight for Ellie's picnic dinner.

What if Chuck was wrong about the outcome of the trial? Loyal and devoted, he had propped her up when hope and despair tore at her with their opposing pulls. But what good was a caring lawyer if he didn't win? .

To satisfy McGillian, she'd have to take the risk this one time; she'd send Ellie to Wes on Monday and pray for the best. How she wished she had enough religious conviction to believe in a divine entity that could change the marching doom of events.

If she couldn't protect Ellie, then her child needed an angel to take care of her.

CHAPTER TWO

On Friday afternoon, Rachel and Ellie returned from the town pool. They dropped their beach bags and toys.

"I'm hungry." Ellie's tone edged on petulant.

"Jelly Belly." Rachel tickled Ellie's stomach. "You ate a hot dog and ice cream. I'll make you a snack. Then it's rest time."

"I don't want to rest. I'm hungry."

"Gerald will come by later; we'll have an early dinner—"

"A picnic."

A demanding knock sounded on the door in the small foyer.

"Here's something you like to do," Rachel said, steering Ellie away. "Put the towels in the washing machine. But don't try to lift the detergent bottle."

The knock repeated. Ellie clomped away, her flip-flops slapping rhythmically. Rachel laid down the copies of *Advertising Age* and *Advertising Week* she should have read at poolside, and sent a longing glance at a novel she had yet to get into. Perhaps tonight, if she finished reading the industry reports, she would immerse herself in a good book.

Whoever was at the door pounded harder. With her foot, Rachel nudged the beach bags on the floor into a tighter pile and peeked through the peephole. She saw a young woman, her brown hair bobbed, with a pair of round spectacles perched on her nose.

Rachel opened the door, and found the woman ready with a business card in one hand and a clipboard in the other. One shoulder was raised to keep her handbag strap from sliding down her arm.

"Department of Child Protective Services," the woman announced.

Again a new caseworker? A shudder zipped through Rachel's body. This one looked twenty years old. Chuck counted on the last caseworker's testimony next week; she had seemed astute and more cooperative than some of the others.

"What happened to the social worker who was here before?" Rachel asked.

The woman shrugged. "I was assigned to the case. Glad I found you home."

"Summer schedule. I get Friday afternoons off. I work home Friday mornings—" She stopped. Here she was already selling herself.

At that moment, Ellie's whining carried down from the kitchen, "Mommy, I'm hungry."

"Come in." Rachel moved aside, opening the door wider. She called back to Ellie, "I'll be with you in a second." She turned to the social worker. "We just got in from swimming. Let me finish with her—"

The woman scanned the small vestibule. Her brows knotted in disapproval at the pile of wet suits and the collection of plastic beach toys that cascaded from the collapsed string bag. She scribbled something in her notepad.

Rachel hurried back to the kitchen. In quick movements, she sliced an apple, slopped peanut butter on it, and placed the sections around a cookie, like an open flower. From the cabinet, she grabbed a plastic cup painted with Big Bird and poured cold milk into it. Ellie continued to whine. A moment later, her crying turned into a scream. She hurled the cup of milk onto the terra cotta floor. White tentacles began a slow crawl along the tiles' crevices.

Rachel held her tight and tried to calm her down. It did not take much to trigger Ellie's tantrums. Speaking in a soft voice, Rachel said, "Ellie, let's go upstairs and rest a while."

As she passed through the toy-strewn living room, carrying the wriggling and kicking Ellie in her arms, Rachel ignored the caseworker scribbling furiously on the clipboard resting against her stomach. Who was this person who suddenly became the judge, jury, and executioner of her life?

Ten minutes later, when Rachel came downstairs, she found the woman taking an inventory of the refrigerator.

"May I help you?" Rachel asked, her voice tight. "Would you care for something to drink?"

"No, thanks, I'm just completing the form."

"What does Ellie's situation have to do with the contents of my refrigerator?"

"Oh, we must determine that the child receives the right nutrition—"

Rachel fished in her mind for the name on the business card. "Miss—Miss Hermon, do you know why you're here?"

"To investigate a case of child abuse."

"It's child *sexual* abuse. No one is complaining about Ellie's diet."

"I have specific instructions as to how to conduct my investigation, Ms. Belmore."

Rachel pressed on. "Where, according to your information, does the abuse take place?"

The woman tapped the form with her pen. "I'll ask the questions, if you don't mind."

"The abuse takes place when Ellie visits her father. Not here. She is well cared for when she's with me—"

"I'll be the judge of that, Ms. Belmore."

Rachel took a deep breath. This was all wrong—as it had been before.

The woman pulled out one of the kitchen chairs and sat down. Her hand caressed the polished oak tabletop. "Nice," she said, and Rachel perked her ears to an envious tone.

She nodded, but kept silent. From the corner of her eye she saw the spilled milk still on the floor, but resisted the urge to get up and clean it. Instead, she turned her attention to the social worker and patiently answered her questions.

Finally, she ventured, "Miss Hermon, have you interviewed Dr. Belmore at home?"

"He is *working*, as you know. I visited him at his office."

Wes worked? And what was she doing, playing tennis? Rachel could just imagine how impressed Miss Hermon had been with Wes's plush office decorated with autographed celebrities' photos. "Surgeon to the Stars," *People* magazine had tagged the handsome physician a few months earlier when they ran their annual "Most Desirable Available Men" listing. Why couldn't Miss Hermon visit Rachel at her office or visit Wes at his apartment?

"I was instructed to file the complaint in your jurisdiction because that's where the abuse occurs," Rachel started again in a softer tone, "When Ellie visits her father in Manhattan—"

The woman examined Rachel's face. "We see thousands of inner-city kids. Rich ones too. Do you know how many don't have a loving father? Or no father at all?"

"It's exactly the loving part that I have a serious problem with."

"Look, Ms. Belmore. It is hard enough for parents who live together to agree on how to raise their children. It is much harder for divorced parents to do that. There's too much animosity. I'd like to find a way for you to cooperate with your ex in a way that will not deprive Ellie of her chance to develop a healthy relationship with him—"

"I don't think you understand. He sexually molests her when she's left alone in his care—"

"We don't know that for sure, do we?"

"Yes, *we* do. I saw it with my own eyes, and this year Ellie finally was able to tell the last caseworker about his sex play." Rachel felt the agonizing words cave in and crush. "It's hard even for me to talk about it. Why does Ellie need to prove anew each time what's happening to her?"

"We are talking cooperation, Ms. Belmore. Dr. Belmore is an intelligent man, and he's willing to negotiate with you. As a physician, he's deeply concerned about what all this litigation and uh—your state of mind—are doing to Ellie's psychological development, and he'd wish nothing more than to stop it. Tell me how you plan to work with him—"

Wes and his Goddamn charisma had done it again.

Why should she be surprised that the sophisticated man with the perfect bedside manner had charmed the young Miss Hermon beyond repair? How could Rachel hope to stay on the social worker's good side if it was already taken? Rachel felt a rage of powerlessness crouch behind her composure.

"You've got your priorities wrong," Rachel told her, "I'm more concerned about protecting Ellie from being molested than I am about cooperating with her father so that he can continue his filthy—"

Miss Hermon cut her off. "You have an attitude."

Rachel heard the note of begging worm its way into her voice, "Sorry. My child is being sexually molested by her father. She needs your compassion—and your help."

"I'd like to talk to her."

Rachel stared at her. "She just fell asleep…. You saw how she was—"

"Yes, I did. She's a difficult child."

Rachel nodded.

"Too much for you to handle, Ms. Belmore?"

With the surprise of a fast burning light bulb when turned on, Rachel saw the trap. She sat up in her chair. "Never—"

Just then the doorbell rang. Rachel, her heart still pounding, got up to answer it. It was Gerald, carrying two grocery bags. There was confidence in the way he shaved his head rather than mourn his hair loss.

He followed Rachel to the kitchen and deposited the bags on the counter. Glancing toward the caseworker, he nodded hello and said quietly, "I'll wait in the living room."

Miss Hermon made a notation on her clipboard. Then she raised her head. Behind the shining glasses, her gaze on Rachel was steady, stern. "How often do you entertain men?"

The blood exploded in a thud behind Rachel's eyes. "What? I do not 'entertain men.'"

"Who is the gentleman?"

"Gerald Rhodes, the man I've been seeing these past eight months. He's a partner at an international construction company." Her tone turned sarcastic. "Would you like to interview him?"

"I might," Miss Hermon said. "You claim your child is being sexually molested. How do you know it's not one of your male visitors?"

"I do not have *'male visitors,'* Miss Hermon. And I strongly resent your implication, which you've now made twice. Gerald does not molest Ellie. In fact, she is so scared of men, she hardly speaks to him."

"That's exactly my point. How do you know that he doesn't molest her and that's the reason she distrusts him?"

Rachel allowed a moment to pass. She had once been whimsical, with a rare sense of the absurd, but she no longer found the absurd funny. Like now, it strung the seconds and the minutes into a nightmare. The air around her, she knew, bristled with intensity and worry. "Gerald didn't meet Ellie until a few months ago—"

"More children are abused by the mothers' boyfriends than by their own fathers."

"Look, Ellie has been suffering—and demonstrating—disturbed behavior for years. You must have enough interviews in your files to that effect."

"I haven't seen the file yet."

"Why not? Isn't someone from your department supposed to testify on Tuesday? It's all there!"

"Don't bark at me. I was just assigned to your case; I'm trying to do my job." She got up. With precise movements, taking her time, she gathered her papers, tapped them until they lined up neatly, and placed them back into the clipboard. The corners of her lips pulled down, and she threw another look at the puddle of drying milk. "If you don't mind, I'd like to go up to Ellie's room and speak to her."

Was she going to wake Ellie? Try to pry information from the cranky child? Rachel felt her fingers clench and unclench. "It would help if I woke her up and introduced you first."

"Aren't you a tad overprotective, Ms. Belmore?"

"How would you like to wake up and find a stranger hovering over your bed?"

"If that's how you want it." She shrugged.

But Ellie woke up from her short nap with a shining smile, and snuggled her warm, sweet-smelling body against her mother's chest. After a brief introduction, Rachel left, despite her anxiety to stay close and overhear the conversation. Would that disqualify the interview—if indeed Ellie agreed to this one more probing by what was clearly another under trained caseworker?

Downstairs, she stood in front of Gerald and looked into his alert brown eyes. He took her in his arms and held her close for a few moments.

"I'm so scared," she whispered. She leaned against his chest, drawing on his strength, her senses numb. Yet she knew more than felt that the many pieces of herself—her corporate career, her home, Gerald's love—functioned underneath the surface like a life-teeming lake thinly coated with ice.

From upstairs, voices carried down. Ellie's reticent laughter was like muted little bells. Miss Hermon took a turn at the toy xylophone. Then they spoke a little, and although Rachel could not hear the words, the woman's conversation with Ellie was less strained.

"Ellie's talking. It's a good sign," Gerald mumbled into Rachel's hair.

"She's too scared of Wes to just spill it all out. He's told her, 'Mommy will put me in jail if you tell.'" She snapped her back straight. "Maybe you'd better drive around the block until this caseworker leaves."

He passed his hand on his shaved head in a pensive gesture. An unfamiliar expression registered on his face.

"What is it?" Rachel asked.

"Nothing. You're right. I shouldn't be here."

"Sorry," she mumbled. She shut her eyes tight, and again furrowed her face in the crook of his neck. "I have to win this time," she whispered.

He returned shortly after Miss Hermon had left. Ellie watched a video in her room while Rachel put away magazines and strewn toys.

With a light tapping on the couch, Gerald motioned to Rachel to join him.

She plopped down. "I can't bear the thought of Ellie going to Wes Monday. I'm worried about the trial. And now I'm scared of what this woman will have to say."

"What's her agenda?"

Rachel threw her hands up. "Three years ago, when I first contacted the agency, it took them months to send someone. The first caseworker was promising. She believed me. Then, before anything was accomplished, she left the agency, 'burned out.'" Rachel shook her head and added, a sad timbre in her voice, "They sent her replacement, a big Mexican man with a huge beard and a booming voice that would scare the hell out of even you. Then a caseworker who believed the rich had it made and what-did-they-have-to-complain-about, then another inept one. They either don't get it, or don't care to spend the time on something that's not obvious enough—"

"Obvious?"

"Like cigarette burns, broken bones—or sperm."

He took both her hands in his. "I hate to even mention this, but have you thought of running away with Ellie?"

She clutched at her throat.

"There's this underground organization in Atlanta," he continued tenderly, "You may not have a choice… "

The words hit her full force, as if a wet canvas had slapped her across the face. She was unaware of the tears until, without warning, they burst the dam. She lowered her head as deep sobs tore from deep inside her, breaking off and washing away more pieces of herself. Gerald held her close, saying nothing, until she emptied out. Hope had become as elusive as trying to pluck moonlight off the water.

"Mommy, Mommy, are you okay?" Ellie's voice came from the top of the stairs where she stood, transfixed, her face gathered in bewilderment.

"Yes, sweetie. Just a touch of hay fever."

Keeping her face averted from Ellie's view, Rachel glided into the powder room to wash up. It was time to prepare dinner.

At dinner, Gerald's attempts to break through Ellie's resistance to all men finally worked. For the first time, she responded to his riddles.

"What's white and black and 'read' all over?" he asked her.

Ellie sent him a curious look that enlarged her eyes. "What?"

"A newspaper."

She giggled.

"Why did the chicken cross the road?"

"Why?"

"To get to the other side."

The giggle gathered resonance. Ellie's face bloomed.

"What's worse than finding a worm in your apple?"

"What?"

"Finding half a worm."

Ellie squealed with delight, and Rachel popped a spoonful of peas into her mouth.

Gerald had to leave to catch his flight to San Diego where his company was rebuilding the airport.

Rachel saw him to the door. "Who schedules meetings on the Fourth of July weekend?"

"Our Japanese investors do. They won't miss a clambake and fireworks display, and, oh boy," he grinned, "the bash on the beach with beer and barbecue will be a blast."

She smiled. "Got it. A list of B's."

He planted a warm kiss on her lips, and held her tight. His voice changed to a whisper. "I wish I could stay and make love to you all night."

"Thanks for trying so hard with Ellie."

"I'm a father, too. I want her to know that not all men are like Wes."

She stretched against his body, connecting in as many spots as she could. "Come back quickly," she whispered.

"Make a list of things that start with an 'S' and are free" he said. "We'll have fun with them."

"'S?'"

"Sky, stars, sunsets, and sea."

She laughed.

"Wait. There's more. The sea also has shore, sand, shells."

He kissed her again on her laughing mouth. "Will you be all right for the rest of the weekend?"

She nodded. "Jacqueline has gigs tonight and tomorrow, but she'll be here Monday."

He stepped out, then quickly returned. "One last kiss." His fingers trailed hers as he left again, wanting to prolong the contact. "I'll call you."

Rachel leaned against the closed door, happiness filling her. How reluctant she had been to rejoin the singles scene. Wes, a man she had loved so much, had been a disappointment too great for her to trust anyone again, least of all her own judgment. How could she have been so wrong about a man? For two years, she rebuffed Jacqueline's coaxing to go out. Until she met Gerald Rhodes.

He had disarmed her with his openness, his down-to-earth love of life's simple pleasures. Gerald and his 'S's. He loved sex, too, but hadn't pressed her until she was ready. It took her a while but after he seduced her soul, she found delight in his inventive touches. He became her expert guide down out-of-the-way paths. Their bodies had reached places that love alone couldn't take them.

They had met at an electronics store where they were both inquiring about a telephone answering machine. The salesman saved his efforts and addressed them together, explaining the different models in the display case.

When Rachel stood at the cashier line to pay, Gerald was right behind her.

"Now I'll have to hope someone will call," he said, his voice warm.

She turned to look at the man, guessing his meaning. He was cute; his baldness, completed by shaving off whatever hair was left, was deliberate. He smelled of clean aftershave, and his charcoal-gray suit had an Italian cut.

"I just moved to the city." He smiled. His teeth were white and strong. "No one knows my new phone number yet."

"And you want me to test your machine, right?" Rachel flashed back a smile. She had long ago learned to engage men's eyes upon introduction. They seemed to remember her striking face.

"Would you?" His expression was winsome. He handed her a gold-embossed business card and scribbled his home phone number with a silver Tiffany pen.

"It takes six months for a woman to know if a man is serious, if he's a *mensch*," the street-smart Jacqueline had cautioned Rachel, borrowing the Yiddish word she had learned in New York. "If after six months he's still interested in you and in your troubles, then he's passed the first test."

Gerald had been in her life for eight months now. He had passed the test.

CHAPTER THREE

RACHEL gasped and averted her eyes. Once again, the moment she stepped into the courthouse, she reentered a world obscured by lies. Distracted, she had let her gaze roam the scene in the small waiting area outside Judge McGillian's courtroom and hadn't noticed her former husband until this moment. No traces were left of the deep scratches she had carved into his cheek that night when she clawed into it, peeling skin. Too bad. She should have left a scar. The shameful mark of a pedophile.

How was Ellie? Had he harmed her during the visit last night? Fear and fury rose up in Rachel like a swarm of angry bees. She got up and sauntered through a small corridor, passing two teenagers in shackles, their faces sullen and defiant, as they were ushered away by guards.

She stopped at a busier section of the lobby. Beyond the metal detector, the spacious waiting hall to the left was filled with the noise of fretful babies and fidgety mothers. Beside a row of soda and snack dispensers, a fat man in a seersucker suit wrangled aloud with his attorney. On the bench in one corner, a couple anxiously held an infant and studied it with love and awe, adoption written across their faces. An elderly couple gaped with fear at a scruffy youth.

For a moment, Rachel stared at a blond, angelic woman whose bruised face read desolation. Rachel wished she could sit next to her, offer words of courage and comfort. But once generous in her attention to people, Rachel now economized on her feelings; she had none to spare. Whatever the young woman's plight was, its desperation reflected her own.

To her right, at the bank of pay phones, Chuck had planted himself. She stopped in front of an available stall and dialed the day care center number. Jacqueline would have passed by earlier to check on Ellie, but she could not reach Rachel to report back.

Rachel trilled her fingers on the aluminum surface while the teacher was summoned.

"How is she?" Rachel asked.

"Tired and cranky. Her hair was uncombed when her father brought her, and she didn't have breakfast."

"I'd lose custody if I sent Ellie to school tired, unfed, and unwashed." Rachel paused. She heard her pulse pounding. "My attorney may want you to mention it when you testify later today."

There was a silence on the other end. Finally, the teacher said, "I'm subpoenaed; I don't have a choice but to be there."

"I'm so sorry to cause you all this trouble," Rachel said, mustering the softest of tones, but the words were too shallow to articulate the guilt that banged away inside her. Why wouldn't the teacher, like many others Chuck plucked out of their workday, resent the disruption? And the school was forced to pay for a substitute teacher.

"I'll see that Ellie gets a quiet playtime and a nap," the teacher said. "Now if you'll excuse me, I must attend to some things here."

"See you later—" Rachel heard the click on the other end. She leaned on the wall closer to Chuck; it was safer near him.

"Ready?" He touched her arm.

"Is this real, Chuck?" she asked. "Is it possible that I could lose custody?" Deep inside, hope and premonition, like two actors, played off each other. "Make this the last round of Ellie's abuse, police reports, new caseworkers, long waits on the court calendar, expert witnesses, psychologists attacking my credibility—"

"If Ortman doesn't pull another one of his schticks, it will be. Now take it easy—"

"You mean, 'Get a grip on yourself?'" Rachel followed him to the double doors of the courtroom. Sometimes she was surprised her legs still obeyed her command to walk.

"Let me handle everything, and think positive thoughts. Don't look too emotional."

"Oh? So McGillian can tell you again in chambers that I look phlegmatic and remote."

Chuck touched her arm again and squeezed. "More like, so Ortman can't claim that you are unstable and delusional—"

She swallowed hard. "I'll be good." To win the judge's Good Mother image award, she'd act cool and collected, as though it were unnatural for a mother whose five-year-old daughter had been molested since infancy to cry.

Two hours later, the overcast sky of the morning had turned darker, and the rain pelted relentlessly on the large window panes. Occasionally, a gust of wind whipped at the falling rain and slammed it across the window with a bang that reverberated in the high-ceilinged room.

With the next gust, Judge McGillian, his smile engraving lines that curved and reached his eyes, said to the two lawyers, "Let's see who's going to run out of wind first—the weather or you." Under other circumstances, Rachel would have found the judge charming, his baritone voice warm, but now he registered as too commanding, dictatorial.

"I'll stick around as long as the court will," Henry Ortman, a tall, thin man with a horsy face and a maddeningly unctuous voice, replied, "We have plenty of ground to cover."

Rachel's jolt of dread at his words was further ignited as, at that instant, her attention pivoted to the arrival of an unexpected witness. She had smelled the cigar smoke on his clothes before her head snapped back to see the pompous man stride down the short aisle and take a seat.

"The witness should wait outside," McGillian said. "Dr. Hoffmann, you know the procedure."

"Your Honor, may I testify out of turn? I have some urgent matters I must attend to."

McGillian nodded. "We'll call you as soon as we hear the next two witnesses."

"I thought Hoffmann wasn't testifying," Rachel whispered in Chuck's ear. "He was unable to interview Ellie. She was so scared of him—"

"He's the court-appointed psychologist. McGillian must hear him."

She fought to suppress her growing panic. Hadn't Chuck said he had tied up all the loose ends?

In the meantime, Miss Hermon took the witness stand. "The mother is paranoid—"

"Move to strike," Chuck called out. "The witness is not qualified to diagnose mental illness."

"Sustained," McGillian said.

"Miss Belmore is obsessed with sexual abuse to the detriment of the child," Miss Hermon declared.

Chuck did not voice an objection. As Miss Hermon continued to answer Ortman's questions, Rachel wished she could seal her ears the way she could close her eyes; to flip a set of lids, valve-like, that would shut off the onslaught of words. The many proceedings had not desensitized her. The negative testimonies, the attacks on her character, pierced her anew each time. Was she the person they said she was? All that remained of the one she had been was her ersatz self, an inferior substitute, driven by a single purpose: to save Ellie. Yet deep down, defiant, unyielding, her spirit hibernated, ready to be revived when she and Ellie regained control over their lives.

Chuck got up to cross-examine Miss Hermon. "If sexual child abuse is proven, would you still consider the mother's reaction an obsession?"

"Well, no, but—"

"When did you graduate from school, did you say?"

"Last year, but I—"

"Have you observed the child with her father?"

"The child has been turned against him. That is not to say he can't establish a relationship with her should the mother allow her to."

From the corner of her eye, Rachel noticed Ms. Edwards, Ellie's psychologist, rubbing her forehead like someone scouring her brains for an answer.

"Did the child tell you what her father did to her?" Chuck asked Miss Hermon.

"Kind of. But no child knows of these things unless told."

"Or unless it happens to them," Chuck interjected.

"Objection," Ortman called out.

"Sustained. Mr. Bernstein," McGillian said, "You know better than that."

Miss Hermon stiffened in her seat and tucked a strand of brown hair behind her ear. "More than half the cases our department investigated last year were without foundation—"

Chuck interrupted her. "So you're basing your assessment on statistics? Not on your field work?"

"Well, that, too."

"Do you disregard the other half of the cases, those that are found to have foundation?"

"It's our policy to try to foster cooperation between the parents. Ms. Belmore has been hostile toward Dr. Belmore. She's been uncooperative with me."

Beyond shock or incredulity, Rachel cringed. Yes, she had been uncooperative with an investigation about Ellie's diet. Jesus.

Half an hour later, Chuck called Ms. Edwards to the stand to testify on her young client's behalf.

"Please state your name and professional credentials," Chuck said.

Ms. Edward's fingers thumbed the edge of a ream of papers, as a card player would a deck of cards. "I have a master's in social work from Adelphi University, and I passed the New York State Board test. I did an externship for three years at Ackerman Family Therapy Institute, and later at the Jung Institute. I've been in my own practice for nine years."

"Have you seen Ellie on a regular basis?"

"Yes, I have. For four months now."

"Is there anything relevant you could tell us about your sessions?"

"My findings conclude that a recent abuse has been indicated beyond any doubt."

"How do you know that?"

"Ellie tells me. I can go through lists of dates of sessions—"

"Not yet. Thanks. Go on, please."

"Also, she has shown me, through anatomically-correct dolls, the games Dr. Belmore introduced her to. She was able to point to the private places where he has touched her."

"How did you respond?"

"I've been teaching her for quite some time to say 'No,' but she cannot yet do it. She's too frightened of him."

"How do you know that?"

"She tells me. Also, whenever we play with these dolls, she ends up throwing the 'Daddy' doll against the wall."

"Thank you," Chuck said. "Anything else?"

"Yes." Ms. Edwards's gaze flitted over the room and came to rest on Judge McGillian. "Ellie has told me her father threatened to punish her if she tells these 'lies.'"

"Objection!" Ortman called out.

"Overruled," McGillian said flatly.

Ten minutes later, in his cross-examination, Ortman asked Ms. Edwards to repeat her credentials.

"So you do not have a Ph.D.?" he said.

"No. The type of intensive clinical training I received is considered more relevant—"

He cut her off. "Thank you, *Ms.* Edwards. Now, let's get back to your testimony. You've mentioned, quote, 'she has shown me, through anatomically-correct dolls, the games Dr. Belmore introduced her to,' end quote. What made you think those were real incidents and not games similar to the ones *you* play with her?"

"She gets very upset. Ellie becomes agitated when a situation is intolerably distressing for her. Not when she's enjoying a game."

"That is not what we've heard of Ellie's behavior in other testimonies. Did you say you know her well?"

"Yes, I do. She behaves well when she is with me, unless—"

"Thank you. You said, quote 'Whenever we play these dolls, she ends up throwing the 'Daddy' doll against the wall.' Does she say anything when she does that?"

"No, she just screams."

"No 'I hate you?' or other such pronouncements?"

"No."

"Could her throwing the doll against the wall without saying anything reflect anything other than her father sexually molesting her?"

"I don't get your meaning."

"Maybe she is reflecting her mother's anger at her father?"

"No, I don't think so."

"But you are not sure, are you?"

"I am sure of my assessment that Ellie is being sexually molested."

"We know you are sure of that. *Ms.* Edwards, I do not doubt you believe it. What I am questioning is your ability to interpret and reach such a professional evaluation based upon your limited credentials—"

Chuck got up. "Objection, Your Honor. Mr. Ortman is harassing the witness."

"No, I'm not, Your Honor. I am simply responding to information presented here by Doctor—no, sorry, *Ms.* Edwards."

"Objection overruled. Go ahead, Mr. Ortman, but please get to the point."

"Thank you, Your Honor." Ortman nodded politely in the direction of the bench and turned his head back to Ms. Edwards. "In previous proceedings we've heard Dr. Belmore testify that he, as a physician, believed in using anatomically-correct dolls and language when playing with Ellie. Are you aware of that?"

"Yes."

"In what way does your presentation of the dolls differ from his?"

"I let her tell me about them, and she says he does these acts. She doesn't just play with the dolls."

Ortman opened a book. "In your testimony you testified last time you said that Professor Hirsch Rosenblum was your mentor. Is he a recognized authority in the field of child development?"

"Yes."

Ortman's long fingers leafed slowly through the pages, even though the green bookmark was visible. "I'd like the clerk to mark the book as exhibit one for identification."

"Go ahead," McGillian said to the clerk. "Please so mark."

"It says here that the typical five-year-old cannot reliably distinguish between the real and the imagined. Let me read you the exact wording—"

"Mr. Ortman, get to the point," McGillian said.

"I've just made it, Your Honor."

Moments later, McGillian asked the bailiff to bring in Dr. Hoffmann.

"Your Honor." Chuck's voice rose up in urgency as he turned to Judge McGillian,

"I ask the court to disallow Dr. Hoffmann's testimony since he was unable to interview the child properly. His assertions would be purely academic."

"He's met the child. He can tell us what he's observed," McGillian said.

"Your Honor, Ellie's terrified of men. There was no interaction; she did not talk—"

"Let's hear him. I'll decide what weight to give his evaluation."

Hoffmann began by reading from his own six-page resume. McGillian asked him to touch only some highlights.

"I have a B.A. from Yale University, and an M.D. from Harvard. After six years training at Psychoanalytic Institute, I joined the staff at New York Medical Center. I left to become the Chief of Staff in Psychiatry at Albert Einstein. In addition, I now oversee the State of Connecticut programs for treating families in crisis."

"Okay, we'll grant Dr. Hoffmann expert witness status," McGillian said in a bored voice.

Rachel nudged Chuck's elbow. She squeezed out the words through clenched teeth. "I don't care what he papered his bathroom walls with. He was no good with Ellie—"

Hoffmann spoke. "The child's disturbed behavior mirrors her mother's negative attitude in regard to the visitation." His small, pudgy fingers tapped on the wooden partition of the witness stand. "Had Ms. Belmore encouraged the relationship between the child and her father, Ellie would not be torn."

"Thanks," McGillian said to Hoffmann. "Bernstein?"

Chuck declined to cross-examine the witness.

"Why don't you?" Rachel whispered, incensed with frustration. "Why not give Hoffmann enough rope to hang himself?"

Chuck shook his head. "Would you like me to argue that Hoffmann never observed Ellie's interaction with Wes? Would you like to have a joint session between father and daughter and hand Hoffmann more chances to throw textbook statements at McGillian?" When she did not reply, Chuck added, "I'll put you on the stand instead."

With pleasure spreading on his thin face, Ortman began to cross-examine Hoffman. He turned to the stenographer. "Please read Ms. Edwards' testimony regarding Ellie's play with anatomically-correct dolls." When she complied, Ortman asked Hoffmann, "Would you please give the court your professional view of the subject?"

The audible sigh Dr. Hoffmann let out contained within it both contempt and dismissal. "We try not to use these dolls; their sex organs are so unnaturally obvious. And they are highly unreliable once a child has been repeatedly introduced to them. There's strong suggestiveness in asking the child specific questions, time and again, to the point of coaching her. We've seen it in the witch hunt of the nursery school trial in California—"

"Move to strike!" Chuck called out. "Your honor, we are not here to discuss general psychological theories. Only Ellie's situation."

"Overruled, Mr. Bernstein. The defense is allowed to invalidate the professional testimony of your witness."

Chuck plopped back down in his seat and began to doodle on the notepad in front of him.

A few minutes later, when Ortman finished milking Dr. Hoffmann, Chuck whispered to Rachel, "This round's not over—"

"Great. We're still in the ring. I'm on the ground, and Wes's counting to ten."

Chuck rose to his feet, his crumpled face closed, and called Rachel to the witness stand. "Please describe your visit to Dr. Hoffmann's office," he asked her.

She kept her voice even, mustering her last shred of strength. "Ellie cried when she first saw him. She hid behind my legs. When I carried her into his office, she became hysterical; I heard her cry throughout the session." She turned her eyes toward McGillian, and said in a pleading tone. "I've asked the court to appoint a female psychologist and not to add to Ellie's anguish."

McGillian did not return her gaze.

When Henry Ortman planted himself in front of Rachel, she stared at his ruddy skin covered by a miniature road map of red veins.

"Ms. Belmore, your perception of the visit is a self-serving interpretation—"

"Objection," Chuck called out.

"Mr. Ortman, this is not TV. What's the question?" McGillian asked.

"I'll rephrase it, Your Honor," Ortman bowed his head deferentially. "Would you say that throughout Ellie's crying—and your reaction to it—Dr. Hoffmann had a chance to observe the interaction between the two of you?"

"Objection, Your Honor. The witness is asked to interpret what another witness has observed or hasn't observed."

"Sustained. Mr. Ortman, do you have any further questions to Ms. Belmore?"

"Yes, Your Honor." Ortman turned back to Rachel. "How many therapists, doctors and caseworkers, in your estimate, have talked to Ellie about 'touching her in the wrong places?'"

Lightening tore the sky outside, followed by thunder.

God! Rachel squirmed. She knew where Ortman was leading. She had lost to this line of questioning before he even started. There had been interrogations since Ellie learned to talk—by four psychologists and two gynecologists—all hired by Rachel and Wes. In addition, the grilling by emergency room physicians, several transient, overburdened caseworkers, a couple of court appointed evaluators, and three policemen would have been traumatic even for an adult.

She stopped counting. "About fifteen."

"Fifteen, I see." Ortman did not lick his lips, but Rachel could hear the note of victory in his voice. "Over how many sessions?"

"I can't recall."

"Try to estimate a range. Fifteen to twenty-five? Twenty-five to thirty-five? More?"

"Fifteen to twenty-five interviews." She said 'interviews.' That would discount the ongoing therapy with Ms. Edwards.

"In how many of these was Ellie introduced to anatomically-correct dolls?"

There had also been games, picture-telling tests, and an occasional coercion of the child locked in a room and interrogated for an hour before being offered a bargain: "Ellie, just answer the questions and you can go to your mommy." Ellie would give the interviewer whatever they wanted to hear in exchange for her freedom.

"In more than half," Rachel replied.

"Thank you, Ms. Belmore." Ortman seemed to gauge her. Her throat was dry. She glanced at her glass of water left on Chuck's table. Ortman went on, "I'd like to go over the list of dates Dr. Belmore was entitled to visit with his daughter, but in which you made Ellie unavailable, starting with your removing her from the marital home—"

"Objection," Chuck called out. "This was long settled during the divorce proceedings."

"Sustained."

Against the pelting of the rain on the windows, for the next half hour, Ortman grilled Rachel. In her replies, she hung on not to his words but to the white spaces around them—all tactics fixated on technicalities. That's what the judge should hear and see, too.

Yet these back-and-forth arguments, words fired at her over invisible lines hurt. She would never get used to the pain they inflicted, a pain that never dulled. It continued to throb like a bleeding internal wound. Too much was at stake. But McGillian must be able to sift through it all. Only he, the gatekeeper of society's rights and wrongs, could reach out and pull Ellie from her nightmare.

Rachel knew what Judge McGillian was about to say as soon as he returned to his bench. He scowled at her from hooded eyes that contrasted with his silver hair. Like his black robe, they looked harsh, unforgiving.

"You're continuing to interfere with the father's visitation rights with unproven allegations. I've warned you that should this continue, I'll transfer custody to him." He paused. "You are leaving me no choice. Mr. Bernstein, have you explained it to your client?"

"Yes, I have, Your Honor. May I consult with her for a few moments?"

"You've had plenty of time."

"Give me five minutes, please."

McGillian glanced at his files. "I'll hear another short oral argument in a case; let's reconvene right after."

Outside, Rachel stood silent. She kept her head turned away from Chuck. In front of her, a row of oversized oil portraits of judges lined the top part of the wall. Dark ocher-colored, their majestic, ornate gold frames were incongruous with the yellow, blue, and red of the plastic chairs and scratched wooden benches. Rachel peered at the somber faces, attempting to decode the workings of their alien minds.

Chuck patted her shoulder. He was only a little taller, and Rachel could almost look directly into his eyes, magnified by his thick lenses. The bushy eyebrows met above the frame, their stern line defying his soft voice.

"Why did you ask for another recess?" she asked. "Let's get it over."

"Didn't you hear what McGillian said? You're practically announcing that you'll continue to deny Wes his rights," he said. "McGillian is beyond giving you more fines. I had to stop before he transferred custody rights—"

"This is not about my rights or Wes's. What about Ellie's rights? She's only five. Can we now try to get a new Law Guardian? Someone who's not a wimp or tied to

Ortman's political connections?"

"After we fought them off so successfully?" Chuck thought for a moment. He motioned with his head toward a young, heavy-set woman with a bursting briefcase, who stood talking to a couple and their teenage son. The attorney's wide feet were planted in spreading pumps, and her bleached hair was gathered on top of her head, looking like a cheerleader's pompon. Her overbite did not permit her lips to close. "Here's a Law Guardian. I've checked out her record; in seven out of ten cases she takes the father's side. In two minutes Wes will trap her with his charm."

Rachel nibbled on the inside of her cheek. "Did McGillian forget about Ellie's gonorrhea last year?—"

"That case is closed. Done with. We've lost the appeal. You heard what they got *our* gynecologist to admit on record. As unlikely as it sounded, he agreed that the term encompassed several conditions—"

She cut him off. "You know it's nonsense."

"And it could have happened in the playground. No factual connection was established to Wes, and his medical records showed no trace of such illness—"

"He's a doctor. He treated himself!"

Chuck waved his hand impatiently. "Look, McGillian is about to hand down a verdict. He's telling you that he won't stand for your disobeying court orders. He's taking your refusal as a personal affront. The way things stand now, we're better off *settling* with Ortman than letting McGillian decide."

"Settling?" Chuck's legal logic never ceased to puzzle and frustrate Rachel. "I can't believe what I'm hearing. You promised—"

"I never promised anything. I told you there are always surprises; there's no way to predict the outcome of a trial."

"Are you telling me we've lost for sure?"

"You'll have to let Wes see Ellie—"

She exploded. "Not for unsupervised visitation, I won't."

"We'll continue to look for new evidence and bring new petitions."

"New evidence? Are you out of your mind? I should let my baby go to Wes so I can collect new material?"

"We're going to criminal court. He'll be dead meat there after the D.A. is done with him—"

"If we wait another year for a court date, that is."

"I'll petition the court to bring in Stephanie." Chuck's arm on her shoulder felt heavy, not comforting. Rachel stepped away from him. He was part of the convoluted system of injustice. The tissue in her hand crumbled under her clenching fingers. She found a dry corner and dabbed her eyes. There was no use. Gerald had mentioned the underground railroad for women who had lost all hope. But how could she? As bumpy and torturous as the legal route was, it was her only option. It had to work. She had to press on, to win.

"A settlement can't be reversed or appealed, right?" she asked.

He nodded. "The alternative is that as soon as we walk back into this courtroom, McGillian will give Wes custody."

"You are not to settle with Ortman," she said, "And that's final."

"You are making a mistake."

"Let's go back in." She turned, feeling less resolve than she showed.

Moments later, she was both elated and disappointed by the news that the case McGillian had started in the meantime would require the rest of the short afternoon. She wanted her case over, but was afraid of the consequences.

"I'll give you a continuance until Friday." McGillian's hand swept magnanimously as he sent a meaningful look at Rachel's direction. "Three days. But no more after that, Ms. Belmore. It will give you time to decide on the wisest course of action." He dropped the gavel on the long oak table. The thud reverberated through Rachel's brain.

"Wait!" She clutched Chuck's arm and whispered fearfully, "Wes is supposed to have Ellie again Thursday. Chuck, you can't accept this postponement again."

"We have no choice." A vein pulsated in his temple. He snapped his briefcase shut. "It's not up to us. You'll have to send Ellie to Wes."

CHAPTER FOUR

THE rain continued to come down in sheets. Rachel stood outside the courtroom doors, unhinged, dazed.

How far did other mothers go? Most women must have fallen by the wayside, short of funds or resilience. Yes, some brave ones skipped town with their kids, opting for life on the run. Until they were caught. The children, fragile butterflies with powdery wings, then were pinned to velvet and handed over to their too-loving dads.

She glanced out the window. The sky had been cloudy that morning when she had left her umbrella in the car. She'd have to run to cover the distance between the building and the end of the parking lot where she had parked her car.

She looked at her watch. Ellie would be home by now. All Rachel wanted was to hold her close, to feel the warmth of the dry cheek against hers, to coo sweet words of assurance into her little girl's ear.

At the main entrance, she dug out her car keys and stepped outside to assess the run through the rain. Large drops fell on the walkway, sizzling on the asphalt. The wise thing would have been to wait until the rain subsided.

She dashed out and closed the seventy-yard distance to her car. She fumbled with her keys in the lock. By the time she pulled open her door, she was soaked.

The interior of the car was hot and humid. Rachel put the key in the ignition and turned. Nothing happened. She tried again. No sound.

Christ. She dropped her head on the steering wheel. Ellie was home, waiting. How was she after a night with Wes? All Rachel wanted was to get to her fast, but now she'd have to run back inside and call AAA.

Back at the courthouse, after she placed the call and was told to wait half an hour for their service truck, she stood by the row of vending machines, unseeing. She should call her office for messages and spend the waiting time productively. Yet she did not move. Her mind filled with unspooled thoughts.

She heard someone behind her.

"Care for a Coke?"

She did not turn, thinking it hadn't been meant for her.

"Would you like a Coke?" a young man's voice repeated. She turned to face a man she had noticed in the courtroom, his kind, blue-gray eyes now gazing down into hers, intently searching her face.

"Oh. Well—"

"Looks like you need a shot of something stiffer, but this will have to do."

Drinking in the afternoon? Her antennae went up. "Are you here on behalf of Henry Ortman?"

"Oh, no. Sorry. I— I mean I feel bad about the way things went." He cocked his head toward the courtroom.

"A savior of damsels in distress, then?"

If he heard the sharpness in her tone, he showed no sign. The pleasant laughter that escaped his lips grooved an elongated dimple on his left cheek. "I just started working here. But I've been sitting through trials since I was a teenager."

He juggled some coins and caught them in his palm. She noticed the long fingers, the fine skin dotted with minor scratches. Signs of the outdoorsy or the handyman type. The bitten nails, though, indicated intensity. Or, perhaps the sensitive male.

"I'm getting a Coke. I'll get you one," he said.

Rachel nodded. She didn't want to drink or eat, but the Coke would chase away the sour taste that filled her mouth.

While waiting for the jingling of the money in the machine, she kept her eyes glued to the window to catch sight of the AAA truck as soon as it pulled into the parking lot.

A moment had passed. No thump announced the released can. The young man hit the button a couple of times. When nothing happened, he smiled apologetically and shoved in the remainder of his quarters. "You win some, you lose some." He stopped and caught himself. "Sorry. I meant quarters, not petitions."

He was trying too hard. "That's okay," she said flatly. She fished in her handbag for more coins and handed them to him. "Try these."

As he bent forward, his shoulders strained the white fabric of his shirt. Energy was coiled in his muscles.

Two cans tumbled out. He popped one open and handed it to her. "I know your name, but you don't know mine. I'm Phil Crawford."

"What's your take on what you've heard?" she asked.

He let out a short, bitter chuckle. "All of us who know how to run the country are busy driving taxicabs or cutting hair."

Whatever his job in court was, why was she bothering with another curiosity seeker who got his adrenalin going when hearing other people's suffering? "Thanks anyway." She walked away. She'd wait in her car until AAA arrived.

A knock on her car window came almost immediately after she had settled down. Through the foggy glass she could not see who it was, but when she rolled the window down, she recognized Phil Crawford's wet face as he leaned forward.

"I saw the lights had been left on when I arrived," he said, "but I had no idea how to locate the unlucky owner. Until now, that is."

"I already called AAA. But they're taking their time."

"I have jumper cables. I'll bring my car over." He began to scuttle away.

"Wait," she called out. "Take my umbrella."

He returned and took it.

A few minutes later, his car—some sporty red number—veered into the empty spot next to hers. He motioned her to unlatch the car hood. Soon, her car was running.

"Wait ten minutes before you drive." He folded the umbrella, opened her back door, and dropped it on the floor. "Let the battery recharge."

But she was in a hurry. She thanked him as he stood in the rain, and drove away, her mind frantically raking over the morning's moments, searching for a revelation, an unspotted alternative to what Ellie's fate might be.

When Rachel entered their small house, Ellie jumped off the living room couch and flung herself against her. Rachel knelt in front of her daughter and held her tight. For a moment, neither moved. Then Ellie wriggled from under her arms, ran to the coffee table, and grabbed a sheet of construction paper splashed with dark colors. In the center were pasted a leaf, an ice cream stick, and some macaroni and beads.

Ellie's face beamed. "Look what I made for you in school."

"That's beautiful! I love it!" Why the black, brown, and gray colors? What happened to yellows, reds, greens, and blues? Rachel pointed to the one purple spot. "I'll hang it in my office. You know I love purple. That's why you added this, right?"

Ellie hesitated, then nodded her head with vigor. "Yes. I love purple too." Then her face clouded. "I didn't make anything for Daddy."

"It's okay, sweetie. He doesn't like purple anyway."

The babysitter was standing at the door, her coat on. She motioned with her head, indicating she wished to speak to Rachel in private.

"Sweetie, Freda needs to show me something," Rachel said to Ellie. "I'll be right back."

In the kitchen, Freda's face was grave. "Ellie threw her toys around the playroom. And she screamed for you." She paused. "There were problems at school, too."

"What kind of problems?"

"Just before I picked her up, she bit another girl. Again."

"God. How is she—I mean, the girl?"

Freda shrugged. "They'll probably call you tonight."

After Freda left, Rachel pulled out a calendar she kept in the kitchen drawer, buried under a pile of recipes. She flipped through the pages. The red notations of Ellie's visits with Wes correlated with the green descriptions of her violent outbursts. Her sweet, beautiful daughter was falling to pieces, being destroyed. At unpredictable moments, unprovoked, she would hit, pinch, and bite other children; then she would throw herself on the ground kicking and screaming.

With shaking fingers, Rachel entered the new report.

The rain had stopped, but the lawn was soaked. Rachel and Ellie spread their dinner on a checkered tablecloth on the living room rug to make up for a canceled outdoor picnic. Afterwards, Ellie chased her mother upstairs and was rewarded with Rachel's feigned shrieks as she let herself get caught.

Rachel half-filled the tub with warm water and dropped in Ellie's favorite plastic toys. She settled on the floor mat next to the tub. She would keep Ellie in the water for thirty minutes of "water therapy," Rachel's own prescription to relax her daughter. The warm water visibly melted away the anxieties and fears, creating a neutralized time zone between her "bad days" and the safety of her bed, where she'd sleep undisturbed by a man's gropings.

Rachel restrained her urge to examine Ellie's genitals or to question her. The intense, unnatural concentration on specific sexual issues kids were never asked about had added to Ellie's distress. It helped Ellie if Rachel evoked pleasant thoughts. Rachel would make no mention of Freda's report.

"Did you see the fireworks last night?"

"I hate fireworks."

"But they're beautiful, Ellie. All those bright colors in the sky—"

"They make scary noises. I put my hands on my ears, like this." Ellie pressed both her hands against her ears and her face gathered into its center like a string purse.

Ellie was also terrified of balloons and hated birthday parties where balloons might pop. Rachel changed the subject. "How was school today? Did you play with the doll house?"

"Yes," Ellie said in a flat voice.

"Did you swing on the indoor set?"

The child shook her head. "It hurts my peepee."

A wave of terror seized Rachel's heart, lurched forward, and reached her throat. Where the hell was Wes's girlfriend?

She kept her tone even. "The water is good for it." It was too late for most physical evidence. If there had been any residual tissue or sperm, it was now destroyed. "I'll put some cream on, okay?"

Ellie nodded, her face down.

Rachel forced a smile, "Let's sing."

"*Row, row, row the boat, gently down the stream...*" Ellie chirped in her clear but subdued voice, pushing a colorful boat along the sides of the tub.

"*Merrily, merrily, merrily, merrily. Life is but a dream,*" Rachel finished the song. For a child, life should be an unfolding dream full of hopes and a sense of well-being. She was helpless to make a dream life for Ellie. None of this should be happening.

After she wrapped Ellie in a towel with a large Minnie Mouse print in its center, Rachel carried her to her room, where white eyelet curtains matched the canopied bed. Playfully, she dropped her on the bed.

"I have the cream," she said, and started to sing. "The wheels on the bus go round and round, round and round, round and round. The wheels on the bus go round and round, all over town."

Ellie joined her while kicking her legs to the rhythm of the song. Rachel gently spread her legs and scrutinized the vulva.

It was inflamed. Two matching dark bruises glared at her from both sides. They hadn't been there Monday morning. Rachel's hands shook and her heart pounded with rage and pain.

How could she ask Ellie how she got those? Ms. Edwards insisted the girl's time with her mother should be her safe haven, secure from prying into raw emotional sores.

Chuck would want her to leave the evidence untreated until confirmed, which delayed healing. Rachel could no longer take Ellie to any hospital, expecting that the chance physician on duty would have enough experience in this field to stand Ortman's cross-examination. Most likely, the doctor's qualifications would be blown to pieces within five minutes. She would need to take Ellie to the one physician whose credentials could not be disputed—and one who had shown eagerness to help Ellie's case.

"Mommy, you're hurting me," Ellie whined, and Rachel suddenly realized that the hand holding the towel over Ellie's head had turned into a fist, catching wisps of fine hair.

"Oh, sorry, Sweetheart." She stood Ellie on the bed and kissed her. "Are you okay?"

But of course Ellie wasn't okay. And she wouldn't be until she was free of her father.

"So tell me about Daddy's friend." Rachel inserted a cheerful tone into her voice. "Was she nice?"

Ellie nodded her head hesitantly, her eyes downcast.

"What's her name?"

"Carolyn." Ellie's voice was small.

"That's a nice name! Just like your teacher."

Ellie didn't reply.

"Did she play with you? Did she read you a story?"

Ellie shook her head and lowered it.

"What's the matter, baby?"

The child's face crumpled and she started to weep quietly.

Rachel held her tight. "What's the matter? Can you tell me?"

"She yelled at him, and Daddy pushed her."

"He pushed Carolyn?"

"And she fell down and cried."

"Then what?"

"She went back to her mommy."

"You mean she left?"

Rachel felt her daughter's head nod against her chest. No adult in the house. No supervised visitation. Wes had seen to it. And he had terrified Ellie after she had witnessed him unleashing his fury on his girlfriend.

"Did he push or hit you?"

"He loves me."

"I'm sure he does. Everybody loves you. You know why?"

"Why?"

"Because you're the best five-year-old girl in the whole wide world, that's why."

"But he hurt me, and I said 'no,' like Ms. Edwards told me to say."

"Where did he hurt you?"

"He said it's a secret. That you'll be mad at me."

"Of course not. Tell me."

Ellie laid her hand on her crotch. After a moment's hesitation she put her other hand on her behind.

Rachel held back a scream. "The cream will be good for it, and in the morning we'll go see the doctor—the nice one, the one you like—okay?" Here was the evidence

Chuck had sought. The evidence Rachel had vowed would never occur again.

She continued to hold Ellie tight and planted little kisses on her head and face. "I promise you one thing: It will never, ever happen again. Okay?"

Ellie put both her little hands on her mother's cheeks, and squeezed. The pudgy padding of the fingers felt warm and soft. "You promise?" she asked, her eyes less than an inch away from Rachel's, looked like a giant bug's. "Cross your heart?"

"Cross my heart and hope to die."

As soon as Ellie fell asleep, Rachel closed herself in her bedroom, pulled the telephone into her large walk-in closet, and called Chuck at home.

"He did it again!" she shrieked into the receiver. Her other hand, clutched into a fist, punched a pillow again and again. "You should see the bruises! You must stop him! I'm going to have Wes killed!"

"I didn't hear that," Chuck said. "You know not to say those things."

"I'll kill the bastard, I'll kill him!" she screamed.

"Rachel, please," Chuck said, his voice strained. "We're doing all we can. You know that."

"We're running out of time! Wes is supposed to have her again Thursday. You know he'll show up with a policeman. Oh God!"

"I'm with you," Chuck said. "All the way. Now try to calm down."

She dropped the receiver, hit the pillow again, then collapsed on the carpeted floor and kicked it repeatedly with her heels. So what if she was acting like a hysterical child?

"Rachel, listen to me—"

Chuck's squeaking voice brought her back, though she felt herself still hanging over the edge. "I'm not listening to anyone who tells me to allow him to see her—"

"Please—"

"I'm telling you, Chuck. I'll take her and run away if this doesn't get resolved!"

"Take it easy, will you?—"

"How can I? Would you if your five-year-old daughter were being raped—?" She heard her voice rising again. "I'm going to call the police. Jesus. Why can't someone do something for her?"

"Promise me you won't call the police," he said. "I may not be able to get you out of another mess."

She was losing it; she must be out of her mind to even suggest getting the police involved. Two years ago, to help the investigation, she had taken color photographs of Ellie's bruised genitals and ordered them enlarged. The next day, the photo lab reported her to the police and she was brought into the station, handcuffed, and was slapped with charges of child pornography.

While she battled those charges in criminal court, the petition for which she had photographed the evidence came up on the calendar in Family Court. But the Family Court judge refused to hear evidence now connected to separate proceedings.

It took Chuck mountains of paperwork and hours of billing time to dismiss the pornography case, saving her from a drawn-out jury trial. Through it all, Child Protective Services was damaging: A new caseworker testified that she had seen a nude 'pitcher' of Ellie on Rachel's bookshelf.

"She was one year old, lying on her stomach and looking at the camera," Rachel gave her counter-testimony. "Wesley Belmore himself took the photograph."

"I saw it in the mother's house. 'Tis all I know. I don't ax who took it," the woman had replied.

Now Rachel held the mouthpiece and sniffled softly into it. Chuck was her lifeline to sanity. He held the end of a loose thread that gathered the frayed edges of her world. There was nothing else she could do except wait. But Ellie didn't have weeks or months to spare.

"Chuck, you have a daughter. You believe in the evidence. Would you send your daughter to Dr. Wesley Belmore Thursday?"

"Of course not."

"Then find a way. You're the lawyer."

He was silent for a moment. "This won't be good, but it's the only one left to try. The Impossibility Defense."

"What's that?"

"It's the one in which the contemnor declares him or herself legally or physically incapable of performing the act required by the judge."

"How do I use it?"

"If Ellie absolutely refuses to go to Wes, you couldn't send her against her will."

"You know what happens. She screams and kicks when he comes to pick her up. You've heard her teacher report.... Well, he does get Ellie when there's a cop present."

"I'll start drawing the defense papers on this one."

"Are you serious? Chuck, if there's this Impossibility Defense, why haven't you told me about it all this time?"

"Because it rarely works; I've seen it only applicable in contract disputes. McGillian will chew my ass on this. You have another tough battle ahead, kiddo."

"Would it delay the end of this trial?"

"We *want* to postpone this coming Friday's trial. We don't want to hear McGillian's verdict because it's not a good one." Chuck stopped for a moment. She could almost hear him thinking. "Do you have a camcorder?" he asked.

"What for?"

"Record Ellie's reaction when Wes comes to the door Thursday. Now, Rachel, it's not yet eight-thirty. Call the gynecologist and take Ellie to see him."

"Tonight?"

"The bruises could be twenty-four hours old. Kids heal surprisingly fast."

"Oh, Chuck— She's already asleep—"

"Do it." His patient voice was at the end of its range. "Can you call your mother to come stay with you?"

She understood. Chuck wasn't being heartless. She was cracking up, and was asking too much of him.

CHAPTER FIVE

JUDGE Robert McGillian entered the anteroom to his chambers, his spirits high. He was greeted by the aroma of brewing coffee.

"Morning, Judge." His secretary's wilted face became radiant. Her barrel-like figure miraculously reshaped itself as she straightened, tucked in her stomach, and pushed out what looked like two pancakes wrapped in a fishnet.

Sylvia was the best secretary he'd ever had.

"Heard a good joke just now?" she asked as she looked at his face.

"Just looking forward to another productive day dispensing justice," he replied, allowing his good mood to spill into his voice. His eye caught the book on the corner of her desk. "*Men Are from Mars, Women Are from Venus*," he read the title, and sent her a quizzical look.

"My niece gave it to me," Sylvia said, her tone apologetic. "It's a '90s thing."

"She's a feminist? Jackie Gleason had the best answer." McGillian chuckled and made a gesture with his fist. "To the moon, Alice, to the moon."

She let out a croaky laugh. "He meant all women."

"Feminists will do. We need the rest. Like you." He sent her a mocking look. "You are the greatest."

Sylvia blushed.

McGillian looked in the direction of the office opposite his own. "Where's our new law clerk?"

"At security. He didn't get fingerprinted yesterday; I sent him to get his ID badge—"

At that moment, Phil Crawford strode in. His chiseled face had the demeanor of a recent law school graduate trying to look confident. He straightened his printed tie and dusted a speck from his new suit. "Good morning," he said with a bit too much enthusiasm, as if to cover up his hesitation of the day before. His eyes, eager with anticipation, sparkled with a grayish glimmer like the scales of the trout McGillian had caught last weekend.

"Good morning, sonny," McGillian said. "Hot to trot?"

"The new horse out of the gate." Phil grinned.

"Filled out the forms for personnel?" Sylvia asked. She glared at Phil with the same guard dog look she gave every new person who came near her boss.

"Yes, Ma'am," Phil replied, his smile broadening.

"Well, then, come to my office. We'll go over the calendar." McGillian sauntered toward his chambers as he called over his shoulder, "Sylvia, what's on for today?"

She waved a computer printout. "The usual. A full docket. And twenty new requests for Orders of Protection, Judge."

"You get that after every holiday," McGillian told Phil, "Fourth of July's no exception. Men drink and think it's fun to punch the little women in their lives."

Behind them, Sylvia balanced a thick stack of files in her arms. To Phil she said, "See that the Judge gives only eight minutes per case. As is, these Orders of Protection will take at least three hours to clear." She laid the files on the judge's desk and marched out.

"Give me your tired, your poor, your huddled masses." McGillian said to Phil and winked. "If you find the answer to why every year we're getting more of these miserable cases than ever before, humanity will be forever grateful to you."

Phil shifted his weight from one foot to the other and smiled a wan smile.

McGillian continued, "People come to court so desperate they have no choice but to trust me. I don't take their trust lightly." He shoved aside the docket. "Here, take Belmore v. Belmore." From his rolling cart, he selected a three-inch-thick file and tossed it in Phil's direction.

In a quick, reflexive movement, Phil caught it. "That's the one I sat through yesterday."

"We need a bright law clerk to handle these messy ones. See what you make of it." McGillian eyed Phil. "Relax, will you? Do you know why you're here?"

"Sir?"

"This isn't a criminal court where, like a Catholic priest, a judge can hold out legal absolution. There, when a suspect's name is cleared, his life's redeemed. Here, in years to come those who ask me for help— losers or winners—will struggle with the fallout from my decisions." McGillian peered at the rows of books on the shelves. He continued speaking as though to himself. "No matter what, I'll fail them in the very thing they want so badly from me. Because I rule not only on matters of guilt or innocence, but on the wisest course of action for love turned rancid, or for children being raised in situations that defy the definition of home." He stopped. "Got it?"

Phil nodded. "Yes, Judge."

"Now, back to my question: Why are you here?"

"You mean, instead of representing wealthy crooks at a big law firm?"

McGillian fixed his eyes on him. The kid would work out fine. "Precisely."

"Sir," Phil put his hands under his armpits, but hastily dropped them to his sides. "I think I've told you I worked for two summers in a Manhattan law firm."

"You could have made big bucks there once you passed the bar."

"It didn't interest me." Phil cleared his throat. "The important legal work is either in Family Court or Legal Aid."

McGillian flashed him a large smile. "That's what I thought. I know the feeling." He changed his tone, "We're going to have a good time together. You play golf?"

"A little."

"Good. And do you fly-fish?"

"Only bait fish."

"Time to learn. Do you know Daniel Webster caught the biggest brook trout in the history of Long Island? Forty pounds."

"Is that so? No, sir, I didn't know that."

"Well, he did. At the Carmen River." McGillian paused. "Now just take it easy and study that file. Tell me why I shouldn't transfer custody to the father."

Phil cleared his throat. "Uh, sir—"

"Speak up." McGillian smiled brightly at him. "If you're going to be a lawyer, you'd better find your tongue."

"Is something the matter with the mother?"

"What do you suggest I do when a custodial parent habitually denies the non-custodial parent his visitation rights?"

"Maybe she has a good reason—"

"Look, it isn't easy to help people make the best of life's tragedies." McGillian paused, and his hand swept in the direction of the courtroom. "Like a dentist who must drill close to nerve endings or a surgeon who must cut into living flesh, a judge must split open the infected soft tissues of people's lives. It hurts, but sometimes there's no choice."

Phil did not reply.

"This is a serious responsibility," McGillian continued, "Don't you ever forget it."

"You bet, sir."

Phil's small office smelled of mildew and old books. The shelves behind the glass doors of the old-fashioned bookcase were felted with dust. His desk was missing a drawer.

The phone rang. Rocking on his tilted chair, Phil brought it back to an upright position. Probably a wrong number; who would call him on his second day on the job?

"Mr. Crawford? This is Charles Bernstein. I'd like to postpone tomorrow's trial—"

"Why are you calling me?"

"Sylvia said you now handle the calendar."

"She did?"

"Look. There has been another abuse, and we need to put together all expert testimony. I'm also filing an emergency petition. Ortman will object, but please explain this to Judge McGillian—"

"I've just started here... I'll find out." Phil's words stretched like a rubber band. What was he supposed to do? He hung up, but remained seated. Unseeing, he stared at the mustard-colored paint flaking from the walls. He got up and yanked the cord of the Venetian blinds. A cloud of dust rose into the air. He coughed and tugged the cord sideways. It snapped, the blinds locking into a lopsided position.

"Our decorator's on vacation," Sylvia called from her desk. "You should have joined one of those fancy-shmancy big firms with carpeted offices, mahogany furniture, and abstract corporate art on the walls to match the upholstery."

"You're not joking. My classmates have all hit the ground running in offices like the ones you're describing." He flashed her a grin. "I'm not so lucky."

"And they have cute little things for secretaries," Sylvia said.

"Well, I'm the lucky one in that department."

"Flattery." Her smile was suddenly shy, exposing little teeth, spaced like a yellowed string of pearls. "What d'you need?"

He got up and walked over. He pointed to a pile in his in box. "What am I supposed to do with fifty cases coming in each day?"

"On light days it's only thirty or forty."

"What a relief."

"Make two piles. Half the cases get to be heard, the other half you find a way to dispose of, close, dismiss, whatever."

"What about emergency motions?"

"The same. It's a trick lawyers use. You outsmart them or they'll run you over with their paperwork." She hid her face behind her computer screen, indicating he had exhausted her good will.

He returned to his office and stared out the window for a moment. Outside, the bright light had a special filtering quality that washed and accentuated the leaves of trees edging the block, the tall government buildings across the street, and the outlines of the cars. He pushed open the window. His self-appointed mission to help children caught in the system had started with no fanfare. Only the shimmering of the scorched asphalt reflected the heat, releasing the acrid smell of tar. The air, heavy with suffocating moisture, threatened Long Island with another brutal July day.

Before closing the window, Phil tossed a last glance at the far end of the parking lot, where his reconditioned red '68 Camaro was parked. Last summer he had treated her to a new engine. There would be no more such luxuries with his public service salary.

More than the absence of luxuries, he still smarted from giving up on his girlfriend, Carole. Since their sophomore year in high school, they had grown up together, then suddenly apart. Her vision of their future together had distilled to specific nuggets—a comfortable home, vacations, cars, a country club, live-in help when they'd have children. Phil disappointed her when his interests veered elsewhere. Hers was not the life he had envisioned for himself nor wished to work hard for, he had told her, hoping she would see things his way, knowing she was incapable of understanding what he had never quite explained. This past year, she had found his pursuing a Family Court clerkship not only romantically naïve, but also lacking in the ambition department. Finally, when Phil had turned down a job offer at the law firm of Leifman, Ellsworth at a starting salary of seventy thousand with prospects of one day making partner in order to work in Family Court, he had made a conscious choice between Carole and his mission in life.

He had expected the breakup, but it still had taken a great effort not to unwrap Carole's framed photograph and place it on his desk. He missed the brilliance of her smile and the softness of her ample thighs. He wished she would call to congratulate him on his new job, as disingenuous as that gesture would be.

Phil plopped down on the frayed upholstered chair and opened the file marked "Belmore v. Belmore."

This was no longer a law school assignment. This was real work. He remembered reading something last year about Dr. Belmore treating the Governor's son after a motorcycle accident. "The Celebrity Surgeon," the newspaper had called him. The thought of the responsibility made Phil dizzy. Should he grant Bernstein his request for another adjournment? More importantly, would McGillian consider his fresh-out-of-school clerk's opinion regarding the transfer of custody to the father?

He leafed through the folder. As he bridged the history in the file and what happened in court, details filled in the blanks. At the trial, it had been impossible not to notice Rachel Belmore's rigid back eloquent with outrage and misery, and the faint trembling of her lips alluding to the struggle to control her emotions. He also remembered her soft cheeks and clear forehead.

The scene had been all too familiar; he'd witnessed people like her—and their turmoil—many times throughout his youth. Like a dog circling a spot, sniffing and exploring the ground, Phil had returned to court time and again to search for an answer to his own pain. He would sneak in after school to observe trials. He crouched in the back, watching, his mind burning as he attempted to understand the system. How was it possible that people like his mother, who sought justice, left feeling they had been kicked in the teeth, punched in the stomach, and shot in the kneecaps?

When Ms. Belmore had lifted naked eyes toward the judge, their deep green had been a pool of pain so familiar to Phil, it mirrored his mother's anguish years before. He detected that same distress in their later exchange when treating her to a Coke. He hoped she'd leave her car lights on next time.

His attention went back to the file. Of course he would do whatever he could to help Ellie Belmore. That's why he was here, toiling in Family Court. Hastily, he jammed the papers back into the file, closed it, and placed it in his briefcase to study at home tonight. As soon as Bernstein's emergency petition was filed, he would take it straight to McGillian.

He hadn't expected a case such as Belmore v. Belmore to cross his path so soon. His mother's lost battle was now his.

Hours later, in his newly rented apartment, Phil struggled to stay at the bottom of sleep. Again, a vivid dream had left his skin gluey with perspiration. He reached across the bed and patted the empty spot where Carole's full body should have been. She had disliked her weight, but he had loved burying himself in her flesh or watching her move with lightness of step on delicate feet. He had adored the freckles that refused to fade away when she bleached them. Now, for a flitting moment of misgiving before wakefulness, he berated himself for his stubbornness. After graduation, Carole had planned to move in with him, but changed her mind when she saw this garden apartment in a poor neighborhood.

It took Phil a while to realize that the pulsating blue light hitting his eyelids and reflecting his accelerated heartbeats was not inside his head. Rather, it poured in through the curtainless window, hit the bare wall where his book boxes still lined up unopened, and then bounced against his closed eyelids.

He opened his eyes at the same moment he heard a banging on a door somewhere in the street. "Police. Open up!"

The crackly voice of a radio operator was followed by the excited noise of people speaking, like disturbed geese.

Phil sprinted from his bed and peered out. Diagonally across the street, outside a red brick garden apartment building identical to his, a dozen neighbors stood in an agitated cluster. Rounding the corner at a dangerous speed, an ambulance approached and came to a screeching halt. Two paramedics jumped out and rushed through the entrance, carrying a stretcher. A few moments later, they emerged. On top of the stretcher, fully covered by a blanket, Phil could discern the outlines of a small body. Very small.

All of Phil's muscles uncoiled into a sprint as he dashed out barefoot, wearing only his boxer shorts and a T-shirt. He took the single flight down two steps at a time. Outside, along with the smell of geraniums and rosemary planted in a barrel, the pre-dawn summer chill hit him in the face and chest. He closed the distance to the scene.

"What happened?" he asked a woman in a faded pink robe who stood under the entrance light, smoking and hugging herself.

"She burned him," the woman replied, her voice shaking with anger. Dexterously holding both the cigarette and the top of her robe, she used the same hand to dab a wad of crumpled tissue to her eyes. "Can you believe this? After all we've told them, they gave him back to her. This time she did it."

Presently, a woman, handcuffed, zombie-like, was led out. She wore a jogging suit, and her disheveled hair stuck out in clumps. Without glancing at her neighbors, she moved like a rag doll as a cop helped her into the back seat of the police car.

The woman in the pink robe edged toward a policeman. "Officer, I'll take the other kids until the morning." She added in a gruff tone, "It won't be the first time."

Mumbling something about social services, she crushed her cigarette under her slipper. Phil watched her as she pushed the glass-and-aluminum door and disappeared into the building. Four families lived at each entrance, close enough to know what was going on. But only if they heard the loud cries. Family secrets were always silent, he knew.

Slowly, taking in large gulps of crisp air, Phil retreated to his apartment house. He felt his eyes mist with sorrow. The words, "They gave him back to her…." echoed in his head like oscillating strobe lights.

CHAPTER SIX

ELLIE sat frozen on the small area rug by the front door, her head bent. Her pink knapsack rested against the wall. Her purple Barney lay splayed over her crossed legs, as mute and devoid of will as she seemed at this moment, closed in her dark and cold dungeon.

Rachel stood by the living room window. Beyond the reflection of her hollow cheeks, her eyes followed a flock of birds flying in formation high in the blue sky, creating a tattered Spanish lace against a gray-blue background, like a mourning shawl. This was the funeral for her daughter's childhood. *Only a monster would allow this to happen to her own child.*

"Mommy, you promised." Ellie raised her head. Her eyes were wide. The feeble protest was worse than crying. The child's submission to her fate sizzled in Rachel's head. Rachel looked away before she broke down. "You said, 'Cross my heart and hope to die,'" Ellie added, her voice pleading and pouting and so sweet. The sacrifice of the innocence. A lamb being led to the slaughter.

Despondency pierced through Rachel. *For the last time. Ever.* She turned away from the window. "I know, sweetie. I promised that Daddy wouldn't do bad things to you again. But the judge wants you to see Daddy."

"Is the Judge God?" There was no cynicism in the child's question.

"No, he's not, but we must listen to him."

"I'll pray to him." Her hands in supplication, Ellie shut her eyes tight.

Rachel walked over and plopped down in front of Ellie. Her fingers combed the wheat-colored hair, the soft strands spilling like spun silk. Ellie inched closer, her movements sluggish, then climbed into her lap. She placed her head on Rachel's shoulder, world-weary. Her weeping was barely audible. "Please, Mommy. Please. I don't want to go."

"We have no choice." Under Rachel's lips, the little face was puckered and wet. With a primal instinct, she licked the tears. She was a declawed animal, unable to protect her young. Her nose ran, and she brought her sweater sleeve up to dab at her face. Lint stuck to her nostrils, torturing her. Moments passed. Sitting still, fear draped itself around her and Ellie, layer by paper-thin layer.

Light footsteps came down the stairs. Jacqueline stopped at the bottom, viewing the two of them. Her eyes caught Rachel's. She brought the camcorder to her face and focused.

"Thank you," Rachel mouthed. Jacqueline had left the office at the same time she had, under the pretense of a dental appointment. The phone would be covered by another secretary. There was no one else in the world Rachel could ask to go through this ordeal with her. Faking cheerfulness, she held Ellie's hand in hers and forced a wave at the camcorder.

Dear Jacqueline, a chipper bundle of energy, had come forward from the periphery of her life when Rachel most needed a friend. Jacqueline, "one CEO away from Prozac," had quit her corporate human-resource position to pursue a singing career. She wanted no management position. Since her endometriosis needed an occasional medical tune-up, she applied for a secretarial job at Sheridan Magazines for the health benefits, expecting to stay for one year. Four years later, she was still there.

Three years ago, the day after that shattering night in which Rachel fled Wes, she checked out of the hotel and moved into Jacqueline's downtown apartment. There, Jacqueline watched the two-year-old baby for a few weekends while Rachel searched for a home to crawl into from under the smoldering ashes of her former life. Soon, she found this small house on the North Shore of Long Island and filled it with printed chintz and pinewood furniture—so different from the gilded antiques she had left behind in Wes's Manhattan penthouse. For that matter, other than Rachel's work, everything in her life was different, herself included.

Now nothing could give her the illusion of safety.

"Let's play patty-cakes," she said to Ellie and raised her palms.

The red light on Jacqueline's camcorder went on, indicating the tape was rolling. Ellie glanced at Jacqueline and turned her head away. She did not move her palms to meet her mother's in a game.

A car horn sounded in the street. Ellie stiffened. Her arms went up around Rachel's neck, tightening their grip. "I don't want to go."

"Sweetie, it's going to be all right," Rachel whispered, her heart pounding. She rose to her feet, hoisting Ellie onto her hip. The little legs wrapped around her waist. In patient movements, Rachel attempted to pry Ellie's limbs from her. But with every released limb, another one tightened further, octopus-like. Ellie's fingers dug into Rachel's neck, pinching her skin.

"Ellie, please," Rachel said quietly but audibly. "You must go to Daddy."

"No!" Ellie screamed. "No!"

A light knock on the door announced Wes's arrival.

"Sweetie, he won't have a policeman with him," Rachel said. "Chuck promised."

Suddenly, Ellie disengaged herself, and jumped down. "No—oooo!" She scrambled up the stairs.

"Where are you going?" Rachel took off after her, Jacqueline following behind.

"No! No!" Ellie's scream tore the air. She scuttled into her room, and glided under the bed. "No!"

Rachel stretched on the floor next to the bed and lifted the edge of the eyelet ruffle.

In the semi-darkness, lying on her stomach, Ellie kicked furiously. "No—oooo!" she screamed in terror.

Jacqueline slid up near Rachel and lifted the other end of the bed ruffle. Aiming the camcorder, she kept it rolling. "It's too dark; the camera can't catch her," she whispered.

Ellie's crying turned to a shrill, long shriek that reverberated in the room. "Eeeee—eeeee—." It went on and on until she was out of breath. She took a gulp of air and started another scream.

"Eeeee—eeeee—." A kinetic shiver penetrated Rachel's bones and knitted itself into them. Ellie was scared as a treed kitten surrounded by barking hunt dogs. And her mother was one of them.

Rachel reached over and clasped Ellie's arm. "Come out, baby," she said, her voice quivering as it pushed past a fast-forming lump. She pulled hard.

Ellie gasped for air and started another piercing scream.

The lump in Rachel's throat turned to a jagged shard. She kept her steady pull on the arm and brought Ellie out.

"Eeeee—eeeee—" Ellie screamed.

"I love you—" Rachel began to say, but pinched off her words. This was not what Ellie should believe love was. Love didn't torture. Love didn't betray.

Downstairs, the insistent knocking on the door turned to foreboding pounding. A moment later, the doorbell, always erratic and unreliable, suddenly came to life. It barged in on the tension with its cheerful ding-a-ling, ding-a-ling, like a clumsy, tasteless joke.

With Ellie wrenched from under the bed, Rachel attempted to gather as many parts of her child as she could. Ellie gripped the bed leg. Her knuckles turned white. But the small fingers could not encircle the leg.

"No—oooo!" She screamed again as her hand lost its grip. "Mommy, no—oooo."

Rachel covered Ellie's body with hers, then tried to collect Ellie in her arms. But Ellie extricated herself from her grasp and ran toward her closet, her shrill screaming uninterrupted. It penetrated less through Rachel's ears than through her entire skin.

Jacqueline's finger pressed the pause button. The red light went out. "Don't you think we have enough?" she asked quietly.

Rachel's adrenalin was dissipating fast. "How long has it been?" she murmured.

"Four minutes."

"That's all?" Rachel gulped. "Keep rolling." Still on the floor, she straightened to a sitting position. Her hair was mussed over her face. She tried to push it off and realized her hands were shaking. She stared at them.

Ellie's screaming came muffled through the closed closet door.

Rachel tried to stand up. Her legs were wobbly, like a newborn calf's. In a moment she would tumble over. She lowered herself down again, stabilized herself on all fours, and crawled toward the closet. "It's okay, sweetie," she called out.

"No!—" Ellie's scream was cut by a violent hiccup. "—No!"

Rachel reached the closet and pried open the door. It was held from inside by the terrified hands of a five-year-old fighting for her life.

Something snapped inside Rachel. She heard its pop, like a guitar string breaking. *No more!* She wanted to scream. *No more!* "You don't have to go," she wept. "You don't have to go. I promise—"

"No!" Hiccup from Ellie.

"Camera off." Jacqueline's controlled voice announced from behind Rachel.

The doorbell was now held in, and the ringing echoed in the house, a rhythmic, joyous jingle.

"Come to me," Rachel cried. "I'm sorry. I'm so sorry." She pushed the clothes aside, reached in, and hugged the cornered child.

Ellie recoiled from her touch. "No—" She hiccupped.

"You won't go to Daddy." She drew Ellie toward her and wrapped her arms around the little body, like protective wings. She didn't know whether the salty taste of tears in her mouth was hers or Ellie's. "Ellie, sweetheart. You won't go."

Downstairs, the doorbell and the pounding on the door continued simultaneously, accompanied by hard kicks. Wes was breaking his restraining order, which prohibited him from such behavior. Ellie's body against Rachel's shuddered with each thump. She wriggled, trying to get away from her mother. But too exhausted, she could no longer muster the energy to fight. Her movements grew feebler.

"I'll go tell him," Jacqueline whispered. "Get ready for stage two."

"Don't open the door," Rachel said. "He's out of control."

"I'll call out through the window." Jacqueline's complexion was sickly olive. "Better me than you."

Rachel's cheek rested against Ellie's head. "Let's go wash up," she told her daughter. "We'll take a ride in the car until Daddy's gone."

Gasping for air, Ellie raised her face to look at her mother. Her cheeks were wet, her fair skin was blotchy with uneven patches of crimson. Her lips quivered.

"Come on. It's all over," Rachel whispered. "I'm so sorry."

There was only time to wash their faces. Ellie's hiccups continued to jolt her head backwards with each internal quake. Rachel splashed water over her own face and flattened her flyaway hair with a wet palm. In the mirror, dark half moons underlined her eyes. The whites were blood-shot, and the green irises around enlarged pupils turned black.

The pounding on the front door stopped. Jacqueline returned. With eyes glazed and feverish, she motioned for them to go. Sweat-soaked curls stuck on her cheeks in a jumble of ringlets.

"He'll be back with the police." Jacqueline's tone swelled with unfamiliar notes. "Get going."

"How about a group hug?" Rachel reached for her friend. Ellie wrapped her arms about both necks. Suddenly Jacqueline disengaged herself. Her hand clasped her mouth, and she ran out, gagging.

Rachel found her in the master bath, throwing up into the toilet bowl. She planted herself over Jacqueline and held her forehead to keep it from hitting the hard ceramic.

"Get going," Jacqueline sputtered between heaving and retching. "I'll be all right."

"You're sick." A two-way traffic of conflicting needs sped through Rachel.

"There's no time. Go."

Rachel hurried back and scooped Ellie up in her arms. Ellie began kicking again. Her arms flailed at the air and caught Rachel's chest and face. "No!" Her voice came out hoarse. "I want to stay with Aunt Jacqueline."

"You're not going to Daddy. We're driving away, but will be back later. Aunt Jacqueline will wait for you." Rachel planted kisses on Ellie's head. "Please be quiet now. I need you to help me."

"No." Ellie shook her head, but she had little power left. Her body became slack and heavy.

In the car, Ellie's crying subsided. Rachel handed her a small container of milk she had grabbed from the fridge. "Here's a straw." But when she lifted her hand, it still shook.

She drove away. Jacqueline would be in the house to show the police officer in as he waved a court order. He would verify that the child he was searching for was not there, again unavailable for a visit with her father.

Fifteen minutes later, in Glen Cove, Rachel and Ellie stopped at McDonald's. Ellie's face was puffed and she glanced around as if Wes would pounce on them from behind Ronald McDonald. Eventually, as Rachel drew funny faces on the placemat, she extracted some smiles from Ellie, but after a couple of bites from her hamburger, the girl pushed the plate away. Rachel got up to buy her ice cream and animal cookies. When she returned to the table, Ellie's head had dropped on the Formica table, her eyes closed.

Rachel carried her back to the car and laid her down on the back seat where an old baby blanket and a faded pillow made a comfortable bed. She drove slowly the few blocks to a beach overlooking the Sound. It was deserted, the cream-colored sand a jeweled relief of thousands of feet that hours before had strolled and jumped in ball games. She stopped the car on the dock and turned off the engine.

The wind caressed the water and left its surface wrinkled. Rachel rolled down the windows a crack to let the breeze in. It came in smelling of salt and fish, damp yet refreshing.

In the back, Ellie slept, her legs twitching.

High in the sky over the opposite shore, a flock of birds, again in the tattered black lace formation Rachel had seen earlier, seemed suspended in the air. Another flock moved in unison above the car. Then another. Rachel tilted the back of her seat to its lowest position. She closed her eyes and listened to the water lapping at the dock. She dozed off and found herself on a boat, back-paddling into the center of her nightmare.

At seven o'clock, she called Jacqueline from a pay phone.

"The coast is clear," Jacqueline said. "For now."

"How are you feeling?"

"I can take it better than Ellie can."

Rachel veered onto her street, her eyes scanning its length for an unfamiliar car. The homeowners kept their cars in their garages and driveways; none was parked at the curb.

Ellie did not wake up. Rachel undressed her and tucked her under the covers.

"I made you broccoli and tomato pasta," Jacqueline told Rachel.

"I'm not hungry."

Jacqueline handed her a snifter of brandy. "I didn't think you'd be. But you should eat something."

Rachel raised the glass. "I hope you had a stiff drink yourself."

"Sure did." Jacqueline paused. "What now?"

"Mission completed. I have to call my lawyer."

"Call your mother, too. She was looking for you earlier."

"Did she say where they are today?"

Jacqueline smiled. "Probably following either the sun, a public concert, a city food festival or a college football game—whichever is closest. Too bad retirees can't log frequent travel miles on their RVs."

Rachel looked at Jacqueline, still pale. "Maybe you should go home. Practice your music. It'll do you good." She could use Jacqueline's company, but she, too, would need to get away from all of this—except that she could not escape her own skin. "How can I ever thank you for everything?"

"Thank me when Wes is tarred and feathered and dragged by a horse."

"Let me pay for a cab to the city," Rachel said

Jacqueline shook her head. "I'll take the train. I need the walk to the station." She gathered her satchel, hugged her and left.

Rachel picked up the phone and dialed her parents' cellular phone number. They had talked briefly Tuesday after she had returned from court and before she had discovered Ellie's new abuse. She had put off speaking to them again, sparing them more pain.

The moment she heard her mother's voice, she burst into tears. Her resolve melted and words tumbled out. She spilled out the most recent events.

"We're flying in Saturday to stay with you," her mother said.

"Oh, Mom. Thank you," Rachel mumbled. She had never fully appreciated her parents' selflessness. Not until now, when her own parenting was being tested. They had never chided her for marrying outside the religion. Further back, Rachel now realized, all throughout her childhood, she had never felt her musician mother's disappointment when both her daughters showed no musical talent. Rachel wept into the receiver. "It's so terrible. I can't take the injustice of it all."

"Rach, darling, it is a nightmare." Her mother sniffled on the other end. "Be strong. There's no choice."

"I love you, Mom."

Rachel stepped into her bathroom to shower. She stayed under the running water for a long time, moving her neck and shoulders in spasmodic movements. Nothing could wash away the virus of dread that had penetrated all her living cells.

She entered Ellie's room and sat at the edge of the bed. In the child's sleep, her face was crumpled. She thrashed about.

"I am so sorry, baby," Rachel murmured. "I'll never put you through anything like this again. Never. I'll be a good mommy. Promise." Then, hoping Ellie would hear her in her sleep, she added, "Cross my heart and hope to die."

She laid her hand on Ellie's back and sang a lullaby. Little by little, Ellie calmed and her limbs relaxed. Her fitful, dry breathing became deeper and more even. By the time Rachel finished the third song, a small smile bunched up Ellie's cheeks. Rachel watched her for a few moments longer, memorizing each line and curve of the delicate features.

Finally, she could not put it off any longer. She dialed Chuck's number at home.

"I have your Impossibility Defense in a neat package," she told him, hearing her own tight voice. Nothing was worth putting Ellie through this ordeal just to prove a legal point. "Video and all."

"Good," Chuck replied. "How long is the tape?"

"About six minutes."

"Six minutes?"

"Yup. Maybe seven."

She heard the intake of breath on the other end of the line. "Rachel, do you expect me to tell McGillian that you tried for a whole seven minutes to send Ellie to Wes? That after only seven minutes you gave up?"

"Chuck, you have no idea what went on here—"

"Let me play the devil's advocate. If I were Ortman, what would I say to this presentation of Impossibility Defense?"

Something buzzed inside Rachel's head. "What do you expect me to do?"

"Next time get half an hour of tape, and then we'll see."

CHAPTER SEVEN

MCGILLIAN tapped his pencil on the long oak table and shoved aside the pile of documents. Some cases provided a twist to break the monotony of human failings and angst. He glanced at Phil, who sat at the side desk, his chair pushed back to accommodate his long legs. The young man exuded energy, something tense and elastic, even when he sat still. Absorbed in a file, Phil's lantern jaw worked as he mouthed points, but the wisps of dark hair playing on his open forehead mocked his solemn demeanor.

"Ready for a recess?" McGillian asked.

Phil jumped to his feet and followed McGillian as he left the courtroom.

"Sylvia's goddamn iced tea," McGillian said. He removed his robe and hung it on the nail outside the door. He began to walk toward the lavatory, talking. "What have you noticed about the way they look in front of the bench?"

"Sir?"

"Don't they look like frightened sheep?" McGillian laughed, but let his laughter die. He didn't like Phil's wince. The young man couldn't take a joke. "Learn to watch them," he continued. "Did you see that man? When he turned to talk to his wife and son, they cringed in fear. It'll never appear on court records, and appellate judges will never know about it, but in this court we've established whether or not to believe this man when he denies being violent." He paused. "How are you managing the calendar?"

"I agreed to postpone the Belmore v. Belmore case. There was a new incident of abuse—"

"You mean *alleged* abuse? Phil, be careful in your choice of words." McGillian waved his hand. "Never mind. Just ease my workload and salvage my summer. If you get me out of here on time most days, there will be plenty of daylight left to go fly-fishing."

"I'll try my best, sir."

"Come with me one of these days. I've got all my fishing gear in the back of the car—a collection of rods, waders, a wide-brim hat. And I keep my fly vest loaded."

"I figured that we've been getting fifty-sixty new cases a day," Phil said, "but we dispose only of half as many. If we don't double the number of cases disposed, we'll fall further behind."

McGillian stopped in the middle of the corridor and patted Phil's shoulder. "You're going to shame me into giving up my golf and fishing."

"I have no such intentions, Judge." Phil smiled. "I'm learning—"

McGillian resumed his stride. "Youth. I envy it. The energy, the spirit, the belief in your ability to change the world." He laughed. "But soon enough, you'll outgrow it. When you are no longer young enough to know everything, you'll figure out which bridge to cross and which one to burn." He stopped and glanced at Sylvia, who had planted herself in front of them.

"Judge, better take a look at this," she said.

"Why? What is it?"

"The Torruellas case. Joseph. The kid is dead."

He sought the support of the cold wall beside him. "The one I wanted to see interact with his mother?" He reached for the newspaper. "Yes, I remember. He clung to her jeans and looked at me with those big brown eyes. He begged me not to tear him from his mom. Christ. What happened?" His eyes began to scan the print, but he had left his reading glasses on the bench.

"She killed him." Sylvia tapped the newspaper. "They found cigarette burns all over his body, and it looks like she banged his head repeatedly—"

Bitter fluids crawled up McGillian's esophagus. He dropped the newspaper back into her hand.

"Judge, Social Services will be here later about the placement of her other kids," she said.

He covered his eyes for a moment.

"Sir," Phil said. "I happened to see some of it. Too late, I mean. I live across the street."

McGillian shook his head. Where and how had he gone wrong? "God knows that as much as I try, I can't hand out good parents to children. We tried to rehabilitate the Torruellas mom so she could make a home for her four kids." He paused. "Sylvia, leave my notes on the case on my desk, will you?"

Ten minutes later, back at the door leading to the courtroom and ready to face the rest of the morning's docket, McGillian gave his court officer a twitch of a sad nod, signaling he was ready. The court officer's key ring, loaded with gadgets to ensure McGillian's safety, jingled as she pushed the swivel door and marched in. Through the closed door, he heard her announce, "All rise!"

He waited a moment longer, his gaze fixed on the wood paneling. The Torruellas boy's large eyes, fringed with thick lashes, stared back at him, accusing. He shook his head as though trying to rid it of cobwebs, took a deep breath, and strode in.

"How are you today, Judge?" an older attorney with wisps of white hair asked.

McGillian smiled. "As a young kid or an old man?"

"As a kid, of course."

"For a kid, I'm only at eighty percent capacity. For my age, though, I'm doing all right," McGillian replied. "Got any bungee events coming up? I'm ready."

The two of them laughed, and McGillian turned to Phil. "We allow levity in court to offset the sad stories." He combed the back of his hair with his fingers. His hair, though short, felt as thick as it had always been. "Ready for your case, counselor."

While the lawyer, now the court-appointed Law Guardian for the Torruellas children, sorted out his papers, McGillian dismissed the press. There were more journalists than usual. He wished he could allow them to sit in and hear the details, to open the file on his desk for public scrutiny. But children's privacy law prohibited disclosure. Reluctantly, he ordered the media out.

Unlike the difficult decision to allow Mrs. Torruellas to try to make a home for her children, this time it did not take long to put the children in the custody of Child Protective Services.

But there was nothing in his power to undo Joseph's tortured death.

"Judge, would you hear an order to show cause?" Sylvia asked.

McGillian glanced at the wall clock. "What's the emergency? Am I the only judge still in on a Friday afternoon?"

"A young man's trying to block his former girlfriend from having an abortion, but the lawyer for the woman claims it should be dismissed."

"Bring me the file."

In his chambers, McGillian reflected on the case and decided not to dismiss it.

The girl's attorney, an apple-cheeked, curly blonde who still looked like a child, began. "Kim Hyon Lee has a constitutional right to an abortion, free from state interference. I repeat our argument that Mr. Mayes has no standing, and that the court should not even entertain this petition."

"Dear counselor, I ruled on this question five minutes ago. That's why we're now hearing it," McGillian replied. "Now, go on."

The pregnant girl was a slight seventeen-year-old with long straight hair that fell down her back and a pale, flat face. She looked no older than twelve. Accompanied by her meticulously dressed Asian parents, she spoke in a small voice.

"I'm a junior in high school, Your Honor." Red blots climbed up from her neck. "I want to have the uh— abortion and graduate. I have excellent grades and I hope to go to college in two years on a music scholarship."

The attorney took over. "Kim Hyon Lee barely knew this boy. She's lived a sheltered life in her Korean community and met him only a few times."

McGillian waved at the nineteen-year-old "man" with an earring and a scraggly patch of unshaved stubble on his chin to state his argument.

Instead, with nods of encouragement from their priest, his parents took the stand.

"If Kim doesn't want the baby, my husband and I would care for and raise it," Mrs. Mayes said in a faltering voice.

Two journalists sat at the back, scribbling notes. This case did not involve a minor, and the press could sit in on it, although they rarely bothered. McGillian glanced at them, then shifted his gaze to the father of the unborn. "Mr. Mayes, I'm not sure I would give you a puppy to raise. How are you planning to be a responsible father?"

"Your Honor," Lee's attorney called out. "If you choose to ignore Roe v. Wade and Planned Parenthood v. Casey—"

McGillian cut her off, his tone rising. "I am quite familiar with the undue burden test of Casey, *counselor*." He looked at the young man for his reply.

The young man shrugged and looked hopefully at the priest.

"We'll give him guidance," the priest interjected.

"I don't like the sound of things," McGillian said, "But what choice do we have?

Miss Lee is pregnant; the baby is here, albeit unborn. And the grandparents—good churchgoing people, the kind this country needs more of—are offering the baby a home."

"Abortion is not illegal! And we have the minor's parents' consent—" Miss Lee's twit of a lawyer called out. "All this is irrelevant."

"We are dealing with the primary interest of another party," he replied. He scanned the faces in front of him. He peered again at the reporters. "Petition granted. Kim Hyon Lee is hereby restrained from having an abortion because of the father's interest." He hit the gavel.

In front of him, Miss Lee, her porcelain face paler than before, dropped her head into her hands and collapsed into her attorney's arms. Her parents exchanged bewildered looks while someone, with exaggerated hand movements, translated to them.

As McGillian rose to leave through his private back door, one of the reporters ran out through the front door. He caught up with McGillian in the private corridor leading to his chambers. "Judge, just one question?"

Annoyed, McGillian stopped with his hand on the door handle.

"Your Honor, has your decision anything to do with your hope for reelection in November? Your party colleagues are running on the pro-life platform—"

"Young man. You may record my stance on the issue, but the law comes first, not politics. Society expected me to be just and fair when they voted me to this bench twenty years ago." He heard the fury creeping into his voice. "In all these years, I've never compromised my integrity for political purposes—"

"Sorry, Your Honor, I didn't mean to imply—"

"—nor my beliefs. And I believe you don't drown unwanted puppies and you don't kill unborn babies. Not if anyone asks me, which they have." McGillian stared into the reporter's eyes. He dropped his voice. "I'm aware that it's a hot-potato issue, but it's the court's role to prop families up in these days of chaotic values."

"What will happen if Mr. Mayes and his parents come back after the baby is born and ask for custody?"

"And the mother still doesn't want it?" McGillian paused. The answer was clear but he was damned if he'd express an opinion before he heard the case, or justice wouldn't be served. "No comment."

Inside his chambers, the court officer stepped forward. "Judge, I need to speak to you." She closed the door behind her. "Channel Twelve is setting up their equipment outside to catch you when you leave. I'm going to have a couple of security guys hang around and walk you to your car. Let's do that whenever you have to leave the building, okay?"

"What do they want with me?"

"The Torruellas case."

"What's the matter, slow news day?"

"Election time, sir— Just let me know when you want the courtroom cleared, and we'll see to it."

In the large ballroom where the Republican fund raising dinner was being held, giant chandeliers sparkled and illuminated three hundred men in dark suits, many in tuxedos. Bejeweled, bedecked, and coiffed women dotted clusters of men, brightening the homogeneous scene, though most were dressed in what McGillian's wife called "a little black dress."

McGillian let Phil open the door for him. He had asked his new law clerk to join him. The contacts could do him good. "It's never too soon to rub elbows with those who count," he told Phil.

But before McGillian could get past the double doors, a young brunette in a black pantsuit propelled herself toward him. She shoved a microphone in front of his face. From high above his head, floodlights instantly washed him. Next to him, Phil squinted his eyes in confusion.

"Your Honor, the Joseph Torruellas case—" she said breathlessly.

McGillian squeezed his forehead. "Very, very sad."

"Are you taking personal responsibility for—"

"Young lady, you know that privacy law prohibits me from discussing the case." He felt annoyance at her not-so-subtle assumption of his responsibility, but he controlled the urge to be rude. Not when the cameras were zoomed in on his face. His fingers still touching the microphone, he smiled. "Now if you'll excuse me—there are some people I must say hello to, including Governor Dunkle."

As they made their way through the crowd toward the bar, someone tapped McGillian's shoulder. He pivoted on his heels. Like his shadow, Phil turned with him.

It was Henry Ortman, an old horse with political aspirations that never materialized. Ortman's thin neck was chafed and stiff against the starched collar of his tuxedo shirt.

"Good evening, Judge."

"Great turnout, Hank."

"We've raised fifty thousand dollars tonight from ticket sales alone."

Ortman extended a knobby hand to Phil. "I saw you in court. Welcome. We like young people to join us; we need new blood in the party."

Phil flinched, but returned Ortman's handshake. "I'm too young to be a Republican," he said with a small smile.

"Time will sweat that liberal streak out of him." McGillian laughed.

When Ortman moved away, Phil asked, "Judge, is it all right for us to talk to a litigant attorney?"

"Sure." McGillian waved his hand. "The core of political activists comes from prominent lawyers and businessmen in each community. I wouldn't discuss a case with him without the other party's attorney present." McGillian paused. "Have I shown any preferential conduct toward Ortman in court?"

"I couldn't tell you knew him outside the courtroom."

"There you are. I never allow a judicial bias—or the appearance of one. They are both equally damaging."

They were about to sit down at their table when Colby Albrecht waddled over. The face that lately beamed at McGillian from the early election posters was round and pudgy and topped with a patch of dark hair. It now gave him a mercurial smile.

"Phil, do you know our town supervisor?" McGillian asked.

"New recruit?" Albrecht laughed more than the comment warranted and his shifty eyes darted about. Without waiting for Phil's reply, he said, "Excuse me." Although he was almost a head shorter than McGillian, he put his arm over the Judge's shoulders and steered him away. They stopped a few steps away.

"It's all set. The county committeemen expect no problem this election," Albrecht said, his voice composed.

McGillian chuckled. "The Democrats can't find a strong candidate to take me on."

"After twenty years of losing, no one with more than a pea brain is willing to put his name on their ticket. What for? To be defeated?" Colby cackled. "Butter. I'm telling you, you'll slide your ass back on that bench like on butter." He tapped McGillian's shoulder. "You're sure you won't consider the Supreme Court?"

McGillian let out a snort. "The answer is still no. I don't care if some think of Family Court as the lowest rung. Someone has to do it. It gives me a sense of mission," he added wistfully.

"You're a rare breed." Albrecht's hand on McGillian's shoulder squeezed. "Just keep your eye on negative media, will you? Even if our constituents don't bother to know the names of the nominees, once you get involved in a business like the one with the dead kid, they'll know your name, all right—and not in a way that would do you any good. The media will descend on you like vultures."

Before McGillian could respond, Albrecht let out a chalky laugh and turned. McGillian watched him disappear in the crowd. Unease crept up his spine. What was the purpose of that warning?

It took a chain of three speakers, each introducing the next, to get to Governor Nicholas Dunkle.

At the end of the affair, McGillian followed Phil to the young man's car.

"Nice car. What is it?"

"A '68 Camaro."

"'68?"

"It's kind of special." Phil opened the passenger door and swatted at the clutter of CDs and a dictating machine on the seat.

After McGillian sat down, Phil revved up the car and put it in gear.

McGillian buckled the seat belt. "Comfy seats. Are they new?" Without waiting for an answer, he continued, "Nice ending to your first week on the job, eh?"

Phil nodded while keeping his eyes on the road. "Your Honor, how do you determine who's the victim in a case and who's the perpetrator?"

McGillian looked at him. "I'd think it shouldn't be difficult to figure."

"I mean, it's not always obvious. Sometimes there can be two victims and you have to decide whose interests should prevail."

"The lines aren't as blurred as you might think."

"The Mayes v. Lee case. Who needed protection—the mother, the father, or the unborn fetus?"

"All three are victims of life's tragic circumstances."

"But your decision, sir, favors life for the fetus, making the mother a victim twice."

"She erred, no question about it. The court can't undo human mistakes, only try to smooth their sad consequences."

"The unborn was never a party to the litigation."

McGillian waved his hand. "The court performs a role that's more complex than merely administering the law. Judges make decisions based on an uneasy mixture of inadequate laws. We're called to interpret what society views as right and wrong."

"Who's to know what's right? The baby will be born to misery. He'll be torn at birth from his mother; he'll be divided between two incompatible cultures. And who'll raise him? Older, uneducated grandparents who did a poor job rearing their own son."

"What's the alternative? Killing him?"

Phil's Adam's apple bobbed as he swallowed hard.

McGillian watched the profile of Phil's open face. "You're afflicted with the most serious malady of youth—that of bleeding-heart liberalism. But it's a condition time will surely heal."

Phil did not reply. A moment later, he began again, "The Belmore v. Belmore case, sir. Why couldn't we grant the mother's lawyer the emergency petition for *temporary* suspension of visitation?"

"Why not grant the father his request for a two-week vacation? It's summer. This may be our chance to give Dr. Belmore time with his daughter. Without the mother's negative influence, things may turn out to be different—"

"You seem to help the father more than the child. This kid needs protection from him."

"Says who? It's unfortunate, but we've got to be careful before we destroy a man by implying that he's at fault."

"Shouldn't we be more careful about a child being destroyed? He molests her. The child's the victim, not the father—"

"If we find the facts to indicate the father an abuser, then you're right. Until such time, the child may very well be the victim of her mother's vicious accusations—as is the father who then becomes a victim. But we haven't determined that yet, have we?"

"Ellie Belmore is clearly the victim who needs protection."

"That's youth for you," McGillian said. "Phil, be very careful not to make a judgment before you hear all the facts. That's what we have trials for. The trial is still on with new material pouring in each week. Don't ever approach a case with such a definite opinion of who's right and who's wrong."

"Your Honor, the testimony of the half-sister, Stephanie Belmore.... I've read the new petition—"

"It's prejudicial."

"But it has probative significance—"

McGillian cut him off. "This case's prejudice is too great. Would you, in fairness to the father, make such a determination?"

"Your Honor, our family law professor at Michigan said that in close cases a judge can stack the facts and find legal backing for his decision no matter which way he goes. Since Ellie Belmore is a minor, we're allowed to use other resources that would support—"

"That's academia for you. Our job, in this courthouse, where we are entrusted with the people's vote of confidence, is to implement the law. Not to make it, not to bend it, not to tamper with it."

"How about interpreting it?"

"That's what implementing it is all about," McGillian said.

"Dr. Belmore seems like a formidable opponent."

"He sure does."

Phil swallowed. "Why would anyone take him on unless she had to?"

"For all you know, she caught him cheating. Women are funny about that."

"So are men."

McGillian laughed. "Look, it takes years of experience, but in time, you'll learn that the majority of women who accuse their husbands of sexually abusing their children drop the charges as soon as they get the money they're asking for."

"This case has no financial demands attached—"

"In fact, if nothing else, some show they're unfit mothers with all they put the kids through." McGillian paused. "You can learn everything from observing the animal kingdom. They have it right."

"They don't have a court system, sir. They just kill each other; eat each other up."

"They keep their young in line, teach them skills,"

"And they copulate with them as soon as they reach maturity."

"Touché," McGillian said, smiling. "I like it when you don't back down. You'll make a good judge one day."

They entered Syosset and drove in silence through the streets that were shrouded in darkness. Within five minutes, they reached McGillian's home at the edge of a cul-de-sac. Phil's car swerved, and came to a stop at the curb.

"Thank you, sir," Phil said. "I'm learning a lot."

McGillian nodded. "You're thinking, and asking questions." Then, as he pulled himself up and out of the car, he added with a smile. "I always welcome a healthy debate."

"Ellie Belmore's situation is not an academic discourse."

"Good night, Phil." McGillian slammed the door behind him.

CHAPTER EIGHT

RACHEL woke up Saturday morning with Ellie's body curled up next to her, a little puppy emanating warmth. Rachel spooned the cuddled, sleeping body and breathed in the sweet smell of baby shampoo, fabric softener, and talcum powder, all misted through the tender scent of her baby's skin.

Ellie stirred and opened her eyes.

"Guess who's coming this afternoon?" Rachel asked cheerfully.

"Who?" Ellie's face clouded. "Dad—Daddy?"

"No, you silly goose. Grandma and Grandpa. And they have lots of presents for you."

Ellie's eyes beamed with relief and delight. "I want a new doll."

"I'm sure they'll get you one."

"With a red dress. I want her to have a red dress."

"I'll bet Grandma will knit her a matching hat if you ask her." Rachel paused. "And guess what else?"

"What?"

"Tomorrow we'll go visit Aunt Josie, and Uncle Howard, and you'll get to play with your cousins."

"They're mean to me. They said their mommy said I'm a brat."

"Aunt Josie said that?" She rose to draw the window shades open only to discover overcast skies.

"Uh-huh," Ellie said.

"They probably misunderstood." Rachel was certain they hadn't. Her sister had been less than gracious about Ellie's problems.

Rachel returned to bed. Lying on her back, her legs extended upward toward the ceiling, Rachel hoisted Ellie up in the air and balanced the small body on top of her feet. "Now, how are Grandma and Grandpa arriving?"

"Airplane," Ellie squeaked with pleasure. "I'm an airplane."

Rachel's wiggling toes against her daughter's plump middle produced a cascade of gurgling giggles of joy. "Now, what would you like to play?" She lowered Ellie down.

Ellie's face became pinched. "I hate the Zoo Game." She lowered her head. "Daddy always wants to play it."

"What game is that?"

"He said it's our secret."

"Some secrets are bad secrets, and you must tell someone."

"He'll be mad at me."

"Sweetie, if you tell me, I'll tell him to stop because you don't like it. Okay?"

Ellie thought for a moment. "It's when the elephant puts his trunk into the monkey's 'tushy,' and the lion roars." Ellie snuggled closer. "I don't like it. It hurts, and Daddy makes those weird noises and then he wee wees on me."

Rachel's heart lurched forward, pounding. It all fell into place.

"I don't know this game," she said, stalling. Outside, the top of the maple tree rustled against the window screen.

"Daddy puts his long, long trunk in my tushy," Ellie repeated. "It hurts me."

"His trunk?"

"His peanut. But he says it's the elephant's trunk."

Rachel's heart gave another twist and settled at the base of her throat. "Don't worry, sweetie," she said. "He won't play that game again. I'll make him stop."

"Promise, Mommy? Cross your heart and hope to die?"

"Cross my heart and hope to die."

Cross my heart and hope to die.

Rachel straddled Ellie on her right hip and strained to see over the heads of other waiting people. Something within her ribs expanded with love as she spotted the approaching couple. Her parents waved, their wide smiles sporting perfect white teeth. With their handsome gray heads, they seemed to have sprung to life from a seniors' vitamins' ad.

Lorena Rayner scooped Ellie into her arms. Her laughing green eyes, so much like Rachel's own, stretched an ebb of moon-shaped lines on both sides of her face. As usual, she wore no makeup yet her face looked fresh.

"My, my, you've grown so big since winter." She gave her granddaughter another squeeze and swung her around. "Say hello to Grandpa."

Ellie buried her head in her grandmother's neck.

"Sweetie, say hello to Grandpa," Rachel said. "He's come all the way from Michigan to see you."

Ellie kept her eyes averted.

"It's all right," Rachel whispered in Ellie's ear, and stroked her hair. She exchanged a knowing look with her parents.

Ellie's resistance to her grandfather melted away in the car the instant he produced the doll in a red dress. A surge of warm feeling spread over Rachel. A retired dentist, meticulous about life's details, he hadn't disappointed her in fulfilling Ellie's last-minute request; he had found a doll on the way to the airport.

"What do you say?" Rachel asked Ellie.

"Thank you." Ellie smiled at him and crawled from her grandmother's lap to his.

As Rachel glanced at the three of them from her rearview mirror, reveling in having them all together, she almost hit the brakes in the middle of the highway. Ellie brought her lips to her grandfather's and proceeded to stick out a little pink tongue and push it into his mouth.

He recoiled. A deep frown creased parallel lines between his brows.

The roots of Rachel's hair went cold. Her fingers clutched the steering wheel. But she kept her voice light and said, "It's nice when you say 'thank you,' Ellie, sweetie, but we don't kiss with our tongues."

"Daddy does," Ellie replied in an argumentative tone. "He said that's how I should say 'thank you.'"

"Oh. It might confuse some people who don't know these things, sweetie. How about if we just say a nice 'thank you'?"

Rachel watched "60 Minutes" with her father while her mother bathed Ellie and tucked her into bed. Through the open door upstairs, Rachel heard her mother's melodious voice telling Ellie a story about the three kittens and accompanying herself on a play keyboard. Even though Ellie could not appreciate her grandmother's talent as a concert pianist, the tale produced squeals of joys from her.

"This is very bad," her father said during a commercial break. "I don't like what happened in the car."

"You haven't heard the half of it. I've been waiting until Ellie went to sleep before telling any more."

He groaned. "There's more?"

When her mother joined them, Rachel recounted her discovery of the Zoo Game.

"He's out of control." A vein pulsated in her father's temple. "Right in the middle of the trial? He just doesn't stop?"

"Russ, Honey, he can't stop. The man's sick. Obsessed," her mother said, then added in a tone as sad as Rachel had ever heard coming out of her, "I never imagined it would hit my own family."

"I could kill the bastard," her father said.

Rachel hit a fisted hand on the couch cushion. "I won't let him have her. Ever!"

"Rach," her mother said. "Does your lawyer believe it's possible this judge might reverse custody because you interfered with Wes's visitation?"

Rachel nodded. "Absolutely. Judge McGillian was about to hand down a verdict, which Chuck diverted. Ortman keeps bringing up my moving in with Jacqueline when I first left Wes, and McGillian gobbles it up. 'Took the child out the marital home. Parental kidnapping,'" she imitated Ortman's unctuous voice. "You'd think I'd disappeared in Brazil. I wish I had."

"You now have the doctor's report. No question that it's sexual molestation," Lorena said. "And the appointment with Ms. Edwards… Ellie can tell her about the Zoo Game."

"There were enough confirmed reports before," Russ said. "Wes's experts have always defused—and refuted—them."

"You saw last year the show Wes can put up in court. But this time not even his experts will be able to convince McGillian to grant him a two-week vacation," Rachel said. She had to force herself to be confident about the outcome of the trial. The alternative was too horrible to consider. "And we're pushing for Stephanie's testimony. The whole thing should finally be over."

Russ leaned forward and put his elbows on his knees. "Be realistic. Your mother and I have talked it over. What will you do if the judge continues to grant Wes unsupervised visits—and this vacation? What if he gives him custody?"

Rachel raised her eyes to look at both of them. "I thought of running away with her. There's this underground organization in Atlanta. They help women escape with their kids." She stopped. "It's too risky. Many get caught, and the child is given to the father for good while the mother goes to jail."

Her parents exchanged a look. Russ asked, "What will you do Tuesday afternoon if you don't get what you expect from the court?"

Her father was trying to make a point, reach somewhere, but Rachel wasn't sure where he was leading.

"I won't let him have her, that's one sure thing."

For a while no one spoke. Rachel bit her lip. "I wouldn't mind the jail part if it meant Ellie was safe."

"If you ran away, where would you go? For how long?"

"Daddy, I haven't figured it out. I don't even know how to get in touch with this organization. And how would we live? In my car? In motels? With no school and no work for years?" She looked at him. "I guess it's better than the alternative. I'll need a flow of cash until Ellie is old enough to return. Oh, Dad, forget it."

Russ asked, "What if, while you're working on getting Stephanie's testimony, McGillian gives Wes his two-week vacation beginning next week?"

"What are my choices? I'll keep her away; I'll hide from the police."

Again her parents exchanged a look, then Lorena spoke in a low tone. "We've talked it over, Rachel. *We'll* take her and disappear."

Rachel stared at them, the words sinking in slow motion into her gray cells. Like a dry sponge, her consciousness absorbed and filled up with the portentousness of the moment. "Disappear? What do you mean, 'disappear?'"

"It means you won't see her for years." Her mother's voice was almost a whisper in the falling darkness. No one got up to switch on the lights. "But Dad and I can hide with her."

Rachel continued to stare. "She'll live with you in the trailer?"

Her father nodded. "Each September we'll stop at another RV park and enroll her in school. It's safer that way. I can't promise she'll be happy without you—or with constantly changing schools—but she'll be free of Wes. And she'll have all our love."

"I don't believe this," Rachel mumbled. "This is so fucking unbelievable."

"Watch your tongue," Lorena said.

"How can you expect me to agree not to see Ellie for years?"

"We're talking worst-case scenario. Do you have a better course of action?" her father asked.

She heard her own petulant tone. "I don't know what to say."

Her mother seemed to choke back tears. "Rach, I feel about not seeing you for years the same way you feel about not seeing Ellie—"

The words hit her hard. "Mommy," Rachel cried out. How selfish she had been. She hugged her mother. "Sorry. I am so sorry for everything—"

"Shhhhhhh." Lorena caressed her hair.

Her father sat, watching. He let a few moments pass. "The pressure on you will be enormous," he said quietly. "It'd be better if no one knows where we are. Not even you."

"What about Josie? And her kids? You won't be able to see them for years?"

Lorena's eyes clouded. She nodded, unable to speak.

"We thought of that, too. It's everybody's loss. Everyone suffers," Russ said. His eyes were red. For a split second he seemed to lose his composure.

"And in the meanwhile, I'll continue the legal battle here?" Rachel asked.

"You must—to the degree that you can," her mother said, regaining her voice. "Without the child to be interviewed by experts, who knows?"

Russ said, "Rach, we have to be packed and ready to leave with Ellie when the court closes on Tuesday. Just in case things don't pan out. Give us Ellie's passport and birth certificate."

"Passport?"

"If our trail gets too hot, we may have to take her out of the country."

Rachel sank back into the couch, feeling herself slipping into a muddy bottom with no foothold. This wasn't happening. This wasn't her life—it was a soap opera taking place in a twilight zone, in another time and place, happening to other people. But a TV program could be turned off if it hurt her sense of credibility, of the absurd. Not so with this one; it was a nightmare borne within a nightmare.

Abruptly, the thought struck her. "You won't be able to use your credit cards, your checking account. You can't leave a paper trail. Maybe you can't even use your own names…. God."

"Honey, it'll all be taken care of. It's better that you don't know how." Her father patted her bowed head.

"I can't believe you have it all worked out."

"Not all. Not the pain of abandoning you and keeping away from Josie. She needs us. Very much."

They should be relieved to stay away from the neurotic Josie. Rachel said nothing.

Lorena took a deep breath. "Monday, we'll transfer more money to your account for Bernstein's fee."

"Do you have enough for all of this? Look what I've brought upon you—at a time you were enjoying your retirement."

"If you must feel guilty, go ahead," Lorena smiled through still-misty eyes. "But it won't be the best use of your energies—"

A shriek, coming from Ellie's room, cut her words in mid-sentence.

"I hate the elephant! I hate the elephant!"

Rachel scrambled to her feet and took the steps two at a time, dashed through the short corridor, and stopped next to Ellie's bed. She held the writhing little body in her arms. The girl's hands covered her buttocks.

"Sweetie, it's me, Mommy. I'm here. There's no elephant. And no monkey, or lion."

Ellie opened her eyes with horror. Then she put her thumb in her mouth and curled up again. She hadn't sucked her thumb in years. Rachel continued to hold her tight, planted little kisses on her face, and stroked the silky locks of hair. From the corner of her eye she noticed her parents' silhouettes outlined against the doorway.

"Oh, boy," her father said. "Oh, boy."

It was after ten o'clock when the phone rang. "Hi there." Gerald's voice was exuberant as always. "How have you been?"

Rachel loved his full voice. She imagined him pacing the floor in his apartment, the phone in his hand, his energy coiled in each of his nimble muscles and sinews.

"Fine, uh, fine. How are you? I've missed you. When did you get back?"

"A few days ago." An unease crept into his voice.

She felt her throat tighten. That wasn't like him. They either spoke or saw each other every day, but he hadn't called from San Diego. And this was Saturday night. He'd never missed spending a Saturday night with her unless he was out of town. Yet here he was, around and keeping away.

"Sorry I didn't call," he answered her unasked question. "It's been tough around here." He proceeded to lament his divorce negotiations. Rachel half listened. Why hadn't he let her know he was back?

"Want to come over tomorrow?" she finally asked.

"Uh, we'll see. I'll be busy with the kids. And the Phoenix project guys are in town."

A fog of disappointment descended over her. Couldn't he hop in the car right now, come over and stay the night after they'd been apart for a week? He'd told her to compile a list of S's…. She bit her lip, uncertain how to negotiate the shifting ground under her feet. Why didn't he ask her how her trial had gone?

He let a moment pass. "I'll try calling you tomorrow," he said meekly. "Good night."

Slowly, Rachel put down the receiver. It clattered on the cradle as her hand kept missing the spot, until it dropped on the table with a clank. She stared at it, listening to the monotone trill of a dead line. She had just walked to the end of the earth and fallen over the edge. Six months, Jacqueline had said. Rachel had felt secure enough with Gerald and, after only two months together, had told him of her difficulties at the office. Subtle as it was, he had understood the corporate culture at Sheridan Magazines, the cutthroat competitiveness of her colleagues, who sought not to improve their performance but, under Vince's leadership, to undermine hers.

Then, one evening, about three months into their relationship, in a flash flood of words, she let down her drawbridge. For hours, she had fumed about her ordeal with Wes and her mounting frustrations with the justice system. That first night, he held her all night. In the morning he looked at her with concern. The deep well of bottomless doom filled with his devotion and love.

And now, inexplicably, he pulled back.

CHAPTER   NINE

ON the walkway leading to the large home of her younger sister, Josie, Rachel trailed behind her parents.

Her father stopped and turned. "Whatever happens, try to take the high road, okay?"

"Sure, Dad, I'll be good," Rachel replied. She never knew what would come out of time spent with Josie, but hoped this visit would be pleasant. God knew she needed a close sister. "I'll be patient."

Her mother kept her gaze straight. Rachel let out a deep breath. The coming afternoon made her feel wired. She continued to walk.

Ahead of her, Ellie skipped happily between her grandparents, holding onto their hands. Every few steps they stopped and swung her up. Each time she rewarded them with shrieks of delight. As they neared the house, though, Lorena handed Ellie back to Rachel.

"We haven't seen Josie in a while," Lorena said, hesitation in her voice. "Give us a minute to say hello."

Rachel understood. Josie had expressed jealousy of the disproportionate attention her parents lavished on Rachel's only daughter, complaining it took away from her own three children.

Next to a large pair of stone Chinese temple dogs, Rachel crouched, pretending to tie Ellie's sneakers. When the door opened, she held Ellie from bounding up the two steps in search of her cousins. When the hugging and kissing between Josie and her parents was about to end, Rachel straightened up.

"Hi, Josie," she said in a cheerful tone. "You look sensational."

Josie's smile was wan, her false eyelashes flapping. Her hand went up to the coiffed hairstyle, each strand sprayed into place. "Do you really like it?" she asked. "You mean it?"

"Of course. It's great." Rachel wiggled her toes in her flat sandals. Josie's hair, makeup, and the tailored magenta pants suit weren't Rachel's notion of an outfit for a Sunday family barbecue. Josie's choice, however, made it clear that in the competition drummed up in her mind, she would not be outshone by her sister's looks.

Josie led them through the huge sunken living room, the cream of its marble floor matching the upholstery of the contemporary furniture and the grand piano. The cathedral ceiling and the room were awash in the sunny afternoon light.

"I want you to see my new painting." Josie pointed at a canvas that covered much of the largest wall. "I did it."

Rachel stared at red splashes and black and navy stains intersected by glued yellow strips. She nodded appreciatively, feeling Josie's expectant eyes on her. "It's great."

"I always said you painted beautifully." Russ's arm rested on Josie's shoulder. "I'm glad you're getting back to it."

"Well?" Josie asked Rachel.

"You're talented. No question about it," Rachel said, wondering how many lies she'd be compelled to tell throughout the afternoon.

"But you don't like it, right?" Josie demanded.

"Of course I do, didn't I say it?" Rachel hated the defensive note that had already crept into her voice.

"Not until I asked you."

"I said it's great." Here they went again. Rachel tried to keep her tone casual. "It really is. There's a balance between the collage and the distribution of colors. The piece brings the entire room into focus—"

"Let's go outside," Lorena interrupted. "Josie, I smell something good."

In the kitchen, in a cloud of fragrant steam, the housekeeper was removing a pie from the oven. She set it on the table next to a large glass bowl filled with tossed salad. Past the double glass doors, in the center of the slate patio, a table was covered with a colorful cloth and set with matching ceramic dinnerware.

"Wait until you taste the vegetable dish I made," Josie gushed. "I got this new recipe."

"A real Martha Stewart," Rachel said.

Her quota for compliments complete, she moved toward the door and spotted her brother-in-law inside the fenced-in pool area. She waved to him. The small-framed Howard stood at the pool's edge in his navy swimming briefs, coaching his oldest daughter as she attempted a dive from the board. The other two children, a twin boy and girl a year older than Ellie, played catch with a beach ball at the shallow end of the pool, their bright arm floaters sparkling in hot pink and yellow.

"Let's get your bathing suit on," Rachel said to Ellie, who came to stand next to her, mesmerized by the scene. A joyous look bloomed on Ellie's face.

In the all-white cabana, Ellie wriggled out of her clothes and into her bathing suit, bubbling with excitement. She ran outside while Rachel grabbed a couple of beach towels from the pile of neatly folded ones.

"Wait, you can't go in until I change," Rachel called out to her. She stepped out to the cabana door to make sure Ellie did not get in the water yet.

"I'll watch her. I'll put her water wings on," Howard called back. He turned to his daughter. "Let's take a break, Nicole, and say hello to our guests." He sauntered over to the shallow end, smiling toward Ellie.

Her eyes wide with fear, Ellie took a step backward.

"It's all right, sweetie," Rachel called over to her. "This is Uncle Howard."

"Daddy! Just one more time. Watch me!" Nicole yelled from behind Howard.

"No—oooo!" Ellie screamed at the sight of Howard walking toward her. She took another step backward.

At that moment, a shriek pierced the air from the direction of the diving board. Rachel flicked her gaze in time to hear a thud and see Nicole slipping and hitting her head on the diving board. Nicole fell sideways into the water at the same instant Ellie took another step backward and stumbled over the steps into the shallow end of the pool.

"Christ!" Howard called out and sprinted back toward his daughter. He dove in.

Rachel had no time to think. She kicked off her sandals, dashed toward the pool steps, and jumped in, still wearing her white cotton pants. Ellie kicked, flailed her arms, and swallowed water. A few feet away from her, the twins stood motionless, their drawn faces small and stupefied. The beach ball floated and reached Ellie, but her arms, jerking in a flurry of motions, batted it away. Rachel threw herself in the water and caught Ellie. She brought up the writhing body while tapping on her back to help her cough out the water.

Across the pool, Howard brought Nicole up. His cheek, chest, and the arm wrapped around Nicole's chest were covered with blood. Something lurched in Rachel's stomach.

"It's okay, baby," Rachel spoke loudly into Ellie's wet hair, trying to overcome Ellie's panicked cries. "I'm holding you. You'll be all right."

The double incident had taken only seconds, Rachel knew, but when she raised her head again, her father was already at the edge of the pool, leaning forward to accept the bleeding and wailing Nicole from Howard's cradling arms. With the water spilling from the child's body, blood seemed to be everywhere.

Russ's delicate fingers checked his granddaughter's scalp. Howard scrambled out of the water, yanked a towel, and tucked it under his child's head.

"She'll be fine," Russ said to him, and turned to Nicole. "What day is today?"

She sniffled. "Sunday."

In Rachel's arms, Ellie's coughs came out softer and in increasing intervals. A minute later, she began to whimper. Rachel, still holding her, broke the water on her way to the steps. "Come on out," she called out to the twins.

They remained standing, their eyes transfixed on the sight of their bleeding sister lying at the pool's edge.

Lorena and Josie came running out of the house, paused for a second to scan the scene, and scurried toward Nicole.

"My baby," Josie cried, and reached a hand, afraid to touch Nicole. "Who did this to you?"

Lorena put her arms around Josie. Rachel could not hear the words, but saw her mother's lips moving.

"She's all right," Russ's voice encompassed them all. "It's only a cut. The water makes it seem much worse." He smiled down at the crying child. "You'll be fine, Pudding, except for half a tennis ball on your head. Let me know when you're ready for a match."

"You hear? She's fine," Rachel said to the twins. She reached over to them with one available hand. "Let's go out and play on the grass."

Suddenly, Josie shook herself loose from her mother's hug and yelled, her pinched face toward Rachel, piercing Rachel with dark, scorching eyes. "It's all because of you!"

"What?" Rachel mumbled, looking around as if someone else standing behind her were the target of Josie's attack.

"It's all because of you and your brat kid!" Josie's voice skipped one octave.

"Stop it," Lorena ordered, "Stop this nonsense right away."

"Ellie screamed and made Nicole fall in the water!"

Rachel gulped. The palm of her hand curved protectively over Ellie's head.

"You're frightening the children," Lorena told Josie, her tone firm, and motioned with her head toward the twins. "Get hold of yourself."

"You're always against me!" Josie cried. "For once, you can admit whose fault this is." She pivoted on her heels and dashed inside the house, leaving behind her splintered air as the four adults avoided looking into each other's eyes.

Howard walked toward the pool entrance, Nicole nestled in his arms.

"Russ thinks she needs a couple of stitches and should get x-rayed just in case," he said quietly. "I'll take her to the emergency room. Sorry to leave you."

"Go ahead," Lorena said. "I'll take care of things here."

"Help me get Nicole in the car," Howard told Russ. Sending an apologetic glance in Rachel's direction, he walked to the garage.

"God Almighty," Rachel mumbled.

From the cabana refrigerator she retrieved cans of Coke and a bag of pretzels. Still wearing her wet clothes, she led Ellie and the twins to a majestic weeping willow, and settled on the lawn under it.

From the manicured flowerbeds and landscaped hedges, the steamy heat carried aroma of roses and honeysuckle. It complemented the picture of the elegant house with green and white striped awnings. Rachel played patty-cake with the three children until her father returned from the garage. He met her eyes in mutual understanding.

She went to him. "Should I just leave?" she whispered. "Either I come back to pick you two up later, or Howard will drive you home."

"Stay with the kids for a while. Let me see how Josie's doing. I'll be right back."

Lorena returned instead. A vague uneasiness wrapped itself in the air around her. "I guess Josie wants our undivided attention since we're staying with you…." She let her words trail.

"It's okay. I understand," Rachel said.

"This is not what I envisioned for my daughters." Lorena's eyes betrayed her sadness. "But the two of you have always been of such different temperaments."

"Mom, this is not a case of 'different temperaments.' You have one crazy daughter, and it's not me."

"She's not like this when she doesn't compare herself to you."

"Compare herself to me?" Rachel asked. "Look at her life. At thirty-one she has it made. A saint for a husband, healthy children, a gorgeous house—and no problems other than the ones of her own creation."

"She thinks you got all the talent and the looks. All she believes she can be is a housewife who dabbles in painting."

"She dropped out of college to get married and produce babies. Whose fault was that, mine?"

"Don't you see? She wanted to be ahead of you in something."

"Well, she won in whatever stupid competition she thought we were in." Rachel closed her eyes for a moment. Behind her stinging lids, bright yellow lights curtained a kaleidoscope of colors. "Mom, I can't deal with this. I don't need Josie's nonsense. Ellie and I will go home and have a good time at the town pool."

Back in the cabana where she changed Ellie, Rachel felt sadness spread over her. She raised her head, as if trying to catch a faraway tune, but all she could hear was the sound of her pounding temples. Was there any place where she and Ellie were welcome?

If only Josie knew she needed her acceptance as much as Josie needed hers, that she needed a sister who was a soul mate, or at least a trusted friend, as Jacqueline was. But in the hazy area between realism and romanticism, Rachel knew she must free herself from illusion. The gulf between her and Josie was just too deep, too wide.

CHAPTER TEN

"I need to practice my presentation on you," Rachel told Jacqueline on Monday morning as they sat down with their cups of coffee. "Here's the story: Baroness has only catered to upscale consumers. They have only a few "doors," as they call their sales counters at selected department stores. By limiting access to their products, Baroness created a shortage of supply, which they followed with a price hike. Baroness's executives pretend to be unaware of a black market for their products in neighborhoods where the company shuns the local stores.

"Now, cashing in on their success, they have concocted a line-extension of moderately-priced skin products, which they magnanimously plan to bring to the awaiting masses."

Jacqueline chortled. "No wonder the competition for their advertising has been so fierce."

"Yup. All magazine reps have been elbowing one another for a share of the new budget. You can't sit in an ad agency lobby without someone trying to dig up dirt on a magazine's editorial personnel, or about printing plant union strikes." Rachel continued, changing her tone to an emcee's. "Ready? Here is the final presentation that will bring Baroness aboard."

She proceeded to deliver the full presentation. The promotion department had helped create it piece by piece, but no one had seen it complete.

Half an hour later, when she was done, Jacqueline beamed at her. "I hope Vince has the sense to use this presentation for all of *Women's Life*'s sales force for the next planning season. This research—simple logic and outright convincing. Fabulous. Seductive."

Rachel shrugged. "I'll show it to him as soon as I can pin him down for some serious work. The promo director must have told him about it. He hangs out at her office whenever he isn't prowling the corridors." The promotion director's work amplified the hype and publicity, which surrounded the selling process.

"He can always replace a couple of the boards and adapt the presentation to any category. Wow," Jacqueline went on. "You know what? Present it to the publisher, too. He'll love it. Anyway, you haven't kissed *his* ass for a while."

"Great idea. I will." Rachel laughed. "The presentation, I mean, not the kissing."

After Jacqueline left, Rachel, nursing a bubble of pride, settled back with a fresh cup of coffee to rehearse her material. It must flow without a single glitch. When she got the account, she would have a serious talk with Vince and the publisher about a promotion. A Category Manager would do; rather than supervising her colleagues, she would only assist them with their projects. Along with the management spot would come the higher income she so needed—but not much out-of-town travel.

She closed her eyes, erased all previous impressions, and reviewed the mounted boards as though she were seeing them anew. She played the multimedia video portion, complete with hired actors and music. Then as she flipped through the boards while reciting aloud the research, she recorded herself on the tape recorder. When done, she listened to her own presentation. It was perfect.

Vince popped his head in. "What's up?"

"Ready for the Baroness presentation?" she asked him. "This will be a home run."

"How about if you go over it with Tom?"

"Who's Tom?"

"Tom Fields, my trainee."

She hadn't paid much attention to Sheridan's training program; she had thought it to be the latest publicity stunt.

She flinched. "Okay. Uh, sure. Where is he?" She wasn't quite up to spending time teaching the young man who had been hanging around the office lately. Pleasant enough and very handsome, he was utterly inexperienced and had not impressed Rachel as being bright enough to even make it into the training program of a major corporation.

"I'll send him in," Vince said.

As he turned to leave, Rachel stopped him, "I'd like to take a vacation day tomorrow."

He looked at her, his eyebrows arched. "Again?"

"The business of life." She smiled.

"Rachel." His voice was strained. "How do you expect to make management if you take so much time off?"

"These are my vacation days," she replied, her tone flippant, forcing herself to sound cute. "I haven't taken even a sick day in two years."

"I haven't taken a vacation day in ten years."

But you haven't worked a single day in ten years either.

She almost said it aloud. She was losing it. Regardless of what else was going on in her life, she must stay on her boss's good side. And get that damn promotion.

Vince gave her a look she could not interpret. "I'll send Tom in," he said, and swiveled on his heel.

The babysitter, Freda, called shortly after. Rachel picked up the phone with apprehension.

"Ellie bit a girl so hard they took her to the emergency room for stitches," Freda reported.

"Do you know who it was?"

"No," Freda replied. "Ellie's having a 'bad day.' I went to get her early. The girl's parents are so mad; they don't want Ellie in school."

"Are my parents home?" They would be able to calm Ellie down.

"They went to your sister's. They left you a note."

Rachel dialed the daycare center number.

"I'm really sorry," the teacher said. "But we're not staffed to handle a child such as Ellie and… and all the problems around her."

Rachel bit her lip. Was the teacher also referring to the three times she had been subpoenaed—two of which she had been sent away from court without testifying?

"It's the middle of the summer program," Rachel protested. Yet what difference did it make if she would be sending Ellie away? If it weren't the reversal of custody, it would be the two-week vacation.

"We'll keep her till the end of August, but not afterward. Some parents are calling… We owe it to the other children to provide a safe environment."

"Thanks," Rachel said, reeling from the sting of the insult. "I appreciate your caring about Ellie so far."

She grabbed her briefcase and dashed out of the office. "I'm going to a meeting," she told Jacqueline. "I won't be back." At least Jacqueline would not be the one doing the lying.

The Rayners' note said they would spend the evening at Josie and Howard's. Rachel held the piece of paper, loving her father's small, meticulous handwriting. If the trial tomorrow brought another disappointment, this would be her parents' last time with Nicole and the twins for years to come.

Rachel stared out the window. The inconceivable thought of losing her case seemed surreal against the flow of normal life outside: Kids played on the lawn across the street, a neighbor unloaded groceries from her car, a UPS truck stopped at the corner. A suburban summer afternoon.

She closed her eyes for a moment. She must steel herself against the possibility that she'd have to send Ellie away. She could almost feel the dripping of the remedy into her veins, as poisonous as chemotherapy that destroyed healthy cells while offering the hope of cure. For too long now time had been measured not by the day or the week, but by the milestones of legal solutions attempted—but instead of bringing the intended relief, they destroyed her in the process.

Ellie came over and wrapped her arms around her mother's waist. "When is dinner?"

"Let's fatten you up." Rachel touched Ellie's mussed hair. "What would you like?"

As soon as they sat down at the kitchen table, Ellie's mood took a turn for the worse. No food was acceptable to her. With songs and stories, Rachel spent a long time trying to cheer her up and coax bits of chicken or vegetables into her mouth. Occasionally, she bent down to the floor to clean up food thrown in fits of anger. She looked down at her T-shirt, stained with peas and carrots. How ironic it was to think of the elegant lunch she had eaten at an Italian restaurant, filling up the quota Vince had set—at least four clients entertained each week. What would Vince make of her not returning to the office this afternoon?

"Sweetie, you don't have to finish." Rachel spoke tenderly with the next eruption of a temper tantrum. "Shall I heat up some alphabet soup instead?"

"I don't want any stupid food!" Ellie shrieked, and hurled herself to the ground, kicking.

Rachel picked up the thrashing body and held it close. "It's all right, Ellie baby," she said tenderly. "Now calm down. Let's take a bath, okay?"

The long soak in the water did the therapeutic trick and restored Ellie's spirits.

It was still hot and humid when the two of them covered the three blocks to Baskin-Robbins, Ellie vigorously pedaling her tricycle, her cheeks flushed in pink.

"Mommy, look! No hands!" She let the tricycle roll forward a few feet, her hands raised above her head. "Look at me!"

Rachel smiled with pleasure at the sight of the beautiful child who had come up for air from her tomb of pain, courageous enough to brave new challenges. Tomorrow, this fragile, tormented spirit could be dealt another stupendous blow, as devastating as an eighteen-wheeler slamming into her. She might lose her mother, her home, her school, her room, and her toys. She might become a fugitive, running away from the law. If caught, Ellie's punishment would be worse than life in prison with no parole— she would be handed over to her father.

At the ice cream store, Ellie selected a sugar cone. "Mix the banana and peach with cherry swirls," she said to the teenager behind the counter and licked her lips in anticipation. "Make it look like the sun." With bright eyes, she pointed at the red ball hanging in the sky outside the store.

"I have an idea," Rachel said as she paid and handed Ellie the ice cream. "Let's say you're someplace and I'm not there with you. Whenever you look at the red sun, you should remember these three words: 'I love you.'"

In response, Ellie hugged Rachel and planted a sticky, sweet kiss on her cheek. "I love you too, Mommy."

"It's a deal? You'll remember?" Rachel insisted.

"A deal," Ellie's voice was like little bells. "Cross my heart and hope to die."

After Rachel tucked Ellie into bed and sang her a lullaby, she went down to the basement to fetch two suitcases and a soft duffel bag for Ellie's favorite toys. The world of a five-year-old could be transported in a few pieces of luggage.

At the kitchen table, Rachel doodled little pictures and wrote simple words on Post-it-Notes. Her mouth felt metallic and sour, as though a cold spoon held her tongue down. She forced her mind into neutral gear; she would not feel, hear, or hurt, or the pain would be too great.

She stuffed the notes in the winter clothes—in the sleeves of the sweaters, in the cushy lining of the gloves, in the depths of the boots. Ellie would find them when her mother and her home seemed as far away as a lifetime—the only mail she would receive from her mother. Would she be starting to read at the new kindergarten by then?

Rachel's silent brooding was broken by Jacqueline's phone call, wishing Rachel good luck in court tomorrow.

"I'm never clear on how your 'final hearing' turns into a 'new hearing,'" Jacqueline said. "Nothing ever seems to be 'final.'"

"Welcome to the club. Here is how I understand it," Rachel sighed. "Custody proceedings in Family Court are a trial, but a hearing is on a point of law within a trial.

My trial is stretching over days because it's postponed due to technicalities, or when we're waiting for a witness, or because we file a new petition with new allegations. But even when I'm done with one Family Court trial, another one may still be open in Criminal Court, or an appeal would be waiting on the calendar of the Appellate Division."

"I'm withdrawing my wish of good luck," Jacqueline said.

"Why is that? I can use every bit of it. If only they sold it in a bottle—"

"Real heroes are ordinary people with extraordinary determination— not luck," Jacqueline replied.

Rachel smiled into the phone. How she wished she could cry out her agony of separating from Ellie, as painful as having her leg amputated with no anesthesia. "Whether I think I can or can't do it—things always come out the same."

"Not forever, they won't. How about praying?"

"I don't even know what religion I am." Rachel said. After her years in Hebrew school and performing in her bat-mitzvah, of which she had been so proud, normal teenage angst over pop music icons and social cliques at school gave way to spending her young adult years in spiritual oblivion.

"I'll ask my Jewish God to take you back, you infidel."

"I married Wes in a ceremony presided over by a Justice of the Peace," Rachel said. It had been an act that stung of betrayal to her Jewish parents, even though in the ensuing years they had made no mention of it. "Is there a religion for single mothers?" she asked.

"That one is 'a calling.'"

Rachel looked, unseeing, into the shadows in the flowered curtains. "It was so overwhelming at first, but ultimately, the challenge doubled my capabilities," she said, wondering what did one call a single mother *without* a child.

"Your challenges are on the heavy side these days," Jacqueline said. "I'm here for you."

"Jacques, I know the office manager gave you a tough time about taking off with little or no notice. You might lose your job because of me."

Jacqueline laughed. "The secretaries are unionized, remember? Sheridan has to put me on notice first."

Rachel's eyes misted. In France, where Jacqueline grew up and studied, corporations routinely used handwriting analysis in the screening of job applicants. Earlier in their friendship, Jacqueline, an astute observer of human nature without this added tool, had examined Rachel's and announced cheerfully, "You and I will be great friends. Perfect compatibility."

If only she had known Jacqueline at the time Wes entered her life. Would Jacqueline have read 'pedophile' in his handwriting?

Rachel hung up and sat still by the phone, hating herself for hoping Gerald would call, wanting to dial his number. Somehow, so harshly, so savagely, he'd yanked himself out of her life. And she missed him. He'd edged out of the relationship just when she needed to feel secure, just when she had turned herself fully toward him—just when she had fallen in love with him.

After Lorena and Russ returned, Rachel sat with them on the back porch. The women rocked on the swing, their fingers laced. Rachel loved the familiar feel of her mother's supple fingers, so pliable, so soft after years of piano practice.

Russ went inside and brought out a bottle of brandy and three snifters. For a while, they listened to the rustle of the treetops and breathed in the fragrance of lavender, geraniums, and freshly cut grass. No one spoke.

An owl hooted somewhere and broke the silence.

"It might not happen," Rachel said. "Judge McGillian may agree to hear Stephanie's testimony and suspend Wes's visits."

Her parents exchanged a look.

"Would he agree to hear the new information about the Zoo Game?" her father asked.

"Chuck thinks Henry Ortman will ask for weeks—if not months—for preparations…. McGillian adheres to procedure above all else, and might grant Ortman's request." She paused. "Tomorrow Wes will demand his two-week vacation."

"Rach." Her mother squeezed her fingers. "We'll do whatever you think is best."

"Why can't I know where you'll take Ellie? Why can't I contact you?"

"With Wes's resources? He'll be on to us in a flash." Her father looked at her. "You know that we can go to jail for this, don't you?"

Rachel suppressed a sniffle. "I just can't bring myself to never see or speak to her again. To never see or speak to you again—" She stopped, and then, as though talking to herself, Rachel continued. "Tomorrow at five, Wes will show up with the police to pick up Ellie for his visit, his court order in hand." Could she then stand there again, heartless, with the camcorder rolling—this time for thirty minutes—recording her child's unimaginable terror? "Ellie can't take any more of this."

Cross my heart and hope to die.

So that was it.

Tomorrow morning, before leaving for court, she would see Ellie for the last time. In a last hug of the little perfumed, compact body, she would kiss the soft cheeks and curve of the tiny nose, she would memorize every line and contour of her child, never letting the school-bound Ellie know those would be their last moments together for a long time, lest she reveal the plans.

Rachel felt her heart snap like a frozen twig. She stood and shuffled her feet toward the stairs. Turning to face her parents, she asked, "Will you tell her every day that I love her?"

Emotionally exhausted, she fell asleep as soon as her head hit the pillow but was startled awake shortly after. Thoughts of Gerald exploded in her head, like a flock of birds frightened by a blasting shotgun. He hadn't called. She had opened herself up, lowered her defenses, but ended up vulnerable and betrayed.

What had happened to the afterglow following their lovemaking—moments that lit up their eyes and percolated their hearts these past eight months? Were passion and ache an inseparable duo in her life?

She must have drifted back to sleep, for startled, she awoke again, swimming up from the depths of the dream. She hit the surface, breaking through it with almost a shock of realization.

She had become a taker. She no longer had anything to give the people in her life—Jacqueline, Gerald, her parents, even Chuck…. In her desperate need, as insatiable as a litter of starving puppies, she had relentlessly drawn on their strength. Her fast-wasting emotional energies were so drained she had nothing with which to reciprocate.

Gerald had been a giver, but she had become too much of a taker. He had had to get away.

CHAPTER ELEVEN

RACHEL could not recall the last name of Phil, the young man with the thoughtful blue-gray eyes who had bought her a Coke and jump-started her car. He sat at a small desk to the right of McGillian's raised bench. Closing a file—was it hers?—he clamped his palms in his armpits and tilted his chair back. His eyes, momentarily filling with twinkles, flicked in Rachel's direction. Then they clouded and shifted their focus to the high ceiling, where they remained fixed as though existential answers had been scrawled across its peeling paint.

In front of the judge's desk, Ortman was deep in a hushed discussion with Wes. Rachel's lawyer seized the chance for a small talk with Judge McGillian. Chuck's ability to switch gears always amazed Rachel. It must be a men's thing, to treat your adversary—or whatever she should call the judge holding a sword over her head—as a friend. Perhaps men were the ones with the gift and knew how to search for the common ground rather than the divisive. Perhaps that's where she had been off the mark in her approach to her boss....

She breathed in deeply and steadied her hands. She felt as powerless and vulnerable as a baby bird that had fallen out of its nest.

"Judge, I've heard you fly-fish," Chuck said.

"Yes, indeed."

"When I was young, my father showed me how to tie a Hare's Ear, a Cozis Devil—" Chuck chuckled. "No luck."

"I use bits of yarn, rabbit fur, feathers, foil, brass beads, and peacock herl—what have you—and wind them around the hook with loops of waxed thread." McGillian's animated fingers emulated the motions. "I shape the thing into a grub, a larva—anything to fool the fish into believing it's the real thing."

"The fish didn't bite mine."

"Ultimately, it's the bond with the river—not the catch—that makes it worthwhile." McGillian smiled, and Rachel winced. How could he be so nonchalant when her life was at stake?

Ortman cut in. "We're ready, Your Honor."

Chuck opened his argument to hear Stephanie's testimony. "Psychological literature indicates that a person who abused one of his children is likely to abuse another. Stephanie Belmore is now eleven years old. We ask that she be allowed to testify as to what her father did to her."

"Objection, Your Honor," Ortman cried out. "The last time she saw her father was three years ago, and her testimony in the New Jersey court dates back two years before that to when she was six years old. Children that age cannot differentiate between reality and fantasy. Those confused memories get imprinted in their minds and can't be reconstructed years later."

"It is up to the court to determine whether Stephanie's recollection is a fabrication of her imagination or the account of a bright, reliable child." Chuck's voice rose as it gathered urgency. "We beg the court to hear her out. An eleven-year-old knows right from wrong, Your Honor. She would know whether what her father did was wrong, felt wrong. She'll be able to impress on the court that Dr. Belmore is a child molester—"

"Objection, Your Honor—"

"A murderer need not murder once a year in order to be called a murderer." Chuck's glasses reflected the fluorescent lighting hanging low from the ceiling. "One murder on his record does it. The same applies to a child molester. A New Jersey court has found Dr. Belmore to be one—"

"That's not true," Ortman yelled. His long fingers poked through a stack of documents. "The judge in the case gave his decision based upon the extreme length of time Dr. Belmore was separated from Stephanie and the deterioration of their relationship by then. Not because it was proven he had molested her."

McGillian turned to Chuck. "Do you agree to admit the New Jersey decision into evidence?"

"Yes, Your Honor, as long as we all bear in mind that the actual trial records are sealed, and we can't obtain transcripts of what the girl told the court."

Ortman handed McGillian the decision and he leafed through it. He lifted his eyes in question to Chuck.

"This isn't a jury trial where there's a concern that a testimony be implanted in the minds of the lay jurors," Chuck pressed on. "I trust that you, Your Honor, can discard Stephanie's testimony if you find it not to be credible."

McGillian raised his hand. "There's another responsibility here that we all seem to forget about: the cross-examination of an eleven-year-old by the defense attorney. It's a horrible experience to put a child through."

"Her mother has agreed—" Chuck began to protest, but the judge interrupted.

"Since I don't believe her testimony can be uninfluenced by the time factor, I won't victimize her to help the case of another child."

Rachel jumped to her feet. "My daughter is being molested!" she cried out. "You're concerned about not hurting everyone except my five-year-old baby!"

"Sit down!" McGillian's voice thundered.

She pounded on the table. "Don't you get it?"

"Mr. Bernstein, please restrain your client," McGillian commanded, but it was not necessary. Chuck had already seized Rachel's arm and pulled her down as he fell into his chair.

"Sorry about that, Your Honor." He turned to Rachel and breathed furiously in her ear, "We'll appeal it."

She lowered her head and steadied her fingers. How could she quarantine her bitterness? Sour and stifling, it gagged her.

Upon hearing the news that Stephanie would not be allowed to testify, Ortman demanded a decision on the two-week vacation and an adjournment of the remainder of the trial.

"Another adjournment?" McGillian asked.

"Until after the father has had time to interact with his child on vacation, at a resort where she can have fun—and have enough time free of her mother's hostile attitude toward him," Ortman replied.

Wes rose to his feet. Even though he was only an inch over six feet, Rachel couldn't help but notice the presence he exuded even before he opened his mouth to speak. She heard her teeth grind.

Wes raised his hand, palm out. "Judge, Your Honor, may I say something?"

"Is Dr. Belmore taking the witness stand?" Chuck asked.

Judge McGillian nodded toward the bailiff. "Swear him in."

"I appreciate it, Your Honor." Wes's voice was barely above whisper yet audible. The master of special affects. He gathered the hem of his suit jacket, and sat down in the witness stand. He began, "I only wanted to express to the court how much I love my child and want to be a part of her life in her growing years. As much as I am pained over the communications breakdown between me and my former wife, I am more distressed over my baby's emotional problems." He halted. His voice seemed to break. "Many people ask for my medical advice every day. I enjoy giving it, and there is no man more proud and happy than I am when I find out that it works; that I've made a difference in people's lives; that I help make their days worth living. Yet I am stumped as to what advice I'd have given myself had I been my own patient. I lie awake at night—"

McGillian stopped rearranging the pencils in front of him.

"Move to strike," Chuck called out. "I don't see the point of this testimony."

McGillian put out his hand. "You'll have a chance to cross-examine Dr. Belmore later." He nodded toward Wes. "Go on, Dr. Belmore."

"Thank you, Your Honor. Sometimes I lie awake at night asking myself, 'How can I resolve this impasse? How can I stop my daughter from hurting so?'" He touched the inside corner of his right eye, then the left one, as if to wipe the beginning of tears. Against his dark hair, the silver sideburns glistened in the fluorescent light. A lifetime ago, when she loved him, Rachel used to cut Wes's hair. Every ten days. He had been so meticulous about it. Now she hated the familiarity, the knowing how each hair had to lie in place on his head just so....

Chuck got up and approached Wes.

McGillian's fingers went back to rearranging his pencils.

But Chuck's cross-examination, going over the same issues, the same points, brought no new information. Then he seemed to move on. "A week ago, Monday, you had Ellie for a visit, is that correct?"

Wes nodded. "Yes."

"Objection," Ortman said. "I know where this is leading. We need time to prepare for the fresh round of accusations of which, unfairly, my client and I only became aware yesterday."

"Your Honor, there was reabuse," Chuck said. "We have two experts who have seen the child. The evidence is irrefutable."

"We need time to prepare," Ortman repeated.

McGillian sighed. "The calendar is heavy and the cases becoming more complex. I'm robbing other cases of the time they deserve, which is one definition of justice not done."

"Justice will be served if we get to investigate the father's version of the disastrous results of this visit," Chuck said.

"The mother is engaging again in the theatrics of the unrealistic and the paranoid," Ortman shot back.

"Theatrics? I'll give you theatrics," Chuck yelled.

Out of his briefcase he fished a Santa Claus doll and placed it on the table in front of him. Then he opened the doll's flasher's coat—and an oversize erect penis sprang out, reaching the doll's beard. Rachel gasped. It had been months since she had handed Chuck the doll. She forgot about its existence.

"Your Honor," Chuck announced, his tone victorious, "I'd like to show the court the present Dr. Belmore gave his daughter last Christmas, when she was four years old."

Judge McGillian was not amused, Rachel could tell. He straightened in his seat, storm clouds covering his brow. "What the hell is that?"

A small commotion at Wes's desk and a quick whispering and shoulder shrugging indicated this evidence came as a surprise to Ortman.

"It never ceases to amaze me how far some litigants will go," McGillian muttered. "And what would the presentation show, may I ask?"

"That Dr. Belmore has an interest in introducing Ellie to a man's anatomy, especially in an erected form that a child is not likely to see—"

"Mr. Bernstein, no pontificating please." The fury in McGillian's voice was unmasked.

"I was answering your question, Your Honor. May I proceed?"

"Hold your horses." McGillian turned to Ortman. "What do you have to say about this?"

"I haven't had a chance to confer with my client, but he's denying ever seeing it—"

Chuck cut him off. "Ellie said her father gave it to her. He also demonstrated how the penis can remain erect by locking it with the small lever at the back."

"My client knows nothing about it."

McGillian shook his head. He rapped his gavel. "I've heard enough. You're disgracing this court, Mr. Bernstein. Please remove that doll, and let's finish the matter in hand."

"Of course it's a disgrace, Your Honor. But one perpetuated by Dr. Belmore. This Santa shows the convoluted mind of a child molester—"

"Objection, Your Honor."

"Sustained. Mr. Bernstein, I'm warning you. Please remove that— thing— from your desk." He hit his gavel.

"Your Honor," Ortman asked, "would you please reiterate the directive to the mother not to interfere with the father's visitation rights? And he needs to make reservations for a vacation—"

"Absolutely not, Your Honor," Chuck called out. "Dr. Belmore shouldn't be allowed to—"

With a raised hand McGillian silenced Chuck. "When is the next visit scheduled?"

"This evening, Your Honor," Ortman said. "Beginning at five. Dr. Belmore will bring Ellie to school tomorrow morning."

"Good. It will give the child time to get used to her father before they take a longer vacation—"

"Your Honor," Chuck cut him off. "The father's right for a vacation has not yet been determined!"

McGillian suppressed a sigh. "Mr. Bernstein, do you have a daughter?"

Chuck nodded. "Yes, but I don't see the relevance—"

"Well, then. You know how it is." McGillian's quiet voice warming up. "A father only has a chance to bond with his daughter before she becomes a teenager. Before her mind is corrupted by TV, hormones, gangsta rap, feminist notions, or thoughts of boys, clothes, and the telephone."

"Your Honor, *my* daughter is not being molested—" Chuck said, but McGillian brought up his hand to silence him.

He leafed through the papers in front of him. "Now may we all agree to reconvene again next week? Final proceedings. Check the calendar with Phil Crawford." He stared hard at Rachel while addressing Chuck. Enunciating each word, he said, "Mr. Bernstein, I don't want to hear that your client has withheld visitation. I will consider it detrimental to the welfare of the child and she could be transferred to foster care until this matter is settled."

It felt as though she were digging a tunnel with a tin spoon. Another postponement. Foster care. The end of her options had been reached.

"I won't allow Wes to have her," Rachel whispered to Chuck. "No way."

"You've heard the judge. As a member of the Bar, I'm required to uphold the rule of law. I can't advise you to disobey a lawful court order."

"Don't talk to me in legalese. What happened to the Impossibility Defense? Can't we argue it with what we have?"

He removed his glasses and rubbed his eyes. "When you give me a video tape that shows Ellie vehemently refusing to go—after you've made sincere efforts for more than seven minutes to convince her otherwise—I'll argue its admissibility."

She swallowed twice. An image of Ellie, her face so close, the pudgy fingers squeezing her own cheeks—and the promise Rachel had made floated in front of her eyes.

Cross my heart and hope to die.

She couldn't do it, but she remained silent. Chuck was no longer on her side. His springing the Santa Claus seemed an act of desperation. Without saying so, he too, had lost faith in the positive outcome of their case.

"Rachel, you have no choice. You want to come back here with clean hands, or he'll have Ellie in foster care."

"That's preposterous. He can't take her and place her with strangers," Rachel said.

"He can and he will. Do you wish to test him? And how would you like to beg Child Protective Services for visits? You'll be lucky if they give you an hour once or twice a week." He swiveled on his heel to leave.

"Wait. Where are you going?"

"To check on the status of our motion in criminal court." Chuck stopped and set his boxy briefcase on the floor. He put both his palms on Rachel's shoulders. His face was craggy, tired. "Those dropped pornography charges, remember? Whether our Family Court case will disintegrate once more or not, in this criminal case we're shooting with all our cannons."

Rachel nodded miserably. "Whenever I'm confronted with a legal procedural maze, my I.Q. instantly drops forty points."

He turned and left. She stood alone in the lobby. Foster care? It was sheer insanity. How was it possible for any decent person to wrench a child out of her home and place her with strangers? McGillian would come through next week. He must. How could he not see it all? Yet what if—as implausible as it sounded—he decided that Ellie should live with Wes?

From down the corridor, her parents walked toward her. Of the options they had pondered the night before, they hadn't fathomed the threat of foster care as an interim legal solution. They hadn't considered another adjournment, only a "yes" or "no" ruling.

The Rayners had arrived in a rented car, ready for a "no" ruling.

"Go home," Rachel said. "I'll meet you there."

Without exchanging another word, they hugged her and left.

She remained planted near the stretch of soda and snack machines, hesitating. Next to her, a man with oozing scratches from ear to collarbone stood transfixed in place. It was only mid-morning. She should go to Manhattan and salvage the afternoon because with the adjournment, she'd have to take another day off next week. Vince wouldn't be too sanguine about her missing work again.

She stepped outside and stood still for a long time. The air above the parking lot was scorching. Its undulating waves quivered, hovered a few feet above ground, and melted back into themselves.

Behind her, she heard the swoosh of the door as it swung open and felt a refreshing blast of air-conditioning breeze past her. Her mind, floating somewhere above, sent faint signals that she was blocking the way. Skirting the edges of her consciousness was an awareness that she must command her legs to move, go down the few steps, walk over to her car.

A voice cut through the fog. "You dropped this."

Rachel turned.

Phil Crawford handed her a yellow folded page.

"Oh, no, it's not mine," she murmured.

His hand remained hanging in the air, urging her. "Please take it." His eyes bored down into hers. He was a head taller than she. On whose side was he?

"What's your job here?" she asked, and accepted the note with trembling fingers.

"Let's just say I lobby for the best interests of children."

"You heard then. It's a circus, not justice."

"Yes. I'm so sorry."

"Sorry is not enough...," she murmured.

"Just do it."

"Do what?"

His eyes shifted to the note in her hand, and with a slight nod of his brows he indicated to her to read.

She opened the piece of paper, but he turned around, flung open the glass-and-aluminum door, and disappeared inside.

She was not up to any puzzles. Without reading the note, she tucked it in her handbag and finally managed to ease down the entrance stairs.

CHAPTER TWELVE

RACHEL opened the door into her home's small foyer and stopped. Her feet felt laden, as if keeping her from making the next and final move. But her mind propelled her body forward to complete the inevitable.

Her parents' subdued voices drifted from the living room. Ellie's suitcases were lined up near the dining table, a reminder that nothing should impede her decision.

The Impossibility Defense. The terror Ellie would have to experience, believing her mother had betrayed her one more time. And what if, to avoid the hassle at Rachel's house, Wes showed up earlier today, at the daycare center, with a policeman?

Rachel stopped at the doorway. Her tongue felt thick. "You'd better leave," she said, hearing her voice tremble. "Today—now."

Her mother got up and held her tight. Her father strode across the room and wrapped his arms around the two of them.

"You won't hear from us anymore," Russ Rayner said.

"You must call next Thursday after the trial to get the results. What if Judge McGillian relents?"

"Your phone might be tapped already. Wes will do anything, you know that," Lorena said. "Don't worry, we'll find out. Just make sure Wes doesn't realize until then that Ellie's actually gone for good."

Rachel stepped back from her parents' embrace. "I'll go get her."

"Mommy, I don't want to go home," Ellie whined when she saw her mother enter the classroom. "We're going to bake cookies for our snack after rest time."

"We have to go now, sweetie." Rachel took the child's hand, feeling its warm pudginess with heightened awareness, and waved a casual good-bye to the teacher's aide.

With small, reluctant movements, Ellie climbed into the car. "I want to bake cookies," she repeated, her tone petulant.

Rachel snapped Ellie's seat belt and turned on the air conditioner. She drove one block and stopped. She took Ellie's hands in both of hers. "Ellie, sweetie, pay attention. Grandma and Grandpa are going to take you on a long, long trip. A wonderful trip to all kinds of interesting places."

"I want to bake cookies first."

"We have to hurry."

"I want to bake cookies. Why can't we bake cookies?"

A small gesture to make her daughter happy one last time. Before her world crashed to a million fragments—to questions for which there would be no answers.

"Okay. We'll bake some at home and you can take them with you," Rachel said.

Instantly, Ellie's face glowed as though illuminated from within.

"I want to talk to you about the trip—" Rachel continued.

"You're coming too, Mommy?"

"No, I'm not. That's the important thing. Remember you said you didn't want Daddy to play the Zoo Game with you? Do you want to see him?"

"No."

"Well, remember I told you about the judge? He's trying to make me let Daddy have you again. If you go with Grandma and Grandpa, Daddy won't be able to find you. Would you like that?"

Ellie nodded vigorously, keeping her eyes lowered.

"But, Ellie, you may not see me for a long time."

"Why?" Ellie's lips again pressed downward, into a crescent shape. "I want you to come, too."

"I have to stay here to talk to the judge. You'll go with Grandma and Grandpa and live with them in a lot of fun places without me. But the one thing I don't want you to ever, ever forget is that I love you very, very much."

For the next hour they busied themselves making cookies. Ellie stood on her Barney stool, squealing with delight as she poured a bagful of chocolate chips into the mix. Focusing all her attention on the task, she shaped the dough into round balls, put them on the greased cookie sheet, and gleefully flattened them with the palm of her hand.

While they waited for the cookies to bake, Ellie licked the bowl and her fingers with a satisfied purr. Rachel glanced at her parents outside. Her father, having loaded the suitcases in the trunk of the rental car, was seated on the patio lounge chair, reading the paper. Her mother, on her knees near the flowerbed, was separating the iris bulbs and replanting them at even intervals. A pastel watercolor of three adults pretending the world was serene and harmonious for the sake of a child. In a few moments, the colors of the painting would blur and run together, never to be recognizable again.

The cookies were still warm when Rachel placed them in a plastic bag and tucked them in Ellie's pink knapsack.

"I'm ready," Ellie announced in her most cheerful voice. She called over to her grandparents, who stood watching. "Let's go on our trip. Bye, Mommy."

"Bye, sweetheart," Rachel said, deliberately keeping her voice pleasant, unhurried. Her hug was warm and tight, holding back her urgency and despair, as though her parents and daughter were off to the playground around the corner. But Rachel's skin memorized the softness of her child's dry cheek, and her neck remembered the contours of the warm arms, as enduring as the imprint of a fossil on an ancient rock.

"Remember to look at the red sunset. Remember the words you should think of."

"I love you, too, Mommy." Ellie's chirping voice was like a bird's as she ran to the door. "Come on, Grandma, Grandpa. Don't make me wait."

Their heads down, they followed their granddaughter outside.

"I love you, Mom, Dad," Rachel tried to call after them, but her lips moved sound-lessly.

The silence in the house had an eerie quality. This wasn't happening. Yet it had.

"No more Zoo Game," Rachel called out to the empty living room. She returned to the kitchen to clean the flour left on the counter and wash the cookie trays. That chore finished, she poured herself a glass of mineral water, then sat down at the table.

Unshed, despondent tears gathered around her heart, and slowly, in a state of stupefaction, turned to rock.

No more Zoo Game.

She willed herself to stop. No dwelling on the tragedy. No feeling sorry for herself or for Ellie. Her child would be safe, and that was all that mattered.

At five o'clock, Wes would show up. When she didn't answer the door, pretend-ing she wasn't home, he'd telephone, screaming profanities. She wouldn't respond. If she lied to him, it would be held against her in court.

After she dialed her office for messages and returned a few phone calls, Rachel turned off the ringer. Let the answering machine handle Wes.

No more Zoo Game.

Her shoulders hunched over, her legs shuffling, Rachel climbed up the steps and stopped at the top landing, hesitating. She made a left turn and entered Ellie's room.

It was still in disarray from the morning rush. Freda had been given the day off, presumably because the Rayners were in town. Rachel would call her later and say she wouldn't need her for a couple of weeks—an unexpected paid vacation—until she was sure Ellie wasn't returning home.

Not returning home. For how long?

She stood next to Ellie's bed, looking down at it. She picked up the pillow and buried her face in it. It was permeated with her baby's body fragrance. She wouldn't change the bed. Instead, she straightened up the cover and lay on top of it. Still clutch-ing the pillow, she sobbed until she felt empty of tears.

She heard Wes's violent banging on the door but willed it to go away, and it finally did.

For an hour, she tried to fall asleep, to escape. It was no use.

Giving up, she arose, went downstairs, yanked the vacuum cleaner from the pan-try, and furiously worked on the living room and dining area. She changed the attach-ment and raked the moldings. She dug behind the curtain rods. She then hit the stairs and the three small bedrooms.

But when the house was clean, the loneliness still enveloped her and moved around with her. This was the time she would normally return from work, would be busy with her evening chores. How often had she wished for a little time to herself? Now she had the time, but she felt too hollowed out to use it.

No more Zoo Game.

She went to the refrigerator. What did she want? She forgot. Perhaps just the wan light seeping through the shelves, or perhaps the cold air to cool off her pulsating skin. She found herself holding up an eggplant and staring at it. An eggplant? She put it back in the refrigerator.

Nine o'clock. She turned on the TV for the news, and flicked through the channels. On CNN the broadcaster was reporting on yet another artillery attack on a kibbutz in Israel. Jacqueline, who had stayed in Israel for several months had once said that the news had nothing to do with how much fun the place was. Rachel pushed the channel button and scrolled through a couple of sitcoms.

Suddenly, a jolt of awareness raced through her.

On Channel Twelve, the local Long Island channel, an interview was just ending. In a frame at the top right corner, Judge McGillian's smiling face was crowned by his distinct silver hair. The mean bastard. The taste of bile rose in her mouth. An Asian girl was seated, another young woman at her side, facing the interviewer.

Rachel attempted to recall the last words, but the anchor cut to a commercial break. She'd missed the whole thing.

If this were any other night, this was the kind of evening she would have spent with Gerald. Dinner would have been followed by slow, deliberate lovemaking in the glow of candlelight. He'd be devouring her body with hungry lips and fingers. Thoughtful, ardent, and sunny Gerald. How she needed to feel his arms around her, his vibrancy to fill her soul.

How could she have been so wrong about him? How could she have—again—made such a wrong judgment of a man?

She reconnected the phone and almost dialed his number, but instead, she called Jacqueline. There was so little she could share with her—Chuck had warned her not to compromise her friend. In the event Jacqueline was subpoenaed, she wouldn't be compelled to lie under oath.

When Jacqueline picked up, Rachel broke in with no preliminaries, "Don't ask me any questions. You don't want to know. But I need a friend."

Jacqueline let out a slow whistle. "It's my girls' night out. Care to join us for a tour of the bars? There's this new place—"

"No, no. Thanks, I'm not in the mood."

"You're back in circulation, aren't you? Gerald is passé?"

"Gone with the wind. Disappeared in the sky like a helium balloon. Swallowed by a whale at sea." Rachel paused and whispered, "I just don't get it. He's not the kind of guy to dump me with no explanation. For no reason."

"Men."

"He was different."

"They all are. For six months."

"This one lasted eight months, one week, and four days."

"That's because he *was* nice. Hung around a teeny-weeny bit longer."

They talked a few more minutes, then Rachel hung up. She would forgive Gerald if he called and gave her any weak, implausible excuse. She would say she had been busy anyway—her parents were in town and the trial…. Later, after they made love, she would cuddle against his chest. He would make her feel safe, protected, and appreciated. Loved. She had so believed he had fallen in love with her. She had reciprocated.

Rachel lumbered over to the bar, opened it, and poured herself a snifter of brandy.

The liquid burned her insides and with it, melted layers of other hurts, melted her loneliness.

No more fucking Zoo Game.

PART II

"NO MORE ZOO GAME"

CHAPTER THIRTEEN

THREE days later, on Friday, Jacqueline handed Rachel tickets for a Sunday tennis match in Flushing Meadows. "They're from the promo director. Vince can't attend and he specifically wanted you to take out clients."

"I'm sure Agassi and Sampras will miss him," Rachel said. "But whom can I invite this late?"

A dozen phone calls later she reached two ad executives, and the women, who had to work all weekend, accepted the invitation with delight. Since Manhattan, with its oppressive heat and humid, dusty air, was no one's place of choice for a summer weekend, they welcomed the chance to break away.

"Bernstein's on the line," Jacqueline cut in over the intercom.

Here it came. The countdown to the unknown. Rachel promptly ended her conversation with the ad executives. "Jacqueline, have a limousine pick up our guests Sunday evening." She pressed the flashing button. "Chuck?"

"Ortman is carrying on about the missed visit; he's demanding Ellie tonight for the weekend," Chuck said. "Did you get another video for the Impossibility Defense?"

"Chuck, there won't be another video tape. Nor will Ellie be available for a visit, a two-week vacation—or foster care. Never. No more Zoo Game."

He was silent for a moment. "Are you saying what I think you're saying? Don't bother to explain over the phone. Tell you what: Can you be at my office within the next half hour? I have an arbitration downtown starting at ten-thirty."

She glanced at her watch. She could make it and still be at her first client meeting fifteen minutes late.

"I'm on my way." Her breath caught in her throat.

As she rushed out, her raincoat and handbag flying behind her, the briefcase batting against her leg, she saw from the corner of her eye Tom's figure rounding Jacqueline's desk. He bent over her stack of Baroness presentation boards. A fleeting thought reminded her how diligent Tom had turned out to be; she had underestimated him. True, he'd had a hard time grasping the concepts, but he had listened attentively when she explained the presentation and had returned yesterday with a written list of questions that he crossed off his writing pad one by one as she answered them.

She jabbed the elevator call button. Once, twice.

"Where are you off to?" Vince, ambling in the corridor, called over to her. Why was he so concerned about her whereabouts while his male sales reps slacked off? If the sun were out today, they would be on the tennis court or golf course with clients.

"I have meetings most of the day. I'll be in and out. Oh, the American Fragrances Ball is Tuesday night. Got your tux ready?"

He gave her the thumbs up just as the elevator door opened. Rachel waved back and hurried into the mirrored enclosure. Leaning her head against the cold back wall, she took a deep breath. Her hands shook, her heart beat in her ears, and her temples pounded. A migraine headache was a luxury she couldn't afford. From her makeup bag she fished two Tylenol tablets, collected some saliva in her mouth, and attempted to swallow them. One got stuck on the roof of her mouth. A biting, acrid taste spread down to her stomach. She gagged.

Out of the elevator, she dashed to the kiosk in the lobby and picked up a bottle of Evian. When she opened her handbag to pay, she noticed the yellow legal paper crumpled in the corner. It took her a moment to remember what it was. The young man from the courthouse. Phil Crawford. She took out the piece of paper to read in the taxi while she scuttled outside to catch a cab.

A strong wind met her the moment she stepped from the swivel door. It rushed down the seventy-block length of Park Avenue and whipped at her, splattering moist beads of rain against her face like shrapnel.

She steadied her breathing. The running motor inside her, a cartoon-like depiction of the way her energy swirled throughout her body, buzzed in her ear, feeding into her mounting anxiety about her meeting with Chuck. She should take it easy or she'd make herself sick.

She hailed one passing taxi after another, and five minutes later, she settled in one. Only then did she look at the crumpled note in her hand. She opened it.

"Take her and run," the note read. "Save her for the rest of her life."

Who was this man? If he worked for Wes, he would not be making such an outrageous suggestion. Did he have anything to do with the Georgia children's underground railroad? Rachel thought of him, tall in his blue suit, his eyes intense over chiseled cheeks. Who was he? A "lobbyist for children," he had said. Whatever that meant.

Well, she had done it anyway, had sent Ellie away. To hell with the rest of them. Yet it felt good to hear this man's urging. He understood and cared.

"How long do you intend to keep Ellie from her father?"

"Forever."

Chuck's inky eyes, like polished river stones, scowled at her from behind his glasses.

Rachel had never seen him so furious. He had been frustrated at other lawyers, indignant at judges, disgusted with court clerks. But not at her. For a split second her resolve wavered. Yet even if she wished to reverse the course of events, Ellie's disappearance had taken on a life of its own; her whereabouts—and her grandparents'—were unknown. Rachel clenched and unclenched her hands. Perhaps her parents were right to keep her uninformed as long as the pressure was intensifying. Someone must be in touch with them to let them know the outcome of next week's trial, but Rachel couldn't imagine who that person might be.

"Now be reasonable. You can't *hide* her," Chuck said, his voice on edge.

"Why not?"

"For one thing, if you're to pursue this line of action, Wes will get custody, and you'll have a much harder time reversing *that* court decision—"

"McGillian is about to give him custody anyway. You've said so yourself," she shot back. "Now even if Wes gets custody, at least he can't obtain physical possession of Ellie."

"Rare are the cases when a child escapes discovery."

"This child will."

"You're taking an enormous risk. I advise you against it."

"Do you honestly expect me to allow my five-year-old daughter to be raped two, three times a week for the next few weeks? Or see her thrown into overcrowded foster care for months as the case drags on in criminal court—so that social services can hand her over to Wes whenever *they see fit?*"

"Rachel, I'm with you. I agree that the law is not necessarily justice and a trial is not a scientific inquiry into truth—only a resolution of a dispute. But that's all we have; there's no other recourse."

"Yes, there is. I have to do for Ellie whatever the system has failed to do for her. It's no consolation for her every time her father sticks his—"

"Don't take the law into your hands."

"Too late, Chuck. I have. From now on, like any normal five-year-old, all Ellie would have to worry about at bedtime is dragons under the bed."

Chuck leaned forward on his desk. His bushy eyebrows knotted into one straight line. "Rachel, I want to be crystal clear on this. A. I don't want to know where she is or with whom. Attorney-client privilege may not apply here, nor do I wish to be considered an accomplice to a crime. Do you understand?"

She nodded.

"B." There was a pregnant pause. "If you decide to continue in this obstinate, illegal course of action, I won't be able to represent you."

The words dropped on her like a shower of pebbles falling on a car hood. She hadn't anticipated Chuck would desert her.

"Chuck, you can't do that."

"Sorry. I truly am. Parental kidnapping is a felony. In addition to criminal charges you could be held in civil contempt." He continued. "Judges throw mothers in jail. But unlike a criminal sentence, a civil one can last indefinitely—or until the mother complies."

For a few moments, Rachel did not speak. A lifetime in jail—or a lifetime on the run. As of next Thursday—if Ortman didn't ask for another adjournment—these might be her only choices. Currents of fear brushed against her determination.

No more Zoo Game.

Tears gathered at the back of her throat. "Surely, you don't suggest I hand Ellie to Wes until the squeaking wheels of justice turn in our favor, do you? Until Ellie's safety is guaranteed, there's no going back." She reached in her handbag for a tissue, but Chuck beat her to it. He pushed a small box toward her.

"Well?" he said.

"I don't have a choice; Ellie's safety is non negotiable. I won't have her touched again. But you must help me fight this."

"Even if I were willing to stick by you on this, I doubt my partners would allow our firm to get entangled in protecting a client who knowingly commits an illegal act."

"You should think of protecting Ellie's ass rather than yours," she said.

He shook his head. "Do you have any idea what the ramifications are to you? Besides jail time, if convicted, you'll never be able to vote—"

"That's the least of my concerns."

"You yourself are not even in hiding." He crossed his arms and leaned back. "You're sitting on a powder keg."

"I have to continue the court appearances for the appeals, right? Chuck, that's why I need you."

He was silent. The rain tapped on the windows. A bleak weekend would match her mood. "This is the wettest July in years," she said abruptly, then felt embarrassed at the inanity of the statement. A police siren bleated in the street, then receded as it rounded the corner. The wall clock marked the passing seconds in loud ticks. Then it chimed the hour.

"I have to go." Chuck jumped to his feet. "Let's see what they do. Start shopping for another attorney, and I'll make some calls this weekend. With the criminal charges we've filed with the D.A., the defense may insist on expert testimony—as invalid as we claim it would be to interrogate Ellie so long after that incident. In that case you'll have to produce her after all. One thing you cannot do: you can't just drop the suit or Wes will slap you with malicious prosecution charges."

"What's that?"

"Just what it says. If you sue someone and then drop the charges, the suing can be held against you as a form of abuse of process." Chuck stepped to the door. "Even if we win in Family Court next week, Wes won't give up."

"For his Zoo Game."

"Ellie also represents his loss of Stephanie. He's determined to prove that the New Jersey judge was wrong. With these criminal charges we're cornering him further."

"We did it because we were sure we'd win. That's what you told me," Rachel said. If she held Chuck to his word, things would turn their way. "'Beyond a reasonable doubt,' you said."

He jiggled some change in his pocket. "Let's not dwell on that now. First things first." Then he paused. "By the way, now we won't be able to use your babysitter Freda's testimony about your mother-daughter relationship with Ellie. I needed her to confirm that you give Ellie a stable home."

"Why can't you have Freda tell it anyway?"

"What is she doing between now and Thursday?"

"She's on a paid leave."

"So if Wes thinks Ellie's only unavailable for visits, but doesn't know she has literally disappeared, Ortman will find out from Freda when he cross-examines her, right?"

Rachel bit her lip and got up to leave. Had she made things worse than they already were?

She tucked her umbrella under her arm. Without Chuck, who would help her fight all this? The enormity of her legal battles was reaching new peaks each passing month, each passing week, day, hour.

At the door, he took her hands in his. She leaned forward and her lips flitted over his cheek. "Thank you," she whispered. "For everything."

"Off the record?" he said.

She nodded.

"Off the record—I understand."

CHAPTER FOURTEEN

"YOU owe me a report on the tennis tournament last night," Jacqueline said Monday morning, while Rachel hung up her jacket. "How did the clients like it?"

"Fabulous. The Weather God was kind."

"I called Him on His eight-hundred number." Jacqueline laughed.

"It turned out to be more glamorous than I had anticipated. You should have seen the Sheridan Magazines hospitality tent."

From outside the air-conditioned white tent, which was surrounded by a symbolic fence of potted palms and a patch of the greenest turf, people had craned their necks to catch through the French doors a glimpse of the celebrities inside. It brought back to Rachel the almost-forgotten feeling that life could be a party, and that she was not only invited, but was the one giving it. Lately, she had been convinced that she was the only one left out.

"The Sheridan family is known for the prices they pay at auctions to stock their wine cellars," Jacqueline said. "But they must have served their homegrown California brands."

Rachel nodded. "The tables were set with fine china and silver; we were served by uniformed waiters—the works. So incongruous with the crowds in jeans and shorts."

"Will any business come out of this?"

"We talked about everything *but* business. It was easy to forget this was supposed to be work." Rachel smiled. She and the two women executives had enjoyed their food and drink and gossiped about the advertising industry. They exchanged notes about their periods and analyzed their relationships with their mothers. Her mother. What would she have done without her parents' help? Rachel continued. "I sometimes underestimate this aspect of the business—to just relax and let things happen, allow them to flow in their own course and hope they'll stumble my way."

"Maybe men here know something we don't, after all." Jacqueline waved a letter opener and slashed the top envelope in the morning mail.

Rachel lifted her curls and gathered them into a loose knot at the nape of her neck. *No more Zoo Game.* The words flashed through her mind like strobe lights. She scanned her to-do list, determined to focus on her work and erase all thoughts of the sense of loss that wrestled for dominance in her mind. Forever—until Ellie's return— she would fight to hold down her web of emotions under the thick layer of details that filled up her days.

Jacqueline continued to sort out the mail. Rachel got up. "I'll get us coffee."

Upon her return, she set the two mugs on the corner of her desk, then settled down again. She opened her calendar. The black-tie affair tomorrow night would be a whirlwind of glitz and splendor to accompany the sumptuous launch of movie star Bridget Morrow's Purple Eyes perfume.

Rachel had purchased a table for ten at the Waldorf Astoria ballroom and had invited several highly visible clients and ad agency executives. *Women's Life* publisher and Vince Carducci, the advertising director, would join her as hosts.

Jacqueline pulled out a card from the stack of mail and waved it. "The guest list's confirmed. Vince will be tickled that no one at your table is your average second in command."

"Since the Chicago trip is on Wednesday, I'll drive in so I can pick up the artist's portfolio with Baroness presentation," Rachel said.

"Good. I wouldn't want you taking the train back late at night wearing your long gown and jewelry." Jacqueline searched her notepad and said in a flat, non-judgmental tone, "We've found a replacement for Gerald on the list."

Rachel said nothing. Was Gerald, at that very moment, staring at his calendar, wondering whether to call to apologize for not being able to attend? The Gerald she used to know would have.

His abrupt, callous desertion stung her anew.

She lifted her eyes from her notes and looked at Jacqueline. "Anything new around here that I need to know?"

"The usual. A bit of this and that and everything."

"Sounds like one of your New Age songs." Rachel smiled. "Any new office romance?"

"You're kidding? No available men here."

"Tom Fields, the new trainee, is cute."

Jacqueline smiled. "He's got the hots for one of Sheridan's daughters—"

"They're all in California. How would he meet a Sheridan?"

"You haven't heard? Bev Sheridan is the new beauty editor."

"You mean *assistant to the assistant editor*," Rachel said over the rim of her coffee mug.

"Editor."

"It's not possible. What happened to Liliana Morgan?" Rachel asked.

Jacqueline sent her a mischievous look. "Actually, they gave Bev Sheridan the title of beauty editorial *director*, so she's now *above* Morgan."

Rachel almost sprayed the coffee she was about to swallow. "I don't believe it. Liliana is the most respected editor in the industry. She won't hang around to see her authority and title usurped by a newcomer regardless of whose daughter she is. What's Bev's background?"

"She's shopped at the best places all her life, has been to every health spa on both hemispheres of our globe." Jacqueline's voice dripped sarcasm. "Unlimited expense account. Isn't that enough of a background for a twenty-four-year-old?"

"This is unreal. Liliana has been courted for years by other women's magazines. One word from her about a product carries more weight with readers than a quarter-million-dollar ad." Rachel stopped and stared at Jacqueline. "How could they risk *Women's Life*'s reputation—and their best source of revenues—for a spoiled brat?"

"When your grandpa and dad own the top ten fashion, shelter, and service women's magazines in the U.S.A. not to mention other leading publications in Europe and the Far East, you have it made."

"Now I'll have to sugarcoat this new development for my Chicago meeting." Rachel felt her teeth grind. Other magazines' reps must have been quick to burn up the phone lines and let Baroness's ad agency know the latest dirt. "For all we know, another magazine is grabbing Liliana with offers of her own chauffeur-driven limousine. Too bad her limousine can't drive right onto her own car elevator like Helen Gurley Brown's so the soles of her shoes will never touch the street pavement."

Jacqueline said nothing.

Rachel continued. "This place is so disorganized; you'd think the least Vince could have done was keep me informed—he has nothing else to do. Why doesn't the publisher fire him for his laziness?"

Jacqueline fidgeted in her seat. A strange feeling crept into Rachel's mind. Why did she have to milk the story out of her friend in the first place?

There was nothing to do but ignore it. "I'll have to field questions about *Women's Life*'s editorial direction if Liliana's no longer dispensing beauty advice to its thirty million readers." Rachel paused. "Jacques, please call the corporate publicity department, get a copy of the press release about this and the Sheridan girl's photograph, and give it to the promotion department."

Jacqueline left, and Rachel gazed out the window. Miniature people seemed to glide on individual tracks thirty floors below. If Jacqueline hadn't told her what was going on, she would have lost face and maybe the account—the budget of the year in the entire industry.

She buzzed the intercom to the promotion director's line to set up a meeting that afternoon to prepare new material.

"Oh, we already took care of it on Friday," the woman said.

Rachel's unease resurged with renewed force. "Really? What did you do?"

"I got a new board ready. I've made duplicates. I'm sending one over with a script. You can talk it out."

Rachel plopped herself into her chair and swiveled it around toward the window. Why hadn't the promo director mentioned anything? Friday, instead of handing Jacqueline the tickets for the tennis game, she could have talked directly to Rachel—unless she purposely avoided her. When, then, did she plan to consult with Rachel about changes inserted into *her* presentation?

CHAPTER FIFTEEN

JUDGE McGillian stepped into his office and settled behind his desk. Sylvia had brought in a ham sandwich at lunchtime. Now its wilted lettuce leaf hanging out and the waterlogged bread made it appear as unappetizing as the floor lamp. McGillian gazed at the stack of files on his desk and shoved it aside. The embroidery of human life. Like his fly-fishing ties, the outside was organized, the stitches close together. The inside was chaotic, knotted, with lines zigzagging and crossing over.

"Judge, you'd better take this call." Sylvia's high-pitched voice broke through the intercom. "The Mayes' lawyer. All hell's breaking loose. Kim Lee got an abortion."

"What? Damn." He snatched the phone, listened to the report, and promptly hung up. "The one thing I hate most is people taking the law into their own hands," he muttered. "It's the surest way to social anarchy."

At that moment, Phil entered the anteroom. He carried a folded newspaper and crossed the distance between them in nimble steps. "Sir, have you seen *Newsday* today? Page seven." He laid the paper on McGillian's desk.

McGillian perused the small blurb mentioning his decision in the Mayes v. Lee case. He got up and paced the room. "Too late," he said, hearing his voice thundering. "Lee got the abortion anyway. She should be held in contempt of court. Jail time. She knew the score. Get her back here."

"Jail?"

"As soon as she recuperates. How long does it take?" McGillian stopped by the window, gazed out, unseeing, then turned back to face the room.

"Your Honor, perhaps you should take a look at this." Phil handed him two lined, legal-sized sheets covered with signatures.

"What's that?"

"A women's group petitioning you to change your ruling in the Kim Lee case."

Without glancing at the papers, McGillian tossed them on the side table. "Sylvia takes care of those things."

"I thought you'd want to know before you take any further action—"

"I don't need to know every time a group of feminists gets electrified by runaway hormones."

"Sir, I don't think that's the reason they're writing."

McGillian took a deep breath. An image of the Lee girl's dark, elongated eyes and slight figure leaped across the back of his eyes. He paced around the room, his hands locked behind his back. His fingers twitched.

"Phil, you win. I'll have to let this one slide. A fine would do." Politically, overreacting was the wrong move. He shook his head slowly and pointed at the folded newspaper. "It wasn't my intention to turn my courtroom into a political forum. My mistake for allowing the journalists in."

"Coming on the heels of the Torruellas case, sir," Phil said, "The Mayes v. Lee case is drawing heat."

McGillian waved his hand with a sign of dismissal. "It'll all die down in a few days as soon as the media get a new subject. Anyway, right and wrong are not subject to popular whims. The threat of publicity would not have affected my ruling in either case."

"I'm not sure we can just forget about it." Phil pointed to a large, white plastic box placed outside the door, the emblem of the U.S. Postal Service printed on its side. "These are all protest letters."

"All from women, I'm sure. You see my point? How would it change things if I read these letters? The baby won't come back to life, will it?" McGillian dropped the palm of his hand on the table. "Idealism is youth's miscellaneous by-product. You young, sophomoric bucks rubbing your antlers against tree bark believe you can change the world."

"It feels good, sir," Phil said, smiling. "Maybe that's why I don't want to outgrow this 'malady,' as you've called it."

McGillian let his body drop into his chair. "When I graduated from law school thirty-five years ago, adoptions were hushed up and no one came forward asking to open his parents' files and cause havoc in other families' lives. Mothers stayed home and, in the rare cases of divorce, men didn't come running to court demanding custody. Gay couples didn't adopt—in fact, no one ever heard of homosexuality—and lesbians did not give birth to a child only to break up and have the mother's lover demand visitation. Parents didn't come to court asking to evict a drug-addicted son turned abusive and violent. There were no surrogate mothers, and no one complained of marital rape. Perhaps the church had a stronger hold on people's lives and hearts, and ministers kept their flocks closer to God."

"And eleven-year-olds weren't allowed to testify about sexual abuse—"

"Are we back to that again?"

"I haven't written your decision yet, sir. You can still change your mind."

"Out of the question. Phil, do you have any idea what eleven-year-olds are like?"

"In what way?"

"Would you trust the words of a pubescent child who hates her father? I have a daughter. Preadolescent girls are the worst. Stubborn, opinionated, critical, ready to accuse their parents of all sorts of imagined things—and that's when they all live together in supposedly functional families." Unfortunately, at age thirty, his daughter hadn't transformed back to the adoring tyke she had once been. With her jumping at his throat over her feminist notions, he was lucky if she granted him the wisdom to tie his shoes.

"Assume for a moment that Stephanie Belmore is bright and knows what she's talking about—" Phil cut in, but McGillian interrupted him in return.

"I'm asked to destroy a man's lifetime achievements based on the words of a minor with a memory dating back to when she was six years old. The only document submitted shows the New Jersey judge wasn't convinced there was abuse." McGillian put his hand up. "Drop it, Phil. This case is taking much too long; we must move it along and wrap it up. Close it. Finito."

He noticed the sudden set of Phil's jaws. "Phil, there's no better way to learn the vicissitudes of the legal system than to immerse the mind in a complex case. The mind, not the heart. One must remain impartial, which you, in the case of Belmore v. Belmore, clearly are not."

"Sir, a five-year-old is suffering—"

"Close the case, I said."

As McGillian stood at his door, ready to leave, a man entered the anteroom. Odd-looking enough to hold McGillian's attention a moment, the man's face was puckered, ending with full, red lips, like twin cherries. He seemed to be teetering on tiny feet.

"Judge, may I speak with you?"

Sylvia rushed over and inserted herself between the men. "Who are you?"

He flashed her a laminated card. "The *City Post*. David Lupori."

McGillian pressed a concealed buzz button, and a court officer expeditiously emerged from behind the courtroom door. She put her hand on the belt where a gun, a pair of handcuffs, a can of mace, a whistle, speed-loaders, a persuader, and a dozen keys hugged her hips.

"If you're a journalist, you know a judge won't talk to you," she said.

"It's not about the Torruellas kid. The injunction in Kim Lee's case—"

"Sir, please leave." She moved toward him.

He stepped aside and his eyes glanced over Sylvia's desk. "May I talk to you then? I understand that a letter campaign has started over the weekend—"

"Leave. Now," the court officer ordered.

The reporter turned, unhurried, seemingly obeying her command yet stealing time. His eyes darted about for any last-minute clue he could use. He smacked his lips and waddled out.

"God almighty, the chutzpah," Sylvia muttered. "So many journalists are calling. You'd think this was the Pentagon."

McGillian practiced his swing. The heat was oppressive, and he wiped away the perspiration streaming down his cheeks from under his cap. He was going to take it easy. All he needed was to aim right, let the steady swing of the club do the work.

He waited until two of his golf partners settled back in their cart, waiting to drive out in search of their balls, and Albrecht, the town supervisor, suppressed his coughing. McGillian readjusted his grip on the club, and hit the ball. On the upswing, he continued the movement in one elegant, effortless sweep.

A few feet behind him, Colby Albrecht polished his golf balls with a damp cloth. "I have a question for you." There was a satisfied chuckle in his voice. "How d'you know when you're getting old?"

"How?"

"You lose the hair on your head and get it in your nose."

"You must be sniffing Rogaine." McGillian laughed.

He relaxed. Albrecht wouldn't mention the Kim Lee case. Usually, from Albrecht's little chuckles and crackles, McGillian deciphered his political cronies' support of the tough stance he took on controversial issues.

He was wrong this time.

"Bob, try to tone things down," Albrecht said, and McGillian was startled by the turn of the conversation. "Too much negative publicity at election time will do you no good. You know we're trying for a larger constituent base."

"Colby, say no more." McGillian felt irritation advancing up his back muscles. He climbed into their golf cart. Albrecht scrambled to join him. Their golf partners followed in their own cart.

It was a long distance on a par five hole. "Remember how Governor Dunkle's son got banged up in a motorcycle accident last year?" Albrecht asked, his tone casual.

"What about it?"

"Ahem, I know it's out of the ordinary to ask—but there's this case of the—"

McGillian raised his hand to stop him. "Please don't tell me. I don't want to know the name of the case."

"I thought so. But Nicholas Dunkle himself spoke to me about his concern for a speedy conclusion—"

McGillian's voice rose. "Please."

They reached the next hole, and McGillian scampered off and walked away to tee off. A fireball of anger formed inside his stomach. Did the Republicans think, after nominating him over twenty years ago, that they owned him for life? A man only had one thing that was entirely his own—his reputation. He should not—could not—compromise it.

He swung, but duffed the ball one hundred feet to the left. It rolled and came to a stop in a sand trap. Damn.

CHAPTER SIXTEEN

UNDER gleaming chandeliers reflecting in the gilded mirrors and columns of the Waldorf-Astoria ballroom, Bridget Morrow glided about with the assuredness of an opulent ocean liner, all flags flying. At her heels, a cameraman and a publicist tossed out orders and smiles.

"She looks like a lobster that's been tossed into a pot of boiling water," Vince said as he eyed Bridget Morrow, the aging movie star whose padded high cleavage and flushed face retained no traces of the internationally famed beauty she had once been.

"What does a lobster feel like when thrown into a pot of water?" One of the guests at Rachel's table threw the question into the air.

"Hot, that's why it tries to escape the pot," Vince replied, a twinkle in his eye. His fingers gnarled, his mouth contorted in a comical expression, he imitated a lobster. "It claws and scrapes at the sides of the pot—stiffens up, like this," he said. "Yak."

Vince was quite a ham. Rachel tilted her head back, laughing. The curls falling on her exposed back felt luxurious. "If I look a lobster in the eye, I can't eat it. I can't put it to death just so I can have a good meal."

Everyone joined in the laughter. Vince rose from his seat on Rachel's right, picked up the bottle of white wine, and began to circulate the table, refilling the guests' glasses.

"Good party," he whispered to Rachel as he finished the circle and stood over her to pour. With his free hand he squeezed her bare shoulder and resettled in his chair.

The wine found its way from Rachel's lips to her throat, filling her with warmth and some lightness of being. Vince and the publisher would see once again how much her clients liked her. That's what office politics was about. Regaining her supervisors' approval each time, as though she still had to pass a test of sorts. Well, she had done it again tonight.

"I'm going to Chicago in the morning for the Baroness presentation at BRT&G," she told Vince, letting her enthusiasm show.

"Oh, yes, a good presentation."

"You've seen it? Really? When?" Rachel threw a quick glance at the publisher, seated across the table. Had he too, seen it without her?

"Tom Fields presented it to management as part of his graduation project," Vince said. "He did an excellent job. After seventy-five years in business, it's rare for anyone to come up with a fresh idea for *Women's Life*."

"Tom Fields?"

"Uh-huh. Impressive. And the promotion department outdid itself."

She was that lobster in a pot of boiling water, trying, with no success, to get out.

"But—I—uh— You know it's my presentation."

"Yours? C'mon Rachel, we're a team here—"

"Vince." Rachel turned to face him. "This was not the work of a committee. You were aware that I wrote the whole damn thing. That I came up with the research ideas, repositioned the magazine, developed an entirely new marketing concept—"

He waved a finger in front of her face in a gesture of mock scolding. "Don't do that." He winked. "That's not a good attitude."

Still seated, she felt herself falling like in an elevator whose cable had snapped. And Tom Fields stealing her ideas and calling them his own was a good team attitude? To think her challenger came out of nowhere, a trainee—

Instantaneously, as though in a pinball machine, a ball bounced from one pivot point to the next, igniting lights and ringing bells. Vince had known about it all along. Hadn't he sent Tom to her, specifically instructing her to take his trainee step by step through the process? *His trainee.*

Of course. That's why the promo director had prepared duplicates of everything— including the last-minute changes in the editorial department. She, too, had known all along that Tom would present the material as his own. But how did usurping her ideas serve them?

Vince's eyes examined her face, a crease knotted across his forehead. She was failing yet another test she hadn't known she was taking—the test of being a good sport when your boss and your colleagues were in cahoots to shit all over you.

"Excuse me." She pushed her chair back and got up, jiggling a leg as though it were numb. Inserting a cheerful tone into her voice, she said, "I should say a few hellos. Be right back."

She could barely contain her anger on the way to the ladies' room.

She pushed through the swinging door and realized, too late, that this was not the place to find solitude. The sumptuous lounge was lined with upholstered settees occupied by famous models, movie stars, beauty editors, and cosmetics and fragrance executives. Facing the huge mirror and a long marble shelf, where fine toiletries and hair accessories were strewn in casual elegance, a group of TV anchor women Rachel recognized was seated on small vanity chairs.

As she stood at the door, dizzy, unsure where to hide, Liliana Morgan, the recently displaced beauty editor, approached her, half a smile flitting over her ruby-red lips. She hooked her eyes silently into Rachel's.

Although they had never been friends—Liliana was higher on the corporate ladder and fifteen years older—Rachel had felt over the years of working on two ends of the same projects that they shared a private wavelength.

Rachel took the older woman's hand. It was supple and reminded her of her mother's. "I've heard," she whispered. Tom's biting a slice off her presentation was minor compared to the Sheridan's daughter grabbing the whole pie. "It's so terrible."

"Not as bad as you think. This may be my chance of a lifetime." Liliana's cultured voice was easy.

All right, then. Liliana was telling her something. She would not stay with *Women's Life* after her loyalty had been betrayed. If only Liliana would not announce her departure to a competing magazine until after Baroness's management decided on *Women's Life* as their advertising vehicle.

But why should she care where Baroness advertised or what was best for the magazine? She had just been dealt a blow. Look what they had done to Liliana.

The two of them edged toward the lavatory section and stopped at the end of the line.

"I hear one of your colleagues is smitten with my new boss," Liliana said.

"You mean Bev Sheridan?"

"That young hunk, Tom," Liliana said. "Word from the fortieth floor is to move him along on oiled tracks."

"I don't get it," Rachel said. "Tom just started his training here, and Bev Sheridan just moved east. When did the two of them meet?"

"Tom Fields happens to be Leonard Fields's nephew," Liliana replied. "He was assigned the honor of taking Bev around to shop for an apartment when she moved her royal tush to New York. He found her one with its own swimming pool. Not a building with a pool, mind you—a *penthouse* with a pool."

"Leonard Fields?" He had been publisher of Sheridan's *Fashion World* until it lost its number one spot to its competitor. When, the following year, it slid down to third place, Fields was kicked *upstairs* to a "corporate position"—an appointment with no job description. "He's been hanging by his teeth at the edge of the cliff. Why take care of his nephew?" Rachel asked.

"'The Old Boy's Club.' Every executive—male executive, that is—is part of it. They're so loyal to each other, it's sickening," Liliana said. "And who cares about the money? Another million or two to take care of their own? The Sheridans trust their operations managers who make them many millions each year. They let them play a bit."

Liliana had never spoken ill of the management circle to which she belonged. She must be taking another job. Very soon.

A sense of powerlessness swept over Rachel again. The harder she worked for Sheridan, the more money she made for the management team, the less it seemed to matter. She had thought of herself as successful, but they refused to credit her endeavors as such, thus taking away the pride of accomplishment. The Baroness account and others she had brought in—even when they represented the only growth for *Women's Life*— were meaningless against the connections of a newcomer. They deceived themselves so Tom would appear more capable than he was.

The line to the lavatories moved at last. Rachel stepped into a stall and closed the door but just stood there, taking deep breaths.

How she wished she could resign; tell Vince to go fly a kite. But too many of her former colleagues were hitting the pavements, grateful for jobs with lower salaries as long as they received health-care benefits.

This year she expected to earn eighty-five thousand dollars before taxes, but her legal bills were mounting with no end in sight. With each passing day, she owed Chuck more money. A new lawyer might ask for a twenty-thousand-dollar up-front retainer.

She must keep her house—double mortgage and all—for when, oh, please God,

Ellie returned. And the car was a business necessity. Dental bills weren't covered by Sheridan's health policy. Whatever was left of her parents' savings would dwindle soon.

She came out of the stall and leaned over the sink, wishing she could go home and crawl into bed, hibernate until it was all over. She dabbed cold water at her eyes, careful not to disturb the fine jade eyeliner that emphasized their color.

A smile plastered on her flushed face, she lifted her head high, tucked her tummy in. She stood in front of the mirror, evaluating her figure. Wrapped in a bottle-green dress, wearing sparkling emerald earrings that hung half way down to her exposed shoulders, she looked spectacular. She should walk out there as though she knew it. She would ask Vince to dance. He loved to unhinge his stiffened joints on the dance floor, a reminder of his days of glory.

If she had to, if it wasn't too late, she'd be a good sport and play their game. She could not afford to get so mad she quit. She could not afford to get fired.

CHAPTER SEVENTEEN

IN spite of the previous night's revelations, when Rachel's plane took off from LaGuardia at seven in the morning, she still hoped *Women's Life* would win the Baroness cosmetics account.

She was met at the reception area of the BRT&G ad agency by *Women's Life*'s Chicago office manager Marshall Hadfield, a man in his late forties. With his fresh haircut and perfectly fitted Armani suit, he looked as though he had stepped out of the pages of *GQ* magazine.

His kiss on Rachel's cheek was more of an acknowledgment of the many years both had worked for the magazine than a reflection of any affection.

"This is going to be tough," he said. "The client-agency team has been watching a four-day marathon schedule of presentations by each of the major magazines, TV networks, radio and newspaper groups, and they are exhausted." He eyed her. "But word is that Baroness top brass has a soft spot for you."

"I got my job at *Women's Life* seven years ago when they recommended me to work on their account," she replied. "Nevertheless, they expect a dog and pony show each time they renew their contract. They hate to be taken for granted."

He handed her a copy of the agency questionnaire. "My secretary completed it a couple of weeks ago. The standard stuff," he said pleasantly. "Rates, publishing dates. For your files."

She glanced at it and something caught her attention. "What's this new Corporate Discount?"

"Oh, it's new—hasn't been published yet. I had Carducci authorize an early release for Baroness. If an advertiser buys x number of pages in so many Sheridan magazines, he qualifies for an additional discount. There are several packages he can choose from."

"Meaning, if we land the account, we bring more ad pages to several other Sheridan magazines?"

"Four to six more. They're presenting too, but the economies of scale are such that we lead the pack."

She nodded in understanding. A deep discount on a page of advertising in *Women's Life* could pay for a full-page ad in a smaller circulation magazine. That free page in the other Sheridan publication might attract new advertisers. Why hadn't Vince impressed upon her the importance of this account? Since when was her client presented with a complicated offer she knew nothing about?

"I wish you had faxed it to me so I could study it," Rachel said, keeping her tone light.

"I figured Vince discussed it with you."

Sure. She heard her teeth gnash.

The two of them walked down the long corridor. Hadfield made a big show of greeting agency executives whose doorways they passed. After several turns, which, if Rachel's sense of direction didn't fail her, took them in circles meant to cover more accidental meetings, she and Hadfield were ushered into a spacious, well-appointed conference room.

They faced the ad agency team, joined by Baroness's president and his New York department heads. They all smiled in acknowledgement, but this was not the time for easy chat. The executives kept a detached tone throughout their question-and-answer period, their locked expressions fighting fatigue and giving away nothing of their impressions.

Rachel lunged into her presentation, the multimedia video followed by her explanation of the statistical charts. She sneaked a glance at her watch. Good; she had paced herself as planned. With a renewed sense of the mission that she was spearheading a huge chunk of advertising for other Sheridan magazines, she tackled the inquiries about Liliana Morgan's and Bev Sheridan's plans for the editorial direction of their beauty and skin care pages. From across the conference table, some heads registered nods of approval. Baroness's president, Rachel's business friend, asked leading questions obviously meant to clarify points the Baroness executives had discussed privately.

After leaving the building, she and Hadfield strolled up North Michigan Avenue. Hot wind rolled down from Lake Michigan and deposited moist air in her hair and on her clothes. Nevertheless, the wide street with its boastful, elegant department store windows was a special treat in any weather.

She slowed down her stride. A long-haired poodle with a pink bow stretched its leash and barked at the little cotton-puff clouds that moseyed above. Rachel stopped. "May I?" she asked the owner. Consent given, she crouched and tickled the pooch's neck. It tucked his wet nose into the crook of her arm, trusting, submitting to the touch of a stranger. The moment gave Rachel the respite from the tension of the morning.

"How do you think it went?" Rachel asked Hadfield when she resumed her stroll.

"First class," he said. "Baroness's president liked you. We ended up with twice as much time as originally allocated."

"When you get the chance, would you please put in a good word for me with Vince?" she asked.

"Sure thing. And if you ever think of transferring to Chicago, let me know." He took her elbow. "Now, how about a celebratory lunch for a job well done?"

She laughed. "Isn't it too soon to celebrate? What if Liliana Morgan leaves before they make a decision?"

He steered her toward the Drake hotel where, under a burgundy-and-gold marquee, a uniformed doorman opened the door for them.

"Sheridan magazines always come out on top," Hadfield said.

Suddenly, she felt small again.

CHAPTER EIGHTEEN

ALONE at his desk, Phil studied the documents in front of him. He had turned off the fluorescent light. Only the green desk lamp threw a yellow glow on the Belmore v. Belmore file. Taking his time, Phil thumbed through the Post-it Notes he had placed at strategic spots, as though a missing clue was waiting to be uncovered. His eyes kept returning to one word. A name. Ellie. A child he had never met but whose mother fought relentlessly for her. Suddenly he realized that the name he had given Ellie's mother, "The Mother Who Protects Her Child," took on a mythical aura, as if life had been breathed into the words. Not all mothers clawed and bit to protect their offspring; he knew it all too well from his own past. But this Belmore mother did.

The next morning, he hoped, at her trial—the final proceedings, according to McGillian—Rachel Belmore might catch the hum of the magnetic field between them. He was frustrated he couldn't do more.

Judge McGillian emerged from his chambers and strode toward the door leading into the courtroom, his steps brisk and assured, a smile gracing his face as though he had just heard a good joke and was still savoring its flavor. As he removed his robe from the hook and put it on, Phil slipped into the courtroom to take his seat.

Today, in the playing field of the Belmore trial, Phil thought, perhaps he would decipher the rules of the game. In the meantime he hoped Ms. Belmore would hear his silent cheering from the sidelines.

"All rise," the bailiff called out.

With the creaking of benches, rustle of clothes and scrambling of feet, everyone rose. Phil passed his hand over at the long list of the Belmore witnesses on the page in front of him. Who was the most valuable player?

Was Ellie, the ball in this game—and the winner's cup?

"Mr. Bernstein, Mr. Ortman," McGillian said in his warm baritone. "I want this wrapped up today. Let's not waste our time on frivolous arguments. Ready?"

Rachel Belmore, elegant yet with her thin shoulders vulnerable, kept her head bowed. Her dusty-pink suit color reflected on her cheeks, heightening their smoothness. Phil wished she'd look up so he could see those deep pools of green. Ellie's mother—who, unlike his own, possessed the strength to battle for her child.

He looked briefly at Dr. Belmore, tall and handsome, his temples gray, more like a dashing soap opera version of a successful physician than a real one.

"Okay, gentlemen." McGillian's tone changed from warm to authoritative as he took his seat on the bench. The elevated platform, his referee's chair, gave him not only an unobstructed view of the proceedings but also established his unequivocal power over the litigants' fates. "Let the record show that you have both objected to assigning a Law Guardian for the minor," he said, "and the reason is?...."

Ortman stood up. His long limbs always seemed coiled, a wound wire ready to spring. "Both Mr. Bernstein and I feel that with the turnover of past Law Guardians, one more would encumber the process—not aid it."

"The two of you seem to do well when united against our justice system. Are you also in agreement on any other points?"

"I'm afraid, Your Honor, that there's no middle ground on this issue," Bernstein said.

Let the game begin. Phil listened as Bernstein took the ball and ran with it. "Since the last trial, the father has committed additional atrocious acts—"

McGillian interrupted. "Mr. Bernstein, please rephrase your words. Be careful in the way you accuse the father."

"Yes, Your Honor. The child has reported—"

Ortman ejected himself from his seat. "I request a hearing on the question of whether the mother should be allowed to report the child's fabricated stories," he shouted.

"No need for that," McGillian said, his tone calm. "We've been listening to testimonies of what the child has told caseworkers and psychologists. Mr. Bernstein, you may proceed, but please be succinct."

Phil felt a slight flutter of hope. One point in favor.

"I'd like to call to the stand Ellie Belmore's schoolteacher," Bernstein announced.

"And the purpose of her testimony?" McGillian asked.

"To show she must force Ellie to go with her father each time he comes for her."

"I accept that the child does not wish to visit her father," the judge said. "It's the reason behind her refusal that I want established."

"Your Honor, there's another reason to hear the teacher's testimony. In the course of this trial my colleague will doubtless bring up the fact that the mother has not produced the child for visitation. I want to introduce the Impossibility Defense and corroborate it with the teacher's testimony."

Phil watched as a dark cloud moved over McGillian's face. The good humor with which the judge had started his day was dissipating. "The Impossibility Defense in Family Court?" McGillian snorted. "You'd better come up with a precedent."

One point against.

The teacher, a pretty black woman with a cropped haircut, took the stand. She confirmed Bernstein's statement but added another. "Ellie acts out these games...." She lowered her gaze.

"What games?"

"Uh, sex games."

Phil thought he heard an audible groan from the plaintiff's table. He darted a glance at Rachel. Her head was down, supported at the temples by two hands, elbows digging into the table.

"Can you please describe them to the court?" Bernstein probed.

The teacher related Ellie's preoccupation with explicit sex games that she believed only a child with firsthand knowledge would play.

Phil awarded her another point.

Ortman led her through cross-examination.

"When did you graduate?" he asked her.

"Four years ago, but I worked—"

"How many children, on average, are in your class?"

"Ten."

"So your entire professional experience is working with forty children at the most?"

One point for Ortman.

"I worked with children before—"

Ortman put his hand up to stop her. "But not as a teacher. From what you do know of children, of whom you know so few, professionally speaking," he said, his tone sarcastic, "is it unusual for a disturbed girl to overreact to a change in her environment?"

"Well… it depends."

"Yes or no?"

"Uh, no, but—"

"Thank you. Now, could you tell us whether Ellie is afraid to visit her father or, is it possible that, perhaps, she's scared of coming to the city—you know, the people, buses, noise?"

"I think it's her father."

"Is it or is it not the father?"

"Your Honor," Chuck called out. "My colleague is being argumentative."

"Let her answer the question," McGillian said.

She shook her head. "Ellie wouldn't make any drawings for her Dad—"

"Yes or no, Miss."

"No."

"Let me be clear on this: You do not know for sure whether Ellie is afraid to visit her father or whether it is something else she's scared of. Is this correct?"

Misery clouded the woman's face as she nodded. "Yes," she whispered.

Another point lost.

"And the sex games you've described. Do you know for a fact that Dr. Belmore has introduced her to them?"

"It's obvious—"

"Did he tell you that?"

"Of course not."

"Did Ellie?"

"Not in so many words, but it's clear—"

"Yes or no, Miss?"

"No," she whispered.

One more point lost. Bernstein must find a way to establish the connection between the sex games and the father.

The gynecologist who had examined Ellie late on Tuesday, after her Fourth of July visit with her father, described bruises and lacerations. He had found the child's vagina exceptionally enlarged for her age, though the hymen, slightly torn, was in place.

The score edged up, but was still four-two in Ortman's favor.

In his cross-examination, Ortman's tactic was to do an end run. He didn't argue the physical findings.

"Can you please tell the court," he asked from his table, forcing the witness to raise his voice when answering, "the age of the bruises at the time you saw Ellie?"

"Between twelve to thirty-six hours."

"Why not six hours? Why not sixty?"

"It has to do with the coloration. We can tell by the range—from reddish-blue to yellow—the approximate age of the bruises."

"Approximate. Uhmm. So you could not determine, when you saw Ellie Tuesday night, whether these were caused early that day at school, late on Sunday at home, or Monday when she visited her Dad?"

"No, I couldn't."

"The lacerations. Could those have been caused by a fall on a hard object in the playground?"

"Unlikely."

"But possible?"

"Without causing other scratches or bruises on her thighs? She'd be impaled without hurting other parts of her body—"

"Please answer 'yes' or 'no,'" Ortman ordered.

"Yes," the doctor said. "If she were dropped from a parachute."

"So between Sunday and Tuesday she could have fallen on a bicycle seat that broke off? Or on a low picket fence?"

The physician held his hands up and dropped them.

"Yes or no?" Ortman asked.

Phil saw McGillian raised his hand in protest—probably because the witness had already answered and should not be asked to speculate further. But the witness kicked the ball into his own team's goal before the judge could stop him.

"Yes," the doctor replied, and shook his head in disbelief.

"No further questions."

Cold sweat tingled Phil's neck. Two crucial witnesses, the teacher and the physician, had failed to connect the physical evidence to the father in a way the judge could not deny.

He listened to every word of two psychologists' testimonies, which canceled each other. Ms. Belmore's witness drew the profile of a man incapable of lasting relationships, given to bouts of violence, and a pedophile. Counteracting it, Dr. Belmore's expert pointed out that Rachel's incompetence was demonstrated by her failure to nurture the relationship between Ellie and her father, that she had in fact turned the child against him. And it was under her care that Ellie was growing emotionally disturbed.

"Often," he said, "children test the borders. We should not reinforce a behavior that gives them power over adults—"

"Move along, please," McGillian said.

"How would you suggest a child who demonstrates this behavior should be handled?" Ortman asked the psychologist.

"A gradual easing into whatever it is that's required of her to do. Both parents, of course, must cooperate, but the custodial parent often has more influence over the child—"

"Mr. Ortman, that's enough. Both lawyers, please approach the bench," McGillian cut in.

In a sidebar, he spoke to them, "This case has had more than its fair share of psycho gobbledygook. Mr. Ortman, what are you driving at?"

"Your Honor," Ortman said. "Please allow me to establish one last point."

"It better be good." McGillian waved the lawyers away.

Ortman asked the psychologist, "In your opinion, could the child have learned the sex games—the explicit movements and vocabulary—from any other source?"

"TV, of course. Afternoon soap operas. Working parents are often unaware of how much their children are exposed to—"

Bernstein interrupted. "Move to strike. We're not here to explore the state of America's working parents. Only Ellie's exposure to certain influences."

"I agree," McGillian said to the witness "You may step down."

As McGillian called for recess, Phil dashed after him. There was still a chance that a bench player, himself, could make an impact.

McGillian came out of his private lavatory. At the sink he patted down his thick salt-and-pepper hair with water until it was plastered flat.

Speaking into the mirror, he said, "The father fails to convince me the mother is not doing a good job with this girl." He washed his hands again.

Another point scored? "She seems very devoted," Phil said.

"Devoted? How can she be if she's working in the city full-time? But I borrow a principle from the animal kingdom. Look at the way baby elephants are nurtured and raised not only by their mothers but also by their teenage sisters who act as babysitters. Females have a knack for baby raising. It's in their genes, and I'm not about to challenge Mother Nature on that front."

No reversal of custody. Thank God. But that was hardly enough. "The issue is beyond this, Judge. The child is being molested—"

McGillian cut him off. "Even if the teacher says the child's play has sexual over-tones, who says it's the father's doing? Bernstein didn't prove the connection. I can't assume that just because a child imitates carnal movements in playing with her peers, it means her father has taught them to her."

Phil wanted to shake him. The law limited the scope of the play. "Preponderance of evidence, Judge."

McGillian stepped back into his chambers. "Each piece of evidence must stand on its own in order to prove a point, Phil. You can't stagger a bunch of unproven pieces and total them as preponderance of evidence."

"When we weigh what's at stake, then it's the only way." Phil pulled his voice back down. "Ortman didn't bring up a real live man—a gardener, an uncle—as the culprit of the child's abuse. All he had was TV—"

McGillian examined the patterns in the imitation Moroccan area rug as though reflecting upon Phil's last words. "It's not incumbent upon the defense to prove who the culprit is; but it would have helped if he had."

Another point? Phil groped for the right curve. "The terror the child feels, Your Honor. That alone—"

McGillian shrugged, yanked the door open. "Let's get back."

The game wasn't yet over, even if McGillian acted like a son of a bitch. But Phil figured the running score was still six-four in Ortman's favor, given the judge's attitude.

Ms. Edwards, Ellie's therapist, took the stand. She was a handsome woman with papery skin who wore a red suit and a large gold pin. In a clear, modulated voice she reported Ellie's secret.

"It's called The Zoo Game," she said.

"Would you please describe the game?" Bernstein asked.

"It's one in which the elephant puts his trunk into the monkey's behind and the lion roars—the trunk being Dr. Belmore's penis, and the monkey is little Ellie."

McGillian stared at her. He turned to the court reporter. "Please read the last statement again."

The stenographer complied. The words, even in her flat, digital robot voice, dropped heavily in the silent courtroom as though accompanied by drums.

McGillian glared at Wes Belmore.

Phil decided it was an ace worth two points. Six-six, even. Preponderance of evidence won. Yup. His heart leaped with joy.

McGillian announced, "Gentlemen, we've heard enough. Unless there's anything to add, we'll reconvene after lunch and wrap it up."

When they returned to the courtroom at one-thirty, Ortman had a surprise up his sleeve.

"Your Honor," he said. "We just got hold of one more witness. We'd like your permission to bring in Freda Cortese, Ellie's babysitter."

Ms. Belmore's sudden jolt of the shoulders and back told Phil it was bad news. If the plaintiff did not give Dr. Belmore the woman's phone number, how did he obtain it?

"This shouldn't be a problem for your client, Mr. Bernstein, should it?" McGillian asked Bernstein. He turned back to Ortman. "But I fail to see what she would add. Don't test my patience, Mr. Ortman."

The small, mature woman clutched her handbag, her fingers clasping and releasing their hold on its sides as she took the stand. In response to Ortman's question, she explained that since the week before, she hadn't been taking care of Ellie.

"Why not?" Ortman asked.

"Ms. Belmore called and told me not to come for the next couple of weeks. But she said she'd pay my salary."

"Did she explain why?"

"Only that Ellie would be away for a little while. Ms. Belmore's folks came to visit, you know. I thought maybe they took her to Disney World or something."

Bernstein took advantage of this unexpected witness to establish that Ellie hadn't been exposed to unsuitable TV programs where she could learn about sexual acts.

Seven-six. Phil's spirits soured.

"Are we ready to close?" McGillian asked.

Bernstein spoke first. "I mentioned earlier this morning the Impossibility Defense—"

"You certainly did," McGillian replied. "I've taken notice. And if you remember, I warned your client last time not to withhold the father's visits. There is no Impossibility if Ms. Belmore has sent the child on vacation, now is there?"

Seven-seven. Even again. If McGillian kept the same tally.

Undaunted, Mr. Bernstein stood firm, his feet planted slightly apart. "Your Honor, we have a video to introduce in support of our claim. Ellie's reactions when her father comes to the door."

"I was not informed of additional evidence," Ortman called out.

"Your Honor," Bernstein said, and pointed at a screen. "It will only take a few minutes of the court's time—"

"We've allowed the defense to present less relevant information." McGillian rubbed his eyes. "Go ahead. Ms. Belmore, please take the stand first."

After the mother testified that she had made the tape, that it was accurate, and had not been altered, the homemade video rolled.

As Ellie's screams tore into the room, Phil peeked up to watch the expression on McGillian's face. It gave away nothing. But Phil's own blood ran cold. The roots on his scalp hurt.

The video was abruptly cut.

"What happened next?" McGillian asked.

"As you could see, Your Honor, the mother was unable to make the child go," Bernstein replied.

"May I talk with your client?" McGillian asked.

"You're still under oath," the bailiff reminded Ms. Belmore.

She answered McGillian's direct question to her. "I had to calm Ellie down. She was hysterical."

"Ms. Belmore. We know Ellie is a problematic child," McGillian said, a tone of compassion in his voice. "We've heard testimonies about her temper tantrums, and now we've seen one of them. I admit, it must be very difficult. But after she calmed down this time, did you explain to her she had nothing to fear? Did you, in any way, try to foster her trust in her father?"

"How could I after she's told me so many times he's hurt her? After I've seen the results of his Zoo Game with my own eyes? Was I supposed to say I didn't believe her? I do believe her, and I hope that finally this court will too."

McGillian leaned back in his seat. He let a moment pass. Then he turned his gaze to the defendant's attorney. "Ortman?"

"If anything, the video shows us the minimal efforts the mother has made in trying to send the child to her father—"

McGillian cut him off. "Don't editorialize. Do you want to cross-examine the plaintiff?"

"No, Your Honor."

A point lost anyway. Eight-eight.

McGillian did not retreat to his chambers to ponder the evidence. "In the matter of custody, I order leaving the custodial responsibility with the mother. I would advise her, though, given the father's profession and education, to consult with him in all matters concerning the child's health and schooling. In the matter of visitation, I find the evidence of sexual abuse to be inconclusive—equipoise. Therefore, I will replace the overnight visits with more frequent, albeit shorter ones. I hope it will put the mother's mind at ease while allowing the child and father more opportunities to develop a continuous relationship. Unfortunately, the supervised visits in the offices of Child Protective Services are not conducive for that type of relationship.

"Dr. Belmore will have two midweek visits from four to seven p.m., and each Saturday from nine a.m. to six p.m. In order to avoid further litigation, I hereby order that for each missed visit as a result of the mother's obstruction, the father will receive an overnight visit." McGillian raised his head from the notes and looked at Ms. Belmore. "Now, is that clear? Don't come back to me asking to cut those overnight visits. It's in your hands."

He banged his gavel, and Phil felt as if he had been punched in the stomach. Equipoise? What kind of Solomonic decision was this? McGillian's words huddled together, keeping their backs to Phil. Years had passed yet nothing had changed. McGillian hadn't changed. Abusers were still handed access to their young victims. The mother hadn't asked to discontinue *overnight* visits. She had asked to stop *unsupervised* ones.

What difference did the time of day make if the father still committed the acts?

CHAPTER NINETEEN

"I'M so sorry," Chuck said. "We did the best we could."

"That's it?"

The rest of her life without Ellie. The weight of the reality carried itself from the moment the gavel banged down in the courtroom, and it would keep floating in the vessel of time. Rachel's brains felt as detached from her scalp as quivering Jell-O from the rim of the bowl.

"What's equipoise?" she mumbled.

"An absolutely even balance of evidence. Fifty-fifty. According to McGillian, we've failed to meet the burden of showing the credible evidence tilted to our side."

"He *does* believe there's a fifty percent chance Ellie's being molested?"

Chuck's jaws clenched and released. "You got it, kiddo. Truthfully, I'm baffled. Equipoise is okay for a real estate matter, or an accident case when you split the tort money—not for child abuse. God almighty."

"But it's legal?"

"Yup. Some would even say it's brilliant—McGillian's reputation for knowing his law at its best."

"Chuck, this is not good enough."

He laid his hand on her shoulder. The deep features in his rumpled face agonized. "McGillian's like many judges in our system. Clueless. He can't grasp the realities that make people's lives. He's a witness to the crisis as it appears in paperwork—never to the human dynamics that lead to those breakdowns. So he fills up the gap in the law with his own prejudices—and yes, legalese."

"He has no business warming the bench if he can't be compassionate. Christ. Fifty-fifty?"

"This equipoise ruling is so absurd they'll be writing about in the law journal." Chuck shook his head. "Rachel, what can I say?" He gave her a quick hug. "I'm so sorry. Will you be all right?"

"Of course not."

"Shall I drive you home?"

"That's not what I meant." Feeling as discarded as an old paperback, she followed him outside. A rush of heat and bright light greeted her exit yet it did not penetrate the chill and darkness she felt inside.

"I'm sorry," Chuck repeated, touched her hand, and dashed down the steps, leaving her standing there alone.

Equipoise.

The new, strange word hung in front of her like a balloon in a cartoon, screaming in a medley of colors and script styles. She felt faint. How she wished to have someone with her now. It was a mistake not to ask Jacqueline. She hadn't wanted to impose on her friend and have her miss a day of work. The office manager had now put Jacqueline on notice, and she risked losing her job—and the health benefits she so needed. But the petite Jacqueline with the permanent sparkle in her dark eyes was a tower of strength.

Rachel walked toward her car. The air sizzled with the odor of baking asphalt. The glaring light shimmered and danced in front of her. She raised her hand to shield her forehead and noticed Phil Crawford approaching her from the tree line.

Take her and run, his note had said. Rachel hadn't been entirely surprised. These past three years, supporters of children's rights had seemed, on occasion, to turn their attention to the Belmore case, but soon, their interest would wane. Simple, clear-cut cases held more public interest, unlike her complex litigation only experts understood.

But there was something in Phil's intense eyes as he stood away from the sun. She examined his face in the shadow of the tree. He cared.

Phil swayed on the back of his heels. "Ms. Belmore, I know it's inappropriate for me to say." His words faltered for a moment. "But I hope you'll do for her whatever it takes."

"Thanks," she replied. She trusted he was not one of Wes's minions. "I will."

When she opened her car door, Phil held it for her. An encouraging smile spread over his face. She noticed again the elongated dimple on his left cheek as she caught a whiff of his spicy aftershave.

She forced herself to smile back. "You can call me Rachel."

It was mid-afternoon, the start of rush hour. Heading west, Rachel drove below the minimum speed, fearing that her instincts, knotted in cobwebs, would betray her. A few minutes after she exited the expressway, the car, as familiar with the charted route as a horse heading to its stable, zoomed into the older section of Green Hills. The streets, eclectic with their styles of one- and two-story homes in red brick, wooden shingles, stucco, or Tudor styles, had an old-world aura. Some flaunted a widow's peak, others tolerated with a wink the embrace of ivy climbing up their sides. Oaks, maples, and weeping willows—tall and proud—arched their tops to canopy the sidewalks. The flowerbeds circling the trees brimmed with perfumed summer blossoms. Rachel could hear Ellie's voice, a note of glee woven through it, as Ellie had noted the flowers blazing in the colors of fire: yellow, pink, orange, and red.

Rachel pulled into her driveway and stopped. Unexpectedly, her little house was unwelcoming in its emptiness the way an off-hours theater felt to an actor. The place she had so painstakingly fixed up and decorated for herself and Ellie, with its three small bedrooms upstairs, and the cozy living area downstairs, now loomed much too big. Ellie wouldn't be bouncing on the front steps after school, burbling excitedly, waving her artwork of the day. Not for many years. Not until she was safe from her father and from the legal system.

A sudden scream of outrage pierced Rachel's guts. *No more Zoo Game.*

Once inside the house, she plopped down on the couch, kicked off her shoes, and leaned her head back. If she'd had the energy, she might have taken a cold drink from the refrigerator.

The red light on the answering machine blinked with its urgent demand. She punched the play button.

Jacqueline's accented voice had a pleasant lilt, which always brought a smile to Rachel's lips. "It's me, and I hope the judge hung Wes by his *chibaberinies*. Anyway, guess what? You and I have grand plans for the weekend. We're invited to Fire Island, to a drop-dead house. A cocktail party at seven-thirty, dinner served on the deck at eight-thirty. Disco dancing from midnight until the wee hours. More details when I see you tomorrow at the office."

For a moment, a wave of warmth toward Jacqueline spread through Rachel, like hot chocolate, smooth and sweet. Gerald had talked about spending a weekend in Fire Island. Gerald again. If only he had explained. His disappearance had left a void like a figure cut out of a photograph.

Jacqueline didn't know Ellie was gone, and Rachel wouldn't be able to divulge any details, but she could unburden herself of her problems at *Women's Life*. From whichever angle she observed her life, it seemed that the "big bang" that had started with Wes's silhouette contorted over the baby's crib went on spreading in slow motion. Her world continued to break into small pieces. Vince's betrayal was one more occurrence in a string of disasters. And the astute Jacqueline knew more about the going-ons at the office than she divulged.

The second message was from Josie, her voice, as always, jittery. Rachel was not up to talking to her sister, but this was one task she must tackle. She punched the callback button.

"What's up?" She kept a casual tone.

"Do you know where Mom and Dad are?"

"I've no idea. They left about a week ago."

"Rachel, I'll never understand you. You didn't ask what their next stop would be?"

"I guess I was distracted. Sorry. I'm sure they'll be in touch with you soon."

"Oh, that. Distracted by your court case? It's all Mom talked about," Josie said in a bored tone. "I'm glad it's over."

"How do you know it's over?"

Josie laughed nervously. "You wouldn't have bothered to return my call otherwise."

Josie's logic was beyond her. Rachel let it pass. "How's Nicole? Is her head all right?"

"She's fine. No thanks to Ellie—"

Rachel held back the impulse to slam the phone down. "Ellie did not cause the accident."

"Who did then?"

"Please, Josie. I'm really not up to arguing right now."

"You never have time to talk to me."

"Josie, please. Not tonight. I have problems—"

"You know what's your problem? You're aloof. You walk around like you own the earth. Even your name is of the Chosen One."

"Naming me after Grandma Rachel meant nothing more than naming me after Grandma Rachel."

"Better than naming me after Grandpa Joseph."

"Come on. They died in the holocaust. Let them be." Rachel could take no more. She had nothing left in her but emptiness. "Please excuse me. I'd like to say good-bye."

"That's what I mean—"

"Have a nice evening." Rachel hung up and sighed. What ate at Josie? Thank God for Howard. He could give his narcissistic wife all the attention she craved. When Josie was the center of his world, she acted much better than she did when her parents and sister failed to wrap themselves around her.

Tugging off her jacket and unzipping her skirt, Rachel wriggled out of them. She padded over to the country-style cabinet converted into a bar and poured Scotch into a glass. On her way to the kitchen to get ice cubes, she yanked off her pantyhose and left them lying on the floor. Then she carried her drink to the couch and settled down again.

No more Zoo Game.

The shrill of the phone woke her, jolting her with the start of a missed flight. The ring persisted—the answering machine hadn't been reset. Dazed, Rachel picked up the receiver. Her eyes scanned with surprise the discarded clothes strewn about.

It was Chuck. "How are you doing, kiddo?"

"Got drunk and passed out."

"I wish I could offer hope, Rachel. But I got you the name of another lawyer. The best. I've talked to her, and she's interested in your case."

Oh, no. "Are you really resigning? Please don't. You know so much already."

"A fresh eye on the case—and a new dose of energy—could do it good."

"Chuck, I appreciate everything. I honestly do. I'm just so tired." She passed her tongue over flannel-covered teeth. "Perhaps I should just stop. Wes can't get hold of Ellie anyway, and why try to prove anything to anybody?"

"When whoever is keeping Ellie is found, he or she could be accused of kidnapping a child." Chuck paused. "You're entitled to a 'woe is me' for about fifteen minutes. Then brace yourself for more. A lot more. Erica Norgard can walk on nails, and that's what you need."

They hung up. Rachel fell back into the couch. Erica Norgard. The new central figure in her life.

CHAPTER TWENTY

"DAVID Lupori's on the phone," Jacqueline announced. "Says he's the brother of your sorority sister, Anita."

"Anita Lupori? There was no one by that name." Rachel reached for the phone.

"Rachel? How are you?" She heard sucking noises, as though the man had a candy in his mouth.

"I don't remember anyone by the name Anita. What year did she pledge?—"

Lip-smacking. "Please forgive me for the fib, but I had to make something up in order to get past your secretary."

The blood left Rachel's head as if through a trap door. "What do you want?"

"I'm doing an article about children taken by a parent when—"

Rachel put her finger on the cradle button and listened to the rescuing click. Wes. The hyena. A brilliant publicity campaign—professionally orchestrated—had catapulted his meteoric reputation as an outstanding surgeon. It would be just like him to hire a PR firm to aid in his legal battle. Was this man a journalist or a private investigator?

There was no time to lose. Her fingers punched Erica Norgard's number.

Ms. Norgard's secretary squeezed her in for an appointment. "How is noontime?"

Rachel let out a sigh of relief. "Great. I'll be there." None of her clients scheduled a business lunch on summer Fridays; they fled the city to the beaches as early as they could—as she would do later today for her weekend on Fire Island.

Rachel fixed her gaze on her new lawyer, a tall and angular woman with a no-frill manner. She was encased in an unconstructed blue suit and white blouse. Her only jewelry—if one could call it such—was a black-faced sports watch strapped by a brown leather band. Yet the determination pulling at the corner of Ms. Norgard's mouth was mocked by the smattering of freckles across the bridge of a straight nose.

Rachel leaned back and let her limbs relax into the soft cream upholstered chair, a shade darker than the carpeting. If most New Yorkers found Manhattan's soot the enemy of light-colored office furnishing, Erica Norgard wasn't one of them.

"Here's what's going to happen." Erica's full voice played at a low-range octave. It nudged Rachel back to face her. "The judge will instruct you to reveal Ellie's where-abouts. You're telling me you'll refuse. He'll hold you in contempt of court."

"What does it mean in practical terms?"

"In theory, he may confine you to jail until you discontinue the act of contempt—and produce her."

The words jolted her. "In theory?"

"It's rarely enforced—and not until a series of warnings is issued— time for the defendant to contemplate his course of action. In the end, though, if you keep to your refusal, then yes, it's possible. I can't keep you out of jail indefinitely."

Rachel's head bobbed in response, up and down, slowly, silently, like a marionette, in tune to a rumbling inner hum. She had known it all along yet, coming out of Ms. Norgard's mouth, it became real. A bright price tag dangled from the package of her legal mess.

"In the meantime we've got work to do." Erica leaned forward, her elbows digging into her desk. "Judges make decisions based upon a mixture of inadequate laws and their own private values. In the crack that allows a subjective judgment call we must erect a buffer to protect you from how an aging conservative Catholic white male named Robert McGillian views your case."

"How do we erect that 'buffer'?"

"He's the interpreter of what he *thinks* society deems as right and wrong. We'll try to control the signals he receives from that society." An errant smile touched Erica's lips, as though she were guarding a secret. "It's called 'public opinion.' With your professional background, you must be good at it."

Rachel gulped. It made sense, but she hated the sound of it. "I— I— never dealt with anything like this."

"Begin to toy with the idea. You must have noticed that McGillian has been sitting in the hot seat these days. Some legal fiasco of two butchered cases."

Rachel nodded. "Yes, but—"

"There you have it. Think how you can turn up the heat." Erica waved her hand. "More urgently, by next week we'll have loads of new petitions to respond to, courtesy of Henry Ortman. Soon, McGillian will transfer custody to your ex-husband; parental kidnapping will justify it. Then we have the criminal action Bernstein has started." She paused again. "My fee is two hundred and fifty dollars an hour."

Rachel stared at her. What had she thought this was going to cost? Forty hours would total ten thousand dollars. There would be hundreds of billable hours. She had stopped keeping count of Chuck's invoices—and he had discounted his fees to almost half the amount Norgard now quoted.

"I'd like to commit to it, but I can't guarantee I'd be able to," Rachel mumbled.

"Rachel, I want you to understand what's at stake: women in your position often lose their homes. Keep pressing the legal battles, or maintain your middle-class lifestyle— it's a financial choice you must make. Don't be surprised that you're faced with it. There are thousands of mishandled cases like Ellie's across the country, but most women don't get anywhere as far as you have, which is why I've told Chuck Bernstein I'd represent you. I care enough to help you go on. But it's not simply my time," Erica made a sweep with her hand toward the door and the offices outside it. "I have rent to pay, plus an expensive operation that I must mobilize on your behalf."

Numbness reached Rachel's throat. "Ms. Norgard, I need you," she whispered.

"Yes, you do," Ms. Norgard replied, her hazel eyes softening. "And call me Erica. We'll work out a fee schedule. You've been getting 'bupkes,' and Ellie is a victim of our very imperfect justice system. Someone must do something about it, for her, if not for our own collective soul as a society."

CHAPTER TWENTY-ONE

SINCE he had committed to half a share on a summer rental in Fire Island, Phil spent alternate weekends in this thirty-eight-mile-long white sand strip dotted with beach communities, inaccessible by car.

He made the drive southbound on the Sagtikos Parkway to the Bay Shore marina in forty-five minutes, and was early for the six-thirty ferry. He bought a ticket and sat on an empty bench on the top deck. Soon, when the commuter train arrived from Manhattan, the ferry would fill up with young executives still in their business suits. He slouched and leaned his head back, waiting for the sprinkle of ocean water to wet his face as soon as the boat pulled out. A blue Dodgers baseball cap, turned backward, kept his hair from being blown in all directions. He thought of his mother, whom he had visited on his way here. Bony fingers at the bottom of her throat, eyes wide in eternal surprise, thin, stooped shoulders, voice like a bird's. Phil had tried talking her into coming to Fire Island with him, at least for a day, but she wouldn't leave her house. Although still young, she was fearful of venturing out, like an old woman who might trip and break a hip.

A commotion on the dock below drew his attention.

"You bitch," a man called, and Phil looked down. With a shock of recognition, he saw Dr. Wes Belmore coming out of a double stretch limousine, yelling, "Where's my daughter?"

Among the commuters pouring out of the van that had shuttled them from the nearby train station, he spotted The Mother Who Protects Her Child, in a red business dress. At the sight of Dr. Belmore, she threw frantic looks around her and turned to flee. People parted to let her through but remained transfixed on the scene.

Dr. Belmore sprinted forward and caught her arm. "Where is she?" he yelled again.

Phil jumped to his feet, took the steps two at a time, vaulted through the ticket gate, and positioned himself in front of the man who continued to shout, dots of froth accumulating in the corners of his mouth, his hand still gripping Ms. Belmore's arm. His other hand was raised ominously, ready to strike.

"Dr. Belmore," Phil called out. "Please take your hands off her. She has a restraining order, which you're violating. If you don't stop harassing her I'll call the police."

"I want to know where my daughter is. According to yesterday's decree I should have her—"

"Whatever the problem is, Dr. Belmore, it won't be resolved now—and not in this fashion. As an officer of the court I request that you leave. Now."

The ferry siren bleated and Rachel, her arm released, lifted an overnight bag and scuttled away. Phil stood watching Dr. Belmore's graceful figure as it folded back into the limousine.

He dashed back to the ferry.

Rachel Belmore was huddled on the top deck near the spot Phil had occupied moments before. Her hands covered her face. The sun ignited sparkles of brushed copper buried in the rich, brown thickness of her hair.

"Are you all right?" he asked, his tone soft.

She shook her head. "No, but I will be." Then she added, her face still buried in her hands, "Thanks for your help."

"I'm a Savior of Damsels in Distress, remember?"

If she remembered their first conversation, she made no indication. She did not lift her head in response. The red blotch on her arm where Dr. Belmore had gripped it matched her sleeveless dress. The thinness of her arms touched Phil in their vulnerability.

The siren sounded again. Phil settled next to her but didn't speak. The ferry glided out of its mooring.

"He has detectives following me," she finally said in a tone so low Phil had to bend toward her to hear.

"So it seems." He paused. The time before last when he saw her alone he had handed her the note; now she'd want to know more. But there was nothing he could say. Or, there was too much. "Do you go to Fire Island often?"

She shook her head.

He continued, "I had summer jobs there while in high school. Nothing like busing tables and delivering groceries to develop character."

She gave no indication that she heard him. Sadness hung around her like smoke. She took a deep breath and tilted her head back to rest it on the bench back. She closed her eyes, allowing Phil to examine her features, as delicate and refined as though drawn by an artist's pencil.

He hadn't felt a rush of tenderness like the one that now swept through him since before his last year with Carole.

"What type of work do you do?" he asked Rachel.

"I sell advertising space for *Women's Life* magazine."

"Sounds interesting."

She opened her eyes. "Most of the time it is, except when it's hell—like this week. The average of a nine, a two and a minus six." She tossed her hair, and a faint fragrance of freshly washed flowers floated toward him.

"One point six, six, six, six," he said right away.

She turned serious again. "Wes and Ortman would tie me to a stake and light fire under my feet if they found out we've talked."

"Any topic but your case is fine," he replied. "Judges, lawyers, and litigants bump into each other all the time. Litigants can't be isolated in a leper colony." Phil remembered McGillian calling Ortman "Hank" at the Republican dinner party.

He relaxed against the seat, feeling her presence next to him. Little by little, she came out of her reticence and they continued to talk. The Mother Who Protects Her Child. Where was the child?

Thirty-five minutes later—much too short a time—the ferry pulled alongside the dock. Rachel joined a man and a woman who were waiting for her. Phil disembarked.

As he was sorting out his duffel bag from dozens of similar ones, he felt someone standing near him. Too near. The whiff of fresh flowers told him who it was at the same moment he jerked his head around.

"Sorry, I didn't mean to startle you," Rachel said. She squeezed a piece of paper into his palm and left.

Two blocks away he stopped and took the note out of his pocket.

It read, "Thanks for caring."

He brought it up to his nose and inhaled the scent.

"Look at the shooting star," Jacqueline called out.

Rachel peered over at the light tumbling quickly through the dark night, its frosty ribbon disappearing with it. Did Ellie, too, at this moment, spot it? She could hear her child's delighted cries as she watched the star's path ending in the water. The ocean's inky surface, covered by frayed gauze, announced its presence in muffled, growling sound like a practicing orchestra of basses and tubas.

Rachel yawned. "Do we have to go out so late?" She rose to clear the dinner dishes.

Dan, Jacqueline's singing buddy and their host, jumped to his feet. "Go take a beauty nap," he ordered Rachel and Jacqueline. "I'll clean up. You'll owe me a foot massage."

Rachel retired to the guest room assigned her. It smelled of potpourri and ocean salt. Floor-to-ceiling windows made up the south wall. Lying on the bed, she watched the white foam of the colliding waves. They crashed in a thunderous racket yet their rhythmic growling was comforting.

Next thing she knew, Jacqueline was shaking her, her touch gentle. "It's disco time," she whispered. Her fingers patted Rachel's hair and tenderly removed a strand stuck to the corner of her mouth.

Rachel groaned.

Jacqueline flicked the light switch on the bedside lamp. In a jaunty jig she made it to the door. "We have a bottle of champagne to wake you up."

"Nothing but a shower could do that."

"Ten minutes," Jacqueline said. "And bring a jacket."

Outside, Dan handed Rachel a bicycle and a flashlight. They rode on the narrow boardwalks, dark and silent in the still of the night. The breeze on her face was fragrant with pine and wet salt and felt refreshing. Her legs, pedaling, were losing their stiffness.

A dozen blocks later, the unlit path merged into a main area of activity, bright with restaurants and boutiques doing fast business at midnight. Summer faces and muscled legs in shorts presented a glow of suntan. People licked ice cream cones, gathered around a street band, sat on the pier to watch the passerby, bantered and laughed.

All around Rachel, the carnival atmosphere spilled out from the side streets and restaurants. But she felt encased in a translucent, impenetrable bubble whose walls prevented her from hearing or touching any of it. How odd it was to watch life streaming by, so normal, so unlike hers. Her world was crumbling, closing on her, the marching beat of a catastrophe loud inside her head.

The three of them settled in a surprisingly uncrowded bar where Jacqueline talked the bartender into pouring their champagne for a corkage fee.

"Let's drink to a better week." Jacqueline touched Rachel's fluted glass with hers.

Rachel hooked her legs on the high stool and leaned on her elbow. Her eyes felt unfocused, glazed over. The feeling of strangeness, of not belonging, wouldn't dissipate even after the second glass of champagne. She felt perched on the edge of a vortex of nothingness. More than sleep, she craved to hibernate until the day Ellie grew up and returned home.

"Here comes your cute friend from the ferry." Jacqueline nudged Rachel's elbow from under her. Rachel hadn't mentioned they had met before. As she glanced at Phil Crawford approaching, his body relaxed, his eyes scintillating, she welcomed his presence. He was a friend, although she was unsure what he wanted with her.

He grinned. "I thought we'd bump into each other in this small place. Like it here?"

"I'll tell you after they let me sleep." Rachel gestured with her hand toward Dan who stood by the jukebox and inserted a coin. Slow music cascaded off the wooden-planked walls decorated with old framed posters. A couple started to move in unison to the music.

"Come join us," they called over.

Phil took Rachel's hand in mock formality. Heat crawled up her neck. She fidgeted in her seat. That was not what she had in mind.

Intrigued and too exhausted to refuse, she left Jacqueline's side. Her body barely touching his, Rachel was conscious of the strange acquaintance they shared. They were six different people interacting on three different planes—in court where she and Ellie had been handed a blow; in the bewildering exchange of notes that told her this caring man was trapped, for whatever reason, in a role he could neither express nor defy; and here, now, his muscular arms making her forget the age difference between them. As they spoke about Fire Island and its people, Rachel felt the stirring of passion whirring in the space between their bodies.

Her resistance was dissolving. But what if, regardless of her conviction to the contrary, he was in Wes's employ? She could put nothing past Wes and his machinations. But then again, Phil had stood up to Wes at the ferry dock; he had rescued her. She should stop being so suspicious of anyone who tried to come near her....

She stopped dancing and pulled away. "I'm sorry. I'm too tired to be good company."

"Yes, after a business week averaging one point six, six, six, six," he said, smiling, ignoring the obvious—her losing in court.

She picked up her flashlight and waved at Jacqueline, who was engaged in a conversation with a new acquaintance with huge muscles bulging from under the sleeves of his T-shirt. But when Rachel stepped out to get her bike, Phil followed.

"I pass by K Street on my way back to N," he said simply.

The dense darkness, soft and rich as mink, curved away the pines, bamboos, reeds and wooden fences and evaporated the outlines of the paths into the night. Only the flashlights threw a muted illumination, vague circles that bounced a few feet ahead of the bicycles' front tires. Past the expanse of blackness that stretched ahead, a streetlight marked a quiet, distant corner.

Suddenly, shadows loomed in front of her, blocking the way. Startled, Rachel hit the brakes. She directed the flashlight and saw a doe and her fawn.

"Hey, Bambi!" she called out.

Phil closed the distance behind her. "Years ago, when the island was detached from the mainland, their ancestors were trapped here. There are hundreds of deer here; they have no natural enemies to disturb them."

The animals stood frozen together as if in a photograph, their bodies at an easy stance. They returned Rachel's stare unafraid.

"A mother and her baby." Phil's voice was ever so low. "They belong together."

A pang of pain zigzagged through Rachel. He understood. "Yes," she whispered. *No more Zoo Game.*

A rustle in the thicket caused the doe to snap her head. She galloped away on light, long limbs, her offspring in tow.

Rachel and Phil rode on in silence the rest of the way. In front of her house, she took off her sandals and stepped on the dune.

Phil followed her to the wide stretch of beach.

They plopped down on the sand, cool as fresh sheets, and listened to the waves breaking against the stillness of the night behind them. With no trees overhead, the silvery half-moon dripped demure light that outlined Phil's profile. His eyes were hidden in the deep shadows above his cheekbones. He seemed so self-possessed. Rachel's fingers raked the sand in circular motions.

"Look at the blue and the red stars," Phil said, surveying the sky.

"What blue and red?"

"The ones transmitting red light are moving toward us. The blue ones are moving away from us."

She scrutinized the dark skies, dotted with millions of lights. "All I see are yellow stars."

"Those are satellites. The brightest ones these days are man-made."

"You mean I can never again swoon over the yellow ones?"

"That's right. But there are plenty of red and blue ones for you to swoon over. They're just not as bright."

She continued to stare at the sky. "I'm not sure I'd want science to replace myths. I'd rather see the stars as cosmic diamonds."

"I didn't mean to ruin it for you."

"It sounds like a cliché, but it does look like gigantic artwork."

The smile in his voice was warm. "'The sky will always be new for lovers.' So said Theodore Holbrook, who died in 1836."

She looked at him curiously. "You just made that up."

"Well, he would have said it had he existed."

She laughed in the darkness. They sat in silence for a long time.

Then they began to talk. She had no idea how long the conversation lasted, and after a while, the subjects just rolled off one another, with Phil in the lead, chattering.

"You have a great public library in Green Hills," Phil said. "I take out foreign movies there. They've got the best collection. Italian, Japanese, Swedish."

Why was he spending so much time with her?

He went on, "I love Czech movies—have you seen any? Before the Russian invasion of Czechoslovakia in nineteen-sixty-eight, the Czechs had the best film schools and movie production facilities. Rumanian movies are catching up."

"I take Ellie to the library for bedtime stories," she told him. "You should see the kids in their pajamas, carrying their favorite stuffed animals. They're like puppies. They huddle on the carpet around the storyteller, someone from the senior citizens' center—" Rachel fell silent. No more trips to the library.

"The reader must have more fun than they do."

Rachel smiled. While Ellie was enthralled in the story, she scouted the best-sellers shelves. She'd let her fingers trail over the crisp covers, regretting all the serious reading squeezed out of her life since she had become a mother. But now she'd have a lot more time to read.

In the long, lonely evenings.

A few minutes into her reverie, Rachel noticed Phil's gaze as it wandered unhurriedly over her face. With the moon now low behind him, she could not see his expression, but she knew her own features were washed by light.

"I have to go," she said, not wanting to.

He helped her to her feet. The touch of their fingers sent ripples of electricity through her.

"Good night, Rachel," he said at the deck, and she heard the caress in his voice. She knew with unshakable certainty that he had spoken her name many times.

CHAPTER TWENTY-TWO

MCGILLIAN cherished his weekends. When he wasn't out playing golf or casting in the river, it was his quiet time to catch up on his professional reading and give the newspapers his full attention. But today, not even those were safe. *Newsday* carried letters to the editor about this Kim Lee business, a matter that had replaced the Torruellas case for public attention. Two weeks after his ruling on the Mayes v. Lee case, it stubbornly refused to fade away.

He put the newspaper aside, and got up. He should pick the apples and pears before the squirrels got them.

The fresh air, although hot, lifted his spirits some. Amadeus, his old poodle, limped toward him, wheezing, his cataractous eyes tearing. McGillian lifted him in his arms. He stood still among the fruit trees, taking in the warm rotting aroma, tangy sweetness spiked with tart tree sap.

"Bob, Colby Albrecht's on the phone," McGillian's wife called out from the kitchen window.

The town supervisor, calling from Governor Dunkle's car, reported they were on their way to a fund raising dinner in the Hamptons. "We're stopping by our headquarters for a series of meetings. The Governor would like to see you if you could drop in to say hello."

"I don't remember my two previous elections to Family Court drawing the attention of the Governor." McGillian laughed. And why should they? Family Court had the lowest image among courts. The Governor would put all his weight behind judgeship elections to the Supreme Court, which ruled on governmental issues.

Albrecht's response was a chuckle cut by static.

But Dunkle did not seem to have anything on his agenda when McGillian was ushered to see him. Dunkle was alone in the room, acting as if he had plenty of time. He spoke with passion about Long Island's potential for economic growth. "I'm reviewing a tax bill drafted to attract more industry to Long Island—a package of tax breaks and utilities discounts for companies with one thousand employees or more," he said. "What do you think?"

McGillian relaxed as he was swept into an easy conversation. After a while, a quick glance at his watch told him ten minutes had passed. His unease returned. The Governor was too busy for this. Any moment now, he would bring up the business with the media circus. The Torruellas case had served Dunkle in scoring public relations points when, sounding like the savior of society's indigent victims, he promised an overhaul of the social system that had no budget.

Sure enough, the Governor brought it up. "The Torruellas committee is proposing to limit the case load per worker."

McGillian said nothing.

Dunkle went on. "And I've assigned it the task of recommending a reform in the privacy law that blocks investigating such tragic cases."

"Had this new measure been in effect, we could have opened up the file to public scrutiny and I wouldn't have received the flak I did," McGillian replied.

"Bob, I'm sorry about the tough time you're having with the media lately. I'm behind you." He rose, indicating the meeting was about to end.

McGillian stood up too and started toward the door. Dunkle scanned the room, but instead of seeing him out, he sauntered toward a collection of framed photographs on the wall. His hands in his pockets, and rocking back on his heels, Dunkle examined them.

The man was dawdling, to what end McGillian could not fathom.

At last, Dunkle turned and walked toward the door. "I'm proud to have you as a judge in our system," he said. "It's a tough job nowadays with drugs wreaking havoc in families."

"We need more support systems—dormitory-style drug rehab programs, special schools for juveniles," McGillian said.

"How's the case backlog?"

"Bad."

"So I hear. My son's surgeon, Dr. Wesley Belmore, has mentioned how tough it is to move things along."

As though a giant frog had leaped at him from the top of the bookcase, McGillian was startled. Damn. Damn. Damn. The blood drained from his face and surged into his heart. Damn. The Governor's flanking maneuver botched all he had worked for—respect for his integrity.

Dazed, he opened the door and stopped. So the Belmore vs. Belmore case was the true purpose of Dunkle's audition. The offense of the meeting felt like the slime left behind by a slug. Unsmiling, he shook the Governor's hand, and left.

CHAPTER TWENTY-THREE

BACH'S melodious notes filled the house with a Saturday morning mood. Rachel woke up from the deepest sleep she'd had in months. The ocean waves roaring outside her window and breaking against the jetties had tranquilized her into a state of oblivion.

Spokes of light shone through the drawn curtains. They bounced off the cedar walls and caught a miniature storm of dust as it swirled and danced to the ocean beat, promising a perfect day.

She arose and let her nose follow the aroma of freshly brewed coffee. She found Jacqueline out on the deck, seated under the striped umbrella and clad in a bikini made of three eye-patches.

Taking in lungfuls of the cool breeze, Jacqueline emitted little purrs and grunts of pleasure. "It's not yet noon," she told Rachel. Her smile was broad, and her teeth gleamed in pure white.

Dan pulled up a chair for Rachel as though she were a patient walking for the first time after surgery and offered her a platter of croissants, flaky and buttery, accompanied by homemade strawberry jam. Then he changed the CD to one he and Jacqueline had recorded, excused himself, and dashed down to catch the game of volleyball starting on the beach in front of the house.

Jacqueline's voice singing in French came on.

"Your friend has been looking for you," she said.

"My friend?"

"That gorgeous hunk you met on the ferry and in whose arms you looked quite comfortable last night."

"Come on Jacques, he's too young."

"Too young for what?"

"For me. That's what."

"Hey, this is the New Age. Role reversal. It's okay when it's the other way, right?"

Rachel mumbled an assent.

"Well, then, voilá."

"What did he want?"

"He was on his way to the hardware store. He's working on a friend's boat and asked us to go on a sunset cruise. I told him you'd go."

"You told him what??"

"I'll ruin the best of promising dates if it's on a boat. I need solid ground under my feet at all times."

"So you're sending me? He's still too young, regardless of what the French say."

"Okay. You've asked for it, so here's the latest report." Jacqueline tilted her head and looked at Rachel from under hooded lids. "Would it help if I told you I bumped into our sweet Gerald Wednesday night at Carrillo's, and he had a starlet—no, a nymph—draped over his arm? Next time, I want you to show up with a man fifteen years *his* junior—and with a full head of hair to boot."

A small dart hit Rachel's heart. What did she expect? "Thanks for the update," she said, and bent over her plate. "But Gerald's bald head was cute."

"The baldness of tycoons has a certain appeal—when the guy is *indeed* a tycoon."

Rachel busied herself with her coffee and croissant.

"All right. Talk to me. You've been mysterious; I assume you have mighty good reasons," Jacqueline finally said. "And where is Ellie this weekend?"

"There are things I can't answer, though God knows I want to talk." Rachel felt the tears pinch the bridge of her nose. "But I do need to hear from you what is going on at *Women's Life*. I just don't get it. I'm one of the best there yet they treat me as if they don't want me to succeed. Am I paranoid, or do I have a reason to feel sabotaged every step of the way?"

"Vince's trying to push you out. You must see that." Jacqueline's voice was quiet, knowing.

"It makes no sense. What about Compton Foods? What about Baroness? These two alone make up eighty percent of this year's new business. With all the other accounts I manage, I bring in over twenty million dollars a year!" She stopped. A sinking feeling—fear—descended on her. The signs had been there but she had denied them. "Have you been running interference for me?" she asked.

Jacqueline shrugged. "No more than any secretary would—"

"Oh, yes. Any 'typical secretary,' you should say. Anyone that happens to double as one's closest friend."

"What's important is that you're not their corporate type. Vince tells you you're not a team player—whatever that means to him—and that he doesn't like your attitude."

"I can't share his nostalgia for his good old Yankee days, and his shield of pretentiousness is made of molded cow dung."

"You've answered it. You don't talk the talk or walk the walk."

Rachel thought for a moment. "Without me, Vince might have to work for a living— He's so incompetent."

"The more he pushes you, the more uptight and critical you get."

"How can I not get uptight?"

"Voilá. Break the cycle. Pretend you're a good sport the next ten times they undermine you. Shmooze with Vince after work at a sports bar. Take our dear promo director to a weekend spa on your expense account; she's more powerful than you've given her credit for. And in the meantime, start interviewing."

Rachel bit her lip. With the economy teetering on uncertainty—and all hell breaking loose around her with one personal crisis after another, how could she start the long and lonely journey of job search? "The stress of looking for another job is more than

I'll be able to handle right now. Maybe old troubles are preferable to new troubles. At least they're familiar."

"You're better off with another job offer in your pocket—"

"Are there rumors? Will I get fired?"

Jacqueline shrugged. "I won't be surprised if, when Tom Fields 'graduates' his training, he'll get some of your accounts."

At that moment, Rachel heard a set of sneakers bounding up the deck stairs. She turned her head to see Phil coming up. His limbs were long and limber in his trunk suit. His hair had blown in the wind, or perhaps he hadn't combed it that morning.

"Will you come for a ride later?" he asked with no preliminaries.

"I don't know."

"It'll be short. Just an hour and a half or so." His eyes were bright with excitement. "We're testing her out."

She hugged herself against undetected chill. Was she compromising her case? What did he want from her, and for what purpose? She should discuss it—him—with Erica. Too much was at stake.

His eager face, awaiting her answer, did it. "All right," she said, hearing her own feeble tone.

"On the dock at five. Wear deck shoes."

Dan led them on an hour-long bike ride along wooden plank paths laid over the dunes and pointed at the beach apples, Japanese pines, Russian olive trees, hemlocks, grass, and bamboos interspersed with wild cherry shrubs. Rachel tuned her ear to the crackling of dry leaves in the thicket. A stag with a magnificent set of antlers came over and ate carrots out of Jacqueline's outstretched hand.

Back on the beach, Rachel closed her eyes and wiggled her toes sensuously in the warm sand. She thought with fondness of Jacqueline, of her careful attempts to smooth the edges of her existence. Jacqueline's warmth recharged her psychic batteries; she reconfirmed Rachel's faith in the goodness of people. This weekend was meant to remind her that life was a ticket to a magic show.

So did Phil. Or, in his case, she should stop analyzing and just enjoy a boat ride later. Just a boat ride, that's all it was.

She was shaken from her thoughts by the light thud of a beach ball landing in her lap. It was followed by two little pudgy hands that scrambled to fetch it. The familiar soft touch of a child scorched Rachel. Merely two weeks ago she and Ellie had spent a joyful Sunday at the park before picking up her parents at the airport.

If only she could hug Ellie just one more time and tell her she loved her, that she would make things all right for both of them. That there would be no more Zoo Game. No matter what.

With a grin of pride on his face, Phil led Rachel to his sailboat. Above a thin blue strip on its side, the boat's name had been painted over in white.

"My partners and I are looking for a name," he answered her unasked question. He touched the shiny surface. "Got any ideas?

Ellie. Rachel smiled and said nothing.

A few moments later they were offshore, heading east in the bay that separated Fire Island from Long Island. Rachel leaned on the back rail and watched the swirling of choppy waters protesting with indignation as they closed on the gash the boat left in its wake.

"How do you like the Dave Matthews' Band?" Phil asked.

"I love 'Satellite' and 'Dancing Nancies.'"

He killed the engine and let the boat drift as he placed the CD in the player and turned it on. "You got one more choice. How about Bonnie Raitt?" He began to sing, "*I can't make you love me.* "

She laughed. "A multi-talented attorney."

"We all have more than one calling."

What was truly his? Lobbyist for children, Savior of Damsels in Distress.

They settled on the yellow vinyl-covered cushions. He popped open two beers— a Lite one for her.

"You think of everything." She laughed. Even the music could not have been his first choice. The Dave Matthews' Band and Bonnie Raitt were not the kind of music young men listened to.

Rachel took a swig from the beer then brought the can to her forehead, soaking her skin with the cool, moist beads. She responded to Phil's chatter. Soon, the connectedness of the night before was there, lying between them as if they had known each other a lifetime before.

When he restarted the engine and held the wheel with sure hands, she perched nearby. "This feels like a vacation," she said over the hum of the engine. "My father used to take us out on a boat on Lake Michigan, but my sister didn't take well to the waves."

"Your University of Michigan team broke my nose." Phil pointed to a small scar. "We played lacrosse against them four years ago. We won. I never got to retaliate because the following year I went to law school there."

Four years ago he had been a college senior? Rachel swallowed hard. He must be twenty-five. So much for her estimate that he was pushing thirty. Even Jacqueline couldn't make a case for a man nine years Rachel's junior. What was she doing on his boat?

Phil went aft to do something complicated with lines and knots. Rachel remained in her seat, looking straight ahead. The sun blazed in oranges and pinks. Sunset.

"I love you, Ellie," she whispered. "Are you too, watching the sunset now and thinking of our promise?" For all she knew, Ellie was not even in the same time zone. Where had her parents taken her? Couldn't they arrange for a meeting just once in a while?

Away from shore, Phil killed the engine again. Rachel heard the clanging of a wrench as he checked something. He dropped anchor and let the boat roll on water slashed open by the passing of other boats, then came over and leaned on the rail next to Rachel. For a while, in the soft gurgle of the lapping water, it felt as though the two of them were the sole witnesses in the world to the blaze of whipped pinks coating the pile of clouds on the horizon.

She felt his physical presence next to her, the hair on his bare arm igniting the fuzz on hers. Gerald had been out of her life for only a month, and she was feeling sexual hunger.

This was all wrong, forbidden and exciting.

CHAPTER TWENTY-FOUR

MINUTES after Rachel entered her office, the phone rang. When Jacqueline failed to answer it after the fourth ring, Rachel picked it up.

"Did you see this morning's *City Post*?" Erica Norgard breathed into the phone.

"Why?" The automatic pilot in Rachel's heart gave a lurch. "I never do. What now?"

"Get it and call me back right away."

She rushed out of her office, but stopped short. At Jacqueline's desk, her friend's figure was doubled over.

"Jacques, Gosh. Again?" It had been a while since Jacqueline's endometriosis had been so excruciatingly painful.

"I'll be fine in a few minutes. I've taken something—"

"Take the day off. Can I get you a cab?"

Jacqueline straightened up. Her forehead glistened with sweat. "Let's wait," she said. For once, her voice was weak.

"I'll be right back." Rachel hurried down to the newsstand.

She stood by the kiosk's newspaper display and stared, stupefied, at a picture of Ellie. The blood pounded in her temples as she read, under the byline of David Lupori, the heart-wrenching story of a father, a famous surgeon, who was searching for his daughter. If Rachel didn't know any better, she would have sympathized with the father's public appeal for help in locating the child he so loved....

Since when did a father who'd missed three visits merit coverage in a major newspaper? Even for the *City Post*, a newspaper that attracted readers by offering them sensational journalism, this reporting was going overboard. Yes, Wes must have hired a PR agency.

Back at the office, Jacqueline, a quizzical look on her face, handed Rachel a couple of messages from reporters asking for her reaction.

Rachel screwed the pink notes into a ball, and tossed them into the wastebasket. She was damned if she would play Wes's publicity game. "How are you feeling?"

"I'll just take it easy today." Jacqueline looked at the ball of pink messages. "I'll order you a cell phone."

"Wait a couple of generations. I can't carry a two-pounder in my handbag only to be frustrated that it doesn't work most of the time," Rachel said.

She fetched Jacqueline a cup of coffee and retreated to her office, where she dialed Erica's number.

Her heart still thumped hard. "This is incredible, though I shouldn't be surprised. Wes has built an entire practice on hype. He knows how to draw every arrow in his quiver."

"We'll respond with a counterattack. Today is the day you're moving from defense to offense. I'll have Lou Kaplan call you."

"Lou Kaplan? You know him? He's too big for this."

"That's who I want behind you. You'll tell him your story—and Ellie's. This is a war in which we'll take no prisoners. Your ex wants publicity? He'll get the kind that will make him want to crawl into a hole."

"What about Ellie? It can't possibly be good for her—"

"Rachel, you have to win. You'd better toughen up and be willing to fight in whatever arena Wes chooses, with whatever weapons it takes—or get out of the game."

"I hate the direction this is taking. Do you want me to splash all over the newspaper what I found in Ellie's genitals?"

"Isn't that the crime we're accusing Wes of?"

Pensively, Rachel laid down the receiver in its cradle. She glanced toward the reporters' crumpled pink messages in the wastebasket. Would a child someplace taunt Ellie about it? How would Ellie ever live it down?

Before noon, Vince popped his head in. "Good news. Hadfield got the Baroness account."

Hadfield got it? With Jacqueline's warning echoing in her head, Rachel struggled to keep her voice pleasant. "How did it come about?"

"He played golf Saturday with the head of the Baroness advertising team at BRT&G. The group liked the Sheridan magazine package."

"Great. Hadfield thought I—we—aced the presentation—"

"Don't get on your soap box, reminding me you personally flew all the way to Chicago and delivered the presentation."

"Oh, no, why should I?" Rachel smiled sweetly but could no longer keep the reins on her indignation. "Not if my developing the concept from start to finish had nothing to do with our getting the account. But it would have made me feel good if you just pretended I did."

He threw his arms in the air in a gesture indicating she was hopeless and walked out.

Forget the promotion. Jacqueline had been right; she should start interviewing.

On the return trip from a late afternoon meeting, Rachel's taxi got stuck in the crawling traffic, its air conditioning out of order. The late-July air was hot and sticky, and she felt her dress clinging to her skin, the light mauve turning purple in the wet spots.

Outside the Sheridan building, a man with a bunched-up face arranged around ruby lips accosted her. When she pushed into the swivel door, he squeezed in with her.

Wedged between him and the glass, she recoiled. "Sir?" She pushed the door faster.

The smacking of lips revealed the man as the one who had called her and whose article she had read earlier. David Lupori. As she escaped on the other end of the revolving door, he produced a camera. Rachel lifted her briefcase to shield her face and moved on. Surely, Erica hadn't meant she should cooperate with the enemy. Lupori was in Wes's camp.

Jacqueline's face was still pale, but her posture, as she stood with elbows resting on her computer monitor, was easy.

"You look like something the cat dragged in." Jacqueline said. With the familiar twinkle in her eyes, she pointed to a magnificent arrangement of exotic flowers Rachel could not name. "From Baroness. Worth at least two hundred bucks. Oh, yes, and Vince asked to see you as soon as you're back."

"If I could just shower first." Rachel's spirits lifted up two notches. If Vince wouldn't praise her for landing the biggest piece of new business of the year, at least her client commended her for a job well done.

In two minutes, she brushed her hair, dabbed powder on her shiny nose, and fixed her lipstick. She threw on a raw silk jacket to cover her disheveled dress, squared her shoulders, and marched to Vince's office.

The spacious room overlooked Park Avenue. From the large windows, the Avenue seemed deceptively cool and crisp in its display of blooming flowers stretching away. The new office decor told Rachel that Vince would soon be promoted from an advertising director to a publisher's position, which meant that another manager—perhaps even two—would be inserted in between the two of them. Not a moment too soon. It would be her chance to hit it off with a new boss.

Artwork from the Sheridan Museum hung over mahogany paneling. Leonard Fields, the displaced publisher who had been kicked upstairs, was married to a talented designer whose work was often featured in *Architectural Digest*. Rumor had it that for each Sheridan office assignment she received, Ms. Fields rewarded that publisher by decorating his residence at no charge. Judging by the way Fields clung to his pseudo-job, which included a new car every other year, country club dues, an expense account, and probably a generous pension fund, the couple was paid handsomely.

Vince gave Rachel a warm grin. "I saw the gorgeous flowers from Baroness," he said. "Well deserved." He closed the door and touched her shoulder in his sure, friendly way. He motioned to the couch. "I wanted to talk to you. Take a seat."

Had he come around at long last? With pleasant anticipation, Rachel lowered herself down and found her body sinking low, too low. Vince towered over her from his spot on a hard-upholstered chair across the coffee table.

Power seating. The man used every trick in the book to unsettle his opponent. He had something up his sleeve.

He left her no time for guessing. "We're very disturbed by this morning's *City Post* report." His eyes bore into hers. "Is it true?"

Jolted, she looked at him. "Which part?"

"Any of it."

Rachel moved to perch on the edge of the couch. The tone of his question placed him in the enemy camp. Why should it be any of his business as long as she did her job well?

"They glossed over the fact that my former husband sexually abused our daughter," she replied slowly, still reeling from the turn of events. "They outright dismissed my evidence—"

Vince shook his head from side to side. "Rachel, Rachel, Rachel."

She winced inside. "What?"

"Don't you see? We can't allow any of our employees to drag *Women's Life*'s name into anything that is scandalous."

The blood rushed to her head. "I beg your pardon?"

"We're a family magazine. A publication for homemakers, wholesome living. You know the editorial content: traditional. No articles about divorce, no high-powered career women unless they leave it to stand by their husbands' side. I don't need to tell you that; you do a fine job articulating it to advertisers."

"Vince, I fail to see the connection between my personal problems and the editorial policy of *Women's Life*. If anything, maybe it's time they woke up on the twelfth floor and recognized that both divorce and child abuse exist in the land of the free and the home of the brave."

"This is not for you and me to decide. The issue here is that I do not want an employee dragging *Women's Life*'s name—"

"I am not the one who gave the interview!"

"That's irrelevant. I don't want our employees dragging us into anything as tasteless as this morning's article."

She heard her voice skirting the edges of her fury. "Tasteless? Vince, I did not pose in the nude for a *Playboy* centerfold. Sexual abuse is many things, but 'tasteless' is not one of them."

He held her gaze and let a moment pass, then two.

Did Wes's colleagues shun him for it, too?

"To set the record straight, *Women's Life* wasn't mentioned." She heard the defensiveness in her words. "Only my name as the mother of Ellie Belmore and the former wife of Dr. Wesley Belmore."

"Can you guarantee me that your place of employment won't be mentioned should this escalate? I don't think so."

If he only knew. Lou Kaplan's story would appear in *The New York Times* tomorrow or the day after. Rachel bit her lip and said nothing.

He leaned forward and placed his elbows on his knees. "I suggest you take a leave of absence until this—this thing calms down."

"Vince, I can't afford an unpaid leave of absence. Besides, time off wouldn't circumvent the magazine's name being mentioned as my place of employment." It dawned on her. In order for his idea to work, the leave of absence must turn into an indefinite layoff.

She was being fired!

Fear welled up in the center of her chest. She kept her mouth shut. Let him say it.

"I'll tell you what," he said. "You still have two weeks' vacation coming. We'll give you two more weeks' pay."

Her mouth went dry. Yes, it was severance. The mess wouldn't clear in two weeks and Vince knew it.

She controlled the shaking that radiated to her limbs. In an even tone she said, "Here's what I suggest. Hold on to your offer until I speak to my lawyer, okay?"

"I hope you are not threatening us, are you?"

"Oh, no, why should I?" She scrambled to her feet and tossed her hair back, looking down at him. "There's no reason to. As I understand your offer, you want me to take a paid leave for one month, part of it being my vacation time. After that I can return to the same job, with the same clients, at the same terms and benefits as I now have, right?"

He gazed at her, his brows knotted.

She had him. Now they were playing the same game. "Vince, I need to get this new arrangement in writing. You know, for Human Resources. I'll never hear the end of it if they don't have it on file." It would be documented along with her quarterly evaluations signed by both him and the publisher, giving her top marks in every category.

And what would it serve? One more battlefront? She had no energy to fight it. She could win a lawsuit of unlawful dismissal, but what would it accomplish? The right to work with heartless colleagues?

CHAPTER TWENTY-FIVE

TUESDAY morning, Vince stepped into Rachel's office, unsmiling, and dropped an open issue of *The New York Times* on her desk.

She did not need to look at Lou Kaplan's article to see the section Vince had circled in yellow, with *Women's Life*'s name underlined in red marker.

Vince's tone, though, was calm, as though he had given up on her. "Why drag us through the mud?"

"My ex did. I only responded."

"Why don't you just settle with him?"

"How do you suggest I do that? Allow him to molest our daughter only once a week instead of three?"

"I'm sure it's not that bad, Rachel. You tend to make a big deal out of things. You're too intense. Maybe this business has gone too far.... Relax a bit, will you? Let's have a drink after work. We'll talk outside the office."

After he left, Rachel dropped his marked paper into the wastebasket. A minute later she retrieved it and tucked it in her briefcase. If *Women's Life* was building a case against her, she would need every scrap of evidence to counter it and prove their motives.

For the rest of the day, Jacqueline fielded her phone calls. Someone managed to get through by introducing himself as a representative of Frederick's of Hollywood, which Jacqueline mistook for an advertiser. He discussed their line of lingerie and described the designs and special fit. It took Rachel a few moments of listening before he asked for her bra and panty sizes and she understood that this was not a prospective advertiser but rather an obscene call. It struck her how articulate the man was. The worst of humanity could be endowed with the gift of gab. As was Wes.

She perused the article again. Lou Kaplan's writing was sensitive and powerful, though at times overly dramatic. The bold headline on page three must have been the editor's touch. MOTHER CHARGES FAMOUS SURGEON EX OF MOLESTING THEIR FIVE-YEAR-OLD DAUGHTER. Describing the series of debacles by the court system and Child Protective Services, the piece included legal explanation by Erica. A professor at New York Law School, supposedly unbiased, was interviewed. He criticized the "equipoise" ruling and its application in such a case. His subtext was that of outrage.

Rachel put the paper aside. The details of her convoluted journey through the legal maze read like a surrealistic tale, no longer hers. Her life had been stolen, packed in a box, and carried away.

Would Judge McGillian see it? His views of this write-up couldn't possibly be sanguine. In a sidebar to the main feature, another writer reported the case of the young Korean teenager whose abortion McGillian had prohibited. According to all legal opinions, he had overstepped his jurisdiction. The quick image of the girl at the end of her TV interview flashed through Rachel's mind, clicking into place along with the letters to the editor she had read and Erica's mention of it.

For a split second Rachel wondered what Phil's opinion of the article was. She wished they could speak on the phone. He wouldn't discuss the trial with her even if it was this very case that had drawn them together. It hung unspoken over their new friendship.

Rachel canceled all her client meetings. Anyone who read the newspaper would not be listening to her presentation, thus fulfilling Vince's prophesy: the publicity had affected her work.

Her in box was empty. No trace either of Vince's offer of a leave of absence or a letter from Human Resources. For all she knew, she could go to court tomorrow, Wednesday, taking it as another vacation day—but it would not mark the start of her new employment terms.

Ortman had managed to secure the new court appearance with unusual speed. Perhaps, when it came to trying a case in Nassau County, her Manhattan lawyer was at a disadvantage.

Erica called again. "What are you doing for lunch?"

"Why do I get the feeling you have plans for me?"

"You're going to speak at 'The Women's Coalition for Child Protection' luncheon. They'll squeeze you in for a fifteen-minute recap—"

"Erica! It's out of the question."

"What's your objection?"

Rachel put her hand on her forehead, scouring for a reply. None came.

"Get going, then," Erica said. "You'd better get used to it, because you have to find more groups to speak to."

Rachel pushed herself away from her desk and gathered her handbag. "I'll be back after lunch," she told Jacqueline.

"Hold it," Jacqueline said. "Here's something to cheer you up." She handed her a copy of *Advertising Age*.

"Time Inc. Launches Liliana Magazine," the headline read.

"How's that for landing on your feet?" Jacqueline's voice sounded as though she were licking honey.

"Good for her," Rachel said. "And a new competitor in the beauty magazine field."

"You don't get it," Jacqueline whispered. "Talk to her about a job. She'll grab you for a sales director position. Double your salary, I'm sure."

Rachel looked at her. "Thanks. It's a thought." She pivoted, then turned back. "Jacques, what women's groups are we associated with?"

"The Fashion Group, Cosmetics Executive Women, Advertising Women of New York."

"I mean more civic or political in nature. League of Women Voters, NOW.... I need to schedule speaking engagements."

Jacqueline's eyes shone with glee. "Right up my alley."

"You can't do it on company time. You're on notice now, remember? I've already got you in enough trouble."

Jacqueline shrugged.

Rachel made it to the luncheon on time. She had no idea what she would say once she took the podium.

"Don't be so jittery," Erica whispered. "You must be used to speaking to client groups."

"That's business. This one's about Ellie's life."

"Just tell your story."

For Ellie. Rachel rose to her feet. "I used to be someone else. Then one night, my life, slowly circling in its orbit, collided with an asteroid. My world screeched to a halt. A split second later, it jerked forward on a new course...."

Fifteen minutes passed quickly. Rachel sat down to a round of applause, feeling dazed, surprised at the reception, at the outpouring of love from strangers. She nodded, shook hands, and smiled, unable to see the faces of her well-wishers through the mist that coated her eyes.

On her way back to the office, she walked down Park Avenue—for a change, at a slow pace. She was in no hurry to get anywhere other than to curl up into a cave deep in her own center. What better place to be alone than in the midst of hundreds of people brushing past her?

She scanned the flowerbeds splitting the avenue. Each block flaunted a different variety, thickly planted and well tended. An urban-style competition. Tilting her face away from traffic fumes, Rachel breathed in. Once, twice. From around the corner came a whiff of a bakery mingled with the scent of flowers. At times, Manhattan air in the open spaces had a deceptively clean smell when the midday summer heat did not cook the garbage in the uncollected plastic bags. Only her hair, when she washed it at night, would tell of the car exhaust that clung to it.

Time for a little game she hadn't played in a long while. Count her blessings. Rachel looked up at the building that towered majestically over Park Avenue. She could not place Vince's windows, behind which a long hallway led to her own office.

One. More than a job paying about eighty-five thousand dollars a year with commissions, she had a career that no one could take away. She had made it in New York, the center of the world. She ticked it off on her fingers. Two, she had her health—all her limbs, senses, faculties, and the sum of it all—her stamina. And she had good looks. It was a gift, her mother had said, to cherish but not to exploit. In New York it was definitely an asset. She had supportive parents, both in good health. And she had wonderful, devoted friends. And she had Ellie, wherever she was, and Ellie would grow up in safety.

She looked down at her right hand, all the fingers expanded, plus one out on her left. Six would do. She felt a shade of a smile quirk the corners of her lips.

At the glass-enclosed lobby of the Lever Brothers' building Rachel stopped to view an art show. After a moment's hesitation, she pushed the revolving doors, stood inside, and scanned the sculptures. She moved slowly from one to the next, savoring them with her eyes, feeling them as though she had one more internal organ designated by nature to make the stone, wood, plaster, and brass come alive and tell her its story. Rounding a corner, one of the pieces caught her eye. She walked toward it, transfixed, pulled by signals transmitted straight into her brain. She stopped and laid her hand on the cool marble, a strangely speckled green with a pink vein twisting and running through its side. Her fingers traced the larger figure of the two intertwined bodies. The arms of the larger one arched protectively, like a bird's wings, over the smaller, less defined figure. Rachel touched the little head.

She lowered her eyes to the brass caption but knew the name before she read the words: "Mother and Child."

"Beautiful, isn't it?" a voice came from behind her. "It's a rare stone from the Urals."

"I'll take it," Rachel cut the saleswoman off in a hoarse whisper.

In the evening, in spite of her resolve to hang onto positive thoughts, Rachel ruminated about her dwindling financial resources. Sitting on the carpet in the living room and using her coffee table as a desk, she sifted through her bank statement and a stack of unpaid bills. As she wrote checks for electricity, cable, insurance, telephone, and garbage collection, she became increasingly aware that she must give serious consideration to selling the house. In a month, schools would reopen, and anyone wanting to enroll their children before September must complete the move. To get the best market value, she must sell the house very soon.

The phone rang. Relieved for the break, Rachel answered it.

"Have you heard from Mom and Dad?" Josie asked.

"Uh-uh. What about you?"

"I had a message on my answering machine. They're traveling and can't be reached," Josie replied. Her tone was meandering, lacking its usual edginess.

Rachel fished for words that would not arouse Josie's hackles. "I liked your painting."

"How's Ellie?" Josie asked.

"Fine, thanks," Rachel replied, perplexed at the sudden concern. Her sister was so unpredictable.

"Listen, Rachel. No hard feelings." Josie's exaggerated inflections suggested practice, the kind one received at a psychiatric hospital before being released to society. "I'd like her to come play here tomorrow."

Like a swimmer being hit by an unexpected wave, Rachel was startled. "You mean Ellie?" she asked.

"Do you have another daughter?" Josie's giggled. "The kids are asking about her. They didn't get to play that day."

The normalcy of the conversation, so unnatural for Josie, unsettled Rachel. "Ellie has this summer program. Besides, I'm working and can't drive her over," Rachel said. Even if Ellie were around she would not have sent her there alone. "Thanks anyway. Give us a rain check."

"I can pick her up any time. What about later this week or the weekend?"

Rachel clutched at her throat. "Let me call you back."

After she hung up, she sank into the couch and let out a puff of air upward, feeling her bangs rise.

The unpaid bills file on the table demanded her attention. Decisions needed to be made. She should search the Yellow Pages for a realtor and at least get the house appraised. Where would she go if she sold it?

A new loneliness enveloped her; pliable, but like a fishnet, it bound her. The empty house seemed to sigh around her. She paced the floor for a while. Then, acquiescently, she sat on her living room couch, nursing a Scotch—a new habit she must shake off—and stared at a blank spot on the wall.

No more Zoo Game.

A knock on the front door made her sit up. She gulped down one more sip of her Scotch. The cold ice and the hot, bitter liquid fought for dominance in her mouth. She let them spread through her stomach. As a second knock sounded, she languorously raised herself off the couch.

Through the fisheye lens of the peephole, she peered at a flattened face but could not, at first, place the dark straight hair and enlarged, blue-gray eye that returned her stare. Then it hit her. Phil.

Phil? She opened the door.

"Hi," he said, in a tone that Rachel was getting to recognize as part of his sunny demeanor. He waved a small package in his hand. "I was in the neighborhood."

She felt her jaw drop but could not find the right question to ask.

"I got a great movie at your library. Want to watch? 'My Life as a Dog.' It's Swedish; it's about a kid—"

Her voice returned. "Phil, I don't think it's a good idea for you to be here."

"It may also be an excellent idea. Depends on how you look at it."

"Is that so?"

"As 'a Savior of Damsels in Distress,' I'm here to find out whether you are, by any chance, distressed?"

His smile sent tingling sensations down her spine.

She tugged at her T-shirt. There was no reason for her to wallow in misery; the worst was behind her. Ellie was safe. The rest was only legal battles whose consequences no longer mattered. She shook her head. "I—I don't know."

"Well, then. If you'd rather I go, I'll leave the cassette here and go home to watch another one all by my lonely self." He gave her a mischievous look. "I'd rather watch it on your VCR, though. What are you drinking?" He peered over her shoulder at the coffee table in the living room.

"Uh, Scotch." She shifted her weight from one foot to the other and stepped back to let him in. "Want some?"

"Any beer?"

In the kitchen she leaned her forehead on the cold enamel of the refrigerator door.

This was insane. She should send him home right now. Yet a quickening of glee some-where inside her told her otherwise.

From the living room, she heard Phil fuss with her VCR. A moment later, the crackling and popping sounds of changing TV channels announced that he'd started it working.

"Statistics show that seventy percent of all VCR owners can't figure out how to operate them," she called out from the kitchen.

"It's simple. Just read the instructions," he called back.

A small laugh escaped her lips. "That's what the other thirty percent say."

Opening the refrigerator door, she reached for a beer and felt a tug at her stomach. She had forgotten altogether about the business of eating. She scrutinized the contents of the refrigerator and the pantry but found nothing more palatable than cheese and crackers to carry into the living room.

Phil was seated on the couch, a framed photograph of Ellie in his hands.

"She's beautiful," he said, and continued to examine the picture. Rachel peered over his shoulder at the picture that came back to life each time she looked at it. Ellie sat at a small desk, her crayons and brushes scattered about, her sweet face smiling at the camera, unaware that paint smudged her cheek and her ponytail was askew.

Rachel threw a glance at Phil. The intensity in his eyes was that of someone in pain. He continued to gaze at the picture as though it were a crystal ball. Gently, Rachel extracted it from his hand and placed it back on the lamp table.

He took in a deep breath and clicked the remote. "Ready?"

She settled at the other end of the couch, her elbow resting against its wide arm, and tucked her legs under her.

"You can put your feet up if you want." She nodded toward the coffee table.

He removed his sneakers, revealing the whitest of socks. She liked neatness in a man. She turned her head away but felt his presence nearby, as a faint, now almost familiar spicy aftershave hung in the air above her. Or was it the zooming about of atoms that electrified the empty space between them?

An hour passed. "Press the pause button," she said. "I'll get us a refill."

"Any pretzels?"

"Nope. Sorry. No junk food because of Ellie. Only carrots."

"Did you have dinner?"

She hesitated. "I have a couple of frozen steaks we can barbecue."

"Great. About forty-five more minutes?"

When she returned with the drinks, she plopped down again, this time in the center of the sofa.

She wished she could lean against his chest.

Damn you, Gerald, for leaving me. And at a time like this.

The movie over, Rachel was surprised to see Phil's misted eyes reflecting her own. His open smile embarrassed her. The sensitive male, for sure.

"This movie falls in the 'good idea' category after all," she said. "Thanks."

"I'm ready for that steak if your offer still stands."

He followed her to the kitchen. She defrosted the steaks in the microwave, then threw in a couple of potatoes. "How about Campbell's alphabet chicken soup?" she asked.

"Any canned peas?" He stuck his head in the pantry and pulled out a can of tomato soup. "I'll make you a delicious French tomato soup."

With Jacqueline's French accent, Rachel said, laughing, "Campbell's?"

He heated the soup and added milk. "My special recipe. Let it boil for a minute." He took a wooden spoon and brought it to Rachel's lips.

"You're full of surprises," she said, salvaging some leaves from a head of lettuce and tearing them up into a salad.

"You ain't seen nothing yet." Phil tapped the end of an imaginary cigar. A moment later he stepped out to the patio with the steaks he had seasoned and barbecued them on the grill.

Rachel had welcomed the feeling of camaraderie the dinner preparation brought, but sitting down to eat, her desire to talk vanished, as though something in her had evaporated. There were no words worth uttering, no thoughts worth expressing. A cloud of bewilderment over tomorrow's hastily scheduled hearing choked her.

If he had noticed her mood change, Phil made no mention of it. "I took a French film course as one of my electives. Saw most of François Truffaut's films. And I wrote a paper about La Cage Aux Folles, comparing four different productions."

He continued to talk, but Rachel kept her eyes downcast. "Sorry," she finally said, "I'm too upset to make conversation."

"That's okay," he responded, his eyes soft on her. "Don't worry about it." He got up and carried the dishes to the sink and loaded the dishwasher.

They cleaned up without exchanging a word. When they were done, she walked him to the door, hoping he wouldn't leave, afraid of the emptiness yet having nothing but her depression to offer.

They stood in the dark foyer. Dim light poured from the living room. She could smell his fresh skin. Phil reached up his hand and touched a stray curl on her cheek then moved it away but kept his fingers laced in her hair. She covered his hand with hers, then lifted her face.

They stood frozen, silent, for a few moments, then he bent toward her. His lips on her neck sent shock waves through her, landing with a thud deep inside her. Without disengaging his contact with her skin, Phil's lips moved up and across her cheek, until they reached her partially opened mouth. There he stopped, his lips almost touching hers, awaiting her signal. She closed the quarter-inch distance. They kissed hard and long, their lips and tongues hungrily searching. Rachel's breathing came in short intakes and she pressed her body against his.

"Feeling better?" he asked.

A moan escaped the depths of her throat as she felt his hardness against her. His arms reached around her and he brought her even closer, holding her tight.

She must be losing her mind; she should send him home. But there was no going back. She wanted him. Now.

"Would you like me to stay?" he whispered, his face buried in her hair, the fingers of one hand brushing the fuzz at the back of her neck, the other hand holding her buttocks, pressing her toward his thigh. "Say yes."

"Oh, yes." The words came out muffled. She wouldn't think just now. Only feel him. Let him fill the void, chase away the depression that spread in the dark cavity that was her entire being.

Once they got upstairs, anxiety suddenly washed over her. She didn't know what to expect from her own impetuous abandonment. She had never given herself to casual sex even if this moment felt right.

"Phil, this is so unexpected—" she whispered, feeling shy as he fumbled with her clothes.

"We'll make it great," he murmured into her open mouth.

She shut her eyes and let herself be swept up again. He planted small kisses on her exposed body, then tenderly laid her on the bed, changing pace. His urgency now restrained, he began to study her body expertly, methodically. He knew it yet his fingers were learning it with awe, as though he were discovering a woman's curves for the first time. His hands did not merely caress her skin, they memorized her lines with the sensitive touch of an artist.

She arched toward him when he placed his face between her legs and allowed his tongue to navigate his way around her folds. Little darts of pleasure shot through her and she moved rhythmically against him. After a while, she lifted her head.

"Are you waiting for me to beg?" she asked in a raspy voice. She reached her arms up.

"You'll never have to." He hovered over her for a moment, looking deep into her eyes before he joined her, filling her with a feeling of raw exhilaration.

From somewhere far away, a woman groaned and screamed, and Rachel realized it had been she. As though in a trance in some ancient dance, Phil rocked inside her, inserting and pulling himself with precision, each time carrying her higher for yet another spin on a spiral of new sensations. When she thought she could bear it no more, he gyrated his pelvis in small, minute circles and brought her to a series of climaxes.

"A Savior of Damsels in Distress," she said, laughing, when at last they lay spent, their bodies wet with each other's perspiration. She felt a rush of luxuriant delight.

"Not too often, I can assure you." In the dim light a smile flickered across his face.

She raised herself on her arm, leaned over, and kissed him hard on the mouth. "My, those lucky coeds."

He traced her nose with his finger. "I've been with only one woman."

"You're serious?"

"I kid you not. My childhood sweetheart."

"Where is she?"

"We just broke up."

Rachel fell silent. So he was getting over a girlfriend. Although he hadn't been a candidate for a relationship, she would rather have known. She tried to brush aside the mild disappointment—her mind too tired to feel. As she stirred and started to get up, Phil put a gentle hand on her hip.

"Don't leave yet," he said.

"I—I— Your timing sounds too convenient— I'm not up to being the transitional woman."

"I want to keep seeing you."

"Phil, for some funny reason, I feel I'm in kindergarten."

"I was hoping you wouldn't bring up the age issue. You're special."

"To think that I'm in competition with a cute little thing…." Rachel could just hear Jacqueline's shriek of triumph if she gathered the courage to tell they had sex—a detail she wasn't about to disclose. "And I'm not up to healing broken hearts."

"Chill out. Mine ain't broken. Or it's already fixed as of this past weekend." He pulled her back toward him. "What makes you think I'm taking us—you—lightly?"

She was overreacting. She let her head drop back on the pillow. "Okay, Phil. I know men find me attractive, but why have *you* pursued me?"

His fingers touched her cheek in the tenderest of caresses, in a touch of untapped love.

"I want to give you an honest answer," he said, his voice feathery against her cheek, "but you may not understand it and I won't be able to explain it yet."

"Try me," she whispered.

"The Mother Who Protects Her Child."

CHAPTER TWENTY-SIX

McGillian rubbed his eyes. Ortman began his oral argument. The ceiling fan hummed. Every few seconds, it came to a rhythmic halt accompanied by a scratchy sound.

Rachel watched the familiar scene with detachment. Her body was hardly aware of the contours of the wooden seat. As though her spirit hovered right below the fan, she observed the proceedings. Things could not get worse. Not with Erica now at her side.

"Your Honor, the child has disappeared. Against last week's final ruling, Ellie has been unavailable for visitation," Ortman said. "Her schooling's been interrupted—in keeping with the mother's capricious treatment of her daughter's education—"

"Mr. Ortman is pontificating," Erica called out.

McGillian turned to her and said in a bored tone, "Counselor, where is the child?"

"In a safe place where she won't be sexually abused, Judge."

His brow shot up. "May I remind you that the father has a right to know the whereabouts of his daughter?"

"My client is acting in full consciousness in this matter," Erica replied.

"Ms. Norgard, have you instructed your client to reveal to the father—and to the court—where the child is?"

"Yes, Your Honor. My client believes that any contact with Dr. Belmore would be detrimental to Ellie."

Ortman got up. "We think Ellie was taken out of the country. The mother's parents are vagabonds of sorts. They have family all over the world."

"I object to that characterization, Your Honor," Erica said. "The mother's parents are retired, distinguished professionals. The father was a dentist and the mother's still a concert pianist."

The judge turned to Erica again. "My dear Ms. Norgard—"

She cut him off. "Your Honor, I respectfully request to be addressed as either 'Counselor' or 'Ms. Norgard' unless you would also address Mr. Ortman as 'My dear?'"

"Yes, of course, Ms. Norgard," Judge McGillian replied in a tight voice. "It is not incumbent upon the father to prove where the child is. The mother must produce her for visitation. Will she or won't she follow this court's ruling?"

"Your Honor, given the aggravated recent history of sexual molestation—"

"Ms. Norgard, we are not here to retry the case. If you want to appeal my ruling of last week, I'm sure you know how to go about it."

He would order Ellie into foster care, Rachel was certain of it. It would make no difference now. She looked behind her, where several women, representing women's groups invited by Erica, sat still. At the far end of the courtroom she noticed David Lupori and a few other journalists whose job was to prey on human misery for the public's entertainment. For all she knew, Wes's publicist was among them, having fed them lies.

Erica stood unmoving, erect.

McGillian continued, "The court has determined that the father will have daytime visits. Have you explained to your client the possible consequences of defying the court?"

"Yes, Your Honor, I have."

The judge turned to Rachel. "Do you understand that any failure to make your daughter available to her father for the set visitation times will put you in contempt of court?"

She looked at him, all her hopes distilled in her eyes. "Your Honor, I don't want to sound disrespectful, but it is my unshakable belief that Wes Belmore has molested our daughter. The 'equipoise' statement of this court has found a fifty percent chance of this having taken place. I can't allow anything further to happen until such time as my appeal is heard at the Appellate Division." Her voice broke down with the last words. "Your Honor, how can you place a five-year-old in a situation where you know there's a fifty percent chance she'd be molested?"

"You've made those allegations before, Ms. Belmore." He leaned forward. "The court has given them serious consideration and has determined the evidence was inconclusive. Unproven accusations are not facts. Nevertheless, to accommodate your fears, I've cut overnight visitation—"

"Judge, Wes—Dr. Belmore—would molest Ellie any time of the day."

"We will not debate this question any further." McGillian crossed his fingers and lay his knotted hands on the table. "Will you, or will you not, produce her?"

Rachel shook her head a couple of times. "I will not, Your Honor," she said, her voice trembling. Then she added, "I'm sorry, I can't."

"I have to find you in contempt of court." He looked hard at her, then turned to Erica. "Ms. Norgard, please take a few minutes to talk this over with your client. Make sure she understands that should she again fail to cooperate, she'll be jailed until such time as she purges herself of her contempt by delivering the child to the plaintiff."

"I ask the court to exercise restraint," Erica replied, "by affording the defendant the opportunity to avoid incarceration."

"It's up to your client. Warnings have been issued many times—she has been fined, too—but she has continuously refused to comply with the visitation orders. Talk to her."

"Yes, Your Honor, I will."

"Make it clear that I'll have her incarcerated as of today if she continues in her stubborn defiance of court orders. We've exhausted all other venues."

"You knew it all along," Erica said to Rachel in the corridor. "You've been so determined. Now it's happening."

"It wouldn't have happened if McGillian weren't so heartless; if he cared about Ellie—"

"Rachel, it's here and now. You're going to jail. Your decision."

Rachel hung her head. This was not possible. "Let's go back in," she said. "Let's get it over with."

Erica's lanky figure, hugged her a bit awkwardly. "I didn't think you'd change your mind."

A few minutes later, the judge's words reverberated, "Please escort Ms. Belmore to Jefferson Correction Facility." His formidable voice did not reach Rachel; maybe she only read his lips. His arm raised the gavel and let it drop silently on the wooden tray.

Sounds continued to swell around her, but they seemed far away. From a huge distance, she heard the mounting buzz of the women in the back rows of the court-room.

Jacqueline pushed closer. Her hand reached out across the two guards, her olive complexion pale, her dark eyes shining like burnished coal. "I'll bring your clothes," she called out.

Rachel stood, her mind numb, as the handcuffs clicked around her wrists. She caught a glimpse of Phil at his small table to her left, his face frozen. She was certain he wanted to rescue her, to take her in his arms and make her forget as he had done the night before. He cared.

Her body shook. What made her think she had been prepared for this? One by one, the lights in her emotional rooms shut down with this latest assault. As a guard snapped the handcuffs to Rachel's waist belt, outrage, fear, and humiliation settled over her, heavier than the cold metal shackles.

Two guards took each of her elbows and steered her forward. The sour sweat of one of them was pungent. Rachel turned her head away, but kept her gaze down.

As the Nassau County sheriff's van sped through the streets to the county jail, she sat alone, staring, unseeing, through the gratings on the windows, her mind floating into a blank space.

Upon arrival, Rachel was fingerprinted, photographed, and strip-searched. She forced her thoughts to remain detached, and they did—until the icy water of the shower hit the length of her bare skin.

And then they took her clothes—her business suit, her high heels, her jewelry, her toiletry kit—leaving her with only the pair of jeans and T-shirt Jacqueline had just brought. At least she didn't have to wear a prison uniform. She was a criminal, but of a different category than those locked up for robbery.

She walked through the recreation room and down a wide corridor, a guard by her side. The inmates bombarded her with sullen stares, jeers, and shouts of contempt that broke through a distant cotton fog.

And then she heard the hollow clang of metal announcing her arrival in her new home—a prison cell of concrete and steel.

PART III

LIVES IN ORBIT

CHAPTER TWENTY-SEVEN

IN the jail cafeteria, Rachel edged her way at the end of the long line. Her eyes burned and every joint in her body ached from the sleepless night on a hard, narrow cot. Although the cell had seemed clean enough, the hot air was permeated with ripe odors of disinfectant, sour bread, and sweat that clung to her hair and clothes.

Someone elbowed her hard in the back. She turned and stared into the face of a large, toothless white woman with sallow skin, darkened in places by pigmentation. Her hair, bleached blond, sprouted five inches of light brown roots. Her foul breath caught Rachel's nostrils. Rachel recoiled, but was instantly sorry for showing her disgust.

The woman let out a malicious laugh. Behind her, the other women watched the scene with rapt attention. "So? What are you here for, Intellectual Cunt? Tried to kill your professor?"

Rachel turned away, swallowing tears that had been stubbornly gathering at the back of her throat ever since she had come out of her emotional coma last night. She had not allowed herself the release of crying. Crying had a way of dragging her further into depths of despair. She needed her strength, or to salvage what was left of it.

This is better than having Ellie molested, she had told herself during the night. *No more Zoo Game*, she whispered as she hugged herself against the chill she felt despite the heat in her cell. For each week in jail, she would save Ellie two or three visits in Wes's bed.

The woman shoved her hard again. "What's the matter, whore, swallowed your tongue? We can get it out, right girls?" With a vicious guffaw, she turned again to the group and orchestrated a chuckle from some of them. She touched Rachel's hair and twirled a curl around her finger. "She's mine, girls," she called out loud. Looking back at Rachel, she said, "One good push up your inte-lec-tual cunt and your mouth opens. Can't wait for that pink tongue on my pussy."

Fear lodged in the pit of Rachel's stomach. A new danger rose in front of her, like an approaching hurricane, and she had no idea how to stave it off.

She stopped in front of a large server filled with scrambled eggs. From behind the counter, a prisoner brought up the ladle to scoop the gooey yellow mix. Rachel had thought she was hungry—she hadn't been able to touch dinner the night before—but the greasy smell was nauseating.

"No, thank you," she said in a feeble voice, and moved on.

"Hear that newbie, girls?" The woman behind her whinnied. "I told you we have an intellectual cunt here. 'No, thank you,'" she exaggerated Rachel's speech.

Rachel darted a look at the guards scattered around the dining hall. They stood about, bored expressions on their faces. The nearest one leaned on the peppermint green wall, chewing gum and swinging her key chain.

"Cut it out, Alegra. I don't want no trouble from you," she said.

"I'm only talking. Exercising my First Amendment right of free speech."

The guard turned away. Rachel stared at her back. As unpleasant as this was, nothing would happen. She must believe it.

At the end of the line, she reached for a piece of toast. Aware that each of her movements was watched by two dozen pairs of hostile eyes, she tried to suppress her fear. Like animals, these women could smell it. In unhurried movements, she filled a tin cup with coffee. Steam rose from the liquid that was watered down to the transparency of tea.

The mug was too hot to the touch. She laid it on her tray. About to turn, she was jolted by a shove, followed by a stinging pain of hot coffee rushing down her arm.

Her tray dropped in a raucous clatter, her coffee spilling on the floor. The toast rolled as if in slow motion as everything around her shifted to low gear.

"Oh, I'm sooooo sorry," the big woman behind her intonated. "Sooooo sorry. Just spilled my coffee unintentionally. Sooooo sorry."

The pain radiated up Rachel's arm, crystallizing all her nerve endings onto one blob of pain. She leaped to the beginning of the line, where she remembered seeing an open container of ice cubes next to the water dispenser. But when she extended her hand to reach the ice, she realized that the women in line had frozen, creating a human wall to block her way.

The pain was unbearable. She stood there, feeling broken and defeated, powerless against the cruelty and hatred written on the faces of the other prisoners. Tears coursed down her cheeks.

No one moved. The guards' faces were glued to an empty section of the dining hall, as though the green-tiled wall were a TV screen.

"Here, let me." A chocolate-brown woman, her head adorned with an intricate web of cornrows, disengaged herself from the end of the line and handed Rachel a handful of ice cubes. Then she turned again and filled up a napkin with more.

"Put this on," she said, her tone matter-of-fact. "Go sit down."

"Thank you," Rachel said, and immediately bit her lip. Being polite had just gotten her into trouble.

The remainder of her energy dissipated through that patch of raw skin. Rachel stumbled to the nearest table and leaned on it for support. Her arm throbbed. The black woman returned with more ice. She covered Rachel's arm with a T-shirt and tied its ends to secure the ice pack in place.

Patting it, she asked, "Better?" She smelled of coconut.

Rachel nodded through misty eyes. "Is there an infirmary here? This burn is, uh—very deep."

The woman shook her head. "Don't go there."

"Why?"

Imperceptibly, the woman motioned with her head toward the prisoners on line. "They're testing you. Them there want to know if you can be one of us."

"I don't care to be," Rachel snapped, simultaneously regretting her words. It was inconceivable that she would be confined to this place for long. Justice must prevail.

"If I was you, I wouldn't have an attitude." The woman scratched her head. "That white trash bitch, Alegra, she bullies everyone to either follow her or stay out of her way."

"I plan to stay out of her way."

"The C.O. will tell you to go to the nurse. They're afraid of lawsuits. You'll say it's nothing and don't go. Alegra won't like it."

"The C.O.?"

"Correction officer."

"How come you won't get in trouble with Alegra for helping me?"

The woman shrugged. "You're her girl. She doesn't want you dying on her—"

"I'm no one's girl—"

"For your own good, don't be stupid." She eyed Rachel. "You need things, and money."

"Money?"

"Yes, that green stuff. Printed with a big number in the corner. Ten, twenty, fifty."

"I had to leave my pocketbook when I checked in."

"Better get some, and cigarettes and candy bars to trade. You'll need it. You'll want drugs, too—"

"I don't do drugs."

"Oh, you will when Alegra fucks you. Or to buy her protection."

This was like an episode from a TV movie of the week, except that this was a waking nightmare. "I need protection *from* her," Rachel mumbled. "I'd like to tell her to get lost."

She held back the urge to wipe her eyes with the back of her hand. How was it possible that in a span of three years—thanks to Wes and the system that supported him—she had moved from being a goddess in a Fifth Avenue penthouse to a designated sex-slave in women's prison?"

"I'm Shelley." Her benefactor sucked on a tooth, withdrew something, placed it on the tip of her finger, examined it, and put it back in her mouth.

Rachel averted her gaze.

"Don't fight her," Shelley continued. "She likes those initiation ceremonies, if you know what I mean."

"No, I don't know what you meant."

"Gets her horny. Girl, where did you grow up, on a tree?"

The shudder that drove through Rachel would not go away. It kept rising in waves as she remained locked in her cell for the entire day, the guards passing by to observe her.

"They won't put you into 'population' until they monitor you in the intake module," Shelley whispered when she passed by on her way to do her chores. "You already caused trouble in the chow hall."

She had caused trouble?

"What's an 'intake module'?" Rachel whispered.

"That's where you're now. Suicide watch. And the guards want to see what kind of prisoner you gonna be. They don't want you killing someone. Liability."

Who did they think she was? The insult pierced through Rachel. Nevertheless, a twenty-four-hour isolation was preferable to mixing with the "population." It kept her protected from Alegra. Rachel sat cross-legged on her cot, staring at her fingers. There was nothing to fill up her time. Sheridan's editorial department shipped to women's prisons boxes of books received for reviews. When Rachel asked a passing C.O. for a book, the woman just kept walking.

She had taken the six Tylenol tablets her new acquaintance had smuggled her, but still, every movement of her right arm hurt. She fashioned a sling from her pillowcase.

In late afternoon, when Shelley passed by her cell again, she tossed a deck of cards and a worn romance novel through the bars. The pink-covered paperback featured a colorful picture of Fabio, his blond hair rolling over his supernatural shoulders.

Rachel sighed and opened the book.

"Your lawyer's here to see you," a gruff female guard said. "You behave yourself, and we won't handcuff you."

The thought of the cold metal brushing against the edge of the coffee burn made Rachel wince in pain.

The C.O. led Rachel to a room in the middle of which was a table. Erica Norgard sat at the side closest to the door, a pile of newspapers at her elbow. Sobbing, Rachel leaned over and almost fell into her. Erica held her for only a second and nudged her away, nodding with her head toward the guard. The guard waved her hand roughly, indicating to Rachel to sit facing Erica, then planted herself against the wall, her legs apart, her eyes bearing down upon Rachel.

"Hold yourself together. You have no choice." Erica's voice wrapped itself around unarticulated emotions. Her brows contracted with concern and she pointed to the makeshift sling that now hung loose around Rachel's neck. The ice-filled plastic bag leaked on the front of Rachel's shirt. A wet stain had begun to spread. "What's that?"

"Get me out of here fast. I'm scared," Rachel whispered.

"What happened? An accident?"

"A deliberate one. An initiation test—one of several others to come, I've been told. These women are animals. You must get me out." Then she added in a little voice. "Please."

"We're working on it. The newspapers are filled with your story this morning. The women's groups we had in court started a telephone campaign to their congressmen and senators—even to Governor Dunkle—"

Rachel sat bolt upright. "Dunkle? Wes did some transplant job on Dunkle's mother a few years ago, and last year he saved his son after a motorcycle accident. Dunkle flew him to Albany. It was in the papers."

Erica's eyebrows shot up. "Why didn't you mention that before?"

"Where was the relevance? Why would the Governor of New York become involved in a Family Court matter? It's one of tens of thousands in the state."

"No longer. The case is now headline news—a 'cause celebré' for children's rights. We'll fight with every weapon at our disposal. Lou Kaplan wants to come here. Talk to him again." Erica paused. "We're also shooting for an interview with Barbara Walters or Diane Sawyer."

"You're kidding."

"What about you? You must have some contacts."

"Well, yes." Rachel thought for a moment. "A former colleague now works for Larry King, and an editor I knew from *Women's Life* is at Dateline."

"There you go."

Rachel tugged a strand of loose hair behind her ear. "What exactly can we achieve? McGillian won't suddenly concede that it's okay for me to hide Ellie. He's already ruled and signed on the custody issue. Could he change his decision retroactively?"

"Theoretically, yes, but I doubt he would. He wrote his decision in atypical haste; he's known for his procrastination. And then, with a huge backlog, when no one ever receives a new trial date in less than three months, Ortman got one in a day. Somebody's lit a fire under McGillian's judicial tush, and I'd be curious to know who it is. When we find out, we'll have him recuse himself."

"Huh?"

"Recuse himself. If it's discovered that for some reason McGillian shouldn't preside over the case, he'd have to step aside and the file will be transferred to another judge. At this juncture, anyone would be better than him."

Rachel let out a bitter laugh. "Oh, yes. Those were Chuck's words about the previous judge until that idiot was finally rotated."

"And if you can think of anything else as juicy as Wes's being Dunkle's family surgeon, please share it with me."

The thought of Phil sounded in Rachel's head like a gong. Would her relationship with him affect McGillian? Not if the judge was unaware of it, not if Phil had never discussed her case with her. If she told Erica, then, less than a month into Phil's new job—his first as a future attorney—he would surely be fired. It still baffled Rachel why Phil would take such a risk.

"Are you with me? Hello?" Erica wiggled her fingers in front of Rachel's face.

"Sorry. It's so hard to concentrate."

Erica patted the fingers of Rachel's well hand. "It'll get worse before it gets better."

"Erica, you don't understand. This—this lesbian is after me. They're going to hurt me, but make sure I don't die in the process." Rachel's heart beat with terror. "I need cash. Quickly."

Erica pointed to a plastic bag. "I had these toiletries checked for contraband. I won't smuggle you money. I don't want you—or me—getting into trouble. But I had money deposited into the jail account for you."

"Anything else you know that I don't?"

"You're in a low-security jail. It has three goals: Keep the bad guys inside. Keep the staff safe. Don't get sued." She paused. "Now about this latest goal: we'll get you medical attention."

"Please don't. Not yet."

Erica fastened her eyes on Rachel's, and said nothing. After a moment's silence, she pulled a fax notice from under the pile of newspapers. She slid it forward. "From Chuck."

Rachel glanced at a rough drawing of a smiley face. "*I'm heading your fan club,*" the note read. "*Be strong.*"

"He's a good guy. A true friend," Rachel said. "My case tore his guts out."

Erica nodded and smiled. "Talking about friends, here's something that may cheer you up. I received a phone call from a man who says he's a friend of yours. He read about the case and wanted me to convey the following message: 'I'm sorry for being such a schmuck. I still love you.' His name is Gerald Rhodes."

Rachel let out a quiet whistle. "Gerald? He said that?"

"Yup. He did. Whoever this guy is, he sounded remorseful."

"Well, I don't know—" Rachel bit her lip.

Erica leaned forward. "Listen. You need to keep all the friends you can. If you haven't yet lost most of them, few will hang around by the time this is all over. Is he worth keeping?"

"He disappeared a month ago without so much as a good-bye."

"What shall I say when he calls again?"

"Well— 'Hello to you too,'" Rachel said. Jacqueline would have had a big, hilarious laugh if the situation weren't so grim.

"One more thing. I wrote a nice, friendly letter to Vince Carducci, explaining that you'll be, shall we say, indisposed, for a little while." Erica's tone turned sarcastic. "I expressed the hope that *Women's Life* magazine, being a publication that chronicles all aspects of women's joys and tribulations, would show the appropriate understanding. Especially for one of their own who, through her strength and tenacity in fighting for her daughter's well-being and happiness, has become a role model for many women."

"I'd love to see his face when he reads it."

"You won't get fired now. It would create a public relations fiasco for Sheridan Magazines. More likely, they'll magnanimously show sympathy by continuing to pay your full salary."

"If I get out of here alive, I'd like to tell Vince to go fly a kite," Rachel said. She had never had the chance nor the nerve to contact Liliana about a job.

"Which brings us to another item. Sorry to bring it up, but my bookkeeper tells me you haven't paid any of our invoices. You must come up with something."

"I thought you've agreed to wait."

"I've agreed I'd cut down on my fee, but my practice is laying out money for you to pay out-of-pocket expenses. And with this latest crisis, my staff and I are spending far more hours on your case than previously estimated." Erica paused. "You owe us fifteen thousand dollars."

How was she expected to get the money while incarcerated? Sell her house from a jail cell?

"Sorry," Rachel mumbled. "I already have two mortgages on the house, but I'll endorse my paychecks to you."

"Now you see why you can't tell Carducci to go hang himself. You'll need your income when we bring Ellie back."

When we bring Ellie back. Not "*if* we bring Ellie back." That was worth everything. The sweet words echoed in Rachel's head. Erica believed in it, and so would she. She must.

"And you're going to have a second full-time job when you're out," Erica added.

"Waiting tables won't pay my legal bills."

"I'm talking about schmoozing with the press," Erica said. "I want you to tend to your publicity campaign as if someone's paying you a thousand dollars a day. Winning the public opinion war is your number one priority."

"When I'm out."

"You can win them all. That pest from the *City Post*—"

"David Lupori?"

"That's the one. The newspaper's under takeover negotiations with an Australian conglomerate. The buyers are stuck with the unionized staff they can't fire so they must get rid of the rest. Lupori, a permanent freelancer, is an old-timer working from a portable typewriter. He's desperate to hold on to his job by doing superb investigative work. He's been snooping outside my office building, and I've seen him around court."

"My office too."

"Here you are." Erica continued. "I can tell by his questions he knows more than anyone about your case—and its cast of players. Either we cooperate with him or Wes will—as he has already in the first article. Let's hook Lupori on our side of the story."

Rachel said nothing.

Erica rose to her feet. "Anything you need from the outside?"

"Do they package air like Chinese take-out?" Rachel scribbled a couple of phone numbers. "Call Jacqueline. Tell her everything she read in the papers about Ellie's disappearance is true, and that I'm sorry I had to keep her in the dark for her own protection. Will you explain to her the legal ramifications if I had told her and she were subpoenaed? Also, Jacqueline has the access to Larry King."

"You're allowed to use the pay phone for collect calls."

"The lines are long—and dominated by the clique whose leader burned my arm." And who'd threatened to force her into lesbian acts.

As Rachel reentered the inner sanctuary of the jail, a guard stopped her for a body search.

"Take off all your clothes," she told Rachel.

Rachel obliged. She handed them to the guard, who passed her hands through them, fingering the hem and stitches for lumps. Then she placed a mirror on the floor.

"Crouch," she ordered Rachel.

"What?"

With the tip of her shoe, the woman roughly prompted Rachel's legs apart. "Now crouch over the mirror and let me look."

A thud banged inside Rachel's head; she must have misunderstood. "I— I—don't get it—"

"Spread your legs, bend as if you're taking a dump, and let me look. Use your fingers to spread your pussy. Like this." The guard held up her hand.

Rachel crouched and shut her eyes tight. The thumping in her temples obliterated all other sounds. The humiliation as the guard scrutinized her private parts for contraband was beyond anything she had ever imagined. It almost made Erica's visit not worth it.

On her way back to her cell, Rachel passed by the pay phone. Several inmates waited on line, their eyes following Rachel with a collective hostile stare. How she wished she could call Phil. It struck her that she didn't even have his home phone number. Did he live with his girlfriend? Was she genuinely a *former* girlfriend?

She wanted him, his caring, his good humor, his warmth—and the sum of all these. But their affair was now his call. The painful yet frozen expression on his face when she was led away from the courtroom flitted again in front of her. It told her how he felt. She recalled their lovemaking, the tenderness with which he had touched her, gazed at her, the dazzle in his eyes lingering. Those were the moments of truth; whatever happened between them was unique, special.

"The Mother Who Protects Her Child," he had called her. There was nothing he could do to protect her from whatever awaited her in this horrible place.

CHAPTER   TWENTY-EIGHT

THE smell of smoke startled Rachel out of a light sleep. Through haze, she opened her eyes, trying to adjust to the darkness of the single-bed cubicle. Against the open bars separating the cell from the corridor, a flicker of bright movement did not register in her mind. It was a small light, like the dance of a candle, and it leaped about not far from her feet. A split second before the realization hit her, Rachel jumped. Fire.

The corner of her mattress was on fire!

Grabbing the bowl of melted ice the guard had allowed her to keep, she poured the water. The fire hissed away.

Somewhere in the darkness, outside her cell, she heard a laugh. "Next time it will be the hair on your cunt, whore." Alegra's voice, unmistakable in its viciousness, reverberated in the empty corridor, sounding like the laughter of a ghost in a haunted cave. "We'll set your intellectual ass on fire, bitch."

Rachel shivered and wrapped herself in the bedcover that reeked of a blend of sour cheese, wet wool, and animal musk. The scorched skin on her arm burnt from the coffee throbbed unrelentingly in rhythm with the thumping of her heart. She scooped the last pebbles of ice scattered about and placed them over the burn. For the rest of the night, frightened and more alone than she ever remembered, Rachel remained vigilant, her back propped against the wall and her ears alert to each sound and rustle coming from the adjacent cells.

Had Ellie been this frightened each time she anticipated her father's "Zoo games?"

In the morning, it was Rachel's turn to shower. The stall area, separated by a low wall from the toilets and sinks, was less crowded than most of the jail public places yet not completely deserted. She had been afraid to shower since her arrival some forty hours earlier, and now her body smelled of sour, oxygenated sweat. Keeping her dignity suddenly became a new goal; it would set her apart from these women and would keep the ember of her spirit simmering beneath the crust of fear and humiliation.

A trustee, a prisoner who'd gained the authorities' confidence, hung about. Unsure where the woman's loyalty lay, Rachel forced herself to assume the woman was in charge of her safety. "Stick around," she mumbled.

"I'm not your maid," the trustee responded, settling that question. "You high-class women think everyone has to wipe your ass."

Holding back a tart reply about the taxpayers' money, Rachel said meekly, "I'll only be a few minutes."

She turned on the water and let it cool her skin. It streamed through her scalp, when Alegra marched in, two prisoners in tow. The three of them carried brooms, pails, and mops. With exaggerated movements, Alegra's minions began to clean the bathroom floor, never looking in Rachel's direction. Alegra stepped toward Rachel, grinning, just as the trustee moved away, her eyes glued to her toes as if she was trying not to step on the wet floor.

Fear gripped Rachel's heart and tossed it down a cavity inside her body. She hadn't yet soaped herself. She had to get away. Now.

Exposed in her nudity to Alegra's scrutiny, she fumbled for the towel that hung on the side hook, away from the splashing water. It was no longer there.

The fingers of Alegra's right hand circled Rachel's nipple. "I bet your cunt is as pink," she said, her voice husky. "You make me horny."

"Take your hands off me!" But Rachel heard her feeble voice betraying her powerlessness.

Alegra's breath was foul. "I'm getting you hot and ready."

"Don't touch me." Rachel turned her back to her. She had to think fast.

Casually, as though taking her time, she squirted large blobs of liquid soap from the dispenser into her palm and spread it over her body. Behind her, gently, with the deliberate leisure of a tiger waiting to lunge at its victim, Alegra caressed her hair, separating the wet tendrils.

Her movements unhurried, Rachel gathered her hair from under Alegra's fingers, collected it, brought it up, and knotted it. She took a deep breath and stood still for a split second, gathering strength, her adrenalin flowing. Alegra's freed hand slid down Rachel's buttock and cupped it. A finger began probing.

From the corner of her eye, Rachel examined the wet floor, a fifteen-foot long black rubber runner cutting through it like a bridge suspended over Niagara Falls. She mustn't slide on the wet floor.

She ducked under Alegra and sprinted out.

Hands reached out to grab her body, but when caught, Rachel wriggled out, like a slippery eel, and bolted away. More hands tried to get hold of her, but were unable to grab the thickly soaped skin.

Rachel reached the corner. She leaped. An outstretched leg slid under her. She vaulted over it. She glided around the partitioned wall. Then her body catapulted into a silent crowd of a dozen prisoners and two guards who stood still, suspense on their faces.

"You're mine, bitch," Alegra guffawed behind the wall. "Wow, I like a hot cunt with spirit."

Shaking, hyperventilating, her ears buzzing, the soap dripping from her, Rachel stood by a sink. Were the women waiting to hear her groans? Her screams? To come to her rescue before she died in her fight with Alegra? The scrutiny was as violating as Alegra's fingers. Rachel rinsed the soap off with her bare hands, letting the water run to the floor around her. Her clothes and towel were nowhere in sight.

She hadn't seen Shelley among the awaiting audience until she materialized and handed her a worn towel. "No one's ever gotten away from her," she said in a conspiratorial tone. "You're her girl. You've humiliated her in front of everybody. You've made her angry."

"Where are my clothes?" Rachel's words were pinched with the effort to speak.

In response to a nod of the head, a prisoner brought her hand from behind her back and handed Rachel her clothes.

A jolt of surprise zigzagged through Rachel. Was Shelley merely Alegra's sidekick, playing the bad-guy good-guy act? Was Rachel the new entertainment in these women's uneventful lives? She felt like a captive explorer among cannibals eying their next meal. It was only a matter of time.

She had to get out. Soon.

When called to the visitors' lounge, Rachel was astonished to see her brother-in-law, Howard. She never had a real conversation with him. Now, at the sight of his slight figure at the desk, her lungs, like a billowing curtain, expanded in relief. Howard's face, so ordinary that she could never quite describe its features, was twisted in concern.

He took her hand. He had never touched her before, or rather, if he had, she had never appreciated human touch as much as she did at that moment. His fingers were small and delicate, like a boy's. Rachel squeezed his hand in return and did not let go.

"How are you doing?" he asked. She detected tears glistening behind his glasses.

"It's horrible." Her voice cracked. "But they promised I'd come out alive."

"It's so awful for you, for Ellie, for your parents."

"Howard, I'm so scared." She still clutched his hand, pouring all her desperation into his. "No one can do a damn thing to help, to get me out. These women terrorize me."

"I have a message for you," he whispered. "They're fine."

"Who?" But she knew before she finished uttering the word.

"Ellie and your parents."

A dam of tears threatened to break somewhere inside her. So Howard was her lifeline to Ellie? The genial man whose existence she had scarcely noticed? Why not? He was a stockbroker, and judging by the expensive lifestyle he lavished on Josie, he knew what he was doing.

"Where are they?"

"They didn't want you to know, to save you trouble, but I guess that's a moot point now."

This was the most important moment in her life, eclipsing all the fear of the past couple of days.

"In Israel; on a kibbutz," he finished.

A sudden electric shock hit her brain. "So far away? Wasn't there a terrorists' attack last week?"

"I wouldn't worry about it. Israel's still safer than New York." He glanced about him, then continued, "It's a kibbutz founded by South African Jews. They speak English. Ellie has playmates—and she gets along with them. But she's picking up Hebrew, too. She hasn't had a—a crying fit since they left."

"This is unbelievable," Rachel mumbled. What had she done that her nearest and dearest had to endure such exile? How long would Ellie need to use the new language?

"Do my parents have to work in the fields?"

"Oh, no. Russ is a medic in the infirmary—he's not licensed to practice dentistry there—and Lorena works in the infants' nursery. She loves it. And she gave a concert Friday night."

Rachel let out a wan smile and sniffled. Jacqueline had family in Israel. It could have been a good choice for her parents. "If they don't get American newspapers, don't tell them I'm here," she said.

He nodded. "They have no living expenses. That's what they were most concerned about. And no paper trail. They asked me to pay another chunk of your legal costs. Bernstein's demanding full payment of the last twenty thousand owed him."

"I don't have that kind of money."

"How much do you have?"

"No savings. Everything I make—after two mortgages and other basics—goes for legal fees. The divorce settlement is all gone; I've spent nothing on myself."

"You need to take out a loan."

"Against what collateral? Even my car is old. And how will I repay a loan?"

"I'll guarantee a three- to five-year bank loan. Monday, I'll mail you the papers to sign."

Rachel dropped her head into her arms. At least she wouldn't be forced to sell her house. For the time being.

A moment later, she straightened up again. "Howard, I need cash, now. Protection money," she whispered. "Make sure no one sees."

With a slight movement, he put his other hand on the table. He had some folded bills ready. "There's two hundred in here."

Imperceptibly, she tucked them into her sling. The guard would check her private parts according to protocol, but might not touch the wound if Rachel made a big deal about it.

"Thanks," she whispered. "I need it more than you can imagine."

In response, Howard squeezed her fingers.

"We're lucky to have you in the family," she said.

"I'm proud to be married to a family like this one."

Rachel gave an ironic chuckle. "I'm not sure Josie would agree with you."

"Josie has a lot of good sides. She just doesn't know how to show them to you."

This wasn't the time to wonder aloud how, over a lifetime, Josie had managed to hide her good qualities from her only sibling. "Don't you think I would have loved to have a sister who's a friend and a confidante? Especially these past few years."

"She craves your approval," he said. "And she's angry at you for ignoring her."

"It's my fault? Am I responsible for Josie's behavior?—" Rachel clammed up. She had almost said "neurotic." Let Howard think his wife was otherwise wonderful. In the meanwhile, rediscovering a devoted brother-in-law was almost as good as having her sister on her side.

Right now, however, the most important thing was that she had money to buy protection if need be. Yet she doubted Alegra could be pacified by money. Nothing but a complete breaking of the newbie would satisfy her thirst for domination.

CHAPTER TWENTY-NINE

FRIDAY morning, McGillian slowly backed his 1987 Pontiac out of the driveway, whistling a marching band tune. After yet another rainy night, the morning was balmy and cloudless, as if an army of elves had labored all night to polish the leaves on the trees and dust the gray off the skies.

There was an unusual commotion in the otherwise quiet cul-de-sac, where a dozen people—women—milled around.

Only when he backed out fully into the street did McGillian notice the placards and signs they held. Just as the trumpets in his head switched to the drums, "Pum-purum-pum-pum," his whistling died.

He stared at the sight. What in the world?—

"With Judges Like McGillian, We're Better Off in Iran," one sign read.

If he hadn't seen his name, he would have thought all this mayhem was meant for one of his neighbors, though which one would attract these crazies was anyone's guess. No, it was meant for him, and he had no idea what they wanted. Christ. His hand reached for the can of pepper spray the security officer had suggested he carry in his pocket.

"*Joseph Torruellas Could Be Alive.*" What the hell. The world was going bonkers.

"We've Had Enough of You." "We Are All Rachel Belmores."

A woman rushed toward his car and plastered a cardboard sign against his side window. "*Stop Ellie's Torture.*"

In front of him, another woman was tied to a utility pole, so it seemed, by an oversized link chain—probably made out of construction paper. A huge sign planted next to her read, "*McGillian Chained Kim for Life.*"

He scoured his brain to figure out who was Kim, but the name did not click.

Still in reverse, he put a slight pressure on the gas pedal and turned. He shifted to drive and inched his way back toward his house. The woman who had plastered the poster on his window backed away, and the others parted. He drove right into his garage.

Once inside the kitchen, he was relieved that his wife was not up yet. He didn't need her anxieties to deal with.

He dialed the office. "Sylvia, any demonstrations outside the courthouse?"

"Demonstrations? No, Judge."

"Send the court security here, will you?"

Less than ten minutes later, a security car pulled in front of his house, and Sylvia emerged, accompanied by a portly court officer who struggled to climb the three steps on the front stoop.

"We have never had anything like this—" Sylvia said breathlessly. "Shouldn't you call the police?"

"During election time? And give these feminists more headlines?" He turned to the court officer who seemed to be still catching his breath. "Just make sure you guys are on top of it."

From his kitchen window McGillian watched the protesters as they formed a circle and began to strut counterclockwise, waving their placards. A van veered and parked at the curb. Half a dozen more women filed out, bringing out a banner. They unrolled it.

It carried an enlarged photograph of an Asian girl. It dawned on him. "Kim" was Kim Lee, the Korean teenager who had upped and gotten herself an abortion, defying his order.

"Christ. It's been three weeks since my ruling on this case." He pointed at the photograph. "I thought it'd die down in a day or two. I should've known better."

"You did the right thing, Judge," Sylvia whispered.

"It's all those pro-choice feminists. They jerk the leash on the media's neck. First they piggybacked on the Torruellas case and now they're exploiting the Belmore case." He shook his head in disgust. "They conveniently choose to forget that this Lee girl didn't want the child. Will you explain to me what harm was done by giving the baby to the grandparents who wanted it?"

Sylvia shrugged. Across the street, a neighbor came out, but promptly scrambled back in. In the window of another house, another neighbor's head bobbed up and disappeared.

Out of nowhere, madness had seized the world, and its alien note boomed inside McGillian. Sunday, he'd take his wife to church. If he had said his prayers more often, perhaps none of this would have happened.

The rest of his morning in court was uneventful. But in the afternoon, as McGillian worked in the solitude of his chambers, he heard a monotonous chanting outside. He tried to ignore it, focusing on a stack of blue-bound court orders. His signature was needed on each before the end of the day, to close another week's glossary of human ordeals. Some were as old as humanity, others as new as the web of social fabric that, when intersected with contemporary concepts of science, economics, and politics, unraveled in ways unimaginable just fifteen years ago. All were packaged into the explicit language of the law and meticulously arranged on the windowsill and in the rolling file cart. Backlog.

After a while, a buzzing broke his concentration. He got up and peered outside.

A cluster of protesters carrying large placards stood under the trees on the far side of a walkway facing his office.

Not again, he thought.

"Ayatollah McGillian: Free Ellie," read one sign.

"Judge McGillian: Pedophiles' Dream," read another.

The words of the chant became clear. "Free Ellie, Free Ellie."

With an abrupt pull of shoulders, he returned to his desk.

The chanting wouldn't stop. McGillian banged his fist on the desk. "Sonny," he called through the open door.

Phil crossed the secretarial area.

"The Belmore case." McGillian pointed at the window. "A cheap trick to make the child the center of attention while the mother's the one in contempt. I've never had a case get out of control like this one."

"It hit a raw nerve with a lot of people, sir."

"What about the newspapers? What do they say?"

"The same thing, I'm sorry to say. Mostly disagree with your decisions, sir."

"I'm not out to win a popularity contest. It's outrageous how far the mother is going to prove her point."

"If there's abuse, I'd say she's doing all she can—as well she should."

"*If* there's abuse. I ruled it was not proven. This publicity is the wrong tactic to take with me." McGillian paused and peered outside again. "Listen, we don't want anything to happen to her while she's in jail. Go out there tomorrow and check things out."

Phil held his breath.

"Would you mind? Even if it's Saturday? Talk to her, meet with the warden. Make sure she's not being treated like a common criminal."

"Your Honor, you could release her. She's been there for forty-eight hours. Surely—"

"No," McGillian drummed his fingers on his desk. "She's in contempt of court, and if we allow flagrant disrespect, where would it lead?"

Sylvia interrupted before Phil could reply. "Colby Albrecht's on the line."

McGillian took a deep breath, then waited a moment longer before picking up the receiver to hear what the town supervisor had to add.

"Hey," Albrecht said, ever cheerful. "How do you know when you're old?"

"How?"

"Your arms get so strong you can bend your hard-on."

"Very funny."

McGillian raised his eyes to check Phil's position in the room. The young man stood by the window with his back to him, his long legs planted apart in an easy stance, his hands in his pockets. Peering out, Phil watched the demonstrators.

Albrecht's tone changed. "I just wanted to relate a message to you. Nicholas Dunkle is very pleased."

Pleased? About what? As the words traveled through the line, McGillian felt the hair stand up on the back of his neck. Did Dunkle truly believe he had bought himself a judge? "I'd like to assure you that no outside influences have in the past nor will in the future determine the outcome of any of my cases," he replied tartly.

He let the receiver drop as unfamiliar rage bubbled up in his stomach. Albrecht's words stung beyond insulting.

It had been his fault. He'd cooperated by moving the case up on the calendar, giving Dunkle the wrong impression. To hell with him.

"Phil," he suddenly said, his voice too loud even to his own ears. "Get the Belmore parties back here first thing Monday morning. This farce must end."

CHAPTER THIRTY

"SMELL this."

Seated in the day room, pretending to read a book in spite of the din, Rachel heard Alegra's dreaded voice. From behind her head, a malodorous finger reached over and flitted under her nose. Rachel jumped to her feet.

"Ever smelled an AIDS cunt? They all smell the same, bitch. A little ex-cha-nge of pussy juice and you'll have it, too. No one will ever be able to tell the difference."

As a white-hot blade lodged in her heart, Rachel swung around and headed toward the corridor. If she could just make it through the long passageway, she would find solitude in the library. She stopped short. Solitude was dangerous in this place, especially on a Saturday, when the prisoners were not working and boredom made them look for new forms of entertainment.

Without glancing in Alegra's direction, Rachel pulled a chair and placed it against the wall. At least Alegra could not surprise her by approaching from the back. But as much as she tried to ignore the woman, Rachel could not help avoid sensing Alegra's anticipating presence. She raised her head to see Alegra scrutinizing her, her lower jaw dropped, her tongue hanging, like a lizard perched on a tree branch watching the approach of a beetle.

In the various scenarios Rachel had conjured, she hadn't imagined that the announcement that Phil was waiting in the visitors' lounge would fill her with the rush of fondness that spilled through her. Illogically, her hopes took flight.

She rushed through the corridors, impatient for the Correction Officer to unlock each of the gates, nursing a fantasy in which she wrapped her arms around Phil's neck and he would hold her against his strong chest, comforting her.

And he was there, in the large room where several Formica tables were scattered about, his long legs planted apart, his hands tucked in his armpits. His easy stance changed when she approached him. The polite expression on his face, the tight smile. He was remote, inaccessible. The intensity in his eyes was gone under the new mask of composure.

"I'm here as an officer of the court," he said stiffly. "To ensure that you're as comfortable as can be under these sad circumstances."

The shift in the room returned to its former balance. "Thanks for coming, but no, I'm not comfortable." She lifted her arm toward him.

"Anything we can do?"

"*'We'* can get me the hell out of here."

They sat down at a far corner of the cafeteria. Screaming children and distraught mothers provided a backdrop. Rachel felt the guards' eyes on her.

"Judge McGillian may be easing his position. He's called the lawyers for a meeting in his chambers Monday morning to discuss the situation."

"You don't understand. I don't have until Monday. These women are torturing me. They set my mattress on fire while I slept!" Rachel heard the hysteria in her voice, but she no longer cared. "They're trying to rape me, for God's sake!"

The quick flicker of pain that crossed Phil's face told her he cared. His tone, though, remained maddeningly formal. "I'll ask the warden to ensure your safety until then. Let's hope all parties involved will reach an agreeable resolution."

"The guards know very well what's going on," she snapped. "And don't give me that legalese talk. I'm not going to hand Ellie over to her father."

"I'm not here to discuss the details of the case." He took out two Snickers and laid them on the table. He began to peel the wrapper from one. "I bet you've never tasted anything as good."

She was edgy and in pain. "Listen, Phil," she whispered, her anger scraping the boundaries of her voice. "If you're here to tell me something—do it. Now. I can't play this charade."

"I wanted to see you," he whispered back. "Very much. I have this one opportunity, that's all."

She got up. "Let's see if they'll let me walk outside. Go talk to them. You're the official who put me in here—"

"Not me. I never would have. And no, they won't allow you outside." Then, following her gaze toward the barred window, he added, "I'm so sorry."

He put his hand out but immediately retrieved it. "Rachel, there's nothing in the world I wouldn't do for you—or for Ellie."

She stared at the unpaved courtyard, devoid of either trees or benches and surrounded by a high chain link fence topped by barbed wire. Dust rose up and swirled away. She craved the barren outdoors, the dry, hot, brown dust blowing in her face.

"There was a demonstration Friday in front of the courthouse," he told her. "About two hundred protesters. The post office delivered two boxes of mail."

"I'm not going to ask you how Judge McGillian reacted."

He smiled. "Today there's a full-page ad in *The New York Times*. The heat is on."

She nodded, but said nothing. For a few moments, neither spoke.

"Chuck Bernstein used to tell me to entertain positive thoughts. I ran out of them," she finally said.

"Here's one for you. Remember a week ago? We were on Fire Island. Getting to know each other."

"Has it been only a week?"

"I tried to peek at your breasts through that striped T-shirt you wore." He smiled, one eyebrow arched mischievously. "No luck."

"You've gotten an eyeful since."

"A mouthful, too." His soft tone tingled her spine.

"Phil, be truthful with me," she whispered. "What if it were found out that you and I have this thing going?"

"McGillian might have to recuse himself—that means to disqualify himself from presiding over the case—"

"I know what it means. But on what grounds?"

"That I've jeopardized the impartiality of the case."

"If you had, I wouldn't be here. Anyway, you and I have never discussed it."

"That's why he only 'might' recuse himself. It's not clear-cut."

She looked around. Could the guard read lips? "What about you? What would the consequences be for you?"

"Tacky, that's all."

"Meaning what? Wouldn't the Bar take some sort of a stand against you when you pass the exam?"

"There's certainly 'the appearance of impropriety.' The Bar's Character and Fitness Committee would make some waves about admitting me. I'd claim that my actions have not prejudiced your case. Obviously, your being here shows that I was unable to affect the outcome."

"What about something more immediate? If Erica Norgard decides to use it, what would happen to your job now?"

"I'll continue to pursue justice." His gaze fell down toward his bitten fingernails. He shrugged. "You do whatever you must do; don't worry about me."

"But of course I will. I can't blow your career to pieces just to get myself a new court date."

"Okay. Here it is. If I leave Judge McGillian's employ, I'll join Legal Aid—I've never looked for a fat paycheck. I've turned down job offers from a couple of the best firms in Manhattan. The kind of legal work I want to do would help those who really need it."

"Am I your first needy case?"

"Ellie is."

"Where do I come in? Am I a bonus serendipity?"

"A thoroughly enjoyable one." He stopped and fixed her with his gaze. Rachel thought she could feel the heat emanating from his body and smell the faint scent of his aftershave.

"Phil, you've taken an enormous risk to your career by pursuing me. Why?"

"I'm in love with you. First I got to know you—to admire you—through the file. Then we met—" He let his fingers slide across the table until they touched hers. "I want you to make room in your life for me."

She felt a small surge of happiness. Then she thought of Gerald. Steady, mature, Gerald, whom, until a few weeks ago, she had believed she loved. How desperately she had wanted him back.

"What happened to your girlfriend? Are you really through?"

"Life has called us in different directions. What about you?" he asked.

"You have some competition lurking in the shadows. But it's over too."

"You don't sound so sure." A sudden smile spread over his face. "But we made love; it must count for something. Or were you just using me?"

She did not reply. Whatever it was about him, about the two of them, that anchored them and made the whole greater than the sum of its parts, she could not yet articulate in words.

"You're welcome to use me again, any time." He paused. "But it *was* special."

"Right now, I'm so scared I can't think straight." She would have to talk to Erica. Phil had given her the green light to use their relationship as ammunition. But how could she do that?

At first, Phil did not notice the man slouching against the entrance of the two-story building in which he lived. But as Phil jiggled the key ring and picked out the one for the front door of the lobby, the man detached himself from the wall and darted over on feet too small for his frame.

"Mr. Crawford? May I have a word with you?" He flashed a business card. "David Lupori, the *City Post*." His bulbous eyes, like a frog's, were too close to his round and inflated crimson mouth.

Phil did not take the card. He was in a rush to call McGillian and see what could be done for Rachel. The prison warden had been of little help. "What's it about?" he asked.

The man smacked his lips. "I've tried to reach Judge Robert McGillian, but couldn't get hold of him today. Figured you might be able to clarify some things—"

Phil's hand dropped to his side. "Sorry. I doubt Judge McGillian would have talked to you if you got through to him, therefore, neither can I."

"How long is he planning to keep Ms. Belmore in jail?"

"I can't comment." Phil inserted the key in the door." How do you know where I live?"

"Oh, it wasn't hard to find." The man flashed a camera and took a quick shot.

"No photographs, please," Phil said.

"Has the Governor responded to the phone campaign to save Ellie? Has he called McGillian to intervene?"

So the protesters had taken their cause to Albany. Good. Phil slammed the front door and rushed up the one flight of steps. There was only one thing to do. Get her out.

Visions of the burn on Rachel's arm, blisters in a whitish-reddish mess, made Phil's stomach contract. And she had been threatened with further punishment. Rape. God. If he could just get McGillian off his ass in the middle of the weekend. McGillian must remove her from danger.

The phone rang ten times in McGillian's empty house. There was no answer. Phil dialed again, checking to be sure it was the right number. Still no answer. Next, he tried to page the judge at his golf club but was informed that the man was not there.

Phil threw a few things into a duffel bag. He had promised his mother he'd come by for lunch. Afterwards he'd pass by McGillian's house and see if, perhaps, he was out in the backyard. If he had no further luck, he'd go to Fire Island and continue calling from there.

By Saturday afternoon most of the weekend crowd had long crossed over to Fire

Island. There were fewer ferries making the outbound trip. When Phil arrived, the next boat was not due for almost an hour.

The salad his mother had served, like the woman herself, had been anemic, as if nothing she ever touched could show itself in full colors. His heart contracted with pity, he had chewed on the wilted leaves, wondering what kind of woman she had been before Parker Crawford swept her off her feet only to send her crashing down to the bottom of despair.

"A Manhattan clam chowder, please," he now said to the young woman behind the counter at a small kiosk.

"Uh, I'm new here." She smiled sheepishly. "Which is the Manhattan and which is New England?"

"Think of the Big Red Apple and then the white snows of New England," he replied. That was his father's tip to keep the two apart. His father was full of funny ideas, told wonderful stories, played imaginative games. Games that turned unspeakable.

Phil settled on a bench to dip his oyster crackers in the hot soup, rich with vegetables and spices, and forced himself to calm down. Parker's charm no longer had a place in his life, only what Phil could do about the memories of those moments in the dark when his father held him tight and whispered loving words in his ears while rocking and rubbing against Phil's tiny buttocks—

That's what seeing his mother's destroyed spirit often evoked. There was no escaping the pain they both endured. Violently, ferociously, Phil shrugged the memory away. It was all over now. His therapist had helped him channel the harrowing experience into a positive, driving force, and that was all that counted. Now he could help children like himself. Ellie, for one. Except that so far he had been powerless to change the course of her case.

A couple with two frolicking puppies whose oversized paws promised they would become formidable animals took the seat next to him. The dogs wagged their tails, ready for play. Kneeling down, Phil scratched the nearest one under its collar. The other dog approached and nudged his wet nose into Phil's other hand for a back rub. Phil let out a laugh. Moments later, he was absorbed in their play.

His equanimity restored, he strolled over to the pay phone. He had promised Rachel he would call her French friend, the petite woman with a mane of dark curls whom he had met the previous weekend at Fire Island.

After he tried McGillian's number—again with no luck—he called Jacqueline.

"You won't believe what's going on," she effervesced. "I spent all day yesterday in Albany at Governor Dunkle's office—most of the time outside it, that is. The phones were ringing off the hook. I got hold of an assistant who said the faxes jammed the line—"

"Jacqueline, I can't get involved in this fashion—Rachel just asked me to say hello."

"You spoke to her?"

Worry for Rachel gnawed in him. He wished he could share it with her friend. "I visited her in my official capacity as a court employee."

"Oh." She paused. "Well. You should report this back to her—we went to the post office and had them lug Dunkle's Friday late mail in boxes—"

"Jacqueline, it's better if I don't get into this."

"Don't give me this crap. You're not calling me in your official capacity."

"Whatever." He assumed a businesslike tone. "It's better for Rachel if we keep our friendship separate."

"So said my last married boyfriend," she replied.

"Sorry, got to go."

He hung up and dialed Judge McGillian's home number again. After ten rings he hung up.

The next morning, Phil pulled himself out of bed, dropped a beach bag at the bay dock, and went jogging. He ran for a dozen blocks west then, drenched in sweat, retraced his track east back to the dock.

In the early hour, the air was cool, and the azure water, in its play of catching and reflecting the light, inviting. Phil dove in, headfirst. He ignored the shock of the cold water on his skin and forced his muscles to radiate their warmth from within. When he broke the surface, he lifted his arms and began a fifteen-minute butterfly-style swim until his shoulders ached and his lungs burned with exertion. He stopped to rest, his arm laced through the dock's ladder, the salt in his eyes and mouth, feeling free, strong, and alive.

After several additional laps, he came out and settled at a coffee shop.

"Would you like *The New York Times*?" a young woman with a reddish ponytail and a tight halter top asked. Her smile was open, inviting. "It comes with the bagels. The editors' invention to increase their Sunday circulation."

Phil returned her smile but ignored her flirtation. His towel draped loosely over his shoulders, he leafed through the paper. His eyes came to a sudden stop on a picture of Rachel.

Unlike the stock photograph released for the previous articles—probably distributed by her lawyer—this one was shot Thursday when Rachel was whisked away into the police van, its barred windows in the background framing her head. The photo captured her glancing toward the camera, an expression of bewilderment on her face. Yet even in this picture, taken in typical journalistic haste, her bright eyes surrounded by dark lashes were clear, her smooth complexion glowing.

He stepped to the pay phone and dialed the judge's number. This time McGillian answered the phone.

Finally. "Sorry, Judge, to call you so early. I visited Ms. Belmore as you asked." Phil gave him a short report. "I think you should let her out, today, before she's hurt any further."

"I don't like the sound of things, but can't it wait till tomorrow?"

"It's not a good idea, Judge. I can pass by the office this morning, pick up the forms, and come over to your house so you can sign."

McGillian laughed. "Still trying to shame me into working overtime? No need to. Let's meet with the Belmores' lawyers tomorrow morning and see what's what."

That laughter pierced Phil to the quick. The same callousness that made McGillian ignore those descriptions in the file. The man understood—or cared about—the realities of everyday life no more than a conqueror of a colonial nation who must determine the fate of a people across an ocean.

Phil called Jacqueline again. "I didn't mean to be rude yesterday," he said.

"Have you seen today's *New York Times*?"

"I'm looking at it right now."

"It's illogical, this American system of yours that elects judges like McGillian because of their political affiliation. What do they know of family issues, psychological forces, social dynamics, and everyday life situations?"

"Judges are beginning to get sensitivity training."

"Too late for Ellie. The best interest of the children? Even *The New York Times* agrees that if Ellie's afraid of her father and has emotional problems, she should have the comfort of her mother and the stability of a steady home. Why can't she have it?"

"Are you asking me as a lawyer, as an American, or as an officer of the court?"

"All of the above."

"Hey, don't go after me now."

"Sorry," she said. "Well, tomorrow should be interesting."

"What's tomorrow?"

"Read the article on page eight. Women's groups from all across the country are joining the 'Free Ellie' campaign. I'll be back in Albany for a huge rally in front of the state capitol."

Could he break confidentiality? Phil cringed. To hell with McGillian. "Jacqueline— er— You should stick around. Don't ask me why, but Rachel may need you on call."

He broke an ethical rule he would soon be sworn to when he took the Bar exam. But in his first month on the job, his mission to help kids had accomplished so little. Nothing, in fact.

CHAPTER THIRTY-ONE

MCGILLIAN motioned with his head toward the lobby where Erica Norgard and Henry Ortman were each absorbed in their documents, probably killing time with work for other clients. For once, there was no petition pending in the Belmore v. Belmore case.

Phil's blood thumped in his ears with the urgency of what he must do. He closed the door behind him and planted himself in front of the Judge's desk. "Sir, you should give more thought to Ms. Belmore's situation at the corrections facility in Jefferson." There was heat in his voice. "The accident was a malicious, deliberate act. It's a bad, infected burn."

"So you said on the phone. What did the prison nurse say?"

"Rachel—Ms. Belmore—was advised, under a veiled threat, not to seek treatment. Judge, the warden says prisoners often don't take well to an educated, high-class prisoner in their midst. He says they'll continue to terrorize her until she's been brought down to their level."

McGillian tapped his pencil. "That wasn't my intention in sending her there."

Phil's words rushed out. "Well, Judge, whether you intended or not, this has become a punitive—rather than a coercive—measure."

McGillian got up from his chair and went to the window. His fingers brushed the back of his head. He kept his hand there a moment longer. Then, with a small wave of his finger, he indicated to Phil to come near.   "There they go again."

Phil stepped closer. In the unloading zone, two women brought out signs from the back of a van and leaned them against the side of the vehicle. Even from that distance, the words "Free Ellie," painted in bright red, were clearly visible. A black pacifier was drawn at the corner of the poster. Phil stifled a smile.

McGillian let out a sigh. "This case is becoming a three-ring circus—what with the media hoopla and all these feminist groups. Did you see that ad in *The New York Times*? We must tone things down all around. I don't want it to seem as though the court is buckling to Rachel Belmore's publicity stunt, but we may have to let her out. I can't allow her to be punished by prisoners."

"Judge, Dr. Wes Belmore was the first one to go to the press with his story. Not Ms. Belmore."

McGillian swiveled around to face him. "Is that so? When?"

"A couple of weeks ago."

"Before Ortman brought the last petition to produce the Belmore kid?"

"Yes, Your Honor."

"You'd think Sylvia would have told me."

"It was in the *City Post*, sir." Phil unclenched his fists; he hadn't realized how tight they were. "Not your everyday reading."

"That Ortman SOB." McGillian shook his head. "I can't remember a case ever causing me so much aggravation. Thanks for taking the time over your weekend. Did you read the Sunday papers?"

"Yes, sir."

"You read, then, that Erica Norgard publicly criticized me—this court. You understand the difference, don't you? This is not a litigant talking to a journalist, but an officer of this court choosing to circumvent the more appropriate channels, and I intend to report her behavior to the Bar's Disciplinary Committee."

At least Rachel would be out. Her lawyer should be able to take care of herself, Phil thought.

McGillian took a deep breath. "Okay, let's get this monkey off my back."

Sylvia's tap on the door cut him off in mid-sentence. "Judge, before the Belmore v. Belmore conference you'd better take a look at this." She waved a document.

"What now?"

"Erica Norgard has filed a complaint with the Judicial Conduct Commission."

"*She* did?" McGillian rose to his feet. "What the hell— On what grounds?" He snatched the papers out of Sylvia's hands.

"She claims Rachel Belmore's contempt of court incarceration is an act of discrimination," Sylvia replied while he perused the papers, moving fast from top to bottom.

"I've never called a woman a 'bitch' before." McGillian's words escaped clamped lips. "But if I've ever met one—Christ." He plopped back into his chair. "Phil?"

"Sir?"

"The woman is making it more difficult for me to help her client. If I let Ms. Belmore go, Bitch Norgard will think her tactics of intimidation have worked."

In brisk movements, Bitch Norgard swooped in, took her seat, and pulled the hem of her skirt below her knees. McGillian allowed himself a peek. In the past several years, female thighs became visible in his chambers as more women were drawn to the legal profession. As he should have known, Ms. Norgard's skirt offered no serendipitous peek.

The conflicting pressures McGillian felt made him bristle. What he had been unable to share with his law clerk was that if he kept that troublemaker Belmore mother in jail, Dunkle would believe he had bought this judge. Such an assumption went right to the heart of who he was. It diminished him as a man, as a person, as a judge.

"Ms. Norgard. Is your client ready to comply with the court order?"

"I'm sorry, Your Honor, but she's determined to protect her child against the father's sexual molestation."

"Coercion hasn't been given its full potential yet, Your Honor," Ortman said. "It's been only four days—"

McGillian cut him off. "We've received a report that Ms. Belmore was severely burned in jail. She was threatened with more of the same. It was not the intent of the court to inflict physical torture on her."

"Then put her in protective custody."

"You're talking isolation. That's another form of punishment—not coercion." McGillian examined the faces of the lawyers. Would the bitch have enough brains to help him free her client?

She was more astute than he had given her credit for, thus unwittingly helping him give Nicholas Dunkle the clear message that he didn't have this judge in his back pocket, doing dirty work for his family doctor. "Ms. Belmore should have the freedom to prepare her appeal," she interjected.

Taking his time, McGillian pretended to scribble a note on the yellow legal pad. "Shall we all agree that from now on no interviews will be given to the press?"

"No problem, Your Honor," Ortman said. "I'm sure my client will agree."

"Why would Ms. Belmore forgo her constitutional right to speak to the media?" Ms. Norgard asked. "Judge, I can't advise my client to accept this restriction."

"Ms. Norgard, it would be better for everyone concerned to bring the trial back to the courtroom where it belongs and not drag it out into the public arena."

"I beg to differ, Your Honor." Norgard's modulated tone was maddeningly calm. "What's good for *everyone* is not necessarily in the best interest of my client—or her child. Since Dr. Belmore has publicly maligned Rachel Belmore, she should be free to exercise her constitutional rights."

"Are you saying that if her release is conditioned upon the request to discontinue this media hype, your client won't cooperate?"

"I cannot see why forfeiting her First Amendment right should be a condition of Rachel Belmore's release from an administrative incarceration for which there is no recent precedent. In the past ten years there has been only one case in which a defendant was jailed for contempt of court—Family Court, that is—without being given weeks or months to contemplate his or her actions first. While I'm sure my client will appreciate the court's decision to release her today, she should be allowed to discuss the gross discrimination she has been treated with when compared with other cases of contempt."

He stared at her. "Ms. Norgard, do I need to impose a gag order? Okay, here it is. I'm ordering all parties not to speak to the press."

For once, she had no answer, but he detected a shade of a smile at the corners of her mouth. The bitch was planning to outmaneuver him. To steel himself, he leafed through his papers. "Ms. Norgard, it is my obligation to see justice done for your client even if you're intent on stretching the limits of my patience and are willing to sacrifice her interests for an esoteric cause to serve your own private agenda."

There. It was done. Having carved an escape route, he announced, "Rachel Belmore will be released today on a ten-thousand-dollar bail."

"I'll see the bondsman outside," Bitch Norgard said.

He nodded, banged his gavel, and turned to the court officer. "Next case?"

CHAPTER THIRTY-TWO

CLIQUES of prisoners idled about the day room. The place was noisy with their arguing against the blaring of the TV. Nothing would happen to her if she just stayed put. Rachel would have liked to write letters in the library. If she stayed here much longer, she might start to write one of the romance novels she was reading. Her life offered plenty of drama. But any quiet place was fraught with unimaginable danger. How long would she be able to stand up to Alegra?

Yesterday, with the short golf-course-style pencil the C.O. had provided, Rachel had started to write to Ellie. Letters that would not be mailed—at least not until she consulted with Erica before handing them to Howard. But it comforted her to breathe words of courage and love to her child.

She held open another romance novel. Instead of reading, in her mind's eye, visions of Ellie playing with her dolls flitted about. Ellie singing in the new kibbutz kindergarten, swinging her legs on the seesaw, giggling in delight when she splashed in the swimming pool. Ellie marveling at the colors of flowers, of ice cream, of the sun. Ellie happy.

A little smile curled on Rachel's lips against her will but was cut short with a tap on the shoulder. She turned with a start.

"Alegra wants to talk to you," a prisoner said to her. "Over there."

The fear took her over again. Rachel scanned the faces about her. In the world she used to know, she would have told the messenger to get lost. But in this misbegotten world of prison, Alegra's wrath was too frightening to fathom.

"I have nothing to say to her," Rachel muttered. The blisters on her arm had erupted, and now they oozed pus and throbbed.

To her astonishment, Alegra ambled over a minute later, puffing on a cigarette.

"Do you mind if I smoke?" she asked Rachel as she sat down, blowing the smoke sideways as a minor concession.

Rachel gave a twitch of a smile. The adrenalin coursed through her. She was developing an animal's sense of danger. Or perhaps it was only a new conditioning to the stench of Alegra's breath.

"Sorry about the other day." Alegra motioned toward Rachel's arm.

Rachel eyed her warily.

"We got wind of why you're here. You're the best."

A glob of saliva stuck in Rachel's throat. She coughed.

"Hey, listen, no hard feelings, okay?" Alegra's smile revealed toothless, gray gums.

"I don't get it." Rachel's heart still galloped.

"You're here because you hid your daughter, right? Her father was raping her, right? We read about it in the papers. Now that's a class act, and I respect that. We all do here." Her hand made a sweeping motion. "These women, me, we all got the shaft from our fathers, brothers, cousins. My mother—she didn't do nothing when her boyfriend stuck it in me and my sisters. It's a good thing you're doing."

Rachel could not take her eyes off the woman, the electronic connections in her brain swiftly scanning through a list of suspicions. Was it possible she was out of danger? Would it be okay to smile at Alegra? Rachel's terror of that woman was too deep. She lowered her gaze into her book. Minutes passed, and she bean to feel a glimmer of understanding toward Alegra. Perhaps, in its own microcosm, the bottom of society had its own value system. Like spokes of sun that lit patches of a decaying forest floor, these women's world was illuminated by bright spots of humanity.

Alegra reached her hand and touched Rachel's fingers. Rachel fought her flight instinct and the revulsion these fingers arose. Alegra had been sexually molested as a child. Like Ellie.

Slowly, Rachel turned her palm up, and responded to Alegra's touch with a light squeeze of her fingers.

"We're daughters, sisters, mothers—even if you think I'm nothing but white trash." Alegra grin was rueful. "We all hurt the same way when men do filthy things to little girls." She halted and theatrically assessed the crowd watching them from all corners of the recreation hall. The features on the ravaged face expanded again. "If anyone tries anything funny, you come tell me. But I don't think you're going to have any trouble. No one I know ever did what you did."

"Thank you—" Rachel bit her lip. She shouldn't be using the words that had gotten her in trouble with Alegra in the first place.

But Alegra smiled again, blew more smoke sideways, and said, "You're okay— even if you're a little too uppity."

She had only a short time to enjoy the new safety from Alegra's threat. An hour later, she was told to gather her things and to follow the guard to the warden's office.

She signed a few documents, found out that Erica had paid ten percent of the bond fee, and was escorted out.

Out! Even the sizzling asphalt smelled good. And there was a honeysuckle climbing an electric pole, sending its fragrance her way.

Jacqueline stood next to the tan-colored Chevy Rachel had left at the courthouse parking lot on Thursday, a lifetime before. Bright beams of sunlight pierced the back of Rachel's eyes. She stumbled into Jacqueline's arms, sobbing.

"My poor baby," Jacqueline murmured as she held her. She removed the strap of Rachel's half-filled overnight bag. "What have they done to you?"

A flashbulb popped nearby, and Rachel glanced up to see several journalists and a photographer. They surrounded her. Remembering Erica's instructions, she struggled to smile at them.

Questions were thrown at her, like darts, but they echoed as though spoken through wax paper.

"I'm sorry," she whispered to a man with bulbous eyes and red, puffy lips. David Lupori from the *City Post* again. In the heat, she was afraid her knees would give way. "Not now. I appreciate your caring, but I can't talk right now."

Jacqueline pointed to the car. "I picked it up and ran it through the car wash. You owe me six dollars, including tip."

A weak laugh escaped Rachel's throat. "I'll go bankrupt if I have to pay you back for everything you've done."

Jacqueline started the engine and pushed the air conditioning control to maximum. "I took a few days off. I'll stay with you."

"Jacqueline, you'll get fired."

"So what?"

"So you need the health benefits."

"Don't worry about it."

"Thanks, but I'll be fine after a shower and a nap. Really."

"Wait till you see the messages on your answering machine. You'll need me to field all those journalists."

"Oh, no," Rachel groaned. "I can't take any more of this."

"There's one you may want to talk to."

"Who's that?"

"Larry King. Your friend was as good as her word. She got her boss interested."

"When?"

Jacqueline shrugged. "They'll let us know."

Rachel fished in her purse for Tylenol. Just to have her belongings back felt like home.

Jacqueline handed her an Evian bottle. "Too late for lunch. We'll have an early dinner. But first let's stop at the emergency room. I don't like the look of this decoration on your arm. It looks horrible, if you don't mind my saying so."

"The day you stop being blunt is the day I lose my best friend," Rachel said, then added, "Thanks for everything."

"Thank me when Ellie's back, or when I shoot Wes—whichever comes first." Her tone changed, its softness matching the mist in her eyes. "Does it hurt like hell?"

"Less than having Ellie in Wes's bed."

When they neared the house after the visit at the hospital, Rachel noticed a huge flower arrangement perched against the front door. Jacqueline slowed down and glanced at it before rounding the house into the driveway on the side.

"Who sent those?" Rachel asked.

"Let me make a wild guess. Your old, faithful Gerald. He's full of remorse; acts like a puppy crawling back with his tail between his legs. He's been calling me twice a day to find out what's going on with you."

"I'm sure you gave him a piece of your mind."

"Didn't deter him."

Rachel did not respond.

"Well? You were pining for him for weeks," Jacqueline continued. "Are you going to take this creep back?"

"I'm in no shape to make any decisions."

"He does have some good sides to him, I must admit."

"There's this question of Phil—" Rachel began to say.

"Don't tell me! That gorgeous hunk from Fire Island? He called me Sunday—"

"You don't even know the half of it."

"I saw him in court too. He said he worked there."

"Jacques, he's only twenty-five."

"I love it! I love it! That will teach Gerald to hang out with young nymphs." Jacqueline stopped. "Hey," she said, her tone grave. "How do you know Wes didn't send him? It would be in character."

Rachel shook her head. "I've already thought of that, but no. This guy's for real."

A note was attached to Gerald's flowers. He wanted to take her out to dinner the next night if she were up to it.

Jacqueline examined the card. "Do you want me to give you a handwriting analysis?"

"Thanks, but I already know about him what I need to know."

An hour later, her arm in a sling, her wet hair up in a turban, Rachel settled in the kitchen with a cup of coffee. "You haven't given me a report on the office gossip," she said.

"I might as well tell you. I was kind of let go."

"Oh, Jacques. Vince was sick of your skipping work."

"He was sick of my loyalty to you. Anyway, the union is negotiating my transfer to any Sheridan magazine of my choice, so I still have a job if I want it." Jacqueline twisted a strand of hair around her finger. "Maybe I'll split. Time to sing—not type—for my supper."

"You should have split long ago to study music full-time."

"But I have been studying. Studying you." Jacqueline smiled. "I've learned tenacity, and determination."

"Great. Thanks." Rachel reached for the phone. "I should call Vince before five; see how my clients are doing. If I still have clients."

"What about Liliana's magazine?"

"There's no way I can give a magazine launch the hours and travel it requires."

Vince's secretary informed Rachel he had everything under control. "I mailed your paycheck on Friday." The new chill in the woman's voice was unmistakable, obviously reflecting that of her boss.

Rachel thanked her and hung up. There was no point in speculating why he didn't come to the phone or what Jacqueline's transfer meant in the larger picture.

Rachel poured her coffee into a tall glass over ice cubes. She added milk and carried the glass out to the patio. She rattled the drink to listen the luxurious sound of clinking ice cubes. The small pleasures in life were so new. She settled into a lounge chair and scanned the flowerbeds she had planted with Ellie. She should send Ellie a photograph.

Jacqueline produced a platter of cheese and crackers along with a thick envelope Howard had messengered over. When Rachel slashed it open, she found the documents for the bank loan.

She read through and filled in the blanks. Forty thousand dollars would hardly be enough. Her hand shook at the enormity of the debt. Tomorrow morning she would go to the local branch, sign for the loan in front of the manager, and get her finances in order. This money would not last long after she paid all her outstanding bills.

From inside the house, she heard the crackling voice of a woman as the answering machine fielded a call. Jacqueline no longer picked up the phone. It might be another reporter or a nasty call from a disgruntled father—a member of a loose group of disenchanted men who had aligned themselves with Wes's cause. Or it could be one of those loonies who got their kicks in life contacting anyone whose name appeared in the news. Rachel had placed an order with the phone company to change her number to an unlisted one, but the process would take a few days.

"It's Larry King's office," Jacqueline called over to Rachel as she snatched the receiver.

By the time Rachel tapped her documents into a neat pile and scrambled to her feet, Jacqueline thanked the caller and hung up. "You got the interview," Jacqueline announced. "We'd better get you to LaGuardia—"

Rachel gasped. "You mean I have to fly to Washington? Tonight?"

"You're hot. That's the only way he'll have it—your first night out of jail."

"I'm in no shape to get on the plane now—" Rachel halted. As Erica had insisted, this was a media battle, and she had to fight in whatever arena Wes dragged her to—and win. For Ellie.

"He suggested you wear red," Jacqueline said.

Rachel plopped down on the nearest kitchen chair. She looked at the wall clock. "I hope my MasterCard's good for a plane ticket."

"You'd better hurry if you want to catch the six o'clock shuttle. They want you at CNN's studio by seven-thirty."

Jacqueline waited for Rachel at midnight when she returned.

"You aced it," Jacqueline said. "A lot of people hate McGillian's guts."

"Larry let some tough callers through. They were ready to chop my head off."

"Without controversy he has no show," Jacqueline replied. "It paved the way for the next level."

"Which is what?"

"Oprah. She's a crusader against child sexual molestation. Her producer is expecting your call tomorrow. They may fit you in her program within days."

Rachel shook her head. "What's the big deal? It's not as if I had a choice—I had to send Ellie away."

"You heard the caller from the Family and Law Organization. Nobody ever hears of the many mothers who end up in jail, of judges that are chauvinistic and cruel, and of the thousands of mothers who give up the fight."

How could they give up the fight? Yet, it could have been her. It was easy to understand how these mothers broke down. Rachel closed her eyes. She had slept on both legs of the flight, but fatigue was still buried deep in her bones. Her body ached all over.

The bedcover, a hand-stitched quilt Ellie had helped select at a country fair, felt more like home than she had ever imagined. She folded it back, crawled under it, and soon dreamed of floating into a silent and opalescent world. Her limbs lowered onto pillowy clouds that enveloped her in tender embraces, closing on her, shielding her. Ellie ran, flying a rainbow kite, her laughter like little bells ringing in the translucent vacuum.

CHAPTER THIRTY-THREE

RACHEL stayed in bed all morning, had lunch on the patio with Jacqueline, then slept again. When she finally woke up at six in the evening, she was ready to face Gerald with a mix of apprehension and curiosity. Mostly curiosity. A little raw patch of disillusion still reminded her to stay guarded.

Jacqueline set her hair in hot rollers and gave her the next dose of vancomycin antibiotics prescribed at the hospital. She helped Rachel get into a white pants suit, and, as the doctor had instructed, rolled up the sleeves to let the blisters dry in the air.

"Wait. Earrings. The knock-'em-dead kind." Jacqueline rummaged through Rachel's jewelry case. She plucked a dangling, oversized pair. "Here. Kill Gerald with these."

Gerald waited at the door. His eyes, edged by softness, were glued to Rachel's face. "You look beautiful," he said, awe in his voice.

"Thanks." Rachel tried not to look at him. His voice alone made her knees weak. She was glad Jacqueline did not seize the opportunity to give him another piece of her mind. Instead, her friend planted good-bye kisses on both Rachel's cheeks.

Outside, Rachel stopped for a moment and took a deep breath of the fragrant evening air as Gerald took her elbow. "Feels like I've been gone for months—not days," she said.

She also wanted to say, "And it feels like you've been gone for years—not weeks."

Only then did Rachel notice David Lupori waiting in the street, his amphibian eyes intent on the scene. She should not have brushed him off outside the jail. Erica wanted him on their side.

"What's next?" Lupori asked.

"I don't know. When I meet with my attorney we'll discuss it. Tell you what. If you give me your number, I'll personally call you if I have anything to report."

He hitched his camera to his face and clicked. "Do you know where Ellie is?"

"You know I can't answer that, don't you?" She smiled. "But she's safe from her father's sexual abuse."

No more Zoo Game.

With a contented look, Lupori handed her his business card, climbed into his Jeep, and drove away.

Gerald had made reservations at Chez Jean-Michel, an elegant restaurant that had been their favorite.

The maitre d' led them to a window table overlooking a sprawling lawn and a lily pond. Gerald's gaze was still fixed on Rachel as he held her chair. "How are you feeling?"

"As well as can be expected under the circumstances." She heard the sharpness of her tone. "And I'm not referring only to Ellie, the trial, and the jail."

"I know. I was such a heel." He took her hand.

She pulled it back. "What is this dinner about?"

"I'm so sorry to have added to your anguish. Would it help any if I explained what went on in my head?"

"I want to hear that. Yes."

She lifted the fluted crystal glass to her lips and closed her eyes for a moment. The champagne tasted better than she had remembered. Tiny bubbles soared in her mouth, tingling her taste buds with flavor both earthly and heavenly.

"I left the house after years of bickering. The last year was the worst. You know all about it. I was heartbroken over leaving the kids. In my search for a more peaceful existence, I met you. And we fell in love." He looked into her eyes. "We did, didn't we? It was real, and beautiful. But suddenly, all hell broke loose around you. The independent, successful executive I had met had problems at work. We all do, but each day brought another crisis that tore my guts out because I cared. Then this unbelievable shit with your ex came out."

"It was there all along, I just didn't tell you about it at the beginning."

"Sorry. This doesn't make me look or sound good, but these are the facts."

"At least you could have told me you wanted to break it off. And why. You didn't even have the decency for that."

"I'm really sorry…."

"Gerald, this is not good enough."

"I wanted peace, not the World War III that was raging all around you. You brought mayhem into my life." He took a gulp of air. "That drive around the block when the caseworker was at your house was degrading…. On the flight back from San Diego I thought about it all. Yes, I missed you, but I had my own baggage to deal with—my own three kids were going through emotional hell but instead of helping them I was wrapped up in your troubles…. So I refocused my energies on them."

"Oh?"

"I'd insult you if I lied now. On another front, I convinced myself that New York was full of beauties. Why did I have to get stuck with the one whose list of problems topped them all?" He patted her fingers. She stiffened. He continued as if he didn't notice her reaction. "I won't pretend I was nice or gallant; I'm ashamed of my behavior. The temptation to ask someone else out—several of them—was too great. The way I eased you out was cruel, and I regret it. But your life was choking me."

"Nothing has changed for the better. You'd better run away now. Fast."

"What I didn't realize was that I couldn't just replace one beauty with ten others—that I was in love with you. I fantasized about you—"

"Please spare me the details," she cut him off. "If it makes it any easier for you, I haven't exactly pined for you alone."

"I guess I shouldn't be surprised."

Why was she here? What explanation would she have accepted? Not this. It simply wasn't enough. Memories of her incredulity over his abrupt departure and of the days and nights she had missed him bubbled in every cell of her body.

They hadn't yet ordered. She gathered her handbag and began to get up. "Well, you told me, now we can leave."

"Please sit down. Please." He waited.

She relented and settled back in her chair.

"I'm truly sorry." His tone turned eager. "If I didn't blow it all to pieces, can we pick up where we left off? Can we start all over again—at the day in the electronics shop when we bought our answering machines?"

"Gerald," she said, her eyes misting, "you've disappointed me so...."

"Give me—us—a chance and I'll make up for it."

How she had craved hearing those words a couple of weeks ago. "I'm so very tired. Physically, emotionally. I'm confused...." She let her words trail.

"I can think of a way or two to 'unconfuse' you." He gave her a sheepish smile, then his tone changed. "Let me love you again. I'll take care of you through the rest of this ordeal." He added with a smile, "I'm ready for the right ride down the rocky road."

She smiled wanly. "Not a very good 'R' list."

"And when Ellie returns, I'd like to move in with the two of you. She began to accept me. In time, I'll be the kind of father she needs."

Rachel looked into the brown eyes she had loved. How she wished she could say "yes." It could be so simple. A neat closure. His offer to be a loving father to Ellie was too tempting to brush off without giving it further thought.

"Don't ask me to answer now," she said.

"Take your time. Now, I'm sure the food is better than what you've had these past few days. I called ahead and asked the chef to make your salmon the way you like it."

They drove back in a comfortable silence of old acquaintants. She was no longer angry, but Gerald's presence failed to bestow on her the sense of elation it once did. His promise echoed with the hollow sound of a coin dropping into a dry well.

At the curb in front of her house, he killed the engine and draped his arm over her shoulders.

His kisses rekindled her desire, but only to the flicker of a candle. Would she ever regain the lost trust in his love?

Reluctantly, Gerald walked her to the door and released her. "I'll check on you tomorrow. Good night, my love."

Jacqueline had Dan over, and the two of them were practicing a duet when Rachel entered. "Phil called. He left a number," Jacqueline announced. "Keeping up with your love life is almost as good as having one of my own."

"Good night, guys." Rachel climbed up the stairs to her bedroom. Even though it was only nine-thirty, she crawled into bed. Her body still remembered the prison cot and was surprised anew to feel the cool, crisp sheets of her bed—life's little delights that she was unaware of until she had them no more. Thanks to Jefferson Correctional, she would never again take them for granted.

With pillows supporting her back and the air conditioner humming in the background drowning the stop-and-go of the singing downstairs, Rachel dialed Phil's number. Her inner core tingled with the anticipation of hearing his warm, delighted voice. He had called the day before to check on her just as she was leaving for Larry King.

He answered on the second ring.

She asked the question she had not been able to ask. "Is this your own place? Don't you live with your girlfriend?"

"I never did. During school vacations I stayed with my mother in Smithtown." He halted. "And as to a girlfriend, I have a new one—if she'll have me, that is."

Rachel clutched the receiver. How could she even allow herself a moment of doubt? There was no question which of her two men possessed the strength of character. "Yes, she will," she whispered, "and she wants you here. Now."

"Give me twenty minutes. Start counting."

When Phil arrived, he had plans.

"There's something I've wanted to do ever since that night on the beach in Fire Island," he whispered against her mouth. She was more beautiful each time he saw her.

"What is that?"

"To make love to you at the water's edge." He gathered all the tenderness he could muster into his gaze. "Are you too tired for a ride?"

Her fatigue evaporated. "I've done nothing but rest all day."

"What about your arm? Can you seal it with Saran Wrap?"

The night was exceptionally warm. Usually, the winds from either the Atlantic Ocean to the south or Long Island Sound to the north cooled the island. But tonight the air did not move. It hovered above them like a huge, moist bubble. Phil pulled his Camaro to a stop near a small stretch of deserted beach.

They climbed out of the car. The sandy beach was on the tip of a peninsula, flanked on both sides by private estates. Few people ever bothered to drive all the way up there even during the day. The sweet, tranquil scent of lavender spiked with rosemary drifted from the estates' flower gardens in their direction.

Rachel took in a deep breath. "Smell the flowers in the air."

He nuzzled her skin. "This is better." He tugged at her shirt, then removed it. He passed his fingertips over her breasts, circling the nipples in a feathery touch. They hardened and produced a similar response in his groin. He wriggled out of his jeans and stepped to the trunk of his car to retrieve a blanket.

He turned to see Rachel's naked figure walk toward the water. In a few large strides, he covered the distance between them.

He took her in his arms, nibbling her neck. Pressing the length of his body against hers, he slowly gyrated against her. His head went down, licking and kissing. "Remember the stars we talked about? Go ahead and swoon over them while I go about my business down here on earth."

At the water's edge, he lay the blanket on the wet sand.

They paddled their toes in the water, Rachel's raised arm resting on his. They let the undulating waves lick and lap against their legs.

His free arm circled her as he turned her toward him. They slid down on the blanket, now soaked and supple, and Rachel lay on her back, letting out a throaty purr. Bathed in the glow of starlight, white and luxurious, her skin satiny, she looked and felt like a mermaid. Phil propped himself on his elbows above her. The water slapped them with caressing sounds, engulfing them, as he felt her warmth enveloping him in hot, pulsating contractions.

Their breathing came short and loud. He would never get enough of Rachel; there would never be a time in his life when he wouldn't want to make love to her.

For a long time, lapping waves banged at his thighs, strokes of splashing, swirling water that upon receding left his skin tingly. Under him, Rachel tensed. Her spine arched and she raised herself toward him. With increased pressure, he moved faster and faster, his breathing coming harder while Rachel's moans echoed in his head. A steady, throbbing beat joined the sounds of the sea.

Sensing a new wave approaching behind him, Phil's rhythmic movements took on a new urgency. He let go.

They lay motionless, catching their breath. Phil lifted her head and rested it gently over his arm.

"I love you," he whispered. "The Mother Who Protects Her Child."

She nuzzled against him. Tranquility enveloped both of them.   "It's time you explained," she said quietly.

"It's not a pleasant story. I promise to tell you when we're both in the mood."

CHAPTER THIRTY-FOUR

"LAZY Bones." Jacqueline shook Rachel awake. "It's ten o'clock and your lawyer's on the phone. Says it's important."

Groggily, Rachel put the phone to her ear. Her other hand patted the empty, rumpled area in the bed. Phil must have left for work while she was still asleep.

Erica Norgard's tone was sharp. "Is it true? McGillian's law clerk spent the night with you?"

Rachel bolted upright as the words reached the hinterlands of her consciousness. "What? How do you know?"

"Lou Kaplan found out it would be making the headline in the late morning edition of the *City Post*. McGILLIAN'S CLERK IS RACHEL BELMORE'S LOVER. What's going on?"

"It's too complicated to explain." The gears in Rachel's head clicked along the process of the discovery. The vigilant Lupori, like a heat-seeking missile, had zoomed in on her house and noted Phil's license plate number. A quick check from his car phone must have matched it to Phil's name—if he hadn't known already. It wasn't hard to put two and two together.

"Now, get on the next train and come see me," Erica ordered. "New strategy. We're shifting gears."

When Rachel came downstairs, Jacqueline met her in the kitchen with a glass of orange juice. "What was that all about?"

"It's Phil."

Jacqueline didn't know this hadn't been their first time together, and Rachel wanted to share the knowledge with no one. The sense of specialness that had enveloped them during the long hours of lovemaking and talking took place as much in the silences as in the words they had uttered. Lupori's intrusion left Rachel feeling invaded, as though a thief had raked through her lingerie drawers.

Jacqueline winked. "I hope Phil was all you wanted him to be and more."

"He's sensitive, witty, caring, and funny." And he stepped forward from the shadows to face the storm of her problems. "He's unpretentious."

"In other words: no money."

"That's beside the point. He's Judge McGillian's law clerk, and it's about to hit the papers."

Jacqueline straightened up in her chair. "So that's why he was in court and then visited you in jail? Didn't I tell you men are everywhere? Everywhere. We only have to listen to their mating calls."

Rachel smiled, but any more talking about Phil would devalue the beauty of their time together. She refilled her glass of juice and started for the stairs.

"Rachel," Jacqueline's softer tone stopped her. "It's not like you to burst through an open door without first checking what's behind it. There must be more to it."

"There is a lot more." Rachel turned to face her. "For three years I only trusted doubt, and the only emotion I could feel was fear." Her voice was barely a whisper. "He's changed that. He needs me, too." As she spoke, she realized the shift in her psyche. She had begun to give, not merely take. Phil, while infusing her with strength, in turn fed on what she gave him. Was that the hidden meaning of his image of her as The Mother Who Protects Her Child?

Fifteen minutes later, comfortable in cream linen pants and a tailored top, Rachel stood at the door. Jacqueline flicked through the TV stations, and the truncated sounds of jingles, cartoon squeaks, canned audience laughter, and announcers drifted out to Rachel when some words made her drop her handbag and rush into the living room.

"Put that on again," she cried out, her hand clutching her chest.

"What's that?" Jacqueline looked at her with arched eyebrows, the TV remote held in front of her.

"What did you just have on? Hurry!" Rachel snatched the remote control and clicked back to the channel.

In the right hand corner of the screen, a small map of Israel was displayed in yellow tones. The muted, gurgled phone voice of a reporter was signing off.

"What was it? What did they say?" Rachel demanded, hearing the panic lodged in her own voice.

"Something about another terrorist attack on some kibbutz. Why?"

Rachel realized that her face, contorted in fear, must have told Jacqueline all that she had concealed these past couple of weeks.

"God almighty, Rachel. I'm so sorry," Jacqueline mumbled. "I'll keep the station on until they repeat the story."

Rachel barely heard the last words. She took the stairs two at a time and dashed into her bedroom. She punched in Howard's number while taking in deep, shuddered breaths. When he answered, she almost cried out from relief. Her lifeline to Ellie was in working order.

"Howard, I—I— There's been some bombing in Israel—"

"Are you going to get excited every time—"

She heard her voice rising in panic. "Call the American embassy, Howard. Where are they? What kibbutz?"

"Rachel," came his quiet voice, "where are you calling from?"

Her knees gave out as a siren sounded in her head at her blunder. If Wes had her phone tapped—illegal as it was—he would know.

"I'll call you later," she said weakly.

"Take it easy, will you?"

Ninety minutes later, she sat in Erica's conference room, where a legal assistant sorted documents, tapped them into shape, and stapled them. More billable activity. Seeing a secretary carrying in a deli lunch, Rachel braced herself for a long working session, but her thoughts were on Ellie and her parents. Howard was right; it was ridiculous for her to get excited every time a bomb exploded in Israel. If only she could get news of them and know they were all right.

"We'll request that Judge McGillian recuse himself, of course." Erica's speckled eyes bored into Rachel's. "We can't protect Phil Crawford from his own foolishness."

Rachel winced. The sense of infusion the two of them shared wasn't Phil's foolishness. She was equally responsible. "It's not what you think. I've kissed enough frogs to know I've found a prince." Rachel stopped. At Erica's rate of two hundred and fifty dollars an hour, there was no point in delving into it.

How was Phil faring at this moment? Although he had appeared unperturbed by the prospect of their relationship being discovered, the media explosion couldn't be comfortable. In the real world, the power of perception was stronger than the power of absolute truth. This business wouldn't look good in his job search.

"All the petitions are ready to be filed this afternoon," Erica continued. "Hopefully, by tomorrow or the day after, Judge Robert McGillian will no longer preside over Belmore v. Belmore."

"Should I assume that all his decisions will be reopened?"

"McGillian's rulings stand. They can be appealed at the Appellate Division on several grounds, the most obvious of which are faulty judgment of the facts, though those are the hardest to prove."

"What good is this switch if I can't bring Ellie back?"

"We'll have better reasons at the Appellate Division to revisit issues pending on appeal," Erica explained. "For one, Stephanie's testimony."

"We were never able to get a trial date at the Appellate Division," Rachel said. "Only Ortman got his petitions on the Family Court calendar."

"We will now."

"Ortman will continue to run back to Family Court," Rachel said. "He'll hammer away at his request for the reversal of custody due to parental kidnapping. For all I know, we'll get another Robert McGillian."

"I'm elbowing our way onto the calendar of a female Appellate Division judge. Assuming she'll be more in tune to the twentieth century's facts of life, then maybe— just maybe— she'll have a heart instead of a ballot box."

A secretary knocked on the door. "There's a Mr. Howard Horowitz on the phone looking for Rachel Belmore. I didn't know whether I could tell him she was here."

Rachel jumped to her feet. "I'll take it."

"It's the blinking one."

She grabbed the phone. "Howard?"

"Bad news," he said. "Your mother was wounded—"

The blood drained from her head as though a plug had been pulled out. "Wounded? That terrorist attack? How bad?"

"She's being operated on now; it doesn't look good. I'm so sorry. Josie and I will fly out there this afternoon."

"Josie too?" Her mother needed Rachel, not her neurotic younger daughter. Rachel sank on the closest chair. She pressed the speaker button so Erica could hear. "Ellie? Dad?" she whispered.

"They're fine. The nursery was hit when Lorena was on duty." His voice choked. "I'm sorry to be the one to tell you this. She was running to the shelter, holding two babies, when it happened. The babies were killed."

"Oh my God. My God." Rachel felt dizzy. The yellow stains in front of her eyes mushroomed and began to infuse. "Howard, I'm going to call my congressman—"

From the corner of her eye she saw Erica waving both her hands. "No, you're not going to call anyone."

"Howard, you call your congressman, senator— Please. Find out what happened. Do something!" Rachel burst into tears. "Please, save her—"

"Rachel, I'm going there. Now let me get off the phone."

After he hung up, Rachel scrambled to her feet, ignoring the darkening clouds behind her eyes, and faced Erica. "My mother was injured. Blown up! Don't you understand?"

Erica placed both her hands on Rachel's arms. Her fingers dug deep into Rachel's flesh. "I understand all too well. I'm sorry. But an American citizen wounded in Israel will be front page news tomorrow. I don't want you to lie to your senator or congressman about what your mother was doing over there. Your brother-in-law will have the information as soon as he gets there. That's all he can do. Think of Ellie. She must come first."

Rachel's knees buckled. She fell into a chair. "I'm going to Israel. My mother needs me."

"You're out of jail on bond. You can't leave."

"Erica, please. Isn't there an emergency procedure you could take?"

Erica shook her head. "Even if we petitioned the court, you'd have to explain the purpose of your trip. Would you like to reveal to the court where Ellie is hidden?"

Rachel sprinted out of Erica's office and took the train back to Green Hills. At the station, she ran to her car and hightailed it out of the parking lot. Instead of driving home, she turned onto the highway. Twenty minutes later, she pressed the doorbell at Josie and Howard's house.

"C'mon," she muttered. "Open up." Memories of her last disastrous visit resurfaced, but she chased them away. That wasn't important now.

Howard opened the door still wearing his business suit. Loosening his tie, he led her into the living room, but did not sit down.

"Josie's upstairs, packing," he said.

"Tell me more of what you know."

"There's little I can add other than to repeat what I heard from your father's frantic telephone call."

"Where's that kibbutz?" The telltale word was an ominous reminder of the possibility that her phone had been bugged.

"In the Galilee," Howard replied. "It's been out of Lebanon's range for years. Looks like a fluke. An Iran-backed terrorist group, Hizbollah, snaked its way through security lines."

She grabbed his arm for emphasis, "I don't want Ellie there. It's a dangerous place. Another 'fluke' might happen. Another shell might hit her kindergarten."

He put his hand over the fingers that clutched at his sleeve. His were warm and dry. "What do you want us to do? Bring her back?"

Rachel bit her lip and shook her head. "Tell my mother that I love her. Very much. Even if she can't hear you, say it anyway." She broke. "And tell Ellie the same thing. Remind her to look at the sunset and remember the ice cream and Baskin-Robbins."

"Sunset and Baskin-Robbins. I'll remember."

Rachel drove away. And she had thought it couldn't get worse.

CHAPTER THIRTY-FIVE

THE speakerphone on McGillian's desk announced that the town supervisor, Albrecht, was on the line. He pressed the button and lifted the receiver, missing the years when each day unfolded into comfortable sameness. Even Albrecht's messages had been predictable.

"How do you know when you get old?" McGillian asked first before Albrecht.

"When you begin your morning with the *City Post* instead of the sports pages."

"Not funny. Are you losing your touch?"

Albrecht's tone was serious. "Send someone to get it, will you?"

Five minutes later, Sylvia hesitatingly laid in front of him a newspaper folded to an article. "You won't like it, Judge."

Not waiting for his reaction, she turned and left.

He glanced at the paper, expecting to see another interview with Rachel Belmore. But the headline caught his attention. He scanned the article and jumped off his chair, knocking it to the floor. His eyes searched for Phil's figure at his desk across the secretarial area.

The son of a bitch wasn't there.

"Sylvia!" McGillian yelled. "Where's Phil? Where's that bastard?"

"He's at the library, Judge."

He dashed to the corridor where his court officer waited.

"Get Phil here. On the double."

He paced his office, his heartbeats pounding in his temples. "This is the stuff that heart attacks are made of," he muttered to himself.

"Are you out of your mind?" he shouted at Phil the minute the young man showed up. "Fucking one of the litigants in a case?"

Phil did not respond. No emotions rippled the surface of his skin; only the tightening of his jaws told McGillian anything had registered.

"Don't you know how to keep your pants zipped?" McGillian shouted. "Do you have any idea what you've done to my reputation—not to mention your own career?"

"Sir, this has nothing to do with you."

A renewed rush of blood reached McGillian's head and exploded in fury. He slammed the door shut and turned to Phil. "Young man! I treated you as my son. Never, ever in my career have I allowed personal considerations to interfere with my dispensing of the law as the people of New York trusted me to. Now you come here, a young Turk, and you let yourself be used by a litigant? To be seduced by an older woman? Don't you see how she and her conniving feminist attorney conspired to implicate you in this mess? They stop at nothing, whether it's publicity or the seduction of my law clerk, you stupid fool! Goddamn fool!"

"Sir, I understand that my actions may seem inappropriate, though I believe they were entirely ethical." His voice was calm. "I'd like to assure you, though, that it was not my intention to undermine you."

"Don't insult me." McGillian passed his tongue over the sides of his mouth to remove the accumulation of saliva. "You're fired! Finish the files you've been working on and get out."

Phil made a gesture of capitulation with his hand.

"And until you're done on Friday, you're not to see or speak to Rachel Belmore. Is that clear?"

"Sir, I'm in love with her and we're both unmarried adults. We can see each other if we want. I promise you though, that I won't deal with her case—"

"Get the hell out of my face! Now!"

Phil stopped at the door, his hand on the brass handle. He opened his mouth to say something, but McGillian cut him off. "Wait till you get to the Character and Fitness Committee. I'll see to it you're not admitted to the Bar!"

McGillian banged the door shut on Phil's retreating figure, staggered a little, and fell back into his chair. He buried his face in his hands. If he had believed Dunkle's affront to his honor had topped it all, here came Phil, and with a new spin, had catapulted an insult into the open.

In the silence that followed Phil's departure, McGillian heard his own heavy breathing.

Sylvia knocked on the door, opened it an inch, then tiptoed in, carrying a glass of iced tea nestled in a saucer. "Are you okay, Judge?"

He muttered something. Of course he was not okay.

She pushed some files and letters to make room at the corner of the desk, and put the glass down. "Maybe you should take the rest of the day off. Go fishing, relax."

He glared at her. She straightened her back, but her stomach remained protruding like a giant wart.

"Judge, I'm worried about you."

"I'm not about to get a heart attack."

"Judge, we've never had a case like Belmore v. Belmore. Maybe you can find a way to get rid of it—for your own good. Rotate it to another judge."

He rubbed his eyes. "I've made a commitment to stay on the case and not let it wander through Family Court seeking justice."

"They don't pay you enough to kill yourself over it."

"Stop clucking at me like a mother hen." He pushed himself off the desk, and got to his feet. "But you're right. I should get out of the madhouse this courthouse has turned into."

He carried his fishing gear to the Potoawa riverbank. His favorite spot was cool and peaceful, and the shallow pool attracted the trout. He sat down to tie a lure, fighting the waves of anger that kept swelling through him each time he thought of

Phil's stupidity, of Dunkle's duplicity, of the Belmore case with its conniving cast of characters, each jostling to outdo the other with publicity stunts or string-pulling.

A large horse stood at the edge of the water, his reins loosely tied to a tree. Other than an occasional swat of its tail, the animal stood heavy and still. Farther upstream, beyond the pile of boulders, McGillian saw a man, probably the horse's owner, aim and cast.

The quiet splashing of water as it eddied and tumbled past McGillian, then bubbled over a couple of rocks into small rapids, filled him with excited anticipation. The trout's silvery scales flickered as they caught the morning sun. It had been a while since he had last been to this spot. He needed to devise new ties to simulate the fish's seasonal diet. Making the fish take his own-fashioned fly was as challenging as it would have been for the Biblical snake to tempt Eve with a wooden apple. It looked good but was inedible.

It was different than the way the feuding Belmores schemed for him, making him bite a wooden apple, frustrating each of his attempts to dispose of the case. Even though he knew better, he ended up falling for their lures—hook, line and sinker.

McGillian cleared his head again and focused on the project at hand. He looped the wax string and tightened it around a section of dark feather until its surface was as shiny as a bug's.

He pulled on his neoprene waders and filled his vest pockets with widgets and a tin box containing a collection of flies. He stepped into the slow-moving water, going deeper, the waders snug against his thighs. He clipped his nippers on a retractable cord and tested his hold on the braided line. With calculated, exact movements he cast the line far into the shallow, long stretch of the river, then leisurely moved his tie about over the water, imitating an insect on its morning flight.

A bird circled the horse's head, and a cloud of flies rose. The horse snapped his massive head to chase the bird away. Then, as though weighing the options between the annoyance of an excited bird and the multitude of flies on his eyes and ears, he dropped its head. His neck muscles trembled a bit.

McGillian wished he could feel less wired, more relaxed, and, like the horse, accept that society had its parasitical insects coming along for the ride. One had to accept that the offensive side effects came with the benefits, the good with the bad. Dunkle was one of the latter.

Phil was another story. McGillian had believed his law clerk to be merely a bleeding-heart liberal touched with some naiveté of youth, which, like the common cold, was sure to take its course and go away.

What was the young man thinking, fucking a litigant in a case? It was more than stupidity. It was insurrection, the undermining of a judge's neutral, unbiased status.

The sharp pull at the end of McGillian's rod brought him back from his ruminations, halting the new wave of fury that surged inside him. With measured, slow movements, he began lifting and dipping the line. The limber rod buckled from the pull. The fish was hooked! In a flurry of excitement it sped from one side of the river to the other, fighting for its life, furious at having been tricked.

"Atta boy, but don't go too far," McGillian called out, presenting his net. He laughed.

"This is your last chance to dislodge the hook. Take it easy."

Minutes later, exhausted, the fish darted right into the net.

Against the tranquility of the river, McGillian heard his own roar of delight. The owner of the horse peeked over the rocks and made a V sign. McGillian grabbed the writhing fish, the metallic glimmer bright in the reflecting sun. He whacked it and slipped it into his creel.

In the break before casting again, McGillian sipped from his bottle of iced tea, his eyes searching for an answer to his troubles in nature and her creatures. Yes, the first requirement for success in life was in being a good animal. Perhaps man, the only animal that blushed—or needed to—stopped blushing when shame, responsibility and guilt had disintegrated. The lost values had not been replaced, leaving nothing but a vacuum, as chaotic as the world at creation. He had thought it was his job, the judge of people, to bring back order and morals into their lives.

He had to admit that there was more to his dilemma. No matter how he looked at it, beyond the appearance of partiality due to Phil's treason lay an indisputable bias due to his own vulnerability to Dunkle. He could no longer treat the case with objectivity. To be true to his own convictions and the high standards to which he had adhered for his entire career, he should not preside over Belmore v. Belmore. The media, society's underbelly, would surely claim victory. Judge Robert McGillian had succumbed to their pressure. Damn.

Trying to compose himself, he felt as though he were stepping off a cliff. But it had to be done. It was still early afternoon; there was time to right the wrong. He collected his fishing gear, and threw it into a pile in the trunk of his car.

Sylvia rushed to pin up her stringy hair as he strutted in, and sent him a questioning look. "I thought you'd take the rest of the day off," she called out. "I've canceled everything."

All he wanted was to remove the muck of scandal stuck in his windpipe. "Get them here," he growled over his shoulder as he hurried into his private lavatory to shower and change. "I don't care how late. Have them cancel dinner plans if necessary."

But that was not needed. Ortman and Norgard showed up shortly after four.

First, McGillian ordered the courtroom cleared of the feminist supporters who multiplied as though on cue, and of reporters clamoring for seats in the front.

"Your Honor," Ms. Norgard said, "this proceeding is not about the minor, and therefore need not be conducted in a closed courtroom."

"Ms. Norgard, you've wrestled control of this courtroom in the most degrading, inappropriate way." The deep resonance in his voice betrayed his fury. "For this last time: this is my courtroom, and I will determine how this meeting is to proceed."

After the court officer had closed the door behind the crowd, McGillian let his gaze roam over the two attorneys' faces. "I'll make it short. Bias appears to have existed in the handling of Belmore v. Belmore—"

Ortman, indignation suspended beneath the cold of his eyes, interrupted. "Your Honor, you were ignorant of the intrigue to trap your law clerk in a wanton act—"

"This is absolutely not true," Ms. Norgard called out.

"Even the slightest appearance of impropriety is unacceptable," McGillian said. "Should I continue to preside over the case, I will reduce public confidence in the fairness of the judiciary."

"Your rulings, Your Honor, were made in good faith." Ortman's voice, on the edge, was accompanied by slender fingers cutting the air.

"Counselor, please do not interrupt me." McGillian's tone rose. "It's an unfortunate turn of events, but I will recuse myself."

He banged the gavel, stood up, and marched out.

CHAPTER   THIRTY-SIX

RACHEL paced the floor throughout the evening, unable to respond to Jacqueline's forced chatter. Guilt and worry over her mother's condition tightened around her chest like a vise.

Phil, working late, called. "How are you bearing up?" he asked, referring to Lupori's revelations in the *City Post* that morning.

The headline seemed light years away. Rachel bit her lip. How she wished she could share with Phil her pain over her mother's injury. The secret she must keep from him felt like some great wheel stuck in the mud of her being.

Struggling to hold down the tremor in her voice, she asked, "What's happening to your job?"

"Judge McGillian is extremely unhappy. I'll manage. Things will look better after I get some sleep." A smile crept into his tight voice. "I didn't get much last night; I'm going to hit the sack."

At midnight, Rachel's new phone rang. Until Wes discovered she had another line, she hoped to be able to speak free of his illegal tapping. Trepidation feeding her heart with renewed horror, Rachel reached for the phone.

Howard's voice was hurried, breathless. "I'm calling from Orly Airport in Paris; we're here for a layover. Now listen carefully. Our friend, Dr. Wesley Belmore, was at Kennedy airport. He pointed us out to a detective who's on the plane, obviously following us. I'm not sure we'll be able to shake him off once we arrive in Israel."

Time stopped. Wes had eavesdropped on their phone conversation. How could she have been so careless? "Check into a hotel when you arrive and don't go to the kibbutz," Rachel said.

"Rachel, we don't have time. I've just called the hospital. Your mother's not doing well." His voice chocked. "Her arm was amputated by the blast. Her abdomen was— was— she has internal injuries. They've fixed her up the best they could. Rachel, she's on life support."

Pain kneaded Rachel's insides into a shapeless pulp. She began to cry.

Howard let a second pass, listening to her subdued sobs. "I'm sorry. So very sorry. I wanted you to know what's going on."

She had to postpone her anguish. "Is the hospital near the kibbutz?" she asked.

"Nothing there is very far."

"Howard, what can we do?"

"I'll have Ellie moved to another hiding place."

"With strangers?"

"Do you have a better idea?"

It was all her fault. God. Rachel shook her head in the dim light of the living room. Then, realizing Howard couldn't see it, she whispered, "Keep in touch. Have Dad call me on this line."

"Don't use a cordless phone. The frequency can be picked up by anyone outside your house." His tone took on urgency. "Here comes my new shadow. Take care."

There was no time to respond to Jacqueline's questioning eyes. In a state of shock, Rachel grabbed her car keys and ran outside, flung open her car door, and swerved out of her street, tires screeching. She drove to Main Street and stopped by a pay phone where she rummaged in her handbag, fished out her phone book, and jabbed the buttons of Erica's home number.

"Will the detective be allowed to take Ellie?" she asked Erica after she outlined her latest predicament.

"You're the custodial parent. Of course he's not allowed to take her without your permission—regardless of what side of the globe she is on. Would that stop him? I doubt it. However, he won't be able to take her out of Israel without her passport. The Israelis can't be casual about their borders."

The Israelis hadn't protected her mother, who was now dying in one of their hospitals, her arm—her pianist's hand—amputated.

She had even forgotten to ask which arm. How she wished she had the sustaining power of religious belief, one that would convince her that there was some higher reason for all this suffering.

"What's the worst-case scenario?" Rachel asked.

"The worst? This is extremely illegal—and the detective risks getting himself a long prison term for it—but it has been done before: He'll kidnap Ellie, keep her somewhere in Israel, and then Wes will negotiate with you, here, for a visitation settlement."

Scared and alone, Ellie kidnapped by a stranger and hidden for an indefinite length of time, until Rachel agreed to give her body back to her father? Rachel staggered. She leaned against the cold aluminum of the phone booth and tried not to inhale the smells of urine and stale beer.

Howard must get to Ellie. He must rescue her before Wes's delegate reached her.

"I won't have to abide by an agreement made under gunpoint, right?" Rachel asked.

"You're talking about countering one illegal action with another. Your kidnapping Ellie and then Wes doing the same—albeit through an intermediary? Very tricky," Erica said. "Once Wes reaches an agreement with you, it is enforceable and can rarely be contested. The assumption is that the parties have reached it of their own free wills."

"That's outrageous!" Tears stung the back of Rachel's eyes. Bright yellow lights laced and haloed the stores' neon signs in a fiery kaleidoscope of colors. "Erica, tell me what to do," she whispered.

"Don't let that detective get to Ellie. But don't you leave the country, either." Erica paused and added in a soft voice. "I'm so sorry about your mother."

Her shoulders stooped, head bowed, Rachel returned to her car, fear seeping through her like corrosive poison. Jacqueline would be waiting for her, but Rachel missed Phil.

She remembered Gerald's promise to stand by her at this difficult time, but his presence no longer offered the comfort she needed.

In tears, Rachel drove through the dark streets, keeping her speed at thirty miles per hour. She had entered a world denuded of possibilities, and she had touched the outer walls of her capacity to cope.

CHAPTER THIRTY-SEVEN

THE cellular phone rang with unrelenting stubbornness. Rachel sat up in bed. The gray light breaking through the curtains told her it was still early.

She picked up the phone. A man with a clipped South African accent identified himself as kibbutz Ramot's secretary.

"Please give my condolences to the parents of the babies." Rachel heard the morning raspiness in her tight throat. "It's so awful."

"We're all devastated." His voice became thick. "I wanted to report that your mother's hanging on; her brain's still registering faint signals." He waited for the words to sink in. "But her critical condition is unchanged. We're praying for her."

"Ellie?" she whispered.

"She's with friends. Ellie's our guest; I'm seeing to it that she's safe." He paused. "Your father is with your Mom at Intensive Care. He sends his love."

Her heart pounding, Rachel pushed herself out of bed.

Barefoot, she padded downstairs and stepped outside. The crisp air blew the last shred of sleep from her eyes. If her arm had healed, she would have gone swimming— anything to relieve the dread that enveloped her. It was so hopeless, and it was all her fault. She crossed the dew-soaked patch of lawn, feeling the cool sensation in her toes. *The New York Times*, wrapped in blue plastic, had been tossed on her driveway. She bent to pick it up, and in a hasty movement, opened it.

A short blurb on page one told of an American citizen critically wounded. No name had been given yet. No doubt the evening papers would elaborate on the story more than Rachel wanted the world to know. When would the connection be made to her own headline story?

Back in the house, she measured ground coffee beans and plugged in the coffee maker. Jacqueline had gone out for a jog. Rachel sat at the kitchen table, her eyes on the newspaper, unfocused.

By the time Jacqueline returned, the sun was high in the sky. She entered through the patio door and slid it shut. She leaned against the wall, panting. Sweat trickled down from under her dark curls, coiled up on top of her head.

"Anything new?" Jacqueline asked.

Rachel shook her head. She got up and took a quart of milk from the refrigerator for Jacqueline. She reached for a glass.

"I can get it," Jacqueline said.

"It gives me something to do," Rachel replied. Anything to keep her inner metronome ticking. Her mother would never get better. She might not live out the night.

"Have faith," Jacqueline said. "Try praying. Go to Friday services tomorrow night."

"You don't seem to practice what you preach."

"God acts in mysterious ways. I get new revelations while jogging. And guess what? She's given me a fabulous idea for my vacation. I'm flying to Israel."

"Whatever for?"

"Ellie must be scared, you've said, shuttled among strangers— Well, she likes me—"

"Jacqueline, haven't you done enough for me?"

"It's for Ellie."

It was the first time Rachel ever saw tears spring into Jacqueline's eyes. "Ellie is the only child I'll ever get to be close to until I'm able to adopt," Jacqueline said.

"Oh, Jacques, oh, God—" Rachel hugged her, a swell of tenderness washing over her. Jacqueline might never know the joy of motherhood. "I've been so self-centered," she murmured. "You never said anything—"

"It was just confirmed recently." Jacqueline shook her curls free and stepped back. Her composure returned. "I'll take Ellie to my cousins. Wes's guy will never find us."

"Your cousins?"

"When the Jews were expelled from Morocco in '56, half my family went to Israel, the other half headed north, to France."

"How long will you stay?"

"At least until your father can care for Ellie again."

Rachel closed her eyes for a second to allow a wave of pain to wash away. Jacqueline didn't say "and your mother is better."

The phone rang. It was Erica. "Call me from the outside," she said.

Five minutes later Rachel dialed her number from a pay phone—and according to Erica's instructions, a different one from the others she had been using.

"Good news and bad news," Erica said. "The publicity in your case has drawn the attention of the New York State Chief Judge. We have an appeal hearing scheduled Monday with Judge Sandra Freeley of the Appellate Division. We'll also present her with our request for an Order to Show Cause why visitation should not be stayed until the appeal is heard. But Freeley's new; her record in considering the welfare of the child is yet unknown."

"She's a woman," Rachel said.

"You'd be surprised. Female judges sometimes lean heavier on women litigants. But more importantly, the Appellate Division is a forum of five judges; Freeley will only sit on the initial hearing. So don't take anything for granted."

Five judges? "I should know that by now. Somehow, I'm never cynical enough to believe that it can't get better."

Erica let a moment pass. "And unrelated to this, you're still charged with the criminal kidnapping of your daughter. But you'll do well with the jury."

"What jury?"

"Whoever told you this was going to be easy? Parental kidnapping is a criminal offense that calls for a jury trial."

Rachel forced her voice to calm down. "What if the Appellate Division finds that I had a good reason?"

"The jury cannot be informed of any rulings subsequent to the crime it is called upon to judge," Erica said.

"Meaning what?"

"Meaning that even if the Appellate Division judges determine McGillian's wrongful application of the law in a way that would now implicate Wes," Erica replied, "the jury should be ignorant of these later facts when deciding on an earlier event—whether you had a sound reason to kidnap your child."

The logic of the law—the law of the land in which she lived—was still a foreign language. Jury trial. "Public opinion is with me now. Maybe we should push for a trial and get it over with? We should win this round."

"The jury is supposed to be unaware of the media coverage."

"It's a wash, then." Rachel sighed. Her logic kept telling her that she should win her right to remove her child from a molester, but here again, "should" was another foreign word that never was translated into the realities of her life.

"Let's wait until we get a ruling from Freeley," Erica said. "We'll try to get the D.A. to drop the kidnapping charges."

"What will happen on Monday?"

"Anyone's guess. Appellate judges rarely reverse a trial judge's decision merely because they disagree with the way he balanced conflicting facts. After all, he's the one who saw the parties and their witnesses in person."

"McGillian didn't agree to see Stephanie as a witness."

"They are more likely to reverse a decision that is based upon the improper *application* of the law."

"Chuck used to tell me that Judge McGillian kept to the strictest side of the law. He was beyond reproach."

"There are plenty of precedents in which an eleven-year-old has testified in Family Court," Erica said. "That's a point of law we're arguing."

"Which of these is the bad news, then?"

"None of the above."

Rachel heard the quick whirlpool in her brain. "So what is it?"

"Ortman is trying to postpone this trial on the grounds that his client is out of the country. Judge Freeley's office pressed to know where and why. It seems your ex is on his way to join his detective in Israel."

Rachel's heartbeat drummed in her ears. "What can Wes do that his detective can't?"

"Neither your parents nor your sister have any legal guardianship of Ellie. Wes, on the other hand, has a recent U.S. court ruling on his parental visits. I am not familiar with Israeli law, but Wes's rights might be translated into temporary custody when the custodial parent is not around."

Cold sweat dripping from her temples and the nape of her neck, Rachel raced home. She bounded up the stairs two at a time and almost collided with Jacqueline as she emerged from the bathroom, wrapped in a towel.

"Got to rush. My flight's at six," Jacqueline said. "I'll be there tomorrow after-noon."

"Wes is already on his way, which means he has at least one full day on you." Rachel followed Jacqueline to the guest bedroom and sat down heavily on the bed.

Would Wes fly there if he didn't know Ellie's exact location? How well was Ellie guarded?

Who would get to her first?

In brisk movements, Jacqueline got dressed. She winked at Rachel. "I'm going home to get my bikini. Ellie and I will have a super vacation."

Her bag stuffed with the few articles she had brought with her, Jacqueline headed out. She handed Rachel a piece of paper. "Have Howard call me at this number—my cousin Stella in Haifa. From there I can be in the Galilee in an hour or so. I'll take care of the rest. Very simple."

"Very simple. With you for a friend," Rachel said.

At the front door, she touched Jacqueline's curls, wet and cascading down her shoulders. Rachel's eyes misted. "These goddamn tears. I can never thank you enough."

"You would do the same for me." Jacqueline kissed her on both cheeks. "Shalom. Au revoir."

"I wish I had time to get Ellie a toy," Rachel said.

"I'll get her a doll at the airport."

"With a red dress." Rachel hugged Jacqueline tight. "Thanks for—"

Jacqueline cut her off. "Thank me when this is over or when Wes disappears to the place where all single socks go—whichever comes first."

Rachel rinsed her face and brushed her teeth. Bitter taste kept forming in her mouth. Ahead of her stretched hours of waiting, of empty time. Fear rumbled steadily underneath the surface of her consciousness, announcing the imminent collision of disasters. Through the iron gates she tried to force shut, visions of the murdered babies in her mother's arms came bursting. The cries of grieving mothers tore through her head.

And merely twenty-four hours after the bombing, Rachel no longer wished her mother saved. Her mother had been too alive to mark off the calendar days of tortured existence, her dismembered body forever connected to machines that replaced her damaged organs. Lorena used to say that in life you stopped at each station instead of merely passing through. What about reaching the end of the line? Had her mother ever imagined what it would be like to find herself alone, lost on a bus at a remote stop?

Phil was unprepared for the sight of Rachel as she opened the door, her lips swollen and her eyes red.

He wrapped her in his arms, his eyes searching her face. His hands moved up and down her thin back, feeling each rib.

"What happened?" he asked, "Are you hurt?"

She shook her head. "I can't talk about it," she murmured, and buried her face in his shirt.

"Is it the article in the *City Post*?"

She shook her head. "Sorry. You're still an officer of the court— I can't discuss it."

"Look, oh, Rachel." She was so fragile, so vulnerable. He kissed her hair. He loved her fresh scent, like a bouquet of fresh flowers. He felt the gathering of tenderness along with the rising of his blood. "I've been fired; there's no longer a conflict of interest or judicial bias. Please."

"Fired? God—"

"Never mind me, right now. Tell me." He led her to the couch.

"My parents are in Israel. My mother was severely injured by a bomb," she told him.

He held her tight as she wept. "What were they doing in Israel?" he asked.

Instead of replying, she stood up, walked over to the powder room and washed her face. When she returned to sit next to him, she had regained her composure. She leaned against him. Her breathing against his neck tingled his skin.

"Ellie's there, too," she finally whispered. "She's unharmed."

He felt relief surging from the center of his being. "So you did it!" he exclaimed. He planted small kisses on her face.

She scrutinized his face, as though searching its features for clues. "The note you gave me.... What is it to you? You've promised to tell me."

Pressure built behind of Phil's eyes, then a secret part of him suddenly unleashed.

"Phil," she said, her tone soft, "I'm listening."

He could breathe the air into which she uttered his name so lovingly. Finally, talking about the little Phil who lay curled up in pain inside him was like responding with his won note of trust.

"My mother should have sent me away. Taken me away," he said in a barely controlled whisper. "But she didn't."

Rachel sat up, tucked her feet under her and drew him toward her, her arms circled around his shoulders.

He began. "My father sexually molested me all throughout my damn childhood—"

"Phil," Rachel's arms around his shoulders tightened.

Details Phil no longer remembered had surfaced. They came elbowing and jostling, barging out of his mouth, circumventing his consciousness. They sought to come out in the open, to be exposed.

"For years, I was torn between devotion and disgust. I adored him and felt guilty about our secret games." Phil heard hysteria creeping into his voice, mingled with a sudden churn in his stomach. "I *loved* him."

He disengaged from her hold and dropped his head into his hands. "I was a willing participant, but I was so ashamed.... And then it turned to rape. Finally I understood...but I couldn't get away."

"Why?"

A deep groan escaped from deep inside him. "Years before, the judge had refused to listen to my mom's pleas to save me.... He said she was neurotic. He couldn't see that her emotional outbursts were the results of being married to my deranged father. She went off the deep end seeing what he did to her boy."

"I know the feeling," Rachel whispered. "Sometimes I wish I could lose my mind just to escape."

"After my mother was free from the marriage, she could have been a perfectly loving mother if the legal system hadn't bulldozed her down. Destroyed her. She lost the capacity to fight for me."

Rachel was silent.

"You see, I am one of the Ellies of the world." Phil pushed himself up and stood on unsteady legs. "Therapy helped me understand, get over it. And like you, I'm strong, resilient. A survivor. Whatever happens to us, we endure, we command our inner resources, and get through."

He inhaled deeply. The words had been said, had been exposed. Suddenly, the emotions accompanying them became silent, like the erased sound track of a motion picture.

"I feel better telling you." He gave himself to the feel of her fingers tangled in his hair. "I'll be fine. I'm going to take a shower." He kicked off his sneakers. In his white socks, he padded toward the stairs.

He stayed under the water for a long time, letting the strong spray of the shower deep-cleanse him. Fitful jerking of his neck and shoulders threw off his unease.

When he stepped out, Rachel, naked, held open a huge fluffy towel.

He stood still, the water dripping into a small puddle at his feet. "There's one more thing I must tell you," he said, looking at her.

"There's more?"

"The judge who handed my ass to my father eighteen years ago was the Honorable Judge Robert McGillian."

Rachel opened her mouth and closed it a couple of times, apparently too shocked to respond.

He added, "There are only six Family Court judges in the county. Four of them have been there for over twenty years."

"How could you stand working for him?" she blurted. "How could you breathe the same air, be in the same room? Why would you want to work for him?"

"Don't you see?" He almost shouted. "I had to stop him from doing it to other kids. The best way was to be right there, before he handed down more of his heartless, evil decisions."

She took another step forward. "Oh, Phil— I know why I love you."

They made love, attentive to one another, desperately seeking each other's most hidden corners, finding them anew. Her breathing, skin, breasts—and all that she was— hurled him into a sensory spiral of passion. Seized by emotions he had never thought he could handle, his love sent him to a new, never-before-explored land of his inner landscape.

The Mother Who Protects Her Child was his.

CHAPTER   THIRTY-EIGHT

ON Saturday afternoon, Colby Albrecht showed up at McGillian's home, unannounced.

"How do you know when you get old?"

"How?"

"You stand at the urinal and you fart." Albrecht laughed.

"Watch yourself. You're turning into a dirty old man." McGillian sat down on his reclining chair and beckoned Albrecht to take the only other seat in his study.

"Here's another one for you," Albrecht said. "You know you're old when at your thirty-fifth reunion all the girls who never gave you the time of the day suddenly hand you their phone numbers."

McGillian smiled. "You're wasting two jokes in one visit? What's up?"

"I came to check on how you are bearing up under the pressure."

"It will blow off." McGillian shrugged. "Notice no one's talking about the Torruellas case any longer?"

"Yeah. Maybe you should lie low for a while."

"How do you propose I do that?"

"Bob, you're lucky; you got it all together. You have your health, a lovely family, your home." Albrecht chuckled. "If I had my wish, I'd be playing golf five days a week. This is a time in great men's lives when they start to travel, or decide to write a spy novel."

McGillian eyed the pudgy man, his new pompadour hairpiece coiffed. "What are you driving at?"

"Don't you want to get away from all of this?"

"I am. Off to Nova Scotia for a fly-fishing trip."

"I mean, end the negative publicity, the press chasing you down the corridors, the demonstrators at the courthouse, at the county seat, in front of the legislature in Albany—"

"What's on your mind, Albrecht?"

The man in front of him searched his fingers, opened and closed them a couple of times, then said, "The elections. This unfavorable media brouhaha must be difficult—"

"It's August. It'll pass by November."

"It's *mid*-August; it won't pass by *early* November. I'm trying to help you avoid more of the same."

McGillian straightened up. Spokes of sun poked horizontally through the Venetian blinds. The truth sank in, sluggishly, as the settling of dust. "Are you saying you won't back me for the next term?"

Albrecht's lips tightened over his upper teeth. "Oh, no, not at all. We're behind you one thousand percent. It's your call, of course, but wouldn't you want to avoid being publicly humiliated—"

"My reputation is much too good to be tarnished by a few weeks of some nasty fabricated media hype."

Albrecht sighed. "Bob, you ain't seen nothing yet. Once your name is plastered all over the county as a candidate, it'll accelerate. There will be public confrontations everywhere you go."

"You guys are making more of it than it is."

Albrecht raised his hands in resignation, a gesture that contained within itself the echoes of words spoken in meetings to which McGillian hadn't been invited. "Bob, it's not in your best interest to run. This publicity business is no longer confined to Long Island. It's statewide. You're getting the kind of exposure that doesn't reflect your record as the great judge you've been all these years. One of our best."

"What am I suppose to do? Retire from the bench?"

"If you think of it, it's not such a bad idea to do so before things get worse for you." He coughed into his coned palm. "Look, you're vested for full pension: a very comfortable retirement."

A huge wave swelled and covered McGillian's head, then receded, leaving him as vulnerable and exposed as a beached fish. He dropped his head and closed his eyes. "Who's behind this? Who's turned against me?"

Albrecht chortled. "Don't take it so personally."

"How shall I take it? Come on, Albrecht, you can't do this to me!"

"I'm your friend. I'm telling it like it is. You want to run again? You won't make it."

"Meaning you're worried a Democrat will get my seat?"

Albrecht continued as though he hadn't heard. "—You'll only embarrass yourself. On the other hand, any law firm in the county will grab you as a partner if you still want to kick around."

McGillian jumped to his feet and paced the room, his arms crossed. "You're talking about my life," he whispered. "My life. There's nothing else for me but to be a judge."

Albrecht got up too. He walked over to McGillian and touched his shoulder. "Take it easy. It's really not so bad. Sleep on it and you'll see the bright side."

McGillian mustered the depth of his voice to sound like his old confident self. "Who will you put on instead?"

"Hank Ortman agreed to be nominated as the next Republican Family Court judge."

"Hank? He's the one who started this media hype in the Belmore v. Belmore case."

Albrecht cleared his throat.

"Friends. You, the others—Albrecht, I've trusted you." McGillian uncrossed his arms. He should shut up before he heaped any more disgrace upon himself. How could they betray him? They all shared the same code of ethics; they had been so well disposed toward one another. It was their values he had distilled into nuggets of law.

He had believed they were loyal to him in return.

Albrecht let himself out.

McGillian remained in his study. He looked around him at the accumulation of odd furniture, add-on bookshelves, piles of magazines and law periodicals, and at his boxes of ties, flies, waxed thread, glue bottles, undressed hooks, chenille, lines, and feathers scattered on the side table. Was this to be his place of forced retirement?

With a groan, he raised himself from his chair and shuffled toward the window. A ribbon of darkness spread outside.

He whispered, "At the end of my career, I am nothing but a name on or off the ballot."

CHAPTER THIRTY-NINE

IN the corridor of her cousins' Haifa apartment, Jacqueline faced her cousins' excited greetings. When they all calmed down, she hitched up her Donna Karan knapsack and picked up the Louis Vuitton suitcase she had dropped off. She followed Stella, her plump hostess, to a small bedroom.

"Has anyone called me?" Jacqueline asked in French.

"An American man by the name of Howard," Stella replied with a glint in her eye. "Is he someone special? Is he the reason we're honored with your sudden visit?"

"It's not what you're thinking. But it's very important. I need to drive to the Galilee tonight. Can you come with me? I don't want to get lost."

"Tonight? It's almost dark."

"Sorry. I must." Glancing at the piece of paper Stella handed her, Jacqueline punched in Howard's cellular phone number. She spoke to Stella while waiting for the lines to connect. "Are these free here? Everyone in the airport and in the street walks around with a cellular phone glued to their ear or snapped on a belt. It's not like this in the States. Too many dead air pockets. We rely more on land lines."

Stella giggled. "Our national trademark."

Howard answered his phone.

"I'm in Haifa. Where's Ellie?" Jacqueline asked without preliminaries. "I'm the only person currently roaming the roads in Israel of whom she is not scared."

"It's not so simple." Howard's words came out slowly, calculating, as though he was breaking some bad news. "We have a legal problem."

Since she had met Rachel there had been nothing but legal problems around Ellie. "Being a law-abiding citizen is the least of my concerns right now," Jacqueline replied. "The sooner I get to Ellie the better she'll be. How's she faring?"

"She doesn't understand why her grandparents suddenly deserted her— she cries a lot— But Josie and I never managed to deal with her. She's scared of me, and Josie, well—" He cut his words. "But that's not the issue. We're in a huge legal mess—"

"You sound serious." Jacqueline's heart began to pound. "What now?"

"Thursday, Wes got a temporary stay. Don't ask me how the hell he pulled it off. Since the child's mother was not in Israel, he obtained on-paper custody of Ellie while they're both here. Neither the Rayners nor me and Josie have a legal standing in regard to Ellie."

"Howard," Jacqueline asked, enunciating each word, "Who has her now?"

"She's still in kibbutz Ramot, where the Rayners have been staying, but Wes's sniffing around the place."

"I thought you'd removed her!"

"It's out of my hands. Yesterday morning, Wes showed up at the kibbutz. He entered with no difficulties—like a village, it's open. He walked into the dining room and located the kibbutz board secretary. The guy wouldn't reveal where Ellie was. He had a bunch of men escort Wes out. But not before Wes—at the top of his voice—threatened the secretary with personal legal liability should Ellie be taken out of the kibbutz."

"But where is she?"

"The secretary won't tell us who's keeping her. He's afraid if she disappears, he'll be named an accomplice to kidnapping."

"Why can't Russ take her out?"

"His wife is dying a horrible death. You can't even talk to him. He won't eat or sleep, let alone leave her bedside. We're afraid for his health. Josie insists we spare him this new development."

"I'm sorry. It's so awful."

"Beyond anything you can imagine." Howard paused. "Anyway, Wes has a detective parked on the road leading to the kibbutz. He would have followed Russ if he had taken Ellie out."

"What a fucking mess."

"I can't hear you," Howard said. "Speak up."

"Never mind." Jacqueline thought for a moment. "Are you telling me that the kibbutz is now holding Ellie? They have less standing than you do. At least you have the grandparents' authorization."

"None of us has more legal access to Ellie than the other. Only Wes. But the secretary knows the history of this case. Thank God, so far, he refuses to release her to him. Today. Tonight. For all we know, Wes will show up again tomorrow—with the police. He has all the necessary documents, except for Ellie's passport."

"Where's her passport?"

"Russ gave Josie all his documents to lock up in the kibbutz vault."

"I must get Ellie."

"There's no way you can just walk in there, search from house to house, and snatch her."

"It seems to me that's the only way." She thanked Howard, and hung up.

"What was that all about?" Stella asked.

"Whom do you know in Ramot?"

"Is that where your new beau is?"

"Howard is a good guy. He is also Jewish, and rich. But he's married."

"Three out of four ain't bad."

"Ramot?" Jacqueline repeated.

"Let me make some phone calls."

Jacqueline woke up with a jolt. Her skin was damp and sticky. She was enveloped in a blanket of heat, even though she lay on top of the bed cover. It took her a few moments to force the room to stop its swaying and to come into focus. From the street below, car horns chased one another in a cacophony of noise. Young people laughed. American pop music poured out of a window nearby. It was mixed with the rapid-fire Hebrew words of a TV announcer that seeped from Stella's living room.

Jacqueline passed her hand over her neck. It was wet with sweat. She yanked out her T-shirt from the jeans she had worn during the flight.

"Ellie." The word crashed into her consciousness. What was she doing sleeping when she had to get to her? She swung her feet to the floor and sprang up, feeling the cobweb of sleep still woven around her eyes. At the entrance to the living room, she stopped. In the sudden chill of the air-conditioned room, her T-shirt stuck to her skin.

"What time is it? Why did you let me sleep?" she asked.

Stella, seated in front of the TV next to her husband, laughed. "It's only ten o'clock. You missed a night's sleep; we thought we'd let you get over your jet lag."

Stella's husband popped a grape into his mouth. "You want dinner?"

"Did you find anyone you know in Ramot? I need to get there. Now," Jacqueline said, unsure of what she would do once she got there.

"Sit down and eat something." Stella was already busy setting the corner of the table with a service for one. "Turns out I know the kibbutz nurse. We met at a public health seminar last year." Stella kept on talking as she moved in and out of the adjoining kitchen. "That was a terrible tragedy last week. No matter how much is happening in this country, we mourn every son and daughter like they're our own."

Jacqueline nodded. "When can we leave?"

"The nurse's away on a class trip. They're due back tomorrow."

She had to beat Wes to Ellie. But it was crucial to have an inside person help them. "At what time?"

"Will you tell us what this is all about?" Stella's husband asked. "We don't see you for six years, then suddenly you pop up out of the blue, all excited about kibbutz Ramot…. If you're not after a guy, what is it?"

"A girl."

Seeing their astonished looks, Jacqueline laughed. "I mean a little girl. My best friend's five-year-old."

She plopped down on the sofa and told them the story. When she was done, Stella let out a short whistle. "What are you planning to do?"

"Get Ellie out. Maybe we'll drive to Jerusalem to see the rest of the family."

"From what you're telling us about this kid, you'd better stay here. She won't take well to meeting many more strangers."

"First thing: how do I get her out?"

"We'll drive up early tomorrow. If we get there before my nurse friend returns, we'll have to play it by ear."

Jacqueline couldn't fall back to sleep. She lay in the dark, listening to the pulsating street noise below. Cars' headlights scrolled across the walls, casting odd shapes, like drunken searchlights. People in the next building argued in Egyptian-accented French about politics. She had forgotten how, due to the heat, Israelis kept their windows open. The voices carried into her room had mysterious yet pleasant, depths of life.

After midnight, a faint breeze from the Mediterranean changed direction and climbed up Mount Carmel. As it wafted into the room, carrying with it a smell of salt and flowering honeysuckle, it lulled Jacqueline to sleep.

When Stella shook her, Jacqueline felt it was the middle of the night. "What time is it?" she mumbled.

"Six o'clock, Saturday morning."

Jacqueline stared at the square of perfect blue sky outside the window.

"Is it daylight?"

Stella laughed. "Your coffee is ready. With no traffic on Sabbath, we'll eat breakfast at Ramot."

Breakfast at Ramot. Instantly it all seemed so close. So possible.

"I'm so sleepy I'll run us off the road," Jacqueline said when they descended the stairs and reached her rented car. She dropped the keys in Stella's hands.

Fifteen minutes later, the car veered into the four-lane road, following the signs to the Galilee.

From the window of the air-conditioned car, the morning seemed crisp and fresh, dappled with promise, as though in this holy land the angels had polished the mountaintops and mixed the purest of blue for today's sky. But when she rolled down her window, a wave of heat hit her nose and throat.

"I've forgotten about your famous *hamssin*. It's like a hair dryer blowing right into your face." Quickly, Jacqueline rolled up the window.

The views kept her awake. A network of raised irrigation pipes intersected meadows of yellow sunflowers, green wheat and white cotton. The colors were soon turned to the monochromatic shine of greenhouses stretching for miles into the horizon and the shimmering of dozens of rectangular fish pools. Arab villages perched on the rocky hillsides. The small poured-concrete houses were painted bright blue and green, alternating with majestic stone homes. Below them, next to patches of olive orchards, sheep grazed on terraced pastures.

Once in a while, Jacqueline noticed signs pointing to turns into dirt roads that led to kibbutzim or agriculture cooperatives.

"Another half an hour," Stella said as they drove deeper into the mountains along roads lined with tall cypress turned brown under layers of dust.

Jacqueline's heart began to pump at the reality of her mission. She was nearing Ellie. She prayed Wes hadn't yet returned to the kibbutz.

The car swung into a small parking lot edged by magenta bougainvillea. Jacqueline climbed out, stretched, and yawned. The air smelled of cow manure, car exhaust and barley dust, but as they turned to walk on the paved path flanked by manicured gardens, it was replaced by the sweet aroma of exotic flowers she didn't recognize. A couple hundred feet later, the path opened to the sight of a building whose marble facade seemed more in keeping with a community center than the dining hall Stella said it was.

Jacqueline scrambled up the few steps behind Stella, and they entered the hall. Instinctively, Jacqueline scanned the room for Wes's face and was relieved not to find it.

A man in khaki shorts, deep in an argument at a nearby table, detached himself from the group and approached them.

There was a brief exchange in Hebrew between him and Stella. Then, Stella turned to Jacqueline and said in French, "The secretary here invites us to sit down for breakfast while he finds out when my friend's expected."

Without saying a word, Jacqueline sat down at a large table already occupied by half a dozen men and women in work shorts and shirts. They spoke in a mixture of Hebrew and South African-accented English. Many had cellular phones next to their plates, reminding Jacqueline of the national trademark. As the instruments rang, the phenomenon seemed to be more like a national plague.

"There seems to be some problem today," Stella said pointedly, alerting Jacqueline with the subtext of her words. "He said they were on alert for strangers visiting; he apologizes."

"You can never be careful enough when it comes to uninvited strangers," Jacqueline murmured. Unsure who at the table understood French, she would not mention the real purpose of their visit.

Someone handed her a platter of cut-up vegetables. A plate of assorted cheese followed.

"What would you like?" Stella asked.

"To find a five years old and scared girl," Jacqueline whispered.

"Food, I mean." Stella sighed. "Eat your veggies."

The cucumbers and green peppers had that special fresh, concentrated aroma Jacqueline had almost forgotten since her last visit to the country.

The secretary returned and spoke in Hebrew with Stella.

"I'd like to take a tour of the infirmary," Jacqueline said aloud in French, cutting into their conversation. Wes might show up any minute.

After Stella and the secretary shook hands and parted, Stella told Jacqueline, "She won't be back until five. But we can visit the infirmary and look around. Whatever it is they're worried about today, we got clearance."

Jacqueline was about to sprint out of her seat.

"Finish your breakfast," Stella said. "We're not in any hurry."

Jacqueline mouthed, "We're not?" How long would she be able to play the game? Jacqueline picked up her fork again. "In that case, I'll make myself an omelet." She went to an open stove where a row of skillets and platters of ingredients had been laid out.

The wait was maddening. If Wes walked in and saw her, it was all over.

Suddenly, a hush fell over the room. Eyes turned to a young couple that made their way into the room, their faces solemn.

"Their baby was killed last week in the bombing," a man on Jacqueline's right whispered in English.

Jacqueline's throat contracted. The same bombing in which Lorena had been hurt. She removed the skillet in which her omelet was frying and dumped the contents into a garbage receptacle at the side.

The young couple shuffled down the aisle, briefly touching hands extended in their direction in a show of sympathy.

Jacqueline went back to Stella. "Finished? We must get going."

Stella pushed her chair away from the table and rose to her feet.

Only when they started to walk, did Jacqueline realize how hard her adrenalin had been pumping through her body. "We're running out of time," she said. "Let's find the kindergarten. Ellie must be there."

"You can't just walk in there and get her."

"What else can we do?

"That's what we're going to find out. We're scouting."

Five minutes later, the two of them entered the clinic's waiting area. Several kibbutz members were waiting, some reading newspapers, others chatting loudly.

Stella studied the announcements on the bulletin board. "Let's see who I know here." She disappeared behind one of the three doors leading to interior rooms.

Jacqueline eased onto a bench. On a wall clock both hands had stopped at six-thirty, as though they had run out of steam before beginning yet another ascent. She glanced at her watch. Almost nine o'clock. She picked up a Hebrew women's magazine and flipped through pictures of summer fashions and food preparations.

At the rate they were going, they were getting nowhere. An hour after arriving at the kibbutz, she had a full stomach but no more inkling as to Ellie's location than when she had awoken that morning. Wes would arrive any minute, and it would be the end of her mission.

Jacqueline tossed the magazine and stood up. Outside, she kept in the shadow of the clinic's patio. A radio played somewhere nearby, and she tapped her foot to Edith Piaf's song. The heat smelled of paint cooking on the wall. Sweat accumulated along Jacqueline's spine and between her breasts and in half-moons on her shirt's underarms.

She stepped onto the path and walked around to the back of the building. Past a cluster of tamarind trees, their gray-green needles soft and pliable in the breeze, a well-tended rose garden extended to a strip of lawn laid in front of a row of semi-detached cottages. Colorful chaise lounges were strewn on grass that was so vividly green it seemed to pulsate in the sunlight.

Was Ellie in one of these houses? Where was the kindergarten? But those were questions no stranger should ask today, when the locals were on alert.

A portable sprinkler squeaked lazily nearby, the curtain of water holding a rainbow. The spray reached the path just as Jacqueline completed her circle. She stopped to allow the water to hit her legs and cool her burning skin.

She began another, larger circle, this time covering the area behind the row of cottages. She was about to round the corner when she heard the sound of children playing.

The playground she sighted was in the shade of ancient eucalyptus trees. Children climbed the monkey bars, played in the sandbox, and swung on the swing sets.

In slow steps, she inched closer. Then closer. She scrutinized the children.

Ellie was not among them.

Behind the playground crouched a low building with a large open porch. A matronly woman wearing a straw hat sat in the middle of a circle of children, reading a story. One child sat in her lap. In the shadow of the porch, Jacqueline could not see the children's faces.

She took another step forward.

She recognized Ellie the same instant Ellie detached herself from the woman's lap, sprang up, and ran forward.

"Aunt Jacqueline!" she called out, an excited smile lighting up her face.

Jacqueline kneeled to engulf Ellie in her arms. When their bodies collided, she straightened up and swiveled Ellie around. "Woooo," she called out. "You got so big."

Ellie squealed with joy. Then her face clouded. "Where's Mommy?"

CHAPTER FORTY

RACHEL put on a navy blue suit and drove to the community synagogue in Green Hills. Many times she had passed the building set back on a knoll, its marble facade lofty as it rose toward the sky. It had been years since she had given any thought to what took place inside the place.

Saturday services had started by the time she tiptoed in and settled on a cushioned bench in the back. She recalled little from her bat-mitzvah days yet there was something oddly familiar in the sound of the strange language Ellie was now learning to speak halfway around the world.

Had Wes reached her? A shudder ran through Rachel. The kibbutz secretary had said only that her daughter was safe. How scared was she, left in the care of people she didn't know?

From behind Rachel, someone reached over and pointed out the place in her prayer book. She followed the English translation, trying to decipher the deeper meaning of the words.

Half an hour later she realized that Jacqueline, as usual, had been right. Praying slackened the rope that had bound her heart. It brought her closer to her mother. For a few stolen moments—moments she did not deserve after having brought this tragedy upon her family— Rachel felt embraced by lightness.

Services over, Rachel rose to leave. As she filed out, the rabbi, standing at the door, shook her hand.

"Will you stay for the 'Kiddush?'" he asked.

"I— I— Thanks," she stammered, feeling like an impostor.

She followed the small crowd to a room where tiny plastic cups of sacramental red wine were spread out on a table along with platters of herring and sliced cake.

She took a cup and a square of pound cake and stood against the wall. The red wine was sweet and smooth in her mouth.

The rabbi approached her. "Are you new in the community?"

"I've lived here for three years."

"Welcome again. Is there anything in particular that has brought you here today?"

Sudden tears sprouted into Rachel's eyes. She hadn't known they were this close to the surface. She gulped for air, but failed to restrain the crying that threatened to break out of her grottoes of pain.

"Let's go into my study." The rabbi's quiet voice was reassuring. His hand gestured at the short corridor to Rachel's left.

The smell of old, dusty books was welcoming. The rabbi waited until Rachel sat down in an upholstered chair and took a seat facing her, away from the desk and the book-lined wall behind it.

"Don't be embarrassed." His tone was soft. "There's usually a reason why people come searching for answers."

"All I get is the Last Judgment." She felt her lips tremble as she fished in her handbag for a tissue. "Every day."

His head moved slowly from side to side as he spoke. "We have grasped the mystery of the atom, but have failed to do the same for the spirit. But spirit has the power to convert despair." He paused. "Would you like to discuss it?"

CHAPTER FORTY-ONE

ELLIE'S teacher dropped the storybook. She scrambled to her feet and called into the schoolhouse. Another woman came out, threw a glance at Jacqueline and Ellie, and without a word, took the teacher's place.

Jacqueline watched as the teacher dashed off the patio, one hand holding down her straw hat, the other clutching the hem of her full denim skirt. She closed the distance to where Jacqueline stood and glared at her through huge dark-framed glasses.

"Ruth, that's my Aunt Jacqueline," Ellie said, pride in her voice.

"We'd better step away," Ruth said in English. She motioned with her head toward the woods to the left.

Jacqueline, Ellie still in her arms, followed her.

"Is Mommy coming?" Ellie asked again.

Jacqueline shook her head. "No, pudding. She's home in the States."

Ellie rested her head on Jacqueline's shoulder. Her hand caressed Jacqueline's cheek as though verifying she was for real. Jacqueline understood. For Ellie, she now represented her mother, the connection to her home, to everything that was familiar and steady in her life.

"Who are you?" Ruth demanded.

"Ellie's mother's friend." Jacqueline could hear her heart beating wildly. "She sent me to be with Ellie since she's used to me."

As if to confirm, Ellie said, "I love you, Aunt Jacqueline."

"I love you too, pudding." Jacqueline put her lips against Ellie's forehead. It was dry and warm. "I'd like to take Ellie—I mean out of here," she said to the teacher.

Ruth nodded. "She's been staying with me, but... maybe not for long." The meaningful look she sent her over Ellie's head brought Jacqueline a new adrenalin rush. She must trust Ruth.

"I'll go get my cousin. We have a car," Jacqueline mumbled. "Pudding, wait for me." She placed Ellie on the ground, annoyed at Stella for having dawdled at the clinic. She dashed back to the nurse's anteroom, concerned about the risk of leaving Ellie just as she found her. Frantically, she looked around. Doors. All she could see were damned closed doors. Where the hell was Stella?

She knocked on one door, then rattled the knob. It was locked. Then she banged on the second door.

Behind her, a waiting patient said something in Hebrew. She ignored him. She didn't wait to knock on the third door. She turned the knob, and it opened.

"Stella—"

Her cousin's astonished look told Jacqueline she'd better get hold of herself. But there was no time. "Quick," Jacqueline said. She grabbed Stella's arm. "Come with me."

Stella followed her. Her steps, on short legs, were agile. "What would I do without you for excitement?"

"I found her," Jacqueline whispered.

When Ruth saw Jacqueline, she jerked her chin in the direction of a path leading into a cluster of pines. Her steps were brisk and short as she walked, holding onto Ellie's hand.

Jacqueline and Stella kept a distance behind.

"I want Aunt Jacqueline," Ellie whined. She struggled to release her hand from Ruth's grasp. Suddenly, she freed herself and sprinted back toward Jacqueline and clutched her leg.

"Stay with Miss Ruth. We'll do fun things once we go away," Jacqueline said in a light tone.

"Are we going to Mommy?" Ellie's chin dimpled into a pout.

Jacqueline glanced around. No one was on the path, but the trees and thick shrubs concealed the turns. Someone might show up any moment. No doubt every kibbutz member was aware of the crisis and would raise hell about a stranger with Ellie.

"Please go," she nudged Ellie toward Ruth, but Ellie's grip on her thigh tightened.

From around a curve, a man and a woman came down, facing them. Seeing Ruth, they stopped. She stopped, too.

Jacqueline hesitated for a split second. She should look natural. She scooped Ellie in her arms and continued to walk.

When she passed the couple, she kept her stare straight as their eyes shifted mercurially between Ellie, Jacqueline, Stella, and then Ruth. They asked Ruth something in Hebrew.

Jacqueline kept her pace, her head high.

"I'm hoping we're not walking in the direction of the father or his detective," Stella murmured in French.

"Or the kibbutz secretary," Jacqueline replied. She resisted the urge to look back as she set Ellie on her feet again. Ruth hadn't yet caught up with them.

They were running out of time.

Suddenly, Ellie tugged at Jacqueline's hand. "Over here." She swerved into a side path.

"What's here?"

"That's where I live." Ellie made for a boxy, whitewashed cottage.

Jacqueline stopped behind a tall hydrangea blooming in pinks and blues. "Whose place is it?"

"And that's my room," Ellie's finger pointed at a window.

"Who lives here?"

"Me."

"Is this your grandparents' place?"

Ellie shook her head.

"Is this where all the five-year-olds live?"

Ellie shook her head again.

"Someone's coming," Stella whispered. She gathered herself closer to Jacqueline. "Move on."

Jacqueline nudged Ellie forward. "After you, Pudding."

They ducked into the shade of a small porch and opened the door. The three of them tumbled in.

"I feel like Goldilocks." Jacqueline let out a breath she hadn't realized she had been holding. "When is Papa Bear coming?"

A moment later, the door behind them opened again, and Ruth rushed in. "Sorry," she said.

"We must get going," Jacqueline said.

"I'll bring Ellie's bag. We'll get you out of here."

"Not through the parking lot," Stella said in French, then repeated it in Hebrew.

"The fruit orchards," Ruth said. In quick Hebrew, her arms gesturing in the air, she gave Stella directions.

"Wait! I didn't understand what she was saying," Jacqueline called out.

"Don't worry. I'll meet you with the car." Stella hurried out.

"But where?"

The phone rang. "Please don't answer it," Jacqueline told Ruth, her tone imploring "Let's go."

But Ruth had already picked it up. She listened for a moment, said a few words, then hung up.

She yanked her hat off her head and tossed it on a chair. Her face paled. "That was our kibbutz secretary. My assistant told him you're with me. Ellie's father is here with Ellie's other aunt."

Pain hit the back of Jacqueline's eyes with a thud. "What other aunt?"

Ruth turned to Ellie. "Your Aunt Josie?"

Ellie shook her head. "I hate her." She buried her face in Jacqueline's thigh.

Something sour and sticky mounted up in Jacqueline's throat. She had never met Rachel's sister, but had heard plenty about her. What was that crazy woman's agenda, showing up with Wes? Where was Howard?

"Listen," Jacqueline whispered, her voice urgent. "This is some kind of misunderstanding. I'm sure it's a mistake. Josie's husband will tell you—"

"The police are there too. We must surrender Ellie—"

"No. Please. No matter what. Please don't hand Ellie to her father."

Ruth put her hand on Ellie's head. "I have to do what's right."

Whatever that meant. Jacqueline had to think fast. "I need to use your phone."

She tapped her foot while she waited for Howard to answer the trill of his cellular phone. Tap, tap, tap. Where the hell was Howard?

On the eighth ring, he finally answered.

"Howard, what is Josie doing here accompanying Wes?"

"Accompanying Wes?"

"You heard me."

"She took a taxi to go back to shower and change… We've been up with her mother all night…." He dragged the words as though reflecting on the situation while speaking.

"I must get Ellie out. Apparently Josie has other plans."

Howard's sigh on the other end of the line was audible. "I'm sorry. Josie doesn't understand…She's so tired…. She believes that with the crisis we're in, we should let Wes take Ellie off our hands and let Rachel deal with it back in the States."

Jacqueline held back a tart reply. "Get your father-in-law. Put him on the phone and have him talk to Ruth, the teacher." She no longer cared if her tone was too sharp. To hell with Howard and his wife if he didn't act now. "He must instruct Ruth to release Ellie to me. Now."

"I can't talk to him. He's in no shape."

"Howard. Wes is on his way to this house—with the police!"

"Give me your number and I'll call you right back."

"I'll hold. Get Mr. Rayner."

She heard the crackling of static on the line, like crashing cellophane in her ear, then anxious voices. Her pulse beat in her temples. She didn't know whether the kibbutz secretary was actually leading Wes over. Maybe he was waiting for Ruth to bring Ellie to the parking lot, the dining hall, the school—

At long last, Howard said, "Here he is."

Jacqueline handed the phone to Ruth.

"How's Lorena?" Ruth asked Russ.

Jacqueline tapped her foot louder.

Ruth listened and nodded. Finally, she hung up.

Jacqueline let out a sigh of relief.   "Let's get out of here," she whispered. "Before it's too late."

Ruth grabbed her hat.

"Where *are we* going?" Jacqueline asked.

"To get a tractor."

"A tractor? Whatever for?"

"Trust me."

Jacqueline cringed. She hated to keep asking questions. "Where is that tractor?"

"Don't worry."

But she did. Her heart beat fast as she rushed behind Ruth through clusters of houses and patches of flower gardens. She had long ago lost her sense of direction and was unable to tell whether they were walking toward the dining hall or away from it. Was Ruth really putting herself on the line? What if she led them right back to Wes waving his court order?

Where was that damned tractor?

The lane ended unexpectedly at a construction site with a gaping crater in its center. The houses around it were missing either a wall or had their windows boarded. One low building lay torn and exposed, its insides sagging, like a splayed butchered cow. On its back wall Jacqueline noticed children's drawings. The blood in her veins ran cold.

"Is this where—eh—?"

Ruth nodded and flicked her eyes over Ellie's head. Without breaking her stride she took to a footpath grooved in the freshly turned dirt.

Jacqueline unglued her stare from the sight and followed. She had to trust this woman. There was no one else.

Ellie stumbled. "I can't walk," she whimpered. "I have little legs."

"Sorry, pudding." Jacqueline hoisted her on her hip and continued her fast pace. Soon her arms began to ache.

"I'm scared," Ellie said.

"Don't be. You're with me."

They left the last house behind and entered the first line of trees in an orchard. The heat hung from the trees like laundry. Jacqueline had to put Ellie down again. Ellie whined.

"Let me carry you." Ruth reached for her.

"I want Aunt Jacqueline."

Ruth handed Ellie back to Jacqueline. Ellie clung to her, her arms circling her neck in an embrace. They walked for what, in the heat, seemed like half-an-hour.

"We grow peaches," Ruth said without breaking her pace. Her words almost drowned in the dry and rasping sound of dead leaves under their feet. "Tomorrow we start picking."

Under a carport, a tractor was parked next to a huge pile of packing crates.

"Where's my cousin with the car?" Jacqueline asked.

Ruth signaled with her hand, but all Jacqueline could see was lines of trees stretching deep into the horizon. She hauled Ellie up on the tractor and propped her on the right rear fender. A huge wheel guard towered over Ellie's head.

"Hold tight," Jacqueline told her as she took her spot on the left fender facing her.

Deep grooves in the mud, cut by trucks and crossed by rivulets, had long since dried. Under the hot sun, they baked into an uneven, hard clay. With each bump, Jacqueline's teeth clanked. Behind Ruth's back, she held on to Ellie's tiny hand, pressing it against the single seat, worrying that Ellie might bite into her tongue.

They left the orchard and rode into fields surrounded by mountains. Dust rose from the unpaved road, swirling in front of them. More dust rose behind the wheels of the tractor. The world almost disappeared except for the hot sun. Jacqueline's skin felt stickier than she ever remembered.

"I'm going to fall off." Ellie's voice trembled. "I want my mommy."

"We're almost there," Jacqueline said. She had no idea where "there" was. "Hold tight."

The tractor took a sharp turn behind a wall of aging cypresses, and Jacqueline almost toppled over. She stabilized herself. Through the clouds of brown dust, she looked ahead at a car.

The door swung open, and Stella stepped out, grinning.

CHAPTER FORTY-TWO

PHIL came in, carrying a Monopoly game.

"This will help you pass the next four hours." He laid out the board game. "It's hard to quit when $200 is awaiting around the corner."

Rachel's entire being was in a stupor. Everything was shrouded in a curtain of sorrow over her mother. "I'm in no mood to play," she said.

But there was nothing else to divert her mind from the looming sense of doom over her mother's condition. As she fought to pass the hours, casting the dice, buying streets and utilities, building homes and hotels, collecting money and paying fines, she brought back thoughts of the rabbi who spoke of the spirit.

"Unrest of spirit is the mark of life," she told Phil as she recounted the conversation. "The strength of spirit is the only lasting security."

"Did he say that the fruit of the spirit is love?" Phil grinned.

Rachel smiled wanly. The rabbi's words continued to pour into her veins, rich with promise, gathering meaning with the passing time. *The spirit is the fiercest of nature's forces.* Her mother's would survive—

She held on to the words when, hours later, the phone rang. It was Howard, with the news of Lorena's death. The announcement dropped on Rachel with a crushing, dreaded—yet surprising—finality.

"I am so sorry," Howard said, his voice breaking. After a few moments, he added, "Josie wants to speak to you." He handed the phone to his wife.

"It's all your fault," Josie sputtered the words. "You and your stupid brat! If it weren't for you, Mom wouldn't have had to come here and get herself killed."

"Josie, I'm hurting as much as you are—"

Howard must have yanked the phone out of his wife's hand.

When Russ came on the line, Rachel could hear her sister bawling in the background. Numb with pain, Rachel clutched the receiver as though hugging her father.

At first, he couldn't speak. The words caved in on themselves in a hushed crash as he wept into the mouthpiece. Rachel's quiet sobs, like colliding mists, met his somewhere at the bottom of the Atlantic Ocean where thick telephone cables lay under tons of water.

Finally he spoke. "Please take care of my baby while I take care of yours."

"Josie?" she asked. Would her sister now become her problem?

"She needs you, Rach. You're strong."

"She needs a mental institution." Rachel sniffled.

"Josie is a different person when you show her love."

"Why are we discussing her?"

"Look how little family we have left," he replied. "We must accommodate everyone's needs. We don't give up on someone just because their problems are too much to handle."

How selfish she had been. "I'm sorry, Dad," Rachel said, feeling ashamed. "You've sacrificed for me more than any parent should ever be asked."

"No more than you'd do for Ellie. I love you."

She dabbed her eyes. "I love you too. Very much."

After a while, when there was nothing more to say, he hung up.

"I love you, Dad," Rachel whispered again into the cut-off line.

Phil wrapped her in his arms.

Rachel sobbed. "I need to be alone," she said, making an effort to speak. "Please leave now."

The moment she heard the click of the door latch closing behind Phil, she unraveled. Stumbling back into the living room, unable to hold off her sorrow any longer, her body folded. She fell to her knees. Her back collapsed into a heap. The pressure of the rough fiber of the area rug felt hard on her forehead, making a painful contact. As she hunkered down like a wounded animal, her chest heaved. Wet strands of hair stuck to her face. Her tongue felt thick and salty. Wetness soaked her face as tears spilled out. Her nose ran, and a thin stream of saliva rolled from her open mouth. Through the stale smell of dust and the lemon-scented wooden-floor polish, a deep, guttural sound escaped her stockpile of sorrows, as though leaning forward she could vomit them all.

Her mother was dead.

It was only many hours later, after tossing in bed until dawn on Monday, that an elusive understanding hit the surface of Rachel's awareness. All those years, her response to Josie had been unkind—perhaps even cruel. The two of them had been young when, due to the six years difference between them, Rachel had squeezed a stake of aloofness between them. She had cared more about her cheerleading practices than playing house with her pest of a little sister. But quarantining Josie only exacerbated her anger and jealousy—two dangerous ingredients in her unpredictable psyche. With the shock of losing their mother, what new truths might loom on the edge of Josie's world, threatening to replace reality?

Rachel rose out of bed and pushed the curtains aside. Over the rooftops of the houses across the street, the sky, light-infused and pearly, was edged with the pinkish ray of dawn. She flung the window open and inhaled the rising mist, smooth and fragrant with lavender, green grass, and peppermint.

Fate had a twisted, conniving way of dispensing her lessons. She fed insights with the fuel of suffering.

These past three years, tentacles of goodness had been reaching Rachel, feeding her on demand. For her mother's memory, for her father's sacrifice, for Jacqueline's generosity—and for Phil, who had stepped out of the shadows to love her and to offer his strength—she would show compassion for Josie. Josie had lost her mother—a victim of Rachel's tortured path. Rachel would replace her. She would tend to Josie's painful needs, infuse them with the energy she had drawn from others. It was time she became a giver.

Rachel inhaled again. Fluttering its powdery wings, a moth of kindness emerged, attempting to take flight. The spirit the rabbi had spoken of revealed itself.

CHAPTER FORTY-THREE

"I got her!" Jacqueline exclaimed over the phone. "She's with me. She wants to say hello—"

"Thank God," Rachel whispered. In the moment it took to hear Ellie's voice, her heart tingled with happiness.

"Mommy? Mommy? When are you coming?"

"Hi baby. How are you?" Longing crawled up in a medley of acute smells, touches and sights of Ellie, unblunted by distance. It was like hugging without hugging. "I miss you so much."

"Grandma's sick. They took her to the hospital."

"I know, baby. Grandpa is so sorry that he can't be with you." The air in the living room smelled of the pine-scented candles Phil had bought and spread around the room. On the table, next to her mother's photograph, Rachel had lit the simple glass-encased memorial candle the rabbi had sent over.

"It's the bomb that hurt her, Mommy. I hate bombs. They're noisy and they make me scared. I want to go home."

How naive she had been when promising Ellie that her grandparents would take her to many fun places. "There won't be any more bombs, baby. And you can stay with Jacqueline for a little while."

Ellie began to weep. "Is Grandma going to die?"

Rachel trembled. Ellie had been through too much upheaval and loss, and each event was experienced in its full potency, magnified manyfold. "There are lots of good doctors working very hard to make her better," Rachel said. There would be time for truth later, when Ellie's daily realities were not one trauma after another.

The conversation lasted but a few minutes. Rachel's heart ached for her child whose future was a series of blanks to be filled up by unfeeling judges. The surfaces of Ellie's life were years away from being smoothed and polished by time.

Rachel could no longer fathom solutions to the current predicament. With Wes so fast on her heels, where was she to send Ellie after Jacqueline's trip? Maybe the time had come for her to take off after all and disappear with her child.

After an exchange of verbal hugs and a flutter of kissing sounds, Jacqueline came back on the line. She recounted the details of her trip to the kibbutz, including the twist about Josie. "When Wes appeared with the police, your sister was with him, wanting to give Ellie to him," Jacqueline said. "This is not just neurotic behavior. This is sabotage. Your sister is a candidate for a brain liposuction."

"That's Josie, all right. Now you know what I've been dealing with," Rachel said.

"Jacqueline, I may need you to come back with Ellie. My attorney doesn't like the sound of that temporary custody ruling Wes has received from the Israeli court. We'll know more in a couple of days, but please hide."

"No one in your family knows where we're staying," Jacqueline replied. "I'm not even using my credit card. I've called Howard from a pay phone."

"Call me collect or send messages through Erica's office."

Jacqueline continued. "More important, I've called Josie about Ellie's passport, but I can't get a straight answer. Because of your mother's passing, I'm trying hard to give your sister the benefit of the doubt."

"Where's Howard?"

"Sunday in this holy land is a regular business day. He's on his way to the American Embassy in Tel-Aviv to make funeral arrangements." Jacqueline paused to speak with Ellie, who was whining in the background. "Got to go. Ellie and I are off to the beach," Jacqueline added.

Jacqueline, thanks—"

But her friend had already hung up.

Rachel dialed Josie's number. Even though it would take time to get the emotional range between them right—and to forgive the new lapses of judgments as reported by Jacqueline—there were words she must utter. It was up to her to move the relationship forward and set it on the right track.

Her sister's tone was guarded, defiant.

Rachel ignored it. "Josie, I love you." She used the patient tone she saved for Ellie. "You're the only sister I have."

"What do you want?"

"Nothing specific other than to have better rapport than we've had. Mom would have wanted us to try; I want to be there for you."

"Fuck you," Josie hissed. "Mom is dead because of you! There's nothing you can ever say or do that will change that."

Rachel searched for another angle. "We're both hurting so much— Maybe when you return we can talk more."

"Go to hell."

It was only a lifetime of feeling rejected that suspended itself beneath the ice in Josie's responses, Rachel told herself. Keeping her tone as weightless as she could, she said, "Well, before I do that, would you please help my friend, Jacqueline, get Ellie's passport?"

"Why are you asking me? Am I your new messenger on Ellie's business? Is there anyone you haven't yet recruited?"

"From what I've heard, Dad gave you an envelope with all his papers to deposit in the kibbutz's vault. Ellie's passport is in that packet, and since you are the one who has deposited it, you are the only one who can retrieve it. Please give it to Jacqueline. She'll meet you wherever is convenient for you."

"I have to go—" The unease that crept into Josie's voice sounded like the growl of a dog, so deep and low that it was inaudible yet it buzzed in her bones.

"Look, are you at the kibbutz right now? Please. I'm trying not to bother Daddy.

Just get the passport out of the vault, and Jacqueline will send someone to pick it up. Can't you cooperate with me this one time? Please."

"I said I have to go. Good-bye—"

Suspicion clutched at Rachel's ankles. It sucked her like an undertow. Before thinking, she blurted, "What did you do with the passport?"

"Wes has as much right as you do." Josie's petulant voice skipped over one octave onto the next, causing her next words to come out in a shriek. "Look what you've put him through for years!"

Rachel felt a tremor begin around her center and ebbing out. "Are you out of your mind???" Still trying to find order in chaos, Rachel wanted to fabricate some logical conjecture that would hold together what was unraveling. But the conclusion leaped at her, unstoppable in midair. "What's with you and Wes?"

"I believe him!" Josie screamed. "He's a good man who's been suffering because of you. We're not finished with you yet—"

"Josie, he's using you, don't you see that?" Rachel shouted. The tremor weakened her knees, and she collapsed on the couch. "He's using you!"

"He loves me! But you can never believe I'd succeed at anything, can you? I'm tired of your put-downs. Good-bye."

"No, don't hang up." Rachel's urgent words tripped over each other. "We must talk. Don't do anything foolish—"

"I'm going to marry him—"

"Don't be ridiculous—"

"You see? You're jealous." Josie let out an ugly cackle, like a witch over her brew. "There's nothing you can do to stop us."

Rachel struggled to her feet and began to pace the room, dragging the phone cord. "Josie, please, listen to me—"

Instead of an answer there was a click, followed by the humming static of traveling silence. Then a dial tone beeped shrilly in Rachel's ear.

She stood still, her left hand covering her mouth and cheek. The only sensation was of her burning eyes, wide open in shock. They blinked. In her head, billions of sparks, containing every thought and emotion, ignited and died in milliseconds.

This wasn't happening. Rachel jabbed another few digits, then stopped. The receiver clattered to the floor as her trembling fingers missed the cradle.

The picture became lucid, irrefutable. Josie, the blight on the family landscape, had outdone herself.

No longer did Rachel need to wonder how Ortman had gotten hold of her babysitter, Freda, that day at the trial. When questioned later, Freda swore that she had never spoken to strangers, nor given her phone number to Dr. Belmore when he had called to speak to Ellie. Nevertheless, the disastrous result was that McGillian refused to hear the Impossibility Defense. It was Josie who had obtained Freda's phone number. How simple.

And that sudden change of attitude, when Josie invited Ellie to visit. The invitation had made no sense in the context of the relationship—except for one explanation: Josie had planned to hand Ellie over to Wes that afternoon. She was going to kidnap her niece!

Blood slammed against Rachel's ears. There had been the speed with which Wes tracked Ellie to Israel. Josie had reported to her lover the minute she heard about her mother's injury. Rachel had believed it was her own blunder, but her phone hadn't been tapped. Her sister had been the one wired.

It also explained Jacqueline's ordeal at the kibbutz. How close the teacher had been to handing Ellie over to Wes when he was accompanied by Ellie's aunt Josie. The mole.

Anger percolating inside her, Rachel's head snapped up. "It would kill Dad if he knew what she's done," she murmured, sending a searching look at her mother's framed photograph on the side table. The smiling face, fresh and bright with love, looked back at her, unmoving. Even the salt and pepper hair, flying in the breeze, was frozen in time.

Next to the picture, the memorial candle flickered, licking its own pool of wax.

Rachel wanted to kick and scream. Her rage sought a place to erupt. Stifling, sour, it gagged her. Bundles of muscles cramped in her chest and forehead.

She leaned against the wall. Too many fears and losses for which no comforts could be offered were running amok. She must grab the loose strings of whatever needed to be tied down.

First she called Jacqueline back to ensure that her friend would not reveal anything to Josie.

Jacqueline was still at home and reacted with a series of denouncements that included the hope that Josie would be kidnapped for a ransom that no one would be willing to pay.

"As soon as I have the right court order, I will apply here for another passport and send it to you overnight," Rachel said. "It might take a while, but don't go to the American Embassy."

"Listen," Jacqueline said. "The last thing your family needs is to have Howard find out his wife's having an affair."

"He deserves better."

"He loves his wife. But if he leaves, you and your Dad will be stuck with her without Saint Howard to manage her insanity. And since Wes is sure to shatter her fantasies, another devastating blow would just knock off a personality already on the verge of a breakdown."

"God. Now it's up to me to save Josie from her own madness?"

"If you don't stop her before it's too late, she and her problems will land at your feet for years to come," Jacqueline said.

Rachel sighed. "What would I have done without your wisdom?"

She hung up, her anger still simmering, but she had to think straight. Josie's betrayal didn't matter now. It was the coming hours and days that Rachel must control before Josie threw her life away. How would she be able to prove to her sister that Wes had no intention of marrying her?

Rachel took in a breath that filled up her whole body. An idea broke through the clutter of random thoughts.

She rummaged through her handbag and retrieved a business card. She picked up the phone and punched in David Lupori's phone number. She would make him an offer he could not refuse.

CHAPTER FORTY-FOUR

RACHEL stood in the foyer of her house and stared at her watch as though timing a three-minute egg. "My mother's funeral's over...." Her voice broke. She felt power-less against the pain that surged through her again. "Instead of going to court, I should be sitting *shiva*. That's the mandatory seven-day mourning."

"I know what it is." Phil pulled her to him and held her tight. He spoke into her hair, "Rachel, this is the worst time in our lives. It'll only get better from here on."

She did not reply, visualizing the procession of mourners somewhere in a place whose landscape she could not begin to imagine. Where would they all gather for the week's shiva?

"We'd better get going. It wouldn't do to be late for the Appellate Division." He eased his hold and steered Rachel toward the door. "Are you ready to face them one more time?"

"Another courtroom. Another place of misery and terror." She straightened her back and gathered her handbag yet avoided checking herself in the mirror. There was no point in seeing again the dark circles under her eyes that made her look more fragile, or checking the simple black dress that emphasized her weight loss.

"I'm here for you. Try to catch my vibes."

Rachel nuzzled his neck. Through pouring out his love to her, he would reinforce her emotional scaffolding for this last attempt to save Ellie.

"I haven't had a chance to tell you about my sister, Josie." Rachel stared at the phone as though someone were about to jump out of it. "She's been having an affair with Wes."

Phil did a double take. "Why would she do that? It makes no sense."

"She wants everything she thinks I want—or which I had and lost. She has drummed up this competition in her head in which she sees herself as a loser."

His arms pulled Rachel close. "Your life is like a Windows computer screen. Each click on an icon opens a new window with a multimedia horror show."

She thought of Gerald who had run away for the very same reason. "Click on Wes's icon, the picture of charisma. He was always so goddamn charming." she said. "He used to listen to Josie's complaints about medical symptoms as if she were on her deathbed. She adored him. Howard's so unglamorous compared to him." Rachel shook her head in disbelief against Phil's chest. "Yet I still don't get it. How could she? How could she?"

"It sounds like she never stood a chance once Wes homed in on her as his source," Phil said. "She's one sick puppy, that sister of yours. Don't think of her as an evil person."

"You're being too kind. You've said the same about McGillian."

Phil's smile spilled into his voice. "Understanding those who are misdirected doesn't mean agreeing to become their victims." He paused. "But it does ease the hatred. Hatred is a poison that will eat you up from within."

Rachel looked up at his face. So young, so familiar, so hers now. He had redirected his anger to a constructive channel. She should do the same. "How do you suggest I keep my promise to my father to take care of Josie? I can't tell him about this."

"You may have to. Only he can talk sense into her head." Over her shoulder, Phil glanced at his watch. "Sorry, but we must leave now."

She disengaged from his embrace, but thoughts of Josie still made her jaws grind with fury. She yanked open the door and walked out.

Tiny silver parachutes of dandelion seeds blew in the soft breeze. In the oak tree, listless birds warbled. One took a sudden drop, then flapped upward again with a shrill sound of fright. Its bewilderment brought back to Rachel her reflections at the early dawn of the previous day—and her decision to be a giver. Now it felt like a decision to become a martyr. She could not see how it was possible to forgive Josie.

Yet a little crocus of feeling broke through her frosted fury. She bent, picked up a pink carnation, and brought it to her nose. Ellie would have been delighted to know how well their flowerbeds had done.

At the curb, Phil opened the passenger door of his '68 Camaro and held it for her.

The Appellate Division building sat across the street from Family Court. Rachel looked over at the white brick building where she had first met Phil. It was hard to imagine that it had been only six weeks ago.

"I must drop these files at the office." Phil motioned at his briefcase. "I promised McGillian I'd finish them."

In the vast lobby, Rachel's eyes scanned the expanse of people: a boy clung to his mother, both of them shrinking in fear from a man standing nearby and darting warning looks at them; a woman wept on an older woman's shoulder while a little girl, crouching between her knees, sent her hand up to touch the wet cheek; a teenage boy with a blackened eye kept touching a gash across his chin as if disbelieving it was there.

"I have to hand it to you, dealing with this scene every day," Rachel said. "It ranks close to a hospital's pediatrics department."

Phil squeezed her hand. "Not quite. There you meet saints. Here you meet sinners—and victims." He veered into the corridor leading to the judge's chambers.

The stillness in the office felt as palpable as the silence. No smell of coffee brewing, no voices filtering from behind the courtroom door. The door bearing Judge McGillian's name was closed.

"He's on vacation," the secretary answered their unasked question. "And he's retiring at the end of October."

"This is Rachel Belmore," Phil said. "Meet Sylvia, the pillar of this courthouse."

Sylvia's nod of acknowledgment in Rachel's direction was minimal. She flashed Phil a quick smile. "If I had known you'd go for an older woman I'd have put the moves on you myself."

"Very funny."

She continued, "You'll be glad—no, ecstatic—to hear that McGillian's not filing the complaint against you to the Bar's Character and Fitness Committee."

Phil let out a sigh of relief. "How come?"

"He's a kind man, Phil. A bit old-fashioned, that's all. "

Rachel winced. Cruel people did not wake up in the morning wanting to be cruel. They just were.

Outside, Phil interlaced his fingers with Rachel's, and excitement tingled in her hand. They walked across the street to the Appellate Division building and wended their way to the second floor.

Henry Ortman was pacing the length of the waiting area, his arms crossed, his Adam's apple bobbing up, stopping at the highest spot before dropping again. His suit pants were rucked up with static around his thin calves. Several court officers moved sluggishly about. The bailiff planted herself in front of the door. In a bored, monotonous voice, she read out a case name, stumbling over its pronunciation.

Ortman motioned to Phil. Self-conscious, Rachel disengaged her fingers from Phil's and took a step back. How much did Ortman know about Wes's using Josie? The thought of her sister needled Rachel anew.

"This is going to cost you plenty," Ortman told Phil. "Do you think you've pulled a fast one, getting Judge McGillian to recuse himself? We'll see who has the last laugh. I'm planning to report you to the Bar Character and Fitness Committee."

"Take a number," Phil replied. "But you'll have to prove that my involvement with Rachel Belmore prejudiced your case when it obviously didn't."

"Your involvement with her—" Ortman spat the word "her" with contempt, "forced McGillian to recuse himself."

"Mr. Ortman, I read in this morning's *New York Law Journal* that you are the next Republican nominee for a Family Court judge."

Ortman's long neck stretched up an inch. His nose and upper teeth moved, rabbit-like, as if tasting the air. "So?"

"So, publicity did McGillian in. Let's see how well you do with your stance on Belmore v. Belmore."

"I beg your pardon?"

"You heard me. The engine is still revving. The same women's groups that opposed McGillian's rulings in this case won't be too happy about your taking his place on the bench. Not happy at all."

"I'm defending my client."

"Would you send your daughter on a camping trip with that client?" Phil raised his hand. "Don't bother to answer."

He spun and steered Rachel along, satisfaction quirking up his lips.

"Great job." Rachel smiled up into his face.

The glimmer in Phil's eyes reflected the blue of his suit shirt. "I'll talk to Erica about these women's groups. I've seen them in action. Maybe I can work with their publicity machine to ensure that Ortman's not elected."

"You're on the right track to fulfilling your mission," Rachel said.

"It's taking longer than expected."

"You're learning the ropes of the system and how to use it to help children." She squeezed his fingers. "Soon, you'll begin to study for the Bar and will do it as a lawyer." She halted. "Ortman's complaint will be vicious. What if the Character and Fitness Committee finds your behavior a breach of ethics?"

"If they don't admit me this year, they'll admit me in another year or two." He stopped walking and hooked his gaze in hers. "And, they'll take a more favorable view if, by then, you'll be my wife."

She turned her head away to hide the happy tears that pushed their way into her eyes.

"Belmore v. Belmore," a bailiff called out, and Rachel's small entourage scrambled to its feet.

Feeling apprehension and mustering the last reserve of courage, she touched Phil's fingers in a gesture of farewell as he stopped at the second row while she followed Erica to her table.

A glance to the left confirmed that Wes was not at Ortman's table. Where was he searching for Ellie? Was Josie, at this moment, sneaking away from the shiva to meet him? Probably not; she was no longer of use to him.

Her poor, confused sister.

Rachel scrutinized Judge Sandra Freeley. She was a rounded woman with a glow of good health in her skin, as though she ate an apple a day. Her dark hair, streaked with gray and wrestled into a severe bun, was mocked by a yellow polka-dot bow that fanned out on both sides of her head.

"Your Honor," Ortman opened. "As I've explained in my petition for an adjournment, my client had to leave the country on urgent business."

"Would you please state, for the record, what that business is?" Judge Freeley inquired. "It couldn't be more important than a determination of his child's custody, could it?"

As though she had been lobotomized, the two sides of Rachel's brain functioned independently of one another. She listened to the discussion while ruminating about the implications of Josie's betrayal.

Phil was right. Josie had never stood a chance once Wes decided to use her. Wes had been aware of Josie's problems. He had picked her because she was an easy prey.

Suddenly, Rachel realized that on some important level, she had forgiven Josie although a raw patch still burned somewhere, like a scraped knee.

The next thought took Rachel's breath with its terror. What if, as far fetched as it sounded, Wes did encourage Josie to leave her husband promising marriage? Would Josie then take her three children to live with a pedophile? God.

Rachel forced that side of her mind to shut down and shifted her focus to the proceedings.

Eight feet away, responding to Judge Freeley, Ortman coughed into a flag-size white handkerchief, then said, "My client flew to Israel to return his daughter to a stable home where she belongs—not someplace in a dangerous land where she can't even speak the language. In the meantime, as parental kidnapping has clearly taken place, we're asking the court to give priority to our petition and award Dr. Wes Belmore custody."

With her hands locked into position, Judge Freeley cut the air to emphasize each sentence. "Before we continue, I'm decreeing that this court remains the sole determiner of the custody issue in this case to take precedence over any court decisions in any other country. The litigants shall not seek other legal venues." She took the room with a sweep of her officious gaze. "That said, I have reviewed all the pending petitions for appeal. I will start with the question of the testimony of Dr. Belmore's older daughter from a former marriage."

Ortman brought up his previous arguments.

Judge Freeley steepled her fingers and let him speak for several minutes before stopping him. "We're not arguing technicalities here, Mr. Ortman. I must determine the validity of your assertions that your client is incapable of molesting a little girl."

"The daughter's testimony is inadmissible if Dr. Belmore was not found guilty of the crime."

"If his older daughter claims he did it, the court should hear her out." She perused the documents in front of her. "I would like to consolidate all the appeals pending." She mentioned some petition dates, then pulled out a document bound in blue. "Oh, yes. This one's quite old…. let's see. The gonorrhea case the child contracted at age three—"

"Thank you, Your Honor," Erica said. "My predecessor could not get a calendar date."

Ortman waved a paper. "It was resolved with the testimony of experts. And it wasn't gonorrhea. Even Ms. Belmore's expert agreed the infection was a general term used to describe several bacterial conditions."

"I'll need to review the records to understand how a baby can contract a *general* STD while playing in the sandbox," Judge Freeley said, "Because if that's the case, we may face an epidemic of catastrophic proportions plaguing our parks and nursery schools."

"It was proven it was *not* an STD, Your Honor."

Freeley lowered her glasses further down. Her stare was imperturbable. "We won't debate it now. That's what the legislature established appeal procedures for—"

"Your Honor, I must differ. An appeal should be heard only if the judge in the case has erred in the application of the law, not over a fact."

"Very well. When we go over the experts' testimonies, I'll show you if and where the judge has erred in the application of the law. Please be prepared to argue how the application of the equipoise finding allows to put a child in harm's way. Now, I want your client here first thing Wednesday."

"The week after would be better."

Judge Freeley looked at Ortman as though he were eating raw snails. "You have one day to get your client back here. Wednesday the panel of judges will reopen the question of the older daughter's testimony whether your client is here or not. I promise you, Mr. Ortman, that the case will be closed by the end of the day."

Rachel felt breathless with the sense of the moment. Layer after layer of something filmy and sheer was shifting, like the disappearing shadows at dawn.

"There has never been a Law Guardian on this case," Ortman said.

"That's ridiculous," Erica shot. "It is on the record—in Mr. Ortman's words—that he and my predecessor, Mr. Bernstein, agreed that it was not necessary to appoint a third party to this litigation."

Judge Freeley pushed her glasses up her nose again and tilted her head with interest as she asked Ortman, "What's the reason for your change of heart?"

"The new developments in the case—the kidnapping might have had additional adverse affects on the child."

"I see." Her movements slow and deliberate, Judge Freeley laced her fingers and laid her joined hands in front of her. "Mr. Ortman. You are doing your client no service by insulting the court's ability to see through another delaying tactic. We have a disturbed child who, by all accounts—yours included—is terrified of her father. She needs a home. Her life must be decided upon—and as soon as possible."

"Your Honor." Ortman's face reddened. "I would like the court to take into account that my client is planning to give Ellie a wonderful, steady home. He's about to get married."

Bile climbed up Rachel's esophagus. What would happen to Nicole and the twins at Wes's home? If only she could grab Josie now, this minute, and shake her and shake her until she understood.

"Dr. Belmore will have plenty of time to tell the court of his wedding plans on Wednesday," Judge Freeley told Ortman.

Rachel hoped David Lupori would contact her soon.

They left the courtroom, Erica smiling and hugging women acquaintances as a small crowd gathered around her. A journalist shoved a microphone in front of her face.

"How do you think the Appellate Division panel will rule in thirty-six hours?"

"Judge Sandra Freeley strikes me as someone who takes no prisoners," Erica replied. "If the others are like her, I have faith that they'll save Ellie."

At these words, someone raised a "*Save Ellie*" banner. Another placard popped up at the back of the crowd.

How could Erica be so sure? Rachel's mouth was dry. She bent over the water cooler and swallowed large gulps of water; she had not realized how thirsty she had been. Straightening up, she forced herself to think of the positive, to try to catch Erica's optimism about the outcome of the appeal. Her prayers, at least in part, had been answered—except that she, and everyone else, was paying such a high price for seeking happiness. Everyone but Wes.

As though reading Rachel's thoughts, Phil asked, "Ms. Norgard, are you planning to pursue Dr. Belmore once you get a favorable ruling on discontinuing his visitations?"

When she responded, Erica looked in Rachel's direction. "First, let's make it clear that we are yet to see what Wednesday will bring, even though I feel good about it." Her eyes began to twinkle with the thrill of a hunt. "But yes, to answer your question,

I won't just drop the ball; I haven't yet started with Wes. When he's found to be a pedophile, then by law, the D.A. must prosecute him."

"Mandatory jail sentence," Phil said, his voice triumphant.

Rachel flinched. Somehow, she could not find enough hatred in her to want to see Wes in jail. Only to see him gone forever out of her and Ellie's life.

"And that's the least of it," Erica said. "I'd like to see the headline in *City Post*: 'Dr. Wesley Belmore convicted of child molestation.'"

Rachel believed Erica could accomplish that. It was okay with her to turn against Wes the publicity he had so diligently courted. She looked around for David Lupori, who hadn't missed any hearing lately; he was nowhere around today.

"While we're at it," Erica turned to Phil, "my firm's looking for someone to work on our pro bono assignments. Why don't you interview for the position?"

Phil's face lit up. "Great. I'm flattered," he replied. "Sure."

Rachel's eyes darted between Erica and Phil's faces. "This is neat."

At the end of the corridor, they almost collided with Erica's assistant as she hurried over, waving a folded fax sheet. She thrust it into Rachel's hands. Erica inched closer.

"Tomorrow's news," the assistant announced.

Under the heading of the *City Post*, a photograph of a beautiful woman with bobbed hair, wearing a white medical coat with a stethoscope hanging around her neck, smiled at them. Behind her, a row of hospital cribs faded into the background.

"*Dr. Belmore's bride-to-be*," read the headline.

The caption introduced the pretty pediatrician who said she was hoping to give Wes's daughter a stable, loving home.

Phil's words about saints working at pediatric wards sprang into Rachel's mind, prophetic, portentous, but with a different meaning. "Thank God," Rachel whispered. This woman presented the solution she was looking for. Josie's savior.

"Wes's publicity machine is working overtime," Erica said. "The piece is perfectly timed to affect this week's proceedings, but I doubt Freeley will be impressed."

"Didn't you tell me to think of public relations as if someone was paying me a thousand dollars a day?" Rachel smiled. "Well, this is a Josie Special. It will bring her back to reality."

Erica's brows shot up. "What did you offer Lupori in return for a favor?"

"An exclusive interview once Ellie returns. Photo op, the works."

"What about Lou Kaplan?" Erica asked. "You owe him big time."

"That's not his kind of beat. He's more of the later-date-follow-up type."

Erica tossed her hair back and laughed. "You've learned the game well. I knew you had the knack for it."

"Wes may be using this woman, too." Next to them, Phil rocked on his heels, his brow knotted. "He's dated this woman while stringing Josie along. She'll be devastated."

Rachel nodded. This piece of news would toss Josie around the walls of her hurts. It would take a lot of swallowing of anger, but if Josie would let her, Rachel would help her sister live through the bitter disappointment.

"I'll have to tell my father the whole story and ask him to break the news to Josie before she leaves Howard," Rachel told Phil. "You were right; there's no way around it."

Erica's assistant cut into their conversation, handing Rachel a second piece of paper. "We have a message from your friend, Jacqueline." She looked at her watch. "With the seven-hour difference, it's just about Ellie's bedtime. She wants you to sing to her."

To sing to Ellie. To talk to her. To hear her voice. It was all so real, so near. Rachel buried her face in her hands.

From both sides she felt arms wrapping around her shoulders. Erica and Phil. She smiled at the two of them through misty eyes. Phil produced a tissue and dabbed her eyes.

"Your last tears," he whispered in her ear.

She drew herself up and started toward the bank of pay phones. She must place that call to her father. There was no time to lose in saving Josie.

And then when she was done, her reward would be singing Ellie to sleep.

THE END

ACKNOWLEDGEMENTS:

To the dozens of women who contacted me to tell me their devastating stories, I give you my thanks and my compassion. I hope that this book will be both a tombstone on the grave of your lost battles and a monument to your courage.

To the Port Washington library, a flagship of libraries, and its dedicated staff that provided me with valuable research resources.

To Honorable Burton Joseph, who turned Nassau County Family Court to a hall of compassion, and to the thoughtful Judge Jerome Madowar, who shared with me valuable lessons from the bench.

To Judge James Gowan from Suffolk County Supreme Court, whose pompousness of the infallible appointed to dispense justice inspired me to speak for all victims.

To Barry Goldstein, Esq., New York; Justice Dennis Adams, Kauai; Charles Van Keuren, Esq., PA, Jay Creditor, NYPD; and Chuck Rappaport, Esq., for their informative advice and reading.

To Steve Emerson, for his carving time to give constructive advice and for his cheering me from the sidelines.

To Peggy Lampert, Oregon, and Judy Epstein, New York, for thoughtful editing.

To Jody Pryor, Alaska, for publishing advice.

Special thanks to my America Online writing buddies. I do not know their faces or their voices, but I know their generosity in sharing their precious writing time and literary insights: Barbara Turner, New Hampshire; Barbara Hoppe, New Jersey; Melodie, The Netherlands; Joan Elizabeth Lloyd, New York, Warren Humbey, Alabama.

Internet surfers assisted me with research—from law enforcement procedures to medical information or the fascinating world of fly fishing: J. Neil Phillips, Alabama; Molly Ryer; Dr. Paul Sokal, Texas; Dick Walle, Ohio; Laurie Sullivan, New Hampshire; Sgt. Walter Frey, NYPD; Sgt. Paul Swanson, NYPD; Lt. Joseph R. Sastre, Milford, CT PD.

To my daughter Tomm, my first audience for thousands of unrecorded and unpublished bedtime stories, who therefore expected nothing less from me. And to my daughter Eden, the fledgling editor whose astute observations leave me in awe.

And lastly, to my husband Ron, with whose love and nurturing I blossomed as an individual, as a woman, as a businessperson and finally, as a writer.

The following questions will help you explore—on your own or with other readers—different viewpoints and reactions to Talia Carner's *Puppet Child*. For a conversation with the author, articles about the justice system, book reviews, an author video interview, a schedule of readings and book-store appearances, and additional discussion topics suggested by reading clubs, please check Carner's website, www.TaliaCarner.com .

Talia Carner would enjoy hearing your own personal stories, comments or questions. Please e-mail her at AuthorTalia@aol.com .

READING GROUP GUIDE:

1. Rachel did not see a "red flag" in the fact that Wes did not visit his daughter from his first marriage. She regarded his fury over that situation as a sign of his love for that child. Should his behavior have tipped her off to his deviant personality? Is it natural for a woman in love, even an intelligent, sophisticated woman, to be taken in by a man's charm and status?

2. Throughout *Puppet Child,* Rachel makes several promises to Ellie, with the full intention of keeping them. ("Cross my heart and hope to die," and "No more Zoo Game"). Is it fair of Rachel to promise things that might be beyond her control?

3. In an interview, Carner reported that she spoke with many mothers, who, broken financially and emotionally, their legal recourse exhausted, deserted the battleground. Their children remained with their abusers. In *Puppet Child*, there is the shadow of Phil's mother as one such broken woman. Can you understand the choices mothers sometimes make? Could you shoulder the emotional and financial load of fighting for your child's safety the way Rachel did to protect Ellie? Would there be other, more effective means to protect the child?

4. Dr. Wes Belmore is described as an upstanding citizen and a man dedicated to healing. Discuss the difficulties inherent in the favorable impression he makes on social workers and the judge. How different would the novel be had Carner not included the prologue in which Rachel—and the reader—actually witnessed the act of abuse?

5. Was Rachel's original lawyer, Chuck Bernstein, as effective as he could have been? In what way was her new lawyer, Erica Norgard, a stronger advocate for Ellie?

6. Judge McGillian is a villain who does not mean to be a bad person. In fact, he sees a mission in dispensing justice and is certain he does good to the world by enforcing social mores. Discuss the evidence presented before him in the Belmore vs. Belmore case. Could he have ruled differently? Was his ruling of equipoise warranted? Should he have removed himself from the case as soon as he felt the political pressure?

7. What ultimately affected the outcome of Rachel's case—her defiance? Publicity? Public pressure? The change in lawyers? Political intervention? The change in judges? Was the final outcome Rachel's own doing or was she just caught up in the events? Would the outcome have been different had she taken another tactic—or none at all?

8. Rachel's lawyer, Chuck Bernstein explains the court decision to disallow the testimony of Wes's older daughter regarding abuse. "If you robbed a liquor store on Tuesday at ten, wearing a ski mask and carrying an Uzi, that doesn't mean you were the one who robbed a liquor store on Wednesday at ten, wearing a ski mask and carrying an Uzi. That's the law in its strictest sense." Please comment on the logic and practical application of this concept meant to protect a defendant from prejudiced jury or judge.

9. Jacqueline is a devoted friend. Is she extending herself too much? What's her motivation for doing so? Would you do this much for a friend?

10. In this novel, Child Protective Services and the legal system come across as callous and chillingly neglectful. Is there enough supporting evidence to substantiate Rachel's despair of ever getting justice for Ellie? Do you know of instances of incompetent judges or incomprehensibly neglectful social services? Would you trust your child to either of these systems?

11. In some states judges are appointed, while in others they are elected. Discuss the pros and cons and the inherent risks of each practice. Do you think that a lifetime appointment shields a judge from being influenced by political play as compared with a judge who must be elected every four or six years?

12. In spite of Rachel's fears concerning Ellie's reaction to strangers, Ellie seems to do well with some people. In addition to her grandparents and Jacqueline, she responds to Gerald and to her new teacher; she does not even hate her aunt who said she was "a brat." Is Rachel overreacting or is she overly protective of Ellie?

13. Rachel encounters problems with her corporate boss. Do they stem from her attitude toward him, from her own personal difficulties, or from her failure to comprehend the corporate culture? Or is it the corporation—as represented by the individual operating within it—that is in the wrong?

14. Phil's heavy baggage is only hinted at as he enters the scene. Discuss his background and his motivation to work in Family Court. Is he reckless in his mission? Do you believe that all do-gooders are motivated by past traumas that fill them with compassion? Compare Phil's perception of justice and the Judge's—their different point-of-views, their analysis of the facts, and the weight given to the evidence presented.

15. Rachel's boyfriend, Gerald, drops out of her life suddenly and unexpectedly. Does the explanation he offers when he returns make sense? Should Rachel have tried to understand his predicament and forgive him? Was his offer to be a father to Ellie and teach her to trust men generous enough to compensate for his previous behavior?

16. Phil is nine years younger than Rachel, yet he manages to gain her trust and love. How does he change her? Is there a base strong enough to hold them together? Discuss their relationship and what each brings to it. Do you believe that the relationship between a younger man and an older woman is more likely to fail than one involving a younger woman and an older man, or is there no difference?

17. *Puppet Child* features a cast of colorful secondary and minor characters, including David Lupori, Vince Carducci, Chuck Bernstein, Sylvia, Colby Albrecht, Josie, Howard, Russ and Lorena Rayner, Freda, Erica Norgard, and Dr. Hoffmann. Staying in Rachel's point-of-view, Carner uses sparse words to describe each of these players. Does her technique work in setting these characters apart? How do these characters—together and individually—contribute to the texture of the novel?

18. Discuss the role of the media in affecting social and moral causes or in bringing them to the forefront of public awareness. Putting a name and a face on an issue sometimes makes it stand out more than more urgent causes. Is this fair? Is there a way around this imbalance of causes?

19. In a tale of angst that is nearly unrelenting, Rachel finds the occasional moment of reprieve. In addition to the walk to the ice cream store and other relaxed times with Ellie, Rachel enjoys the tennis tournament, spending a weekend in Fire Island, strolling down the street in Chicago, laughing at the beauty industry ball and having rapturous sex with Phil. What role do these times play in the overall story? How do you perceive the total sum of these ups and downs of Rachel's life?

20. In a surprise twist, the women in prison show compassion and solidarity with Rachel. Discuss their culture, their initial response to her, and their attitude toward Rachel when she leaves prison.

21. Both Rachel and Lorena are mothers who sacrifice much for their children. Discuss the subconscious role model Lorena might have presented to her daughter. Discuss the dynamics between Rachel and Lorena also regarding Josie and what each must do. Which mother made the *conscious* ultimate sacrifice?

22. Rachel was probably a giving person until she discovered Wes abusing of Ellie. She turned into a desperate parent whose focus was on her child. Relying on others to help her in her plight, she became a taker. How did that personality change affect her relationships? What was it that transformed her back into a giver? Were being a giver or a taker conscious choices, or were they reactions to

Had a good reading experience? Now order author Talia Carner's more recent novel, China Doll.

A riveting journey to save one life.

An American music icon, Nola Sands, is on a concert tour in China when a baby is thrust into her arms. Resolved to save the infant from death in a Chinese orphanage, Nola finds herself on a collision course with her husband/manager, with her record label company's interests in China—and with the world's two super-powers determined to silence her.

In a story of an adoptive parent's unwavering love, Nola's flight across China is a tale not only of human rights abuses running amok in an astonishingly picturesque land: It is the gripping self-discovery voyage of a woman coming into her own.

ISBN# **978-0-9773821-2-5** $13.95
- Greatly discounted on Amazon.
- For <u>reading group</u> discount, please contact the publisher at <u>MecoxHudson2@aol.com.</u>

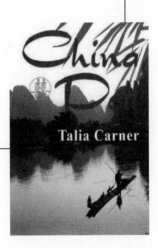

Talia Carner